Under a
Sapphire Sky

Susannah Bates was born in Suffolk in 1970. While reading English at Durham University, she co-wrote her first play, *Smoke*, for the Edinburgh Fringe, where it was nominated for the *Guardian* Student Theatre Award. She then went on to study law in London and qualified as a solicitor in 1997. She practised law in the City until she gave up to become a full-time writer. Her first novel, *Charmed Lives*, was published in 2001 and selected for the WHSmith Fresh Talent promotion. She is also the author of *All About Laura* and *Honor & Evie*. She is married with a young son and lives in London.

Under a Sapphire Sky

Susannah Bates

arrow books

Published by Arrow Books 2010

2 4 6 8 10 9 7 5 3 1

First published in Great Britain in 2010 by
Arrow Books
Random House, 20 Vauxhall Bridge Road,
London SW1V 2SA

www.rbooks.co.uk

Addresses for companies within The Random House Group Limited can
be found at: www.randomhouse.co.uk/offices.htm

The Random House Group Limited Reg. No. 954009

A CIP catalogue record for this book
is available from the British Library

ISBN 9780099445449

The Random House Group Limited makes every effort to ensure that the
papers used in its books are made from trees that have been legally
sourced from well-managed and credibly certified forests. Our paper
procurement policy can be found at: www.rbooks.co.uk/environment

The Random House Group Limited supports The Forest Stewardship
Council (FSC), the leading international forest certification organisation.
All our titles that are printed on Greenpeace approved FSC certified paper
carry the FSC logo. Our paper procurement policy can be found at
www.rbooks.co.uk/environment

Typeset by SX Composing DTP, Rayleigh, Essex
Printed and bound in Great Britain by
CPI Bookmarque Ltd, Croydon, CR0 4TD

For Alec

ACKNOWLEDGEMENTS

Thanks to the following for the help they have given me in the research and writing of this book: Oliver and Annabel Bates, Charlotte and Tim Booth, Charlotte Bush, Helena Crawford, Rob Drummond, Cecilia Duraes, Laura Fallowfield, Tom Gillum, Ameen Hussein, Watadeniya Jayarathna, Edward Johnson, Clare and Peter Kemp-Welch, Arjan Kirthisingha, Anna Latham, Ramani Leathard, Oliver Malcolm, Vanessa Neuling, Claire Panta, Kate Pelham Burn, Menaka Perera Arangala, Harry Peto, Marian Reid, Olivia Richli, Zoë Robinson, Shakuntala Schott, Annabel Sebag Montefiore, Stephanie Sweeney, Henrietta Tatham, Rob Waddington, Ruth Waldram, Tom Williams, Jen Wilson, Sian Wilson.

In particular, thanks to Kate Elton and Georgina Hawtrey-Woore – my editors at Random House – and to my agent, Clare Alexander, who have all worked so hard on my behalf, and whose continued support and encouragement gives me the confidence to keep writing.

But most of all, thanks to my family – to my parents, for being so interested; to my son, for being so easy, and to my husband, for making me so happy.

PROLOGUE

It was hot in the lecture hall that afternoon. Black blinds were down – dark, against a street of summer brilliance. And in that closed cocoon a class of twenty sat silently at their microscopes, examining the day's stones under small clean circles of light.

They'd been studying corundums that week. Marianne had hoped to catch the start of the final session but lunch had run on, and as the door swung shut she felt momentarily blind. The contrast was too sudden. The outside street held a sensory inner imprint – of massed footsteps that, minutes earlier, had been bubbling out of the Underground; of drilling at the corner of Tottenham Court Road where some water main had burst – and it took a few seconds for the images to weaken, the echoes to fade; for Marianne to adapt to subtler stimuli.

And then, through the darkness, came a pinprick of blue: a cabochon sapphire – its star off-centre, imperfect. Other details started to take shape. To the left of the sapphire, sketched against a greyer outer orbit of microscope light, a hand was making notes. Then the half-lit student put down his pen. Frowning, he adjusted the lens, leant over, and took another look.

All across the room, a multicoloured trail of corundums – and fake corundums – sparkled under microscopes. Yellows, pinks, purples, and all shades of blue – from palest putty to murky indigo . . . Marianne looked down the row, stopping at a pink: much closer in, directly to her left. A watery pink – waiting on the clinical tray of Gabriella's microscope as she filled out the last box on her classification form and smiled up at her friend.

'Good lunch?'

Marianne took the empty chair beside her. Taking off a denim jacket, she reached down in the darkness, feeling around the rough interior of her canvas bag for the various pens and papers she needed for the session.

'Where's Rogerson?'

Gabriella didn't know. 'This one's a pink sapphire, isn't it, Marianne? I'm pretty sure it is. I just—'

'Let's have a look.' Marianne took the stone. She didn't really need to check. Of course it was a sapphire. How could Gabby doubt it? She might have missed Tuesday's session and spent most of Wednesday's too hung over to take in much. But look at the precision of those facets! And those straight growth lines that – with the stone being so pale – were even visible to the naked eye . . . what else could it possibly be?

Gabriella watched her friend holding the stone. She watched the steadiness of Marianne's hand and the warm look in her eye – more appreciative than assessing. She noticed the way Marianne hadn't bothered to use the microscope. Just a pair of tweezers and an old triangular loupe she kept with her at all times – safe, in a zipped inner pocket of her bag.

Turning to the classification form that Gabby had

been filling out, Marianne ran her eye down Gabby's list of answers, checking and nodding.

'. . . this is fine, Gab. You're getting the hang of it.' Looking back at the stone again and smiling now, 'It's all about the growth lines, see? That one, there, across the bottom . . .'

But Gabriella wasn't listening. She'd seen something else in Marianne's bag – something that had slipped out of the inner pocket with the loupe, something with a flash that quite eclipsed any other stone in the room: a brilliant solitaire diamond, attached to a platinum ring. Marianne's hand was swift over the bag, swift over the flap, but she wasn't swift enough. The ring was free – it was rolling about in the palm of Gabriella's hand, now oddly grey and dull in the penumbra of the microscope. Gabby looked at Marianne for a moment, while Marianne looked back, impotent in her plastic college chair.

Grinning, Gabby tried the ring, slipping it on to her wedding finger. She turned briefly to check – 'Paul, right?' – and was back with the diamond again, shaking her head. 'Of course, Paul. I knew this was coming. I *knew* it!'

Still Marianne said nothing – watching as her friend whipped off the ring and laid it on the tray of her microscope, under the direct light; watching as, chameleon-like, it transformed itself from the low-watt of the shadow into a thing of such celestial whiteness and purity that it was impossible not to blink.

Gabby examined the magnified version. 'So go on, then,' she said, eye locked to the microscope. 'Where did he take you? Nobu? Or was that a little too inventive for poor old Paul? Claridge's, maybe? The Ritz?'

She didn't need to go on guessing. Nobu was spot-on. But Marianne, unsettled by this – by the suggestion that Paul was somewhat obvious in his tastes and that she, Marianne, wasn't the only one to have noticed – had yet to admit it when the door opened and Dr Rogerson returned to his afternoon class.

'I think you'll find we did diamonds last term, Miss Franklin,' he said, standing over Gabby, taking a leaflet from the pile of photocopies he'd just made and holding it out.

Slowly – deliberately so – Gabriella looked up from the microscope. Ignoring the proffered leaflet, she gave the lecturer a stare that was both childish and superior.

Rogerson shrugged. He was used to girls like Gabriella Franklin – every class had its share of spoiled princesses. 'And if you must use the institute's equipment to assess your own pieces,' he added, putting the leaflet on the table and moving away from her down the line of students, 'at least do it in your own time.'

By four o'clock, the session was over. The blinds were released – rattling cheaply up their rolls and opening the room to natural afternoon light. The stones were carefully boxed away, the classification forms were collected up and left in a leafy pile for Rogerson to mark as – in various groups of twos and threes – his class left for the weekend.

There was a wine bar directly opposite the building and a pub at the end of the street. Students from the institute would flock to one or the other – especially on a Friday night. It was a great way to build up future contacts in the trade, and Marianne had no wish to pass up on that kind of opportunity. But there were times when it was tempting not to join them – especially when she had Gabriella in tow . . .

As a 'spoiled princess' – and, more particularly, a

4

spoiled princess with a complete inability to tone it down – Gab struggled to be taken seriously at the Gemmology Institute. And while there were undeniable advantages to the label (money, confidence, contacts and the possession of an automatic social life that hardly needed amplifying with friends from the pool of earnest students on her course), the ensuing air of social independence did not make her popular there. It was all too easy for Gab's classmates to read arrogance into the indifference, the reluctance to add any more names to an already-bulging address book . . . and it had taken a profoundly contrary nature like Marianne's – with her instinct for the opposite direction, for the most unlikely projects – for the two to become friends. Marianne was the only student to bother with Gabriella, the only person on their course sufficiently perverse to find something of interest in the very detachment that put the others off. It was chance that they happened to be sitting next to each other that very first morning, but it was more than chance that kept them close. That Marianne was amused, instead of shocked, by the whispered commentary Gab poured into her ear – commentary that was invariably at someone else's expense but somehow always funny enough to override the nastiness – would probably have been enough for Gab (who loved an audience) to want her as a friend. But it was really the way Marianne had engaged with Gabby that first year – challenging her attitudes, lifting her boredom, opening her mind to the beauty of stones and settings she might have overlooked . . . giving her a sense of respect, even love, for the things she was learning – it was these things that laid the ground for the kind of friendship that would outlast the course. For there was something very flattering about Gabriella's willingness to listen to Marianne and learn from her – a surprising humility that belied the cocky surface. Marianne had no intention of finding herself a more 'sensible' friend.

Not that it was easy – mingling with the other students, trying to build up contacts while Gab, beside her, radiated the bored air of an obedient toddler forced to sit through an adult conversation, drinking, fidgeting, swinging her legs, checking her telephone for messages. Not easy – keeping in with the gem school crowd – when there was such an alluring after-hours alternative: namely, the smart London townhouse that Gab shared with her brother George. This house was minutes from the institute. And with its large sofas, high ceilings, and a kitchen that was more than adequately stocked with fine alcohol and food, it sometimes made the other option – queueing along with the other students at some dirty bar for a pint of mediocre beer, then having nowhere to sit – seem more like punishment than reward. Especially on a hot July evening such as this, when Gabby and Marianne had rather more vital matters than course-work gossip to discuss.

For Paul, having made his proposal, was now off on a business trip and wouldn't be home for a week.

'I don't want an answer,' he'd said to Marianne, as he put the ring on her finger and paused to admire the sparkle. 'Don't give me one now. Just promise you'll think about it while I'm away . . .'

Marianne was relieved. It was an easy promise to make – she was hardly going to put it to the back of her mind. And in spite of removing the ring on her return to the institute and zipping it safely away, in spite of planning to keep the matter secret, Marianne was glad in a way that her plans had been foiled. She wasn't naturally reserved. She liked the idea of having someone else to talk it through with, even if that someone wasn't Paul's greatest fan. And so now, turning left, and left again, she and her friend walked away from the bars and restaurants, into the residential heart of Fitzrovia.

'Excellent,' said Gabriella, as the latchkey failed. With the door double-locked and the alarm to disengage, it was clear that the house was empty – clear that George and his family had left for the weekend. Gabby wasn't expecting them to be there. In this burning weather, Helen, her sister-in-law, was sure to have bolted off to Hampshire as soon as possible – performing sleek lengths of that new swimming pool while the children and their nanny kept a satisfactory distance. But her brother wasn't so easy to rule out. He had a disconcerting habit of working late on Friday nights, especially when closing a deal, before coming back suddenly at ten or eleven o'clock – tired and hungry in his dull day-worn suit – to cramp Gabriella's style. Or else he'd be wooing some prospective client with a long, expensive lunch and then, at four o'clock, he'd decide it wasn't worth going back into the office again and return to Fitzroy Place to spend a few hours at his state-of-the-art desk which – somewhat thoughtlessly – had been placed in the main drawing room.

This desk wasn't the only example of George's selfishness. Indeed, his behaviour and attitudes invariably gave the impression that the house belonged to him outright – that he and his family were only letting Gabriella stay there on sufferance – and Marianne often wondered why she never objected. Why did George and his family have what seemed to Marianne to be the complete run of the place – with their monochrome good taste infecting every

7

corner, their smug wedding photographs on the drawing-room piano, their scented candles marking territory in the air – while his sister was demoted to the basement? And when Marianne discovered that George and Helen already had a house in the country and were often only in London for a couple of days in the middle of the week, it seemed to her bizarre. The property had been left to them both equally. Marianne knew this. And okay, so there was a distant half-brother to consider – a half-brother named Jay, who was living somewhere abroad with George and Gabby's stepmother; a half-brother who might also have had a claim on his father's London house and whose name was invariably raised by Gabby every time Marianne grew overly indignant on her behalf. 'Compared to poor Jay . . .' she'd say, never finishing the sentence.

But it seemed to Marianne, reading between the lines, that 'Poor Jay' and his mother had been more than adequately provided for, under a separate trust. She had no doubt that it was easy for Jay, the baby of the family. His beautiful long-haired boyhood, with parents who'd clearly adored each other, was more than evident in the many photographs about the place. His reportedly charming disposition, artistic bent and indifference to things material was undoubtedly the natural result of his place in that old cycle of love breeding the lovable. Easy for him to be generous in such circumstances. The sons were both fine. But the daughter . . . the daughter seemed somehow to have lost out.

And the more Marianne discovered about her friend's complicated family life – how Gab's father had left her mother before Gab had even been born, how she and Jay were almost twins and the awkward truth underlying that situation, her mother's subsequent bitterness and drink problem which was in direct contrast to the joyous world of her father's new love where the sun always shone and laughter filled the air – the more she sensed Gab's need for security, both financial and emotional. Gab was vulnerable, off-balance, short of natural judgement. There were distortions in her mindset – she was frequently too loud but could equally be too silent; too smart, or too scruffy; too close, too distant; too jolly, too glum – distortions that revealed an inability to read the moment and led to a certain sort of isolation, a social disconnection, which in turn explained the growing fondness for alcohol, while simultaneously blinding poor Gab to the lessons she might have learnt from her mother. George was all right – he had his own family now, his own lucrative career. He ought, Marianne felt, to be giving more to his sister at this time of her life. Not pushing her aside like some sort of weakling runt. Just because Gab might not have spent her inheritance as wisely as her brother, it didn't mean she had no right to it at all. Wasn't the obvious solution to sell up, split the proceeds, and embark on normal, separate lives? She didn't even have her own sitting room down there.

'I know, I know,' Gabriella had said, back in January, as she poured Marianne another glass of wine and settled into one of Helen's beige silk chairs. 'But I do get certain benefits –'

'Like?'

Gabriella grinned. 'Like never having to open a printed envelope,' she said, indicating the pile of mail that sat on her brother's desk. 'Like never having to speak to a lawyer or a fund manager. Or having to find a competent plumber . . .'

Marianne could manage only a superficial smile in return. It was true that Gabby was hopeless when it came to anything administrative. But this was only because her family had encouraged it and the girl was too lazy to resist. She could write a charming thank-you letter. She could – if pushed – pay her credit card bills. But when faced with perfectly standard correspondence from HM Revenue and Customs, or the Electoral Commission, BUPA, her car insurance company, her fund manager's quarterly statements of account . . . or indeed anything remotely serious, she was lost. Barely knew what they were. And while Marianne could see that it was convenient for Gabby to leave such matters to her brother, it was hardly an excuse, she felt, for George to take such blatant liberties when it came to the house itself. It seemed to Marianne that he was using Gab's desperate need for family love – for the sense of paternal support she got from his handling her administrative affairs – as a way to grab the lion's share of their inheritance. And the more Gab declared herself satisfied with the arrangement, the more it irked Marianne.

'I couldn't do it on my own.'

'Of course you could.'

'But—'

'Come on, Gabby. It isn't difficult.'

'Not for you, maybe –'

'Not for anyone! And think of the control you'd have – think how nice it would be to know exactly how much money there is in your portfolio, to know how it's being invested, and—'

'Not as nice as having someone do it for me.'

Marianne had let it go. But with the amount of time she'd spent in Fitzroy Place that year – coming back with Gabby after evening seminars and chatting into the night about their plans for setting up a jewellery business together – such thoughts were never far from her mind. She'd met George and Helen. And oddly, on first acquaintance, they hadn't seemed so bad. While George had spent much of the time on his mobile, he was clearly at a critical stage in some business deal, and at least he'd had the manners to take his negotiations outside. And Helen, softened by pregnancy, had been positively disarming with her compliments. More than once, she'd admired the necklace that Marianne had been wearing – one of Marianne's bolder designs . . .

But it was easy to be flattered. And, to Marianne, such moments only added to the niggling sense that while Gabby was of course lucky to have an inheritance at all, lucky to have a brother willing to manage it for her, lucky that 'work' entailed little more than turning up to the Gemmology Institute once or twice a week, somehow she was still being short-changed by this charming and efficient couple.

Gabby, meanwhile, was far less bothered by her own circumstances than she was by this new threat to Marianne's.

'I'm not saying he's a disaster as a *person*,' she said, opening one of the drawing-room windows. 'I like Paul – you know I like him. But as a friend, Marianne. Not a husband. Not for you, at any rate. Not now.'

Smiling, Marianne waited for Gabby to come up with yet another reason why she and Paul shouldn't get married. For sure, his proposal was a shock – Marianne herself was far from certain what her answer would be – but the idea was not unattractive. Paul was attentive, charming, good-looking, young. Marianne had met him the previous year at the British Museum – attending the first night of an exhibition of Ancient Egyptian jewellery . . . an exhibition Paul's bank happened to be sponsoring. For him, it had been a coup de foudre, love at first sight. For her, it had taken a little longer – but he was admirably persistent, admirably confident, admirably grown-up beside her student friends. Different. Not afraid to be romantic. They'd been together for a year with no arguments – none at all – and, in various ways to varying degrees, a great deal of pleasure. Apart from the fact that it had been almost too easy, what wasn't there to like?

'It's just too soon,' Gab went on. 'I expect I'm being selfish here, but you can't dangle such a totally delicious business idea in front of me, Marianne – the two of us setting up together – and then bugger off and marry Paul. Don't you at least want to *try* for a career before you sink for ever under a pile of nappies?'

'We wouldn't have children immediately. Even if we did—'

'I'm sure Paul wouldn't object.'

Marianne felt a surge of irritation. 'What's that supposed to mean?'

'Only—'

'You've spoken to him about it?'

Gabby sat at her brother's desk. 'I don't need to speak to him about it, Marianne, to tell what kind of marriage Paul Farage has in mind for you.' She toyed with George's paperwork, his orderly in and out trays, his gleaming photograph of Helen. 'You must have seen the way he glazes over when one of us mentions the business plan – it's like he thinks it'll never happen, that it's just some girly fantasy. And you only have to look at that awful rock—'

And then, noticing Marianne's expression, Gabby checked herself. 'I don't doubt it was extremely expensive,' she went on, carefully. 'I'm sure most women

12

would be thrilled with a three-carat solitaire from Graff . . .'
She waited for the point to hit home, for Marianne's
expression to show that involuntary flicker of offence at
the idea she was 'most women', that pride in herself for
being different – a pride Gabby knew she nursed – before
adding, '– but is that really what you want?'

'What I want, Gabby, is a man who—'

'Understands you? Loves you? Takes time to think
about what you might like on your finger, as opposed
to finding some sort of status symbol that reflects how
successful *he* might be? A man who's prepared to put a
bit more effort into your ring than a few scrappy
seconds in Bond Street and a quick swipe of his card?'

Marianne swallowed.

'He could at least have given you a stone with *colour*.
This ring, this stone, it's – why, it's the jewellery
equivalent of Helen, for God's sake!'

Stung, Marianne looked around the smartly neutral
room. Helen's room. She glimpsed herself, just the top
of her head, in the elegant Venetian mirror that Helen
had chosen to put above the mantelpiece . . . and saw the
familiar gypsy corkscrew curls and the stretch of
beetroot-coloured silk she'd found in Mexico last year –
twisted round and round itself, holding the bulk of her
hair in place . . . too much, too bright, too dense a dye
against the delicate brie and biscuit tones of the
wallpaper. Then she looked at the brilliant on her finger.

'It's only a ring, Gab.'

'Yes, darling. Of course it is.'

Marianne sat on the calico sofa. She undid her lovely
beetroot scarf and wound it, ropelike, between her
hands – pulling at its length, testing the tension in the
weave of the silk.

'And anyway, why would I want an engagement

ring that reflects me? How egocentric is that? Surely I should want to be reminded of Paul! He's the one who matters. He's the one—'

And Gabby, sensing that this was getting serious, that she might lose her friend altogether if she pushed the point too far – leant forward and, smiling fondly, touched Marianne's arm.

'Then that diamond will be perfect,' she said.

It was supposed to be conciliatory; a neat, light attempt to agree to disagree. It was supposed to say that if this ring worked for Marianne – if it signified what was most important about her relationship with Paul – then that was all that mattered. But as soon as the words were out, both women knew that Gabriella had said far more than she'd intended.

Marianne closed her eyes. She thought of the diamond trade, of its dark industrial mines, its shady reputation – the barbed wire, the watchtowers, the culture of fear . . . and of how those dazzling crystals of light – that whiteness, that purity – seemed only to drive men in the opposite direction. She thought, too, of the rather more ordinary showrooms down the road in Hatton Garden – the sense of something seedy behind closed doors, the grubby underside of glamour. Then she opened her eyes and, looking down, saw the impressive multifaceted solitaire that Paul had chosen for her. She remembered all the scientific facts she'd learnt last term about diamonds . . . about the hardness, the status, the promise of 'forever' – or was it more a threat? – in that icy brilliance. And the more she looked, the emptier it seemed. Perhaps it was the room they were in – the safe lighting, the neutral colours – but all she could see, through the expensive flashes, was a glassy blank and a disconcerting absence of character.

PART ONE – SRI LANKA

Chapter One

He'd wanted to wait until everyone else had left the church. He'd wanted his private moment with God – alone in the little hexagonal building, without disturbance, so that he could give the matter his proper attention. It was important. He might not have been in Sri Lanka at the time, he might not have known any of the victims or their grieving families, or seen whole communities swept away, but still – along with the rest of the world – Paul Farage had felt touched by the Boxing Day Tsunami of 2004. He'd gazed at the news footage with horror, still wished that there was something constructive he could have done to help – something more significant than giving his credit card number to someone at the end of a charity donation line. And this, in a way, was it. It hadn't involved money, not unless he counted the airfare or the hotel bill. He hadn't – as yet – so much as rolled up his sleeves. Three years might have elapsed since that appalling day but, damn it, at least he'd bothered to make the journey.

*

And now he was here, on his knees, in a windswept church of freshly laid bricks which sat, awkwardly new, amidst the litter and dirt lining the road from Colombo to Galle. Travelling along that road yesterday in an air-conditioned taxi, Paul had stared out through the window – out, through the small rectangle of glass that separated him from what was happening on the other side, with the dislocating sensation that he was merely watching a film on television. He'd had to remind himself that it wasn't just a scene that had been staged; that, once his car passed, the mothers of those discarded-looking kids wouldn't be sweeping them away to be cleaned and brushed and taken off to McDonald's for tea; that the tuk tuks and rickshaws, the dusty billboards, the shacks and stalls, and the strangely beautiful slices and curls of Sinhalese script trailing over every wall and poster and truck . . . it was all for real.

Paul had wound down the car window. With the humid air against his skin, he'd continued to gaze at the roadside scenery – and as he gazed he felt a rising horror. For here and there he began to notice ghostly grey-green streaks on the lower sections of some of the buildings. And the further he travelled, the darker and more prevalent those streaks became. Eventually the driver explained what they were but, by then, Paul had no need to ask – for it was all too clear that this was the stain of the tsunami, and that these brave concrete structures, structures which had miraculously withstood the initial blast of water, had somehow failed to shake the infections that went with it. Each surviving building was now marked by an intermittent horizontal line – stagnant green below, clear above – no more than a few metres high, for a few tragic metres was all it had been . . . a line of death that ran parallel to the coastal road, all the way from Colombo to Galle and, no doubt, beyond. And it was only the new structures – the bright temporary communities set up by global conglomerates, the startling skyscraping Buddha of gold that he'd seen the day before, and this modest little church – that broke the line.

All these things he'd noticed and considered. All these things – and more – Paul wished to bring to God that day. But the moment had been ruined, on account of sniffing from the row behind. Somebody had been sniffing, and it hadn't been anything as poetic or forgivable as tears. It had been the mundane attempt to clear a nasal passage – he could tell by the determined regularity of the sniffs, by the phlegmy, intermittent cough – and whoever it was had decided to perform this unattractive bathroom function right in the middle of a church service. It had taken all Paul's strength not to show his irritation.

'Paul?'

It was Sophie – prayer sheet in hand, turning back from the crowd at the door, aware that he was lingering. She didn't need to say more. The single syllable of his name was enough to remind Paul that his girlfriend and her parents and, no doubt, other members of the congregation would all be waiting, that someone would have arranged for transport back to the hotel, that this wasn't the time for a private moment with his Maker.

Paul followed her out of the church. He stood with the others on the patchy grass, with the old graveyard behind them and the clouds gathering above – for the monsoon season was not yet over – and waited for Father Perera, the local priest, to say a few final words and a quick closing prayer by the memorial stone that stood outside. The wind was rising, the sea was rough. Paul had to strain to hear what the priest was saying.

'. . . and of course, as we all know, this beautiful new church would not be here at all' – a graceful arm was raised in the direction of Sophie's father – 'without the splendid efforts of my very good friend the Reverend Charles—'

Charles Mostyn demurred. 'Really, Rex. I only—'

'– of his wife Victoria, his charming daughter Sophie, and everybody at St John's in London. On behalf of the parish of St Mark's, I welcome you here today – all of you – and we thank you from the bottom of our hearts!'

Father Perera's affectionate smile wandered over the group and came to rest on Paul who – for some reason impossible to explain, even to himself – completely failed to respond and instead looked limply at his feet. He couldn't understand it. Why the embarrassment? Surely, by now, after everything he'd been through since Marianne Cooper had turned him down – the emptiness of his life, the decision to quit working for LKPC Investments and find a more meaningful occupation, the drifting into his local church one cold London Sunday and the complete spiritual transformation which had followed – surely he could manage a sincere Christian smile in return. Hadn't he learnt anything? Wasn't he beyond those lily-livered attitudes of the past, that allergy to Christian fervour, that stiffness that used to come over him when being urged to exchange a 'sign of peace' with his equally unwilling father in church at Christmas?

Obviously not. Obviously, there was still room for improvement. And Paul, grateful now for Sophie's hand in his as the monsoon rains descended and they hurried towards the cars, was struck by a familiar sense of his own weakness – and an equally familiar sense of distance from, and admiration for, his girlfriend.

'. . . so what about tomorrow?' Victoria Mostyn was saying as she stood on the steps of their hotel – under the verandah, out of the downpour. She was talking to one of Father Perera's friends, an expat voluntary worker in her thirties – one of many who'd arrived in Galle over the last few years in the hope of contributing to the many aid projects that had sprung up in the wake of the tsunami – who was driven by the same ache, the same sense of emptiness that Paul had experienced recently. Victoria had met a number of them at the thanksgiving service and was interested in learning more about certain local projects – particularly those involving children.

'I'm not sure what Soph and Paul have planned,' she went on, glancing up at the others – waiting at the top of the steps, 'but I could certainly make lunch if that's any good for you. Or—'

'I'm around,' said Sophie, quickly.

Victoria nodded. She turned back to the voluntary worker. 'And I know Charles would be interested. He was heavily involved with setting up exactly this sort of reciprocal arrangement between a couple of schools in Fulham and Romania – we have friends in Bucharest who were keen to get something started – and I have to say it's been a huge success. They even managed to arrange a trip to London recently, to meet their pen-friends from the kids in Sophie's class . . .' She turned to Sophie, who hesitated.

'It was quite an operation, Mum,' she said, coming back down the steps. 'I'm not convinced that the kind of schools that Kate's been talking about would be right for something so ambitious, especially with the distances involved. But –' smiling now at the voluntary worker – 'but what about some sort of coordinated class project? I don't know . . . something very simple . . . maybe we could look at agriculture? Compare your tea plantations with the arable farming methods in the UK – something like that – and get each side to draw pictures and write some segments about how it's done in their own country and then send them over, and we could stick them up on the walls . . .'

Paul stood listening, a half-smile on his face. It was typical. They might have come to Galle to attend the service of thanksgiving at Charles's friend's church. It might have provided a focus for their trip – certainly, the fundraising had taken up a huge amount of his time these last few months and Paul had no wish to play down the importance of what they were ultimately here to do. But it was also supposed to be a break. The idea was that, after a day in Colombo with Father Perera, a day of travelling south to Galle to his church, and then the day of the service of thanksgiving – after all that, it was to be a vacation.

September was an ideal time for them to have come. It was still out of season so the prices were temptingly low, and Paul – the old Paul, the luxury-loving treat-seeking Paul who'd once enjoyed a six-figure salary and knew a thing or two about restaurants and hotels – couldn't resist it. Lured on by the figures on the website, he'd grabbed at the opportunity, persuaded Sophie and her parents to let him make the booking, and gone straight for the town's most prestigious establishment.

'. . . *stunningly situated,*' read the first paragraph on the hotel's Home Page as image after image of paradise unrolled in a slideshow before Paul's dazzled eyes, '*a whole new standard of elegance and luxury . . .*' Flash! There it was: crisp sheets, balconies, vast stone bathrooms and open showers. '*A truly world-class spa . . .*' Flash! Again! Two beautiful smiling therapists beside a perfectly prepared daybed, with piles of neatly folded towels just out of focus, and an artful strand of frangipani resting on the pillow. And so it went on: '*. . . a vast tranquil swimming pool . . .*' Flash! He could almost feel the water rippling at his toes, '*. . . and an extensive range of international cuisine fused with local inspirations . . .*' Flash! A close-up of a flaming pan of sizzling prawns, scattered about with coriander. Paul salivated. '*With our dedicated team of staff attending to your every need . . . and all just moments from some of Sri Lanka's most celebrated beaches.*' Flash! Flash! Flash! '*Settle in the shade of our whispering palm trees, wander at your leisure along our golden sands, refresh yourself in the sparkling water, soak up the very essence of Sri Lanka beneath a vibrant sapphire sky . . .*'

He hadn't put it quite that way to Victoria, of course. He'd merely said how comfortable it sounded – historic, too, with its Dutch colonial origins and subtle Vermeer-influenced interiors – how nice it would be for them all to have a holiday, a proper holiday, together. With its ancient fort, its charming streets, and its growing reputation as a twenty-first-century Riviera – a reputation driven by the small group of boho-aristos who'd settled there, benign new-colonials who, in search of some of the privileges that their ancestors might once have enjoyed, and perhaps with a dash of inherited entrepreneurial spirit, had made significant property investments there in the last decade . . . Galle was, tsunami notwithstanding, a serious destination for the discerning traveller. Knowing this, Paul had assumed it would have been a pleasant surprise for his girlfriend and her parents to discover just how on-trend it was – this smart hotel he'd found for them. He'd imagined how pleased they'd be, how grateful. Perhaps even a little impressed by his style and taste.

Instead, it was now blindingly obvious to him that, far from being thrilled, the Mostyns were embarrassed to be staying there. They said all the right things. They marvelled at the luxuries – the green-tiled swimming pool, the range of spa treatments on offer, the elegant dining rooms, the attentive service – but their tone lacked the requisite note of awe. It was too gentle, too kind, more that of parents humouring a child. And when, that morning, Paul overheard Victoria telling Father Perera why they were staying somewhere so glamorous and expensive – finishing with an affectionate, 'Dear thing – plainly used to something rather more sophisticated than our usual B and Bs and caravans! I hope we don't embarrass him . . .' – Paul understood too late that physical luxury wasn't such a comfortable experience for the soul; that such things as an Ultimate Double-Handed Ayurvedic Massage were tantamount to torture when there were children begging on the streets outside and local projects to learn about. Style and taste? What a joke. How wrong could he possibly have been?

He waited for Sophie and her mother to finalise their plans with the voluntary worker and join him in the lobby and for Victoria to collect her room key and disappear, before suggesting to Sophie that they go upstairs for a drink. There was a bar on the top floor with views out to sea.

'Sure,' said Sophie from the armchair to his left – scribbling vigorously in the back of her diary. Sudden ideas that were occurring to her, ideas about the schools project which she didn't want to lose. Then, returning the pen she'd borrowed from the hotel receptionist, she smiled suddenly at Paul. 'So come on, then,' she said, nudging him. 'Where's my glass of champagne?'

The upstairs bar was deserted, but the views – as he'd expected – were arresting, in a gusty grey-washed out-of-season way. Paul and Sophie stood at the windows watching the dark wet spikes of the palm leaves thrash against the buildings. There was no beach to speak of. At this time of year the sea level had risen to the fortress walls, and all they could see was an expanse of pewtery water – heavy, cold, dark – right up to the horizon.

Paul left her there for a moment and went to get their drinks and, as he did so, a group entered the bar. Two women and a man. Paul watched them as he waited for the barman. He noticed the purple dye of the man's shirt; the well-considered looseness of the apple-green kaftan on the woman to his left; the subtle strands of silver thread in the wrap-around skirt of the other, slimmer, woman who was sitting with her back to him. By the standards of his former life, they were – to Paul – unmistakeably superior. There was something about the way they'd entered the bar – a confidence of direction, a lack of interest in the view – which, together with the sort of clothes they were wearing and the complete absence of redness in their tans, told him they weren't average tourists. And there was a part of

Paul that longed for their acknowledgement; longed to be as interesting to them as – strongly, unsettlingly, against his will – they still managed to be to him.

'God this is boring,' said the man.

The woman in apple-green rubbed her eyes. 'Malika seemed to think it might start improving next week,' she said. 'Something about low pressure and high pressure. But,' sighing now, 'I have to agree with you. We should have waited a month. There's fuck all to do when it gets like this. The place –'

'It's a dump.'

Silently assenting, the woman lit a cigarette. Outside, the rain fell harder. 'It's the dirt,' she said at last. 'It's that revolting black wet dirt. And with the roads a disgrace, and the dodgy drains, and puddles everywhere . . .' She closed her eyes. 'I *know* it's a Third World country. I *know* it's wrecked. And of course we all feel sorry for them, but – honestly. It's not as if the tsunami happened yesterday . . .'

Giving his room number to the barman, Paul took their champagne glasses over to the window. Sophie was still there, still looking at the grey seascape. She stood with her profile to him, lost in the outside world. She hadn't heard a word the others had been saying, hadn't even noticed them. And as Paul joined her, he realised that it wasn't the sea that was holding her attention – that she was looking down, right down into the street below, to where a small boy no more than three or four years old was heaving laundry inside out of the rain.

He passed her a glass.

'Thanks,' she said, smiling suddenly at him. It was the same open smile she'd given him downstairs – a smile he adored. It righted his soul.

'. . . and when you think of all the money that's been raised – it must be into billions by now – I mean, what the fuck are they spending it on?'

Paul looked at Sophie.

'What?' she said, amused.

'Will you marry me?'

Chapter Two

That night the weather cleared. And Paul, opening his curtains the following morning, found himself in the brochure-perfect paradise. His room overlooked the hotel gardens, and the vast green palm fronds that had been thrashing at his windows as he'd gone to bed . . . those same fronds now rested, dry and calm, against the glass. The colour of the sky – with its very particular cornflower hue, its rich glistening clarity – it was the promised sapphire. Paul opened the window. After the controlled neutral atmosphere he'd been sleeping in, it felt good to inhale something more natural – sea air tinged with the smell of drying earth, sunlight burning into fresh green foliage. And then, more faintly, drifting over a discreet wall to his left along with the muted clatter of knives and forks and murmuring from the staff, Paul was pretty certain he could also smell his breakfast. It was as if he'd walked right into that slideshow on his computer – he had a sense of windows opening, and opening again. Dimensions extending, like some clever advertisement – with Paul, Mr Ordinary, dressed in jeans and a T-shirt, strolling through the magic.

*

Paul closed his eyes. He said his morning prayers. And then, turning back to the empty bed, he began getting dressed. This empty bed was, unsurprisingly, a source of some frustration for Paul – but it was also a source of pride. For in the six or seven months that he and Sophie had spent together, they'd yet to share a bed, or a sofa, or even the back seat of a car; and with a wedding around the corner, both were now determined to hold on. They were into the home straight now. Just a few more months to go, and then . . . only think of the reward! A bride who really could wear white. He had a sense of quiet restraint, of virtue, of feeling 'right' with God. Paul liked these things. He liked this new set of old-fashioned rules in his life, liked to think he might be earning the approval of Charles and Victoria.

'Good night, my darling,' he'd said as, late last night, he'd stood with Sophie at the door of her room.

Sophie had smiled. 'Are you sure?'

'Of course I'm sure! At least, I am if you – I mean, if you . . .' He'd trailed off, suddenly uncertain, until Sophie, laughing, had kissed him fondly and put her key in the door.

'Well *I* can wait,' she'd said provocatively.

Paul had raised his eyebrows. 'I'm very glad to hear it,' he'd replied.

Returning to his room, alone, Paul had felt a little heady. Listening to the rain outside, to whip-wet palm leaves scraping at the windows, he'd taken some time to fall asleep.

He hadn't expected her to say yes. Hadn't, in truth, intended to ask her at all . . . certainly not so soon. Sure, he was serious – her values, her background, her love for him . . . all these things had made it pretty clear to Paul, within weeks of knowing her, that Sophie Mostyn was the wife for him. And then, of course, there was the equally important regard he felt for her parents – for the childhood they'd given her, the attitudes and all the minutiae of daily family life in the Mostyn household . . . those things were now very important to Paul. Almost more important than the woman herself. For they told him what sort of instincts she would have, and what sort of family they, in turn, would raise.

He'd never had a girlfriend without sex. And while such a state of affairs might well have precipitated an early proposal, this wasn't the case for Paul. It wasn't that he didn't fancy Sophie. She might not be the most glamorous woman he knew, but Paul no longer found female glamour attractive. On the contrary, he found it slightly seedy – particularly when it came to wives. He liked the straightforward looks of his girlfriend. He liked the sandy eyelashes, the freckles, the knowledge that Sophie's knickers would be pure white M&S cotton. Soft. Unintimidating. She was taller and broader than any of his exes, but – again – what was wrong with that? He liked the idea of her being physically strong, of never getting tired . . . it was, indeed, a fantasy of his to imagine a day when he'd come back from work and find her at home with four or five children crawling over her and everyone laughing and looking pleased to see him. Really and truly, that was all Paul wanted from life these days. And he was looking forward to being as intimate with her, physically, as he was spiritually. At least he knew she'd look the same in the morning as she did the night before. Probably better. But (perhaps he was getting older) he didn't feel desperate. There were moments, sure, but those moments could be quickly sated. It was more as if he were savouring something. Taking it slowly was part of the pleasure. And somewhere in the back of his mind he must have known it was his for the asking.

But he'd been in no particular hurry. And it was only that trio of strangers in the bar – intimidatingly glamorous, utterly indifferent – that tipped Paul over the edge, triggering in him such a deep and violent need to reject such people *for ever*, that his proposal – his need to turn in the opposite direction – was knee-jerk.

But in spite of it being involuntary – and while still slightly taken aback at the alacrity of Sophie's, 'Yes!' – Paul was also, in the soothing air of morning, starting to feel rather proud of himself. Charles and Victoria, on learning of it over supper that night, had been flatteringly delighted, pleasingly impressed with his decisiveness. And Paul, on a roll, was all for finding an engagement ring. Here. Now. Today. Sri Lanka was famous for its gemstones – he'd learnt that much from his year with Marianne – and Paul, with his reduced income, was hardly averse to a bargain.

But a bargain wasn't so easy to find. And for laymen like Paul and Sophie – neither of whom was in a position to know if a stone was even genuine, far less whether it was worth the price tag – it was well nigh impossible. They spent that first day trawling Galle's jewellery quarter, getting hotter and hotter as the day wore on. And as Paul became increasingly frustrated with the market, Sophie grew ever more depressed. All she wanted was for Paul to be happy. She didn't particularly care what kind of stone it was, or even if it was a fake. Anything half pretty would be great.

'That's not the point.'

Isn't it? thought Sophie. Unhappily, she reached for another 'sapphire' that had caught her eye. 'What's wrong with this one? I like it, Paul. I really like it.'

'Ah . . .' The jeweller smiled kindly. 'Madam has good taste! That one is very good! Expensive, but—'

'Or this one,' said Sophie, quickly. 'This one is fine.'

'That one is not so good, madam.' Confused, the jeweller looked at Paul. 'What you want? You want something cheap, we have these ones here – see? And—'

'Come on, Soph.' Paul took her hand. 'I've had enough.'

The next day – first thing – he took her to Hassan's, a small, smart emporium close to their hotel, a place that had been recommended by the manager. Paul didn't doubt that commission would be involved but, after a short internal battle, understood he had no choice. After yesterday, he needed somewhere reputable. And as a man who'd once felt that only Bond Street was good enough for an engagement ring – a man whose old inclinations still simmered beneath the surface – he acknowledged that any residual misgivings at the sense of being manipulated by the local system would surely pass if the end result was a local ring that was genuine.

Standing outside Hassan's shop, waiting for it to open, Sophie was optimistic. After the bewildering array of makeshift stalls of yesterday, the place seemed positively Cartier. With its black velvet cabinets, its air conditioning, its double-doored security and its private room at the back, there was no doubt that the owner was a man of substance – a man who valued his relationship with the New Oriental Hotel, a man that Paul would be able to trust. Quickly, they were ushered in and stood at the display tables, gazing through the glass at rows of glittering rings, waiting for Hassan himself.

'He is coming,' the assistant said. 'Would you like some tea, madam?'

And as they waited for tea and Hassan to materialise, Paul and Sophie began looking with more focus through the glass. Some of the rings had price tags – all, Sophie noticed, significantly more expensive than yesterday's. She glanced at Paul, at the sunken way he'd leant on the display table, at the weary finger drawing a slow line over its glass surface, as if crossing out each ring it passed. Her optimism wavered. She wondered what, if anything, she should say to him – and as she hesitated she became aware that they weren't the only couple in the shop that morning. It hadn't been immediately apparent – on account of the showroom being L-shaped – that there were other cabinets beyond the bend, and other people looking at them. But as the minutes ticked on, Paul and Sophie found themselves witnesses to an increasingly heated discussion.

'*Tariq*'s coming?' said a woman's voice.

There was a short, deep laugh. 'Well, I'm not going to Ratnapura without him.'

'Jesus.'

The man let out a long sigh. 'I didn't promise you a scenic trip to the hills. I never said it would be fun.'

'I wasn't expecting—'

'This is business.'

'Yes, Jay,' said the woman. 'I know. And, believe it or not, I have a business to run as well. But that doesn't mean I've got to put up with three hours of that *weasel* in the back of your jeep.'

There was a pause. 'It's the front, actually.'

Silence.

'I'm sorry, Gab. He simply wouldn't understand it if we made him go in the back. He'd find it insulting—'

'Jay, *please*.' The woman sounded close to tears. 'You know what Tariq's like. You *know* –'

'If you've got a problem with the way Tariq Ibrahim looks at you, get a headscarf. Deal with it. I'm not your bodyguard, Gabby. I'm trying to give you some contacts, some experience. I'm trying to help you. If you want me to treat you as an equal, if you want professional respect, then this is where it starts. Okay? Now—'

'Please, Jay?'

'No.'

Paul and Sophie looked at each other.

'You'll thank me for it later,' the man went on, his voice a little softer. 'Honestly, Gab, he's a genius. We're lucky he's coming. And it's only a day – just a few hours – you can handle that, can't you?'

Silence.

'When you see him at the auction, you'll understand. Tariq knows his stones. More importantly, he knows those guys up there. So if you can't cope with the idea of coming with us, then—'

'*Us?*'

Then the shop bell rang. Outside, through the glass, they could see a slim, small man wearing dark glasses and smoking a rolled-up cigarette.

'Hey, Chanaka,' he said to the assistant. 'Jay here?'

34

And in the general movement that followed, with the security doors admitting this new arrival, the man from around the corner coming forward to greet him, together with sudden activity at the back of the shop – the arrival of Paul and Sophie's tea; followed by Hassan, politely introducing himself . . . it took a moment for Sophie to realise that Paul's attention was elsewhere, that he was talking to someone he knew, and then a moment more for her to realise that the woman they'd been listening to was some sort of friend of his.

'I can't believe it!' he was saying, shaking his head. 'So – so what are you *doing* here, Gabby? I mean—'

'Business, mainly,' came the reply. 'Marianne and I set up together.'

'Of course!' said Paul, recalling snippets of girlish pipe dreams – usually after midnight, over a third bottle of wine in some godforsaken club that Gab had found . . . shared dreams about starting a business together . . . fantasies that had seemed so unlikely at the time. 'Just as you planned.'

'That's right.' Gabby smiled. 'It's going well. And I'm just here to stock up, and learn a bit about the trade, and Jay's been helping me. Jay – see? Over there? The tall one, talking to that idiot in shades?'

'Yes, I see.'

Gabby sighed. 'They tell me I'm lucky to have a brother in the business. Especially one who's a dealer. But' – rolling her eyes – 'depends on the brother, right?'

Paul couldn't help himself. Double-checking Jay, whose dark skin and rich black hair were a million miles from Gabriella's distinctly Scandinavian colouring, he failed to hide his disbelief. Yes, the man was taller – at nearly six feet four inches, significantly taller – than any Sri Lankan Paul had met. Yes, his jeans, his trainers, his tailored shirt . . . they had all the stamp of Western privilege. But Gabby Franklin's *brother*? Surely that was—

'Half-brother, I should say,' Gabby added, amused. 'Perhaps that's where I've been going wrong. He lives out here, or – or used to . . . his mother does. But of course he's a stone dealer so he doesn't really live anywhere, and – and anyway . . .' Trailing off, she looked at Sophie.

'Oh,' said Paul, hurriedly, 'oh, Gabby, this is Sophie – my . . . blimey. I suppose I have to say you're my fiancée now!' Laughing, Paul put an arm round Sophie's waist. 'We only got engaged on Sunday,' he explained, almost as if it were a confession.

'Engaged?' said Gabby, eyebrows disappearing up behind her fringe.

The room fell silent. Even Jay and Tariq stopped talking routes and road maps, and turned to look at the couple.

'Then you'll be needing a ring,' said Hassan, smiling.

At first it seemed a mad idea. What possible advantage was it for anyone for Paul and Sophie to take Gabby's place in the jeep, and go with Jay and Tariq, right up into the hills, to the gemstone mining region, to the distinctly untouristy Ratnapura market itself? Hassan had hundreds of rings and stones on offer – many of them suitable for Paul's and Sophie's purposes. Jay and Tariq had business to do, stones to find, prices to negotiate. They didn't need a couple of wide-eyed hangers-on. It wasn't, as Jay had said to Gabby, 'a scenic trip to the hills'.

But Paul was getting desperate. And while it was clear to Sophie that he still liked the idea of a local ring at a local price, she could also see that – in spite of the smart display cabinets, the hotel recommendation, the obvious advantages of Hassan's emporium – the reality of doing any sort of business in a foreign town, with foreign people he couldn't read, was proving almost unbearable for him. And now this sudden encounter with a familiar face, a familiar face who understood the local trade, was more than Paul could resist. Especially when it was Gabby – with her huge distaste for Tariq the rough-stone expert; her need for some excuse, some face-saving way of extracting herself from the expedition – who came up with the idea.

Hearing Paul say to Hassan that what they really wanted was a stone that would remind them of their time here in Sri Lanka – the place he'd proposed in, a place they'd love forever – followed by Sophie's tentative request – perhaps – for something a little unusual, something different . . . Gabby stepped in. Loudly, she said that if they wanted something *really* different, something that would give them a memory all right, why not get one in Ratnapura? Jay could take them in his jeep.

Jay frowned. 'I hardly think—'

'Why not?' said Gabby. 'There'd be room enough if I don't come. And it would certainly be "different",' she went on, smiling now at Sophie, who smiled back in simple relief at this possible answer to Paul's problems. 'Jay would find you the most awesome stone. Something properly rare. At a fair price.'

'Except it would be rough, Gab,' said Jay. 'I'm not entirely sure that's what your friends have in mind.'

'Tariq could cut it for them.'

37

'Tariq's a busy man –'

'I'd do it for a lakh,' said Tariq, lighting another roll-up.

'A lakh all in?' said Gabby, swiftly. 'Selecting *and* cutting?'

'What's a lakh?' said Paul who, in spite of his time in the City, didn't feel confident enough to assume that Sri Lankan lakhs necessarily equated to Indian ones.

Tariq rubbed his left temple. 'Or the usual percentage,' he went on, giving Paul a sidelong glance. 'Cash. Whichever is most.'

Confused, Paul looked at Gabby – who, realising she'd reached the limits of her knowledge of the Galle stone trade, looked in turn to her brother.

Jay sighed. He needed Tariq. And Tariq, with his debts and his women, was always on the lookout for ready cash. It was in Jay's interests to keep Tariq sweet. And then, glancing from Tariq to Paul and guessing, from the mischievous look in his sister's eye, that this Paul was Marianne's Paul – the bloke she'd dumped at stone school, the flashy one with the City career and, no doubt, more than enough cash in his pocket – Jay decided to run with it. For while commission in these circumstances should really depend on the price of the stone, and while Tariq was certainly pushing his luck – a lakh was steep, for it was unlikely they'd find a stone of such value – it was also true that they'd be pushed to find another cutter of Tariq's experience at such short notice. And then there was that soft-looking woman holding on to Paul's arm . . . it was clearly going to make her day if he agreed to help them find a stone in Ratnapura . . . and Jay was always a sucker for gratitude. Deep, respectful, female gratitude. It made him feel heroic.

Speaking Tamil – the somewhat rough-and-ready Tamil he'd picked up from years of dealing with the local Muslim jewellers after learning, the hard way, that his own Sinhalese counted for nothing in that quarter – Jay told Tariq that a lakh, in cash, was more than enough for his services, no matter what kind of stone they found. He wasn't in the business of thieving from his sister's friends.

Tariq said nothing.

'And you're to cut the thing tonight, Tariq. No hanging about. They'll want to take it with them on the plane.'

'I'll cut it when I'm paid.'

'Oh, you'll be paid.'

He turned to Paul. 'A lakh is a hundred thousand rupees. It's a fair price.'

Paul barely had time to convert it into pounds. His nod was more obedient than authoritative.

'Great. Let's go.' Finishing his cup of tea, Jay gathered together the broken folds of road map that he and Tariq had been perusing and stood up. 'I'm sorry,' he said to Hassan – again, in halting Tamil. 'I'll look out for those moonstones. I'll get a good price . . .'

Hassan shrugged his shoulders with the indifference of prosperity, and left Chanaka to see them out.

Chapter Three

Five hours later, Sophie found herself sitting alone in the passenger seat of Jay's jeep, waiting for the men to return from the auction. It had been parked in the shade at the side of the road, but the heat was still extreme. No matter that it was a good few hundred feet above sea level, Ratnapura was inland – surrounded by a combination of dense jungle and flat stretches of paddy fields, miles away from the coastal breezes. Even with the windows open, Sophie's healthy Celtic body was covered in a thick film of sweat. The skin on her back and arms slipped against the faux-leather upholstery. The sunglasses that had looked quite chic in the airport now slid down the bridge of her nose. Pushing them back up for the umpteenth time, Sophie noticed her reflection in the wing mirror and – laughing grimly – put her wet head in her hands.

Jesus. She shouldn't be swearing, but – *Jesus!* What on earth had she been thinking? How had she imagined that an expedition into the unknown, with some half-brother of a friend of a random friend of Paul's he hadn't seen for years . . . how was this a nice way to go about finding an engagement ring? How had she managed to let what should have been a charming and companionable stroll – ending in an easily acquired ring and a few happy memories – turn into some sort of endurance test? Worse, a solo endurance test. For while it wasn't unheard of for women to attend stone auctions, Tariq didn't want Sophie. Didn't want Paul, either – a snow-white tourist with a fat money-belt would hardly advance their bargaining position – but Paul had been adamant. He'd wanted to see the stone in question. He'd wanted the complete experience.

'Fine,' Jay had said, slamming the door – checking his watch. 'But don't draw attention to yourself, Paul – or the fact that you're with us. Don't talk to me. And certainly don't talk to Tariq. Don't even *look* at him. Pretend you're writing for a newspaper, or – I don't know . . . taking photographs for a gemstone journal or something –'

'Okay, okay.'

'. . . and maybe we'll be all right.'

So Paul went with them while Sophie, aware that Tariq had been overruled, that pride was involved, agreed to stay in the car – not realising quite what this entailed, or how long she would have to wait. She couldn't even go for a stroll – Jay had been very clear about that. Not down this deserted lane. It wasn't safe. So here she was – confined, alone, bored, in this oven of a jeep. Could it be any less romantic? They'd already been gone an hour with no sign of a return – not even a text from Paul. And now . . . well, if he came around that corner right now and saw her as she was, Sophie rather doubted he'd be interested in giving her an engagement ring at all.

41

Noticing that Jay had left the keys in the ignition, she turned on the car radio – but the chatter of Sinhalese and insistent Bollywood music did nothing to calm her. She switched it off. And then, after three or four attempts to relive the moment he'd asked her to marry him – a moment that seemed to get shorter and shorter with each repeat – Sophie opened her eyes, and reached for the handle to the glovebox. Perhaps Jay liked reading. Perhaps he'd have a book in there, or maybe a newspaper. A boiled sweet would be nice. A different pair of sunglasses to try on. Although, in her sweaty state of boredom, even a car manufacturer's manual would be better than—

Sophie's hand shot back into her lap. Her jaw dropped open and dangled there for a moment, in parallel with the dangling glovebox door, before she quietly closed both again.

A handgun? Tentatively, Sophie reopened the glovebox. She didn't take the gun out, she had no desire to move the thing, but there was something about it that fascinated her. For, in spite of all the movies and television dramas she'd watched over the years, Sophie had never seen a gun at first hand. It was a pistol. It lay nonchalantly on its side – blackened steel, small, discreet – together with a couple of strips of shinier steel which, she assumed, were refill magazines . . . on top of a pile of papers that she had no intention of looking at now. Idly, she wondered what it would be like to hold – it seemed so neat and would easily fit into her handbag, along with a mobile and a bunch of keys. Almost glamorous, in a Charlie's Angels way, until someone's blood was actually spilt and a man lay dead in the road.

*

'. . . back by eight, Paul. Eight at the latest. It's faster going down. The roads will be emptier—'

Sophie flicked the flap back up.

'You're here!' she cried, getting out of the car. Paul looked wonderfully out of his depth – his hair every bit as limp as hers, his shorts badly crumpled, his cheeks almost purple, his expression confused. She gave him a sweaty kiss. 'Any luck?'

He felt in the pocket of his shorts and removed a small paper package. Unfolding the paper in the shade of the jeep and balancing it in the palm of his hand he revealed a small matt dirty-pink lump.

Sophie took it from Paul's open hand and held it in her own. It was warm.

'It's a padparascha.'

Sophie frowned.

'Padparascha,' said Paul, again – pronouncing it *padpa-racha* as the others did. 'It means "lotus flower".'

Jay put a hand on Sophie's shoulder. 'It's all right,' he said, smiling down at her. The smile was wide – almost elated. 'It won't look like that when it's cut. In fact, it'll look astonishing. A blend – a real blend – of pink and orange, which might sound nasty, but trust me. A decent padparascha, a natural one like this, the colour . . . it's extraordinary. The reason you've never heard of them is because they're rare. You only find them here in Sri Lanka – they're very special, Sophie. Truly unusual.'

Sophie looked at the small misshapen stone, at its dull surface, its lack of presence.

'We don't know exactly how good this particular one is,' Jay went on, reaching through the open window of his jeep and taking out a torch, which he then switched on and placed underneath the stone to show Sophie a little more of the interior. To her eye, it still looked decidedly murky. '. . . which, of course, makes it even more interesting to someone like me. We've taken – or rather, Paul has taken – a bit of a risk. There's a chance it may not be a padparascha at all. Just an ordinary pink sapphire –'

Ordinary pink sapphire? Sophie glanced at Paul.

'. . . which is what makes the thing affordable.' Jay tossed the torch back through the open window. 'And why it's even for sale on the open market. In fact, I should probably warn you that Tariq doesn't think it's a pad. There was no mention of it at the auction. It was sold to us as a slightly overpriced pink which, I have to say, may well be all it is.' Jay turned to his expert. 'Not convinced, are you?'

Tariq leant over the bonnet of the jeep – chewing betel. He didn't bother to reply.

'Never is,' said Jay, amused. 'Thinks I don't know what I'm doing. Thinks I should stick to dealing – he's probably right. But,' suddenly serious, 'I've just got a hunch about this stone. At certain angles, there's warmth in here – to my eye, at any rate. And it'll still be pretty, Sophie – even if I'm wrong. *Please* don't look so anxious. Whatever it is, it'll be beautiful. A lot will depend on how Tariq cuts it. We think there may be a couple of inclusions at one end . . . this one, see? Where it's darker? And it may be better for you to end up with a small stone that's perfect – rather than a bigger one with visible flaws . . . but I suggest you leave all that to Tariq. He'll know how to get the best out of it.'

Sophie looked again at Paul. Beside the flushed, thrilled Jay and the deadpan Tariq – inscrutable behind his shades – poor Paul seemed wan, pale, out of his depth. She hoped he hadn't spent thousands.

Jay gave her back the stone. He got in behind the wheel. 'But it's a good one,' he said, starting the engine. 'I know it. I know it in my gut.'

Chapter Four

It was a fast ride back to the coast. The air was cooler, and by the time they were out of the jungle the sun sat low in the sky: blinding, when they were driving into it ... but to look in the other direction, the impression was quite different. The reduced light threw a dusty pink haze over the villages and tea plantations they passed; over places and people that, in the midday glare of their outward journey, had seemed almost one-dimensional, poverty and hardship flatly exposed. The whole landscape seemed relieved that the day was done, stretching and softening like a worker coming home. But as Jay's jeep hurtled through it – rough, aggressive, overtaking blind with only the briefest double-toots from the trucks in front to signal that the way was clear – such scenic subtleties were lost on Paul and Sophie. He felt for her hand across the back seat of the car.

'You think we should call your parents?'

Sophie shook her head. 'I sent Mum a text. They won't wait – Father Perera's having some sort of party tonight. I expect they'll go to that. She seemed pretty relaxed ...'

'Great,' said Paul – jaw tightening as, once again, Jay tried and failed to pass the bus in front of them.

Sophie felt his discomfort. Paul was an uneasy traveller at the best of times – always worried about being late, or running out of fuel, or taking the wrong turning. She'd seen him checking co-passengers on their flight out from London, secretly searching for possible terrorists. Still holding his hand, she leant forward and asked Jay how much longer he thought the journey was likely to take.

Jay looked at his watch. 'Once I get past this bus, it shouldn't be more than half an hour. There may be a bit of traffic getting into your part of town. It's the New Oriental, isn't it?'

'Or – or anywhere,' said Paul, quickly. 'Really. I'm sure we could get a taxi from your place, if that works better for you.'

'Don't be silly,' said Jay as the road reached a corner and the bus ahead tooted that the way was clear. With a brisk spin of the steering wheel, he pulled out once more on to the other side of the road, heading at speed into the path of oncoming traffic. It was hard to tell how far away it was; confusing, with the headlights in the gauzy air and the rattling, rusty body of the bus to their left. And then, in the middle of this manoeuvre, Jay decided to answer his mobile. 'Yes?' he said, fixing the thing between his chin and his collarbone. Paul closed his eyes. He needn't have worried – Jay did it with yards to spare – but the changing grip on Sophie's hand, the way it moved from tender to vicelike, made her smile.

'Sorry, Ma. Can you say that again?'

For a moment or two, there was silence. The car sped on into evening shadow – leaving the bus far behind.

They could see the glow at the end of Tariq's cigarette, and the distant lights of Galle.

'Sure,' said Jay at last. 'I'll ask them now.' Turning round now – smiling at Paul, 'You guys free for dinner?'

Paul and Sophie looked at each other.

Telling his mother he'd call her back, Jay put the mobile down and reached for his cigarettes. 'There's no pressure,' he said, offering them around. Neither Paul nor Sophie smoked. Tariq had his own. 'Mind if I – ?'

'Not at all.'

'Go ahead.'

Lighting one, Jay cleared his throat. 'The thing is,' he went on, 'she's been gossiping with Gab . . . who made the mistake of telling her about you both, and now of course she's desperate to meet you.' He coughed again. 'Poor Ma. She's a bit starved of romance at the moment, what with Gabby still single, and me . . . well, me being me . . . any possibility of talking weddings and rings and dresses and so on, while simultaneously introducing you to a bit of Sri Lankan cuisine . . . she just can't help herself. Gabby'll be there. And George – my older brother George. You met him?'

Paul hesitated. He had met George Franklin – once, briefly, at a party. It had been at the height of his relationship with Marianne. He hadn't realised, until it was too late, that George was the Franklin of Franklin Asset Management – a highly respected specialist investment-management firm which had been much in the press at the time, due to its pulling off a coup by going into partnership with the powerful Kau Lung Banking Corporation. Paul had rather dismissed the guy, taking him to be as lightweight and irrelevant as

48

his sister. Worse, he had been showing off to Marianne about some deal he was working on at the time – a deal that had been about to hit the financial press. George Franklin had stood there for a moment or two, saying nothing, and had then drifted away. And it was only a week or so later, as he read a profile about dynamic new faces to watch in the City – and saw the accompanying mugshots – that Paul understood his error. The Franklin name still invoked in him a fleeting sense of shame – the sort of shame an amateur musician might feel when, having volunteered some impromptu entertainment at a friend's dinner party, he suddenly realises he's in the company of a virtuoso.

'Well, anyway. He's around, plus wife and kids – although I expect the kids will be in bed. Helen's rather strict.' Jay put the cigarette back to his mouth and dragged on it, heavily. 'As I say, no pressure. You've probably had enough local colour for one day . . . but if you like the idea of joining us and being interrogated to death about your wedding plans . . .' he was grinning now at Sophie through the rear-view mirror – 'then of course you're more than welcome.'

Which was how, a few hours later, Paul and Sophie found themselves sipping mojito cocktails on Anusha Franklin's verandah, listening to the crickets and to Jay telling the others about their day.

Anusha's house sat a little out of the town, on a shady hill with views across to the old Galle Fort and on to the ocean beyond. It wasn't directly on the beach and, in many ways, its detachment from the main tourist attractions gave it a certain serenity – an air of belonging to the community – which the modern villas lacked. Not that Anusha needed any boost to her sense of belonging to Galle. For while her villa had originally been built by a Dutch merchant back in the eighteenth century, while its origins were colonial and its influences European, it had still, at the end of that same century – shortly after the Dutch were ejected by the British – found its way into the hands of Anusha's great-great-great grandfather. He'd been a Sinhalese shipbuilder who knew a thing or two about collaboration with settlers . . . and the villa had remained in the family ever since. It was large, but not especially so. And even though the local term for such establishments, *walawe*, was, strictly speaking, a distortion of the original *walawes* (which were ducal in scale, vast palaces, richly staffed, remnants of a once-thriving feudal system long predating any Dutch settlements), these 'new *walawes*' were mere miniatures – with a section of Sinhalese society considering their owners poor pretenders to the grandeurs of the past. However, the villas still had beauty and dignity, and something historic – albeit colonial – that lent them a particular charm. Like many of the others, Anusha's was square in structure, with a low tiled roof that was covered with bougainvillea. It had been set around an inner cobbled courtyard where an ancient fig tree occupied the centre. And all around the outside lay a large tropical garden full of frangipani and flame trees, fuschia and hibiscus. It had terraces and steps that led down to a subtle grey-stone swimming pool. It needed three full-time gardeners to keep it going, and Anusha was more than happy to employ them.

But, while she was willing to pour effort and resources into the garden, her approach to the interior was rather more restrained. With her Western education and natural sense of style, she understood the charm that came from rooms that had evolved, rooms that hadn't simply been stripped down and redone from scratch. Yes, she had the money to make it all new, but she preferred to patch up her grandmother's hand-painted wallpaper, repair those creaking colonial fans, plaster up the filigree latticework in the walls, keep those heavy old Dutch chests in the library . . . while simultaneously introducing a pair of broad modern sofas, widescreen televisions and bookshelves filled with anything and everything from eighteenth-century bird books to bright, shiny catalogues from the latest exhibitions at the Metropolitan Museum of Art. Anusha was proud of her Cambridge degree, proud of her early days as a translator at the United Nations headquarters in New York and subsequent marriage to Archie Franklin. She liked her house to reflect the eclectic nature of her life, and the lives of her forebears. She was proud to come from a line of travellers – travellers who still knew where they came from, and the importance of coming home.

Sophie loved it. After the trauma of the road, the sensation of tranquillity that she was now experiencing was close to exquisite. Watching the moonlit surface of the swimming pool through the dark twisting branches of the frangipani trees – their clean lines making a kind of abstract pattern against the silvery water – she realised that, in spite of initial misgivings, she was glad that Paul had accepted the invitation; glad to have stepped out of the guidebook, off the tourist trail, and into something unique.

And it wasn't such a big party in the end. Aside from herself and Paul, and Anusha and Jay – who was talking about the stone, explaining to the others that they didn't have it with them because Tariq had already taken it back to his workshop, charged with the task of cutting and polishing it overnight – the only other people on the verandah that evening were George and Helen Franklin.

Gabriella was absent. A hastily remembered prior engagement found her leaving the villa, dressed to the nines, just as Jay and the others pulled up at the gates. Only mildly embarrassed, she wound down the window of her air-conditioned car to explain.

'Rory's leaving dinner – so awful – I totally forgot.'

Jay didn't bother to reply. Shaking his head, he simply pulled his jeep to one side and waited for his sister to close the window of her car again, and drive past them, out into the road.

In many ways Sophie was glad of Gabby's absence. It was awkward enough sitting next to Helen Franklin – who was exuding an air of simplicity that could only be achieved by a grooming regime that was anything but . . . with smooth toffee-coloured legs stretching all the way down to perfectly graded toenails. In the candlelight, they looked more like matching strings of pearls than caps of hardened flesh. And then there was Anusha, who was so phenomenally young-looking it was hard to believe she was the mother of a fully-grown man. She sat opposite Sophie – darkly beautiful, and covered in the most amazing jewellery. Even George, in a soft pink shirt and a pair of linen trousers that had, undoubtedly, been sourced by his wife, even he had a certain sort of glamour. And poor Sophie felt as out of her depth with these gleaming people as Paul sometimes felt – for widely differing reasons – with her family and friends. All of a sudden, her worthy economies in the field of body-maintenance seemed almost disgustingly neglectful. How could she have failed to get a pedicure before coming on holiday? How could she have laughed at dear, sweet Maggs – her friend from teacher-training – for suggesting she try a bit of light fake tanning? And as for those unsightly nicks on her shins – if she chose to use a razor, an old one at that, Sophie only had herself to blame. For, in spite of the twenty minutes that she and Paul had just enjoyed in Anusha's Victorian-style bathroom – in spite of the pretty fresh kaftan she'd been lent, the chic wooden hair-clasp, the sparkly flip-flops – Sophie knew herself to be a cut below. She could tell herself it didn't matter, she could chastise herself for minding – for being so silly, so vain, so self-absorbed – but the sense of herself as inadequate, of her femininity as having been some-how annihilated by the others' beauty . . . it rocked her. And while she had nothing against Gabby (indeed, had rather warmed to what little she'd seen of her in Hassan's store that morning: the stream of childlike outrage at the idea of taking second place to Tariq, the shameless hassling to get her brother to take Paul and Sophie with them in the jeep, the lack of interest in maintaining decorum . . . there was a natural energy to Gabby's egotism that stood in refreshing contrast to vicarage virtue) – yet, for all that, Sophie knew that the presence of yet another well-groomed woman that evening would probably have finished her off.

She took a large minty gulp from her mojito, turned a little in her chair – so that Helen's beautiful legs were no longer immediately, offensively, visible – and launched herself into the padparascha conversation.

'I can't wait to see it!' she said, overdoing the fervour. 'How long do you think Tariq will take?'

Jay smiled. 'Well, if he's doing what he should be doing, and there's no reason for him not to be, not when there's a lakh on delivery, then I don't see why you and Paul can't pick it up tomorrow.'

'Oh, how exciting.'

More smiles. Jay put down his glass. 'And then the only thing you still have to consider is what you're going to do about getting the thing set.'

Paul and Sophie looked at each other.

'It would certainly be cheaper to have it done out here,' Jay added. 'Much cheaper. Although I doubt we'd find someone who could do it for you in time – you'd need to have it sent back separately, and then you get all the tiresome complications and expenses involved with getting it through customs and so on – whereas, if you take it through yourselves . . .' He smiled at Sophie's innocent face. 'You can declare it if you want, sweetheart. You just—'

'What does that cost?' said Paul, unconvincingly casual, sipping his mojito as he waited for the reply.

'Well, on top of the whopping seventeen point five per cent VAT you pay on arrival in London, there are various local charges here – a basic duty . . . point seven per cent, I think it is . . . and insurance costs, postage and so on, which no doubt would take them for ever to process, with masses of paperwork . . . it's incredibly boring and time consuming, and you'd probably end up paying more than you would if you bought the thing in London. Which is why it makes sense for punters like you, with one-off pieces, to bring them through yourselves. Take the risk. It's so tiny.'

'And then?'

Jay smiled at him. 'Well,' he said, 'if I were you, I'd probably take it straight to Marianne. She's genuinely talented. Still cheap-ish – might even give you a discount. Still relatively unknown . . .'

Jay let his sentence drift – struck by some sixth sense, some strange instinct for caution that sometimes hit him when reaching the climax of a deal. He glanced at Sophie. How much did she know?

'Who's Marianne?' said Sophie.

Paul told her. 'She's Gabby's business partner, darling. Remember?'

'Of course. I'm sorry.' She smiled at the others.

'She's also Jay's girlfriend,' said George, getting up from his chair and heading over to the table for a refill. 'Which might make you question his bias a little. She—'

'George . . .'

'I'm not saying she's second-rate,' George went on, ignoring his brother and speaking, very deliberately, to Paul. 'Far from it. I'm only saying you might want to look around a bit, get a sense of the market, just in case there's something you prefer. Something you—'

'Girlfriend?' said Paul, stupidly slow as he turned from George to Jay. 'Marianne Cooper's your *girlfriend*?'

'I think she's a little bit more than a girlfriend,' said Anusha, also getting up, and giving her son a look he'd come to recognise in recent months. 'Don't you?'

Jay looked back at her, saying nothing, while Paul ploughed on.

'Your – your fiancée, then?'

Anusha couldn't help herself. 'One would have hoped that to be the case,' she said to Paul, 'when the girl's expecting their baby in the New Year. I'm telling you! If Jehan hasn't asked her to marry him by then, I'll damn well drag that boy to London myself and force them up the aisle. They – honestly, Paul, why can't they do it properly? Like you and Sophie . . .'

55

Paul looked at her.

'What's stopping them?'

There was an awkward moment. Startled, Paul looked at his hostess. 'I don't know,' he mumbled. 'I – I guess everyone's different . . .'

Muttering, Anusha disappeared inside. Even the crickets were silent.

'But she's a good designer, you say?' said Sophie, grabbing at what was left of their conversation.

Jay nodded, amused. He was used to his mother's ranting. She only called him 'Jehan' when she knew she was losing. 'Of course, a lot of it is down to personal taste,' he said, 'but even so, I can't think of anyone as good as Marianne.'

'There's Mark Jardine.'

'Yes, George. And there's Tiffany, and Asprey, and Cartier, and Theo Fennell. But that's hardly—'

'You should still look around,' said George, ignoring his brother. 'I spent months making sure I had the right person for Helen's.'

'Let's see it,' said Sophie, turning, smiling, leaning towards Helen's outstretched hand. 'Oh, it's beautiful! Paul, look at this!'

Paul came over, and the pair of them looked at Helen's diamonds – two of them, nestling yin-and-yang against each other in a horizontal sixty-nine.

'It's nice,' said Helen, in qualified tones – tilting her wrist so that she could see it too, 'Mark did a good job. But I have to say, if we were doing it again, I'd seriously consider Marianne. Have you seen the necklace Anusha's wearing? That's her. And,' turning now to George, 'you remember that amazing emerald she set for Miles's sister?'

George looked back with a neutral expression.

'You liked it, didn't you? I'm sure you said—'

'I did. You're right.'

'Then—'

'Absolutely. I'll go to Marianne next time.'

Helen sat back satisfied. And then, realising what her husband had just implied, suddenly sat forward again. '*Next* time?'

Inscrutable as ever, George leant forward – over a garden candle that had flickered out. 'Anyone got a match?'

And Sophie, full of sudden pity for George – who was only trying to make sure they didn't rush at it, that they got it right; and who'd clearly spent a fortune on his wife's beautiful ring, all for a lukewarm 'nice' – said quickly, 'What's the name again?'

'Marianne Cooper.'

'No, the other one,' said Sophie, indicating Helen's ring. 'Your one. This one.'

'Oh, Mark. Mark Jardine. He used to work at Mappin and Webb, made a name for himself there first, got properly established, and then set up by himself – about ten years ago . . .'

'And you've still got his number?'

George smiled at her. 'Of course I have.'

Later, after dinner, as they waited for the taxi to take them back to the hotel, Sophie prompted Paul to take Mark Jardine's number from George. But they also took Marianne's and it was clear, to everyone, which designer she really preferred. It wasn't simply that Marianne would be cheaper than Mark Jardine – although that was, of course, a factor. It was the jewellery itself. Helen might have been careless of her husband's feelings, but there was no mistaking the eye-catching beauty of Anusha's necklace. And her earrings, her bangles, her anklet . . . all by Marianne. All exquisite. Sophie had observed them closely throughout dinner.

'I just hope she isn't too expensive,' she said, snuggling – childlike – into Paul on the back seat of their taxi as it headed home to their hotel. 'I hate to think how much you must have spent on that stone.'

Paul smiled. 'Then don't,' he said, thinking of the calls he would need to make tomorrow to transfer funds from his savings account into Jay Franklin's. The idea of that savings account getting smaller didn't thrill him, but Sophie had a bit of cash put by, he knew. They'd be all right. 'It's none of your business.'

Sophie fell dutifully silent, but her brain was buzzing. 'One more thing,' she said, 'and then I promise I'll shut up about it, darling. But please don't go to Mark Jardine. Don't think I was really keen, or anything. I was only—'

'Being kind.' Paul stroked her hair. 'I know you were.'

And Sophie, nestling against him as she looked out of the window at the rooftops and telegraph wires, speeding by, and at the moon far above them, steadily keeping pace – Sophie couldn't help but feel a flicker of guilt at her own happiness, at the unfairness of it all.

'Poor George,' she murmured.

Poor George? Shuffling a little – her head was digging into his shoulder – Paul thought of the man's detached air of success, of the way he'd disappeared in the middle of dinner to take a telephone call, of the brisk way he'd dealt with his wife's gaffe. He thought of how he'd once looked up to men like George – seen them as role models – and of how that had all changed.

'I don't think you need to feel too sorry for George Franklin,' he said, kissing the top of his fiancée's head. 'Pray for him, by all means. But don't, for God's sake, fret about his ego.'

'They *must* have done it! Nobody would get engaged without—'

'They're Christians.'

'I'm a Christian.'

Jay coughed.

'I am!'

The others all looked round at each other, all failing to suppress their mirth as Jay continued, in a shaky voice, 'Gabby, darling – I love you. I really do. But – honestly – you're as much a Christian as I am the Pope! You *can't*—'

'I believe in God, and Jesus, and so on. I pray. I go to church.'

'When?' said Jay, crying now with laughter. '*When* did you last go to church, sweetheart?'

'The Eyres' wedding.'

'In June.'

'And we went at Easter, me and Mum –'

'Only because there's nothing better to do in Basingstoke.'

Crossly, Gab lit a cigarette. 'Anyway,' she said, wishing she hadn't come home so early. 'What's church got to do with it? I'm still a Christian, I still believe in God, and I have to say I've no *intention* of marrying someone without knowing what he's like in bed. It's madness! In this day and age . . . What if they—'

'They're saving themselves,' said Anusha.

'Paul hasn't saved himself. I know that for a fact. He and Marianne were at it like rabbits.'

'That was before he met Sophie.'

Gabby shrugged. 'He's hardly a virgin.'

'Bet she is, though,' said Jay, stealing one of his sister's cigarettes.

There was a moment's silence while the five of them considered the state of Sophie's virtue.

'Probably never had the opportunity,' said Helen, catching Gabby's eye.

'Now, now.' Gabby giggled.

'I didn't mean—'

'Of course you did. Not her fault, of course – poor girl. Could probably do something about her skin, a haircut would help, but she's never going to look like – like Marianne, now, is she?'

Yawning in the lamplight, Helen looked at her ring again. 'So what do you think Paul sees in her?'

'It's more what she sees in *him* that baffles me,' said George, from behind an old copy of the *Observer*.

The others looked at each other.

'You're serious?'

'George?'

'Mm?' said George – still screened by the paper, still seemingly lost in the article he was reading.

'What's wrong with Paul?'

George put the paper down. He looked up at the whirring fan. But before he could answer, Jay cut in. 'There's nothing wrong with Paul,' she said. 'George just can't see why a man who is only moderately successful on the business front—'

'Moderately successful?' said George, amused. 'The man's a total failure. He couldn't hack it at LKPC, he had some extremely dodgy-sounding job at SwissBank, which he left after three months, and now he's some sort of charities consultant for an outfit I've never heard of, and which probably doesn't exist.'

Triumphant, Jay looked at the women – as if this remark had completely proven his point. 'He just can't see why such a man could ever be attractive!'

George picked up the paper again. 'The God Thing doesn't help.'

'She sounds just as bad,' said Gabby. 'From what you've been saying . . .'

'At least Sophie isn't fake. Her father's a vicar. It's in her blood. Paul, on the other hand . . .' George looked as if he'd eaten a lemon. 'I'm sorry, but the sight of him sitting there, hogging the high-ground, pretending that he left the City for moral reasons . . .'

'Perhaps he did.'

George snorted. 'Believe me, Gab, the City would have had the measure of a phoney like Paul Farage infinitely more quickly than Paul would have had the measure of the City. He was sacked. Or as good as sacked. And now he's using the Church as some sort of refuge –'

'Isn't that rather the point of the Church?' said Helen, feeling clever.

'He's *flaky*, my love.'

'I see. Because he thinks there's more to life than balance sheets and profit-and-loss accounts, and – and due diligence, and so on – because of that, he's a flaky do-gooding monster?'

'I didn't say he was a monster.' George sat forward, clasping at his head. 'I just think – Church aside – no decent man would consider going to an ex-girlfriend for an engagement ring.'

'Even if the ex were as talented as Marianne?' said Jay – studiously casual – helping himself to one of his sister's cigarettes.

61

Hair awry, George looked at him. 'You *can't* think it's okay!'

'I don't think it's so terrible, George.' Jay lit the cigarette and sat back. 'And if it means that Marianne and Gabby get a bit of business their way . . .'

'Then everything's all right?'

Jay rolled his eyes. 'Well, it would be, if you would only shut up about it for a few fucking seconds, and stop interfering.'

Astonished, George stared at his younger brother – a brother he loved – who was normally so laid back, so easy-going, so slow to lose his temper.

'Honestly, George! How can you accuse Paul of being holier-than-thou, and then get all self-righteous yourself about where the poor guy gets his stone set?'

Silence.

'How would you like it,' Jay blazed on, 'if I had a friend with a business needing financial services, and I went *out of my way* to send them to one of your rivals?'

George looked up at the fan again, spinning above their heads. 'I wouldn't like it,' he admitted. 'I'd feel let down.'

'Then don't do it to Gab and Marianne.'

'But it's not—'

'Back off. Let Paul make his mistake – if mistake it is. Show a bit of loyalty, can't you? And let your sister get her business off the ground.'

Chapter Five

Paul was getting jittery. He hadn't really expected that the stone would be ready the next morning – he knew how things worked in countries like Sri Lanka, he wasn't particularly surprised. But when it still wasn't ready by the end of the day – or even the day after that – he started to worry. The funds had gone through now, and there was nothing to show for it. Even Sophie was concerned. And as they waited, it became increasingly clear that they'd be lucky to have the thing in time to take with them on the flight back to London.

Jay was full of remorse. 'You will have it tomorrow morning, Paul. I promise. In the meantime, all I can do is say how incredibly sorry I am. It never normally—'

'We're leaving at midday.'

Jay reached for his cigarettes. 'I know,' he said, taking one out. 'And believe me, I'm not at all happy with Tariq about this. He's got a lot of explaining to do. But he has sworn to me, on his son's life, that he'll have it for you in time. He's done the cutting, it's just the polishing left now, and the best news, Paul, is that it *is* a padparascha!'

Paul's legs stopped swishing at the swimming-pool water. He sat at the edge, with the hotel telephone tight against his ear as Jay explained the significance of this. The stone, he said, might be smaller than Paul was expecting – apparently, Tariq had needed to cut it that way to preserve the purity – but it was, for sure, the right decision. A small, pure padparascha was infinitely more valuable than a large one with a visible inclusion. And Tariq had gone for a cushion-cut design which, again, was the perfect choice for the stone. In short, they had a great deal!

'And?' said Paul.

Jay was confused. 'Well – well, it's a beautiful natural stone,' he said. 'Compared to a pink sapphire, which is easily what it might have been, it will have a certain extra quality – you'll understand when you see it – a magic—'

'But what are we talking? A grand? Two grand?'

Jay lit a cigarette. 'No,' he said, wearily. It was always money at the end of the day – no matter how exceptional the stone. He hoped this padparascha wouldn't be wasted. Hoped that Sophie, at least, would be deserving. 'No, Paul – if you wanted to buy something similar on the open market in London, you wouldn't get much change from ten. Maybe even twelve.'

For a moment or two, all he could hear was the drone of the hotel swimming pool filter – and the soft splosh, splosh of water, lapping against the side.

'*Twelve grand?*' said Paul at last. '*Sterling?*'

'Happy now?'

'Very happy,' said Paul, calculating – from the price he'd actually paid for the rough stone that day in Ratnapura – that he must have made close to eight thousand pounds. 'So long as the damn thing gets here.'

Jay closed his eyes. He was starting to think that George might have had a point – certainly, this was a very different Paul from the one he'd had in his jeep. 'Tariq will be at your hotel at ten o'clock,' he said. 'I've told him you're leaving at eleven – you've got an hour's margin – and of course I'll make sure my mobile's switched on, so if you do have any problems you can—'

'Hang on, there.' Paul was out of the water, padding back to his sun-lounger, footsteps wet and sloshy on the hot tiles. 'You're coming with him, aren't you?'

'I'm sorry, Paul. I can't. I've already made plans.'

'But how will I know it's real?'

'Real?' said Jay.

'How will I . . .?'

'What exactly are you saying?'

'Twelve grand, Jay! Twelve fucking grand!'

Jay stiffened. 'Tariq wouldn't pull a fast one, if that's what you're implying. He might miss a deadline, might push for a better price, but—'

'How can I be sure?'

Jay held the telephone away from his ear for a moment. He looked at it before answering. 'Well, Paul, apart from Tariq's innate honesty, his track record here in Galle, his reputation as a top rough-stone expert, his place in a family of Muslim jewellers stretching back centuries, it's not in his interests to ruin the lucrative relationship he has with me.'

'I'd still like you to be here.'

'I'm sorry, Paul. That just isn't possible.'

Silence.

'I can send Gabby, if you like.'

Still, Paul was silent.

'You want her?' Jay waited. 'It's Gabby or nothing. You decide.'

The following morning, after breakfast, with just over an hour to spare before their departure, Sophie and her parents decided to pay a final visit to the little church on the side of the road. Their bags were packed, their bill was paid, and only the business with the stone remained outstanding.

'You're sure you don't mind?' said Sophie, wiping her mouth with a hotel napkin as she turned to check with Paul. 'I could easily stay with you. It wouldn't be a problem. I'm only—'

'Go,' he said, smiling at her.

Still Sophie hesitated, hands uncertain on the rim on the table.

'Go!' he cried, shooing her off. 'I don't need you, darling – don't even want you, if I'm being honest, not when we're talking money and so on. It's better you're not with us.'

He was expecting some sort of row. Certainly, he was expecting Tariq to be late. And Paul was still in the hotel dining room finishing his coffee when, at five to ten – Tariq was ushered in by a waiter.

'Tariq! Good heavens! Here, take a seat. You've got the stone, then?'

Tariq took off his sunglasses. 'Where's Jay?'

Paul looked at him. *Where's Jay?* And then – slightly baffled – said, 'Didn't he tell you?'

'Tell me what?'

'He couldn't make it.'

Leaning forward, Tariq poured himself a cup of

coffee from the Mostyns' pot. He seemed deflated. And Paul, looking at this reaction, began to understand why Jay might have left his cutter in the dark. Tariq was no doubt under some sort of three-line whip. He'd clearly bust a gut to be there on time, to show Jay he was reliable, and now, after all that effort, the main man wasn't even here. Suspecting that if Tariq had known that Jay had no intention of being there that morning then Tariq himself might not have bothered either, Paul realised how close it had been.

'But we are getting Gabriella,' he added, for his own amusement.

And Tariq was still looking disdainful when Gabby herself appeared at the door.

'There you are,' she said, sitting beside them on one of the smart striped chairs, busying herself with her bags. 'Now, this has got to be quick. I have a massage in ten minutes and I can't be late. Where is it, Tariq?'

Tariq passed her the package.

'Thank you.'

Gabriella opened the package. Inside was a stone softly saturated with a colour approaching that of rosé wine. Taking it out, holding it between forefinger and thumb, Gabby lifted it to the light. Slowly, she turned it – letting the newly polished facets twinkle and sparkle in the morning sun. She and Paul gazed at the gentle hue, both trying to decide: pink or orange? It was impossible to say. Too knowing to be pink, too innocent to be orange . . . the blend was perfect. Wonderfully unresolved. Plainly, obviously – a perfect padparascha. Even Paul could see it.

He reached out. 'Can I?'

'Sure you can.' Smiling, Gabby passed it to him. 'You like it?'

'I love it,' he replied.

Neither of them noticed Tariq – sitting at the breakfast table, head bent, fiddling with the hinges on his sunglasses.

PART TWO – LONDON

Chapter Six

Marianne looked at the array of jewellery boxes set out along the counter, struggling with the unfamiliar sensation of not being able to make up her mind. It was lucky she'd already chosen the outer fabric – watered silk of catmint green (to Marianne's eye it held the right balance of classic and vintage, duchessy and thrifty, timeless and fashion-forward, pretty and intellectual) – long before this pregnancy took hold of her brain. Lucky that she and Gabby already had their business logo in place, for it had been easy to convert the intertwined lettering of Cooper Franklin they already used for their stationery into something they could use on their boxes. No problem there. The Box Company had everything ordered and printed and ready to go. It was just this final decision – about the box shapes themselves – that failed her. Not so much the ring boxes, where there was comparatively little choice, but what to use for the bigger pieces? Should they have regular square ones, or hexagonal ones, or round ones? Fat ones? Narrow ones? Spring-hinged? Magnetic? Or just stick with the pretty old-fashioned little hooks?

And would they ever need these beautiful giant tiara boxes?

Holding one of them on her lap – opening and closing it as she mulled the matter over – Marianne toyed with the idea of leaving the final decision to Gabriella. Gab wasn't pregnant. She had time on her hands – and had always shown far more interest in the packaging of their project than Marianne had. Why not pass the decision on to her? Except that Gab wouldn't be able to resist ordering more tiara boxes than ring boxes, just because they were prettier. Gab would have no qualms about taking the nine or ten different-shaped box types on offer, instead of a perfectly serviceable three or four. Marianne understood there was a certain sort of female mind prone to obsessions with stationery and linen. She knew that for such women – Gab included – the sight of a wide range of boxes in the showroom cupboard would certainly press the right buttons. And no doubt it would be nice to take them out from time to time and stroke them – while balance sheets and profit-and-loss accounts festered away in some back drawer. But would it bring in the business? In sheer desperation, Marianne would probably end up making pieces to fit the boxes, simply to justify the expense.

Not that they were struggling. On the contrary, Cooper Franklin had made good progress this year. It was more than ready for branded boxes and a proper showroom – no question. And Marianne was delighted by the fact that their success was finally showing signs of extending beyond the cushioned world of Gabby's contacts and word-of-mouth, into the real market. The decision to present at the national trade fairs had been instrumental to this success, particularly at last year's

International Jewellery London show at Earl's Court – where they'd won the Best Newcomer prize in their category. This award had made a big difference to thier business – eliciting serious approaches from some of the major buyers in the country. Of course there was still some way to go before they'd be able to get a stand at the super-prestigious Basle fair, but after only five years' trading, it was still quite a coup. And the website, too, was gathering interest . . . according to Gabriella, at any rate. It was early days, and their presence on the Internet was really more Gab's responsibility than Marianne's. She couldn't do *everything*. But as for letting Gabby loose on these delicious tiara boxes, she . . . no. It was better for Marianne to choose them herself. Here and now. Better to keep it simple.

'We'll take a hundred of these,' she said, picking out the style of ring box she liked and handing it to the man. 'Fifty of these square ones, thirty of the fatter bracelet boxes – that's right – and ten of those big round necklace cases you showed me earlier. No, the round ones.'

The man put them to one side, and then embarked on a slightly protracted conversation about payment and delivery details – for Marianne, fully prepared for a fight on the matter, was disconcerted to hear that her order could be turned around overnight, that the boxes could be delivered to her showroom as soon as tomorrow afternoon if someone was there to let them in.

'Don't you need more time?' she said, suspiciously.

The man checked her paperwork and shook his head. 'Up to you, of course,' he replied, with an amused glance at her bump. 'I've no doubt we could ask the factory to faff about for a few more days if that's really what you want. But we do find that, on the whole, most of our clients are delighted with a quick turnaround. So unless you have a particular problem—'

'It won't cost more?'

'No, madam. Although – again – we'd be more than happy to up the charges if that makes you feel more comfortable.'

Marianne grinned. 'I don't think that'll be necessary,' she said. 'Thanks all the same.'

Reaching for her bag, she got to her feet and – to her horror – wobbled. Quickly, her free hand grabbed the desk. She steadied herself. The moment passed. But the sting to her pride remained. Marianne didn't need to look at the man to know that he'd be wondering how to help, and whether to help, and all the rest of it . . . only, instead of gratitude, she felt overwhelmingly defensive. Refusing to acknowledge what had just taken place – refusing even to meet his eye – she pretended to search for something at the bottom of her bag, blocking his concern with a curve of her shoulder.

Oh, how she hated it: the elephantine vulnerability. From the outside, she looked neatly pregnant. But inside – especially for a woman used to lightness in her carriage – it was starting to feel very different. Recently, Marianne had caught herself reaching round to the small of her back and rubbing at it like some sort of caricature. It wasn't as if anything ached. It was more that she couldn't quite get used to the fact that she was changing – she was continually surprised by this new body of hers, with its different shape and balance. She would realise too late that she couldn't fit past someone's chair in a restaurant. She'd misjudge her energy. Bump against doors. And barely six months' gone. It was ludicrous.

Leaving with the details confirmed, and the man opening the door for her with sympathetic courtesy, Marianne walked the two hundred yards or so around a corner and into Hatton Garden itself – to the workshop where her two-dimensional designs were converted into three-dimensional works of art. And as she got closer, she started to run. Fuck it. She wasn't an invalid. Irked by what she perceived to be the mad mother brigade – the women who *never* drank and *never* ate gooey cheese or raw meat or pâté or, frankly, anything half tasty, women who'd leave the room if anyone was wicked enough to light a cigarette, women like her mother, and those yoga nutcases whose articles she read in magazines – Marianne had recently found herself actively embracing any opportunity to flout their edicts. She enjoyed her sprint to the workshop.

And in any case, it wasn't entirely unnecessary. With a six o'clock appointment fast approaching at the showroom – Paul and his fiancée were coming round for their preliminary engagement-ring discussion – she didn't have much time.

The prospect of this appointment had created, in Marianne, an uneasy fascination. Paul and his fiancée wanting to see her about a ring was weird. But it was also somehow irresistible. The date had been fixed for a couple of weeks now, and she'd even spoken to Paul a couple of times since the original call . . . though not for long and always quite specific, getting straight to the point: dates, times, prices, directions; it all seemed very civilised and normal. Too normal perhaps. It meant that the underlying oddness – which had yet to be brought into the open – was generating a strange sort of energy simply from lack of acknowledgement.

More than that, there was something compelling about this opportunity to dip into the past: a certain challenge it posed to the status of the present that – like that of a school reunion – Marianne found hard to decline. She liked testing herself. And, with her present life so very fine and bright, she felt confident of a happy result: the reinforcement of a personal trajectory in the right direction. She wasn't worried. Certainly not on her own account – not with Jay, and the baby, and the flourishing business. If anyone was going to find that evening's meeting difficult, then it was surely Paul.

But while Marianne would have preferred to be back at the showroom in time to let them in herself – she had no desire to add to Paul's discomfort – her dash to the workshop was, in truth, driven more by a practical imperative to be there before it closed than it was by thoughts of Paul and Sophie. Gabby could always let them in and get them started on the books and magazines until Marianne appeared – there was always some leeway at the showroom – but the workshop was a different matter. Those boys packed up on the dot. Tools down, radio silent, fans off, lights darkened, windows closed, dust settling in the evening light, clunk-shift-clunk with each heavy door, beep beep beep as the alarms were set . . . and off they'd go to the pub. Clients notwithstanding. Even Marianne.

The workshop was an intensely male environment. There were girls, now, in the high-security reception booths – and it was often a woman in charge of the more administrative areas of these Hatton Garden workshops – but the essential skilled work that went on in the inner sanctums of such places was invariably done by men. Men's men. East End- or Essex-born – with practical right-wing cab-driver ethics, and clothes and accents that often belied their true wealth. Men with tans from fancy holidays in the Algarve, who still had the rough-and-ready appearance of a market trader. It was, in many ways, a time warp to be in that environment. *The Sun* still did its daily round. And while the girlie calendars and posters that adorned the walls featured the likes of Jordan and Paris Hilton, it could, just as easily, have been Linda Lusardi and Samantha Fox. Car magazines sat on the windowsills, and no one cared very much about the facilities – so long as there was enough loo paper, Nescafé, sugar, and fresh milk.

Gabriella found these men tricky. They could be charming, flirty even – complimenting her on her appearance, or admiring the jewellery she'd chosen to wear that day – but tricky nonetheless. They'd tell her Wednesday, and still not have it ready by Friday. They'd shrug good-naturedly when she complained, but do absolutely nothing about it. They were always de-prioritising her deadlines – or suddenly making themselves unavailable when she really needed to explain exactly what she wanted for the adjustments to Lady Butterworth's brooch. It didn't help that their workshops were invariably in old Dickensian build-ings that were riddled with complicated passages and little rooms leading off one another and staircases where you wouldn't expect them to be . . . and Gab had no way of tracking them down; no way of creeping up on them unobserved – what with the security doors, the high-tech camera systems, and those stupid, sulky girls at reception.

Marianne often wondered what it was that Gabriella

did to make those girls choose to appear stupid in her presence. Melinda was a jeweller in her own right. Kerry and Faith were only there for the extra money while they studied for degrees in engineering and law. Hardly dumb. And as the sisters or nieces or daughters or even granddaughters of established silversmiths and polishers, these women often had an extra air of authority and entitlement. They knew the score. They were confident about refusing admittance to this jeweller or that courier if the right documents weren't produced. They certainly never questioned the sexist tone of the workshops. And while this only added to the whiff of mafia that pervaded Hatton Garden, again, it was hardly surprising. When one thought of the priceless items that passed through those work-shops on a daily basis, the need for trust was paramount. Marianne had no complaints.

'Melinda,' she said – a little breathlessly – into the street-level intercom, 'don't suppose Lee's still there, is he? We spoke this morning—'

The door buzzed open.

Marianne climbed to the top of the building, up to the workshop that she and Gabby had been using since their institute days. It was a shabby building. The stairs were narrow, badly lit, and lined with a frayed carpet of indeterminate colour. Marianne had long stopped notic-ing it. Today she was looking at her mobile as she climbed – waiting for her emails to come through. Midway up the second flight, she noticed that one of them was from Jay – and, smiling, paused to read it while she caught her breath. Jay's emails were never long.

'– but not a patch on you, Smidge,' he'd written, 'not unless virginity's an asset! xx'

Smile fading, Marianne continued slowly up the

stairs. Ever since Jay had told her about bumping into Paul and Sophie in Sri Lanka, they'd exchanged a number of merry emails on the subject. Marianne had learnt all about the trip to Ratnapura. She knew that Paul was engaged, and that he was bringing a padparascha back to the UK to be set – preferably by Marianne herself – long before he actually rang to make the appointment. Jay was tickled by Paul and Sophie's earnest Christianity – he'd been teasing Marianne about it, asking what she'd done to the poor man to send him hurtling into the chilly embrace of the Church. And while Marianne couldn't now remember exactly what she'd said to Jay in her last email, there was something about this latest one that didn't make her smile quite as much as the others.

'You there? I'm sorry, Lee . . .' She was out of breath.

Lee's tanned face appeared over the top banister. 'Hello,' he said, amused. 'You want me to come down?'

'No, no . . .' Marianne panted her way around the final corner. Meeting Lee's eye for a moment, she smiled, shook her head, and attacked the final flight. 'What's wrong with me? Only six months, and already I'm . . . Jesus. How am I even going to get up here in January?'

Lee laughed.

'I'm serious!'

'I know you are,' he said, rapping at the porthole so that Melinda could let them back in. 'We'll install a Stannah.'

'But how did Sam cope? And what about Kerry, with her twins . . .' she said, ignoring him and addressing the question to Melinda, who was waiting on the other side of the doors.

79

Melinda reached for her bag and coat. 'Kerry didn't try,' she said, passing Lee the entry book and an old blue biro, and letting herself out. 'She – don't you remember, love? We had that useless niece of Mike's . . .'

The doors clanged shut behind her, leaving Marianne and Lee alone together in the old, familiar workshop. Marianne could see that a rare attempt had been made to tidy it that evening. Melinda must have swept the floors – dust was everywhere. Tools had been put away in the open wooden boxes that lined the worktops. And the bigger items of work-in-progress, the pieces that couldn't go into the safe, the silver candlesticks and soup tureens and sporting cups and shields and plates, all sat – in varying stages of 'finish' – on shelves at the far end of the room.

Lee took the little brown envelopes that Marianne produced from the depths of her bag. There were three of them: an order for a christening bracelet with five turquoises to set; a pair of amethyst earrings; and an outsize tourmaline ring – all with accompanying designs and instructions. He checked the first two, and paused at the third.

'*Another* tourmaline?'

Marianne nodded. 'She needs it for Tuesday, Lee – asked me specially to make sure that you'd have it for her by then. You can do that, can't you?'

Lee pursed his lips.

'It shouldn't take you long. Just a—'

Lee shook his head. 'There's no problem *doing* it, love. I just . . .' – shaking his head – 'Nothing's straightforward with that Gabriella. Everything has to be finished yesterday. It does my head in.'

'This one really is urgent, Lee. She's going to the

States with it at the end of the week. She needs it—'

'When, exactly?'

Marianne tried to remember. 'Thursday? Friday, maybe? But—'

'Fine. You tell her she can have it Thursday morning. I'm sorry, love. But if she can't even be bothered to collect that Butterworth brooch – even after all that fussing and all that begging, and the *please, please, pleases . . .*'

'Didn't collect it?'

'Didn't even send a courier.' Going back into Melinda's office, to the safe that sat in the corner, Lee tapped a few numbers into the panel, pulled open the door, and produced another brown envelope – identical to the ones that Gabby had given him – with 'BUTTERWORTH' scrawled along the side.

Marianne looked at it in silence. There had been definite advantages to setting up the business with Gabriella. It wasn't just the glamorous contacts. Gabby also had access to a level of capital investment that Marianne simply couldn't hope to raise. Her father, a structural engineer, had died from cancer when Marianne was still a teenager, leaving her mother with an adequate pension for living expenses, but nothing spare. Even if she had been able to help fund her daughter's business, Marianne wasn't sure that her mother would have done so. For Patricia, who'd adored Marianne's father, had never really forgiven her daughter for directing that wonderful talent for design – a talent she'd clearly inherited from Neil – towards something as frivolous as jewellery. Why hadn't she become an engineer as well? Why wasn't she doing something more serious and worthwhile?

But Marianne's interest in bridges and tunnels was – at best – limited. And even if she had found more to excite her in engineering, there was something about her personality that would not have thrived on parental blessing. Indeed, Patricia's rejection of the jewellery business – far from making Marianne think twice – had inspired, if anything, the opposite effect from the one her mother intended. Sure, Marianne had an innate love of gemstones and design. Indeed, there was a part of her brain that, like the brain of an addict, would burst with delight at the moment of seeing light pass through a crystal: the purity of colour it generated, and then all the possibilities that followed, the subtle arts of how best to display that beauty, how to arrange it and set it off in such a way that it could be worn round the neck, the wrist, the finger, or set into the earlobe . . . all these things could absorb her mind indefinitely. A new design idea would keep her awake at night – searching, testing, imagining, pushing herself, on and on, until it was perfect. And the compulsion to create with such materials – the gemstone in the metal, and then how that combination might sit against the human form –was riveting, quite riveting. Responding to the challenge – in terms of design – of how best to expose the natural beauty of a stone was every bit as vital to her as food and sleep and sex. Often more so. Marianne would have been a jeweller, even if her mother had supported her. The fact that Patricia didn't, while sad from a personal point of view, was, from a purely creative perspective, perfect provocation. But Marianne still needed funding . . .

And that was where Gabriella had come in. Except that Gabby was, at best, a mediocre jeweller. Stylish, sure. Well-groomed. Glamorous. But none of those things guaranteed much talent in terms of gemmology and jewellery design. If anything, they were a hindrance. Gabby couldn't understand that designer clothes and regularly blow-dried long blonde hair did her no favours on the professional front. She didn't see that Marianne's scruffiness – that pencil in her cork-screw hair, that loose thread on the hem of her skirt, those sloppy boots with the trodden-down heels, that old black frock coat she lived in – all those things gave her credibility in Hatton Garden. It wasn't a place you dressed for – unless it was to remove your jewellery, or wipe off that lipstick. Gabriella couldn't grasp the essential duality of a jeweller's life. She had no sense of why the clothes and make-up she wore to seduce a client weren't necessarily appropriate for the boys in Hatton Garden. How was it possible to push for a discount, standing there in cream Chloé, with a TAG Heuer watch on her wrist?

Ever since her year at the institute, Gabriella had been determined to set up her own business – desperate to win the respect of her brothers, to be taken seriously and prove the likes of Dr Rogerson wrong. She just wasn't interested in grafting, she couldn't see the link. She wanted quick results. And with so many funds at her disposal, Gabby was in the enviable position of being able to make the business dream an instant reality. She knew that Marianne had something special. She knew she wanted Marianne as a partner. And Marianne – restless, after three months of dogsbodying at a place in Bond Street that had taught her nothing more than how to make a proper cappuccino – had been too tempted to turn down such an offer.

There was, however, a price to pay for this arrange-ment. Over the years, Marianne had come to accept her situation – gently edging Gabriella out of the more serious aspects of the business, allowing her the status without 'boring' her with essential details. And leaving Gab in charge of the website, while not ideal, was absolutely part of this tactic. It was only recently that the website had shown a return on all Gab's efforts – in the form of an enquiry from a Manhattan jeweller named Hoffmann Sawyer interested in stocking Cooper Franklin pieces (an enquiry that had so excited Gabriella that she was making a special trip to meet them). Marianne didn't believe it would lead to anything – she hadn't even heard of Hoffmann Sawyer – but if it kept Gabriella occupied and out of trouble . . .

There were, however, certain professional situations she simply couldn't avoid. On at least three occasions in the past five years, Marianne had been forced into the embarrassing position of having to renegotiate unfavourable deals which Gabby had struck. She was constantly obliged to clarify her partner's instructions, check her invoices, confirm her orders. It hadn't so much mattered at the start, when each commission was a one-off, when the scale was comparatively small. But as they expanded it was becoming clear to Marianne that this state of affairs was unacceptable. She sensed that it wouldn't be long before the association would start to affect her own reputation. Perhaps it was already doing so. There were only so many favours she could ask – even from Lee and his gang.

Apologising now, she took the Butterworth envelope, signed for it, and said that there was absolutely no hurry for the bracelet or the amethyst earrings. Any time in the next month would be fine by her. And Lee, entering the new envelopes into the workshop order book – together with their deadline details – closed the safe again, smiled at Marianne, and told her that wasn't the point. She could have *her* pieces whenever she liked. And Marianne, knowing this, could only say again how terribly sorry she was.

'Except you're not the one pissing me off,' said Lee, reaching for his coat. 'Now. Can I give you a lift anywhere? Or is that Jay downstairs?'

Marianne laughed. 'God, no. He's on the plane to Thailand now. Or should be –'

Lee's eye flitted to the bump beneath her coat.

'– and then it's Bogotá,' Marianne went on, proud of her intrepid lover. 'Then New York – possibly. Then Amsterdam. He won't be back until November.'

'Busy man.'

'I know! Sometimes I don't hear from him for weeks . . .'

'And you don't mind?'

Marianne smiled. Of course she didn't mind. But it was strange just how many people – even men like Lee – seemed to think that it was necessary to be constantly in one another's company for a relationship to work; couldn't see that there was a freshness, a freedom, to spending time apart. Marianne loved the way Jay lived his life – loved not knowing exactly where he was, or when he would come home. She loved being surprised by a sudden return – the element of wildness, the lack of predictability. It was sexy.

And then, aware of the Butterworth package still in her hand and the fact that it was well outside their business insurance policy to use public transport for items of that value – thinking that this was what Lee was worrying about – Marianne gave the envelope a brisk tap.

'I'll take a cab,' she said. 'It's only to the showroom. You don't need to worry.'

Lee shook his head. 'It's rush hour, love. You'll never get one. Come on.' Pressing the exit button, he opened the door and stood aside for her to leave first. 'I'll drop you. It's almost on my way . . .'

Chapter Seven

Marianne and Gabby were delighted with their new showroom. Instead of the old basement office in Fitzroy Place, the constant collisions with George and Helen on the stairs, early evening meetings being interrupted by children in pyjamas, potential clients having to tread around shopping bags that invariably ended up being dumped by Helen at the bottom of the steps . . . the business now had a small area of independent space. It was neatly located up a quiet mews in the heart of Kensington in a house that, while central, was completely uninhabitable for domestic purposes – it was much too close to the Underground – and therefore comfortably within their budget. These premises had, in the past year, been converted from a tired, poky house into a smart showroom with additional basic living facilities – a bathroom, a bedroom, a small box kitchen . . . and then comprehensively secured to meet the requirements of the insurer. All the alarm systems, the fancy double-door arrangements and automatic locking devices, all the safes, the security cameras, the intercom system, the reinforced steel doors that were now routine for Hatton Garden premises . . . all these things had now been installed in Kelso Mews. They gave Marianne and Gabriella's business an instant air of establishment, of professional standards, of containing something serious to protect. It made Marianne feel responsible – properly responsible – for the first time in her life.

Lee dropped her at the entrance to the mews, leaving her to walk the final few cobbled yards, past an unfamiliar pair of bicycles that she guessed belonged to Paul and Sophie, up to the showroom entrance. Marianne looked at her watch: only ten minutes late. Not bad. And then, looking for her keys, she noticed that – like a late-night cab driver, waiting to be certain she was safely inside – Lee's car was still there at the end of the mews. He waved at her though the open window, and Marianne waved back – masking her irritation. She knew he was being kind. She knew he'd gone out of his way. But still . . . why couldn't people treat her normally any more? Why did they make such a fuss?

The showroom wasn't large. Greatly against Marianne's artistic instincts – but in line with her reluctant business sense – it had been decorated in calm, neutral tones that ensured their clients remained focussed on the matter in hand. At the far end there were a couple of beige sofas and three glass bookshelves containing a number of classic volumes dedicated to the arts of gemmology and jewellery design. Together with images from old museum and auction catalogues, and five years' worth of jewellery magazines, this small collection of publications provided more than enough material to whet a client's appetite.

Paul and Sophie – who'd clearly been let in by Gabriella and were already onto champagne – were seated side by side on one of the sofas, flicking through a photograph album of Cooper Franklin's latest engagement rings. Their backs were to the door, and – at the moment of entering the room – all Marianne could see was a pair of heads, equal height, bending together to examine a page. And then, in unison, they both looked round.

'I'm so sorry.' Closing the door, Marianne waited for the extra click that ensured it was properly shut before coming towards them – glowing, friendly, coat coming off, bag thrown aside, hands up to the spiralling hair, redoing it as she stood, greeting them: with both arms raised to fix the pencil, her belly visible – nicely round – not too big, but obviously still a baby in there under the multi-patterned peasant-style dress . . . and light slim legs in opaque black, down to easy flats.

'It's been a mad day. Nightmare at the Assay Office. Nightmare with the alarm this morning – poor Gabby had to wait three hours for the man to come and fix the wretched thing! And then we—'

Drop it, Marianne, said a voice in her head. *No need to bang on. Just smile – that's right.*

'Paul . . .'

Kiss him now – nice and neutral – left cheek, right cheek – done – move on.

'And – Sophie, right?'

Kiss her too. Why not?

'Do – please – sit down.'

The three of them sat: Paul and Sophie, back on the sofa where they'd been before, Marianne directly opposite. She leant forward over the glass coffee table, to see which of her portfolio albums they had. And

89

then – sneaking a first proper look at them both, now that the greetings were over – knew instantly, and with a guilty surge of relief, that Jay's assessment of Sophie's appearance was spot-on. Sophie wasn't unattractive but it was also painfully obvious that the woman had no *allure*. And while, of course, Marianne was glad for Paul that he had found someone else, that he hadn't taken too long – truly, sincerely, she wished them well; she had Jay, Paul had Sophie, it was all very satisfactory – on some animal level, somewhere in the sexual pecking order of things, in that hard subliminal evolutionary realm, Marianne sensed an easy dominance. She wasn't proud of feeling this way – of finding herself so very susceptible to that residual sense of territory towards an ex, an ex that she herself had spurned. She had no claim to Paul, no interest in him, no need to trump poor Sophie in this way, and yet, and yet . . . Marianne accepted it would take a better woman than she – a smaller ego, a bigger heart – to remain immune to this particular sense of victory. She couldn't control such primary instincts. She could only control how she reacted . . . and, to that extent, Marianne wasn't worried. On the contrary, devoid of any sense of rivalry, it was now possible for her to enjoy a real sense of goodwill towards Sophie, a sense of safety in the latter's presence that, paradoxically, would only bring out the best in herself . . .

There was a low rumbling sound beneath the building – a sliding screech of iron – as another train went by. Marianne barely heard it. Her smile was warm, keen even – it was easy to be kind in such circumstances – as she waited for the rumbling and the screeching to subside, for the train to go, so that she could be properly heard.

'You found anything you like?' she said, as peace resumed. 'It can be tricky – especially if it's . . . do you wear much jewellery, Sophie?'

'Not really.'

Liking Marianne's quirkiness, her easy manner – relieved that she was nothing like the glamorous women that had so intimidated her that evening in Sri Lanka – Sophie presented her fingers, unadorned; neck, ears, wrists . . . similarly empty. She gave Marianne an apologetic smile.

'Well, I have to say that's great, from my point of view,' said Marianne, who understood the importance of finding something positive to work with in a client. 'Really. It means I don't need to worry about tailoring your ring to anything other than your own tastes and personality.'

'And this,' said Paul, feeling into the corner of an old grey envelope, and pulling out the padparascha stone.

'Of course!' Marianne put out her hand. 'Let's see?'

The stone fell plum into her palm. And even in the early evening light of the showroom – with the day fading outside and the mellow glow from the sofa lamps making the conditions for inspection hardly ideal . . . even then, Marianne sensed she was holding something special. She'd already heard the basics from Jay and, in a way, it wasn't quite as remarkable as he'd led her to expect. But then, Jay had only seen it rough. He also harboured a passion for stones that ordinary mortals found hard to understand. In a few months, some other stone would catch his eye and this padparascha would be forgotten. In the meantime, his interest bordered on the obsessive. And, like a Lothario driven sleepless with desire for a woman he hadn't yet seen naked, the fact that Jay hadn't actually seen the finished article would only have added to this fixation. All he knew was that his instincts had been right – that the rough stone they'd found that day in Ratnapura was indeed a padparascha. He was desperate to hear what Marianne thought.

Marianne smiled. Expectations aside, it was still a great stone. She and Gabby did a fine trade in commissioned rings – engagements were their bread and butter – but everyone wanted diamonds. Occasionally, they'd get a request for a ruby or a blue sapphire – but it was all so dull, so conventional. At the beginning, Marianne had tried to steer her clients towards something braver – but the efforts had proved futile and it hadn't taken long for her to accept the inherent nature of commissioned work and save her true talent for exhibition pieces and magazine promotions. And the irony that it was Paul – Paul of all people! – bringing her this stone wasn't lost on Marianne.

She looked at him – noticing, with interest, that he seemed to have lost some of the thrusting confidence of his City days. Sitting there on the sofa, slouching a little, making himself smaller, slimmer, narrower . . . it was, she felt, the body-language of a different man. A weaker man. And the clothes he was wearing – fine sludge-green cords, with worn knees and a little too short in the leg and a soft shirt of heavyweight cotton, a weekend shirt, intended more for strolls in the park than boardroom business – all spoke of someone less ambitious, less muscular somehow. Reduced. His hair was longer. His shoes were old and brown. In the intervening years, Paul Farage had acquired the floppy air of an antique dealer or a university lecturer. And while, for some people, that transition might have been a positive move, Marianne wasn't so sure with Paul.

And she couldn't help but feel concerned; concerned that this faded beta-male look – while, in many ways, more appealing than the cropped, pinstriped, go-getting, undentable Paul of yesteryear – suggested a man who thought of himself as inadequate. A loser. She began to see why he'd become so involved in the Church recently, and why he might have chosen a girl like Sophie Mostyn as his bride.

'It's beautiful.'

Paul smiled. 'Well, you have to say that, don't you . . . but I hope at least that you think you might be able to set it for us. We—'

'I mean it, Paul. It's a dream for me to be able to set something like this. Something completely unique . . .'

Marianne talked on, tactfully avoiding any comment on dull diamond solitaires, while praising the padparascha. And then, moving the subject easily towards what kind of setting they might like, flicking through the albums, the books and magazines, she began the process of narrowing and refining their ideas, building a picture of what ring might best display the padparascha's beauty on the finger of a woman like Sophie. And while, to Paul and Sophie, it seemed that they had Marianne's absolute attention – while they fell completely for the impression that they were getting something tailor-made to their own unique circumstances – it was, in truth, something rather less than that. How could this ring have her full attention while there were so many other calls upon her mind? How could she concentrate on the job in hand while wondering – for the umpteenth time – what had driven Paul to choose her for this ring? Was he trying to make a point? Was this new mousy fiancée supposed to make her jealous?

Marianne allowed herself a small inward chuckle. Well, if that was his aim, she was confident – had been confident *long* before today – that it would fail. She'd never regretted turning Paul down. He might have changed since then . . . certainly, the things that had once attracted her – the confidence, the relative maturity beside her student circle, the air of being different – had fallen away – but even if he hadn't changed, she wouldn't have wanted that kind of man. She didn't want the sophisticated banker he'd once been. She didn't want the corduroy wimp he now was. She wanted . . . she wanted what she had: a man like Jay. Someone exceptional – not only in himself, but as a match for Marianne. Someone who shared the same aspirations. The same principles. She and Jay would never choose marriage; never enter into a contract on their love – a contract that, to both of them, seemed more like a coward's charter than a source of pride. It was, they felt, something people hid behind, or – perhaps more accurately – leant on, when there was something missing at the heart of the matter. And now, with this wonderful unplanned baby – irritations and complications notwithstanding – Marianne felt truly blessed. For it was clear to her that there was something in the natural order of things, something deep and right and true, that approved of her decision to be with Jay.

She'd walked into the room full of defiance, geared up to defend the choices she'd made. Paul was just so conventional, so terribly by-the-book, and, no doubt, his future wife was too. They were bound to disapprove of Marianne. Indeed, she'd have been more than a little disappointed if they hadn't disapproved. She liked to define herself against such people, pit herself against the flow. But now, looking at Paul and Sophie – side by side on the sofa, signing up to a lifetime of rules – the fight left her. Marianne felt only pity for Paul, with his plain little fiancée, his weak little job, his clinging to religion; and just as much for Sophie, with her poor, unfortunate looks, her place as his 'second choice' (for why else would he be letting the poor girl remain ignorant of the past that he and Marianne had shared?), her misplaced faith in marriage as some sort of haven from the ills of the world.

'What about this one?' Sophie was saying.

Paul frowned. 'It's not too fussy?'

Sophie put her empty champagne glass back on the coffee table. She looked again at the album on Paul's lap. She was getting tired. She didn't know what she wanted any more. Just a pretty ring. A regular, pretty ring. It was kind of Paul to involve her in this way, but – honestly – she'd have been every bit as happy if he'd just gone off and got one, like most other men seemed to do.

'I'm not saying I don't like it,' Paul added, quickly. 'I'm only thinking . . . would you be comfortable wearing something like this in school, for instance? Or on Help the Homeless nights?'

Sophie giggled. 'I'm not going to wear it *then*, darling! And I certainly wouldn't wear it to work. I'd only lose it, or bash it against something, or—'

'When would you wear it?'

'Parties. Dinner with my parents . . . that – that sort of . . .'

Sophie trailed off. Noticing Paul's expression and realising that he'd imagined her wearing it all the time – reading the disappointment in his eyes at the idea of his precious hard-won padparascha not on permanent display – she was torn between an ever-present desire to make him happy, and a certain horror at the idea of appearing showy while at work or in the church. It was an impossible decision, rendered all the more impossible by the knowledge that nice Marianne was looking at her, waiting. Sophie hesitated. There had to be an answer, a compromise, a neat way through. She just needed to be alone for a moment or two. Needed space and peace to collect her thoughts . . . a bathroom, perhaps? It was better than nothing.

'Of course!' said Marianne, in answer to her request. 'It's just up the stairs at the end – that's right. Then second door on the left, and then . . . Gab'll show you. Gab?'

The kitchen door opened and Gabriella emerged, munching buttered toast.

'You couldn't show Sophie the loo, could you?'

Finishing the toast, Gab licked her fingers. 'Sure,' she said. 'Come on up . . .'

The pair of them disappeared up the small spiral staircase.

Paul and Marianne looked at one another.

'So, how—'

'I'm thinking—'

Both stopped.

'You go.'

Marianne bit her lip. 'No, you go, Paul. I'm sorry. Go on – what were you saying?'

Paul shrugged. 'It's not important,' he said. 'I was just going to ask you how you are, how' – he waved an awkward hand in the direction of her belly – 'how the pregnancy's going – that sort of thing. You're feeling okay?'

'Oh, great!' said Marianne, over-bright – busily

96

sorting through the albums and magazines on the coffee table. 'It's great. Can be tiring, of course. But I think that's perfectly normal at this stage, and at least there's no more morning sickness . . .' She grinned at him. 'Three months were more than enough!'

Paul nodded. 'And – and Jay?' he said, very gently.

'Jay?'

'He . . . I mean, is he . . .?'

The grin disappeared. 'Is he what, Paul?'

Paul floundered for words. And Marianne, staring at him, began to realise what lay behind his question. Little by little, it dawned on her that Paul – New, Moral Born-Again-Christian Paul – didn't merely disapprove. He actually viewed this pregnancy as some sort of failure. He really believed – she saw it in his eyes, a chilly purity, a certain blankness that came with strict adherence to rules . . . really believed that it was a man's duty to propose marriage in such circumstances, that Marianne would be longing for it, and wondering why Jay wasn't 'making an honest woman of her' – insulted, even. With growing horror, Marianne – who'd been fully prepared for Paul's condemnation, and was all for defending her corner – now understood herself to be merely an object of his pity. Possibly – God forbid it – worse than pity, for, wondering now if Paul was actively ashamed of their past intimacy, it occurred to Marianne that perhaps *this* was the reason he hadn't told Sophie about it. Not because Marianne was at the top of his list, but because – sullied and dirty – she'd fallen to the bottom. In spite of the blatant differences in their physical appearance, perhaps Paul had other priorities these days. He'd shown not a flicker of the old desire.

'I'm sorry,' he said. 'I didn't mean to upset you. I

97

just,' – sighing now – 'wanted to be sure you were okay.'

'I'm more than okay, Paul. I've never been happier.'

He didn't believe her.

'I feel – *we* feel – completely thrilled about this baby. It's the best thing, absolutely the very best thing, that's ever happened to me!' But her voice wasn't entirely joyful. It had a defensive edge.

'That's great, Marianne.'

Silence.

And then, taking a deep breath, Paul tried once more to explain himself. 'I was only worried that – what with Soph and me turning up together, all happy and engaged and . . . you know what I'm saying – I just didn't want to make things worse for you, Marianne. Didn't want you to feel you had to go along with making this ring for us if it was all going to be too much for you . . .' Paul sighed again. 'You're so brave,'

Brave?

'. . . it can't be easy.'

'But it is!' she cried, as another train rolled underneath the building. She almost had to shout. 'It is easy! It's the easiest thing in the world!'

Paul merely smiled.

He and Sophie left soon afterwards. Coming back downstairs – recomposed, decided – Sophie complied, absolutely, with Paul's ideas about the ring. Of course he was right: something simple, something easy – or easier – to wear. He wouldn't need to know the ins and outs of exactly when she wore it, or when she took it off. She didn't need to spell it out.

They chose a design they liked. It was a design that Marianne would still need to adapt. Her drawings would then need to be approved, they'd need a second meeting, so there was more than enough time to change their minds. In any case, Marianne herself needed to check her diary, and to check with Gabby, to be sure they had the time and resources to take another commission . . .

Sophie's face fell.

'I'm afraid it does get busy at this time of year,' Marianne explained. 'And if we're looking at a December wedding, that's . . . well, what with Christmas around the corner and the baby due in January, and – and then we've got an exhibition in March . . . I won't bore you with the details. But now I know the kind of ring you're after, I'll be able to see if we can fit it into our schedule – we'll speak in the next day or two, shall we, Paul? And we haven't even *discussed* wedding rings. But . . . exactly. I'm sure it won't be a problem. You haven't asked for anything complicated. I just want to be sure I can deliver.'

Chapter Eight

'And as for those bikes,' Gabby was saying, as – laughing now – she opened the little fridge. 'Did you see them? The his and hers, with God-Squad stickers on the bars? Jesus, Marianne, that was a lucky escape for you . . .'

Marianne smiled back. She was still smarting from the things that Paul had said. Or maybe it was the things he hadn't said – hadn't needed to say – for, of course, it was all there in the clothes he wore, the woman he'd chosen, the pity in his eyes as he'd looked at her bump, the Jesus stickers on his bicycle. And it was balm for her to listen now to Gabby's cheerful irreverence. Gabby took out a bottle of champagne. It was the one she'd opened for Paul and Sophie, and it was already – Marianne noticed – virtually empty. Prattling on, Gabby dribbled the remains of the bottle into her own glass, opened the fridge again, and reached instinctively for another.

'. . . not that I'm against bikes. But the *sight* of them, Marianne, bumping over the cobbles, with those ludicrous bits of plastic on their heads!'

The cork popped. The champagne fizzed and frothed and overflowed ... out of the mouth, down the neck and – shrieking – Gabby leapt aside. She was about to go out to dinner with George and Helen and some new man they wanted her to meet. She'd changed into an immaculate black silk tea dress. Her hair was up. She was wearing heels. She smelt of gardenias. And the ensemble – which was elegant, if not entirely in keeping with the wearer's usual style – would not have been improved by a wild, wet splash across the front. She was lucky it had missed the dress, lucky that her own sudden movement hadn't sent both glasses flying. And Marianne, aware that tonight was supposed to be important for Gabby – aware, too, that her friend had already drunk too much to be trusted around liquids and glass and hard kitchen surfaces – shooed her back into the showroom.

'I'll do it,' she said, putting a full glass of champagne into Gabby's hand and nudging her firmly through the door. 'Just go and sit down somewhere. Stay nice and clean and out of trouble. At least until your brother gets here.'

Gabriella did as she was told while Marianne, opening the cupboard under the sink, reached for the old floor cloth. She began mopping up the puddle of champagne. As she mopped, and soaked, and rinsed, and squeezed, she thought of Gabriella ...

Gab wasn't an alcoholic. Yes, the girl liked a drink – and sometimes a line, a pill or two – but nothing to worry about, nothing extreme. No worse than Marianne. It was a natural pattern of behaviour they'd picked up as students, a heightened way of socialising, fun – vaguely naughty – but hardly cause for concern. Gab never got drunk or high by herself. She was

101

always sober by the morning. It was, in Marianne's opinion, entirely normal behaviour for someone of her age and background. Indeed, were it not for Gab's poor mother – whose decades on the bottle had given her a profound insecurity, warped values and a rampant self-pity, who, all too clearly, *did* have a problem with alcohol – there would be no issue. No justifiable issue, at any rate. No excuse for the Puritan expressions that George would pull every time he saw a glass in his sister's hand, every time her laughter grew too merry, her appearance too chaotic, her fun too apparent. He never said anything. He didn't need to – his face was enough. And Gab was too unsure of herself, too aware of her mother's sickness and the ever-present shadow it cast over their lives.

Not that it stopped her drinking, of course. On the contrary, there was something about George's sober presence that gave his sister a particular craving for it . . . and tonight was a classic example.

Gab's dinner dates with George and Helen had become something of a feature in the last year or so. On the surface, it seemed a perfectly nice thing for a brother to be doing, taking his sister out to dinner from time to time, introducing her to potential boyfriends, showing that he cared, that she wasn't forgotten. With their father now dead, their stepmother living permanently in Sri Lanka, and their real mother damaged beyond repair . . . Gabby was, effectively, parentless. And it was clear that George saw it as his duty to look out for her – take on the role of a father – until Gabby was established with a young family of her own. And while Marianne could see that he was trying to do the right thing by his sister, she couldn't help finding it all a bit patronising . . . almost as if

102

George hadn't realised that Gab was a grown woman of nearly thirty, and more than capable of taking control of her life. By taking her on dinner dates and introducing her to a string of suitable men, he clearly felt that marriage was the answer for his sister. Not for darling Gabby a job, a business, or the fulfilment of genuine independence. Oh no. What Gabby needed was a nice husband who would look after her, steer her into the safe waters of motherhood and home-making, and – ultimately – relieve her brother of further filial duties.

And the more Marianne thought about it, the more incensed she became. George had shown little or no support for his sister's career. He'd laughed when they'd told him about the showroom. And even though it had been up and running for nearly a month now, he hadn't once bothered to come and see it. To him, this jewellery business was just a happy hobby; an adult – and somewhat expensive – form of dressing up that shouldn't be allowed to get out of control or embarrass the family, financially or otherwise . . . a precarious way of treading water until the proper work of marriage and babies appeared.

Tonight was to be George's first showroom visit. And for all Gabby's careless attitude, her drinking, her munching toast, her laughing about Paul and Sophie, it was clear to Marianne that, underneath, the girl was tense with longing for her brother's approval. From the outset, Gabby had been obsessed with the new security system. It was a system that had been installed very much with George in mind – for when the man did bother to dredge up some sort of opinion on the subject of his sister's business, it invariably concerned the extreme value of the materials she worked with, and what might happen if something went astray . . . and Gabby was determined to show him she'd addressed the matter. With this in mind, she and Marianne had spent a good deal more than was necessary on the technology – ending up with something so sophisticated that it was hard to understand. It hadn't helped that, testing the system that morning to be sure it was ready to show George, Gabby had been unable to switch the alarms back off. And so a calm day of preparation had morphed into a nightmare of policemen and technicians, of jangling bells and sirens, together with bursts of intermittent beeping and – of course – those ever-present underground trains . . . no wonder Gab was wobbly. No wonder she was drinking. Sometimes, it seemed to Marianne, that, far from steering his sister away from the fate of their mother, George was, in fact, exacerbating the problem.

Giving the cloth a final squeeze and tossing it back into the cupboard, Marianne picked up her own glass of champagne and returned to the showroom. She found Gabby standing at the desk, looking at the padparascha that Paul and Sophie had left behind. Gabby looked round at her, and smiled.

'So what do you think?' she said – indicating the stone.

Marianne took it from her. Sitting at the desk, she switched on the lamp to her left and held the padparascha – steady and professional – under the bulb. In truth, she was a little annoyed that the thing was still here. She'd tried to persuade Paul and Sophie to take it away with them, but Paul had been oddly emphatic. He wouldn't be going to any other jeweller until Marianne had made a decision and, in the meantime, he would be grateful if she could keep it safe for them, properly safe, here at the showroom.

'But—'

'At least let us *hope* that you'll take it on . . .' Sophie had said, giving Marianne a beseechful smile as she lifted her chin for Paul to tighten the strap of her bicycle helmet. She looked like a child.

Marianne couldn't help smiling back. 'All right,' she'd said. 'But please don't think it means anything. I—'

'I know! I know!'

It wasn't an entirely foolish move. With the pad-parascha in her possession, Marianne would be able to use it for any preliminary designs she might make. She'd be able to see it in all sorts of different lights – get a feel for its details, its nuances of colour, its personality. For, unlike the stones she normally worked with, this one would certainly have character – and, for all her reservations about Paul and Sophie, Marianne was still strongly tempted to accept the commission.

Both women looked at it – at the gentle blend of rose and apricot as it turned in the fall of light. With none of the sugary girlishness of pink, and none of the sultry vulgarity of orange, it rested in the balance. There was a restrained degree of saturation, an infusion of colour that – again – was neither passive nor aggressive, neither watery pale nor angrily vibrant. To the gem-schooled eye – to anyone who understood the rarity of its positioning on the spectrum – the stone was instantly special.

Marianne bit her lip. 'I love it,' she said, putting the stone back down. Reaching for the box of cigarettes that sat by the telephone, she offered one to Gabby – who took one – before helping herself.

Gabby lit hers. 'And the setting?' she said, holding the match to Marianne's. 'You like their ideas?'

Both women inhaled deeply.

'Enough.'

'So what's the problem?'

Marianne's laugh was small and wry. 'Where do we start?' she said. 'It's – what – mid-October, now? We've got two months until Christmas. We've got . . .' she took the order book from the top drawer of her desk – '*all these* still to finish, Gab,' turning a page, 'and those,' another page, 'and those. We've got the showroom exhibition to think about—'

'That won't be—'

'March will be here before we know it. And then there's the small matter of a baby in the offing.'

Gab's eyes widened. 'You're turning it *down*?'

'I don't know.' Marianne picked up the stone again. 'I just don't know . . .'

And Gabby, looking at her, at the way she was holding the stone, at the expression in her eyes, and knowing, too, Marianne's enthusiasm for the business, for her willingness to say 'yes' at all possible junctures, her near-fixation with taking on as much business as possible, of making money – especially with all these new expenses to consider – Gabby knew that there was more to this uncharacteristic hesitation than a backlog of work, or an exhibition deadline. It wasn't the baby – Gabby was certain. Indeed, if the prospect of motherhood had affected Marianne's business approach at all, then it was to make her rather more ambitious, more work-hungry, than she'd been before. Something else was involved. Something more particular to this latest commission.

Angling round, Gab looked at Marianne more intently than before – willing her to look back.

'Is it because you and Paul were—'

'In a way.'

Gab scratched her head. 'But it's been years,' she said. 'Years, Marianne. Don't you think that if Paul's okay . . .'

'Then it's all right?'

Gab nodded.

'It doesn't matter?'

'It—'

'What? Even though he clearly hasn't told that poor girl that he and I were even involved?'

Gabby looked a little startled. The tone was decidedly sharp.

'. . . far less that he actually asked me to *marry* him? It's – Christ. I'm sorry, Gab. I know we need the money. I know it's an easy job. And yes – all right – I would quite enjoy working with a stone like this. But – honestly, in my position – would you do it?'

Gab stared back at her, unsure what to say. It seemed to her that Marianne was being oversensitive. Unnecessarily proper, somehow. Almost as bad as George. It wasn't as if Marianne and Paul had anything left over from their time together. Nobody was being unfaithful. Nobody was being betrayed. It was all water under the bridge. What possible benefit would it be for Sophie to know now about their past?

But before she could give voice to these thoughts, there was a sound of tyres on cobbles and a flash of headlights at the window.

George and Helen.

Gabby let them in while Marianne lingered at the desk. This desk was a large, leather-covered, antique affair that had been left to Marianne by her father. And while – to Marianne – it still had deep sentimental value, both she and Gabriella were also conscious that

107

a sensible brown CEO-style desk did not fit with the image they wished to convey. They agreed that they would only keep it at the showroom for as long as it took them to find – and afford – a more contemporary alternative. But as the days and weeks went by, Marianne's father's desk began to look like staying. It had weight. Like the high-tech security systems and the discreet beige walls, it sent an important subliminal message to their clients. It counteracted the youth and femininity of their partnership. It showed that the girls meant business – and tonight, more than ever, Marianne was glad of the gravitas.

She toyed with one of the drawers. Having hurriedly stubbed her cigarette out – sliding the ashtray well down the length of the desk so that it gave the impression that only Gabby had been smoking – she now felt a little annoyed with herself. No doubt, the perfect Helen did yoga every day of her pregnancies, and only ate organic food, and never touched alcohol, and followed the prescribed regime to the letter. For sure, those pretty pink fingers wouldn't have gone near anything as yellow and as evil as a cigarette . . . but why should that affect Marianne? Why should she care what these people thought?

'It's just up there. See?' Gabby was saying.

George glanced up at the alarm sensor.

'And now . . .' Gabby's voice had the slow drama of a drum roll – 'all I have to do . . . is . . .' she waved her arms about like a mechanical doll until a red light flashed. 'Da na! There! See? It's sensitive to any movement. And it's linked to the police station, so—'

'Like the one we used to have at Winchfield, I expect,' said George to Helen, *sotto voce*.

Helen smiled. 'What, the one that went off by

mistake so many times that the police stopped coming out altogether?' Kissing Gabriella, kissing Marianne, she filled the room with cool citrus scent.

George stood underneath the sensor, squinting up at the brand name. 'Actually,' he said, 'maybe not . . . I don't recognise the name.'

'It is a good one,' said Gabby quickly. 'We've had it checked out. And – see next to it? That's the CCTV –'

For the briefest of moments, George looked almost impressed. Then he raised both eyebrows and said, mischievously, 'Well, I hope you remembered to put a film in, Gab. These things don't just work by themselves, you know.'

'Of course I did. It's—'

'I'm joking, Gumbo!' He ruffled her chignon. 'Don't get so wound-up! Now. Are you ready? The table's booked for eight . . .'

Gabby's face fell. After a day of anxious anticipation of this visit, were George and Helen really going to disappear without even seeing the kitchen, or the rooms upstairs, or the pieces on display? Was it really so irrelevant, so totally beneath their interest? Her face was painfully transparent. And Marianne, reading it, could no longer remain quiet. Pointing out that as it had only just gone seven, and they still had half a bottle of champagne to get through, it would be rude of George and Helen not to stay at least for a drink, she came out smilingly from behind the desk into the centre of the room.

'Champagne?' said George. There was a trace of censure in his tone.

Marianne struggled to maintain her smile. Unsure exactly what it was that had prompted the man's disapproval – whether it was the unsuitability of alcohol with pregnancy, or a desire to restrain his sister's burgeoning drink habit, or simply a comment on the extravagance of the business serving champagne over wine – perhaps all of the above? – she knew only that it was typical. Typical. Unnecessary. Unkind, even. George surely realised how much Gabby valued his opinion. Was it really too much for him not to humour the girl, at least for this one night? Most people, most normal people, would be grateful and happy at the offer of champagne. A kinder brother might even have brought a bottle himself, in celebration of this business milestone – a house-warming gesture. It wouldn't have gone amiss. Suggesting to Gabby that she get a couple more glasses from the kitchen, Marianne led them towards the sofas. Explaining that it was a bottle left over from Paul and Sophie's visit – that it would be a shame to waste it – she set about filling the glasses.

'Ah,' said George, taking a glass. Again, his voice had that unpleasant trace of censure. 'Paul and Sophie.'

'That's right,' said Marianne.

George said nothing.

Gabby sat beside him. 'Actually,' she added, 'Marianne may not be able to do it. We're just so busy at the moment – booked right through to Christmas. And I'm off this Friday to New York to meet with a retailer. Manhattan. Upper East Side. The buyer there has expressed real interest in our designs – all from the website, apparently! So that was definitely worthwhile – I'm taking a few samples over – and then there's the showroom exhibition of course . . .' On she rambled, talking of trade fairs, silversmiths, business development and future publicity, while George and Helen made a bad pretence of interest.

Marianne saw both looking at their watches. She saw Helen looking at George, discreetly trying to catch his eye. She saw George look up and smile back at his wife.

'. . . though not with all the grovelling we have to do at the workshop these days. Honestly! It's like getting blood out of a stone! And they *never* give us any sort of credit . . .'

George stood up. 'Come on, Gab,' he said, draining his glass. 'Thanks for the drink, girls. It's great – finally – to see your little studio . . .' He felt the edge of the sofa, testing the quality of the material as strings of additional internal calculations and figures passed through his mind. Marianne could see it in his eyes – in the slight hesitation of his hand; in the way he surveyed the room. 'It's certainly smart.' He smiled at Marianne. 'And, I must say, I'm relieved to hear you're not going to make that ring for Paul and Sophie. It never struck me as the best idea. '

'I didn't say I wasn't, George. I said I was thinking about it.'

George turned for his coat. 'Well, I'm sure you'll make the right decision,' he said, kissing her goodbye. 'Right, Gab – have you got your bag? Keys? Mobile? Good girl. Now,' – turning to leave, puzzling over the sophisticated series of catches and handles and buttons on the door – 'bloody hell. How on earth do we get out? I thought it was supposed to keep the business secure, not to incarcerate your poor unsuspecting clients! It . . . oh, I see . . . okay . . .'

Picking up the abandoned glasses, Marianne took them back into the kitchen and gave each one a perfunctory rinse before returning to the empty show-room. She stood in the kitchen doorway for a moment, looking at the scene: at the silent pools of lamplight on the spotless caramel carpet; at the mellower bookish effect they'd created around the sofas in the far corner with those large museum catalogues stacked along the shelves, the neat piles of gemstone publications . . . and then, just beyond, at the discreet wall cabinet of bulletproof glass that – today – displayed a pale emerald pendant, suspended round the neck of a velvet headless bust. It was all easy enough to look at. All attractive. All – as George had commented – 'smart'. But none of it was as compelling as the padparascha gemstone on her desk, with that strange fusion of colour – rose-tangerine, tangerine-rose . . . a restless compound – caught and bound in a concentrate of crystal no bigger than her fingernail. It was a blend of colour that, for all its pastel softness, seemed also to carry an inherent volatility, suggesting imminent separation, yet never quite reaching it . . .

Another train went by – more rumbling, more screeching, more racketing down the line. And then silence. Somehow, a deeper silence than before.

Marianne sat at the desk. She pulled the lamp a little closer, angled it even lower over the surface and, taking a small black velvet tray from a drawer to her left – it was one she used when discussing stone options with clients – placed the padparascha lightly in the middle and guided it under the hot, bright beam.

She thought of Paul and Sophie urging her to take it on – thought of George, pushing the other way – and sighed. Perhaps it didn't really matter what she did. It was only a ring. But the idea of Paul viewing her as some sort of object of pity – as he surely would if she said she couldn't do it, with his: *just didn't want to make things worse for you, Marianne. Didn't want you to feel you had to go along with making this ring for us if it was all going to be too much for you – you're so brave* . . . all made her inclined to take the job, if only to show him she wasn't bothered. How *dare* he talk to her like that? How dare he imply that Jay – her beloved Jay – was somehow inadequate because he wasn't asking her to marry him, or fussing over her like – like Lee, or Graham, or all those other sweet, but frankly silly, and deeply unsexy, men she dealt with on a day-to-day basis.

And then there was George, with that schoolmaster air of weary disapproval that he seemed to have acquired recently – so judgemental, so middle-aged – as if Marianne had just walked into assembly with her skirt hemline marginally above the regulations, and making it more tempting than ever for her to hitch the thing still higher and saunter up to the front.

Certainly it was becoming hard for her to remember those good, original reasons she'd had for hesitating about accepting the commission – especially with the stone now before her, a stone that seemed to have managed the impossible feat of capturing both the grandeur and the delicacy of a fine dawn sky within its crystal confines.

Already, she had a pretty clear idea of what she'd do with it. The setting Paul had liked would be easy to adapt. And if she could lead them away from the more traditional claw mechanism of holding the stone – a mechanism that invariably made a piece look Victorian – and persuade them to take a simpler line with a sleeker, slightly more modern effect – it wouldn't be difficult, especially with them wanting something more practical . . . and she'd still get that all-important lift on the stone which, while making it seem bigger, was really more about getting maximum light into the heart of the thing, and making the most of those beautiful facets that Tariq Ibrahim had cut. In fact . . .

Marianne shifted the desk light again and bent to get a better look at the gradients on the side of the stone – at the depth she had to work with.

. . . with a bit of skill, she might even be able to do without so much metal around the stone itself – she could open out the setting, perhaps even create an outer ring, and suspend the stone inside – and create the kind of space around the stone that would expose it to maximum light from the maximum number of possible directions . . . if she could just persuade them to trust her . . .

She smiled. Pushing the desk lamp aside, she reached for the order book – together with the business diary that sat beside the telephone – and looked at the winter schedule. Then she looked at the stone, twinkling on its tray, thrilling her with its juxtaposition of innocence and seduction. Then at the diary. Stone. Diary. And with George's words ringing in her ears – *I must say, I'm relieved to hear you're not going to make that ring . . . It never struck me as the best idea* – defiantly wrote it in.

She had to wait for another train to pass before calling Paul's number and leaving a message to let him know that, after consideration, she would be delighted to proceed with the commission, assuming that he and Sophie were still keen. Could he call her tomorrow? '. . . or whenever you've a moment, Paul. I'd just like to talk through a couple of details and we'll need to set up another appointment for some time in November, for you to approve my drawings so that we can get the thing off to the workshop and on to Sophie's finger as quickly as possible!'

Three hours later, Marianne was still at the showroom – still at the desk – rubbing her eyes as she grappled with a number of outstanding administrative matters that had started to bother her, invoices and receipts . . . it was important to get these things in order before she left to have the baby. Yes, she had a few months in hand, but it didn't hurt to get the systems up and running well in advance of her departure. For if Gabby was to stand half a chance of handling things while Marianne was on leave, then the systems really needed to be as simple and as clear as possible.

She was also waiting for a call. Jay had promised her he'd make contact when his plane landed in Bangkok – which should have been at around ten o'clock, London time – and it made sense for her to work on until he rang. That way, she could call him back on the office line, at office expense, and have a good long chat. They hadn't spoken properly in weeks. There was a lot to say. Not just baby stuff, stuff she knew was boring but still needed to consult with him about . . . doctors, hospitals, scans, and what all that ghastly baby equipment was likely to cost them, and was he prepared? And then all the latest gossip about Paul and Sophie, for there was nothing like laughing with Jay to put the rest of her life in perspective. And while it might not have been a perfectly legitimate business expense to use the office line in such circumstances, nor was it entirely illegitimate, she reckoned. After all, Jay was every bit as much her stone dealer as the father of her child.

Only it was now almost eleven, and still Jay hadn't called. Marianne checked her mobile: nothing. She checked the office line: open and clear. She rang the number at her flat, just in case, but again, there was nothing. No messages, no previous caller withholding their number, no activity at all. The plane must have been delayed, she reasoned. Poor Jay. However much they both loved to travel, it was no fun waiting around in airports or – worse – sitting on some runway in some foreign land, with tinny, tacky airline music playing overhead. Marianne didn't envy him. Resigned to the disappointment – she couldn't hang about all night – she called a cab and cleared the desk of paperwork. Then she lifted Paul's stone from the black velvet tray and took it over to the safe, only to discover that she couldn't easily see the dials. She needed better light.

And so it was that, crossing back over to the other side of the room so that she could switch on the rather less forgiving overhead lights that had been installed by the previous occupants, Marianne was just returning when the telephone rang. At last! Reminding herself that it might just be the cab firm calling back, or something equally prosaic, Marianne stopped at the desk and, with the padparascha still in the palm of one hand, picked up the telephone with the other.

'Hello?'

'Oh,' said a woman's voice. 'I'm so sorry. I—'

'Sophie?'

'Marianne. I – oh, how embarrassing. I thought I was calling your work number! I – I'd no idea –'

Marianne closed her eyes. 'It's okay,' she said, resting her bottom against the side of the desk. 'This is the showroom. You're absolutely right. I was just—'

'I didn't wake you?'

'No, no – I was just doing a bit of extra work on the accounts.'

There was a short silence at Sophie's end as she looked at her watch.

Marianne read her thoughts. 'I know,' she said, amused. 'I'm a bit mad – Paul should have warned you. But there's no need to worry, Sophie. I like working late. And anyway I'm stopping now . . .' Idly, she opened her hand and observed the little pad-parascha, rolling about in the brighter bluer overhead glare. '. . . so, in fact, you couldn't have called at a better time.'

'Oh good.' Sophie sounded genuinely relieved. 'Great. You are brilliant. I mean – no wonder you're doing so well, you and Gabby. You've got to work hard, haven't you? It's a lesson to the rest of us. And – well, anyway, Marianne, I won't keep you. I just wanted to say that we got your message and of course we're thrilled you can do it! And yes – please, please – let's fix a time for Paul to come in again and okay your drawings. We think it's better if he comes by himself next time – I don't want to be pulling in different directions like we were today. It must be maddening for you, and I'm sure I'll be thrilled with whatever you and he decide . . .'

But Marianne wasn't listening any more. She was looking at the stone. And her expression had shifted from pleasure to scrutiny as – in the flat, ugly light – a flat, ugly thought went through her mind.

'. . . pretty much any day is good for him next week. Evenings are better, I suppose. But, really, anything would work. He . . .'

She couldn't be sure, of course. She'd have to take it

117

to an expert. Probably Dr Rogerson – he was as good as anyone else in London at the moment. Certainly, she could trust him. After all, he was the man who'd originally lectured her on this subject: on the extra-ordinary beauty of genuine padparaschas and the legends surrounding them, and the extreme rarity of such stones, and the sad fact that – following a random mistake in Thailand in the late 1990s, where someone had routinely heat-treated a few inferior pink sap-phires, but had forgotten to first remove a chrysoberyl from the kiln, a chrysoberyl that had then thrown off a micro-fine deposit that, in turn, had diffused into the surface of the sapphires, tinting them orange . . . because of this, there now existed treated stones that looked exactly like padparaschas – so much so that it was only possible to determine the true colour by having the stone re-cut. Such stones had flooded the market in recent years, and any student of gemmology needed to be aware of this fact. Yes, the professor was the man to ask. And Jay, of course – when he came home. Better still, leave a message. Jay would want to know as soon as possible – that much was certain. It wasn't wise to hang about in these situations. Action was key. It . . . Christ, what a nightmare. What a monstrous embarrassment.

Hoping she was wrong – but knowing, somehow knowing, deep down, that she wasn't – Marianne held her breath. The stone was lovely but it wasn't magical – not now, not in the blank even light. It didn't thrill her eye. And while she wasn't an expert – wasn't even a stone dealer – Marianne still had a feel for these things, for when something wasn't right. And it was screaming.

'. . . we'd quite understand if you can't make it,'

Sophie was saying. 'And, of course, if Jay is away, please do come by yourself – we don't need to be even numbers or anything! It would just be great to see you. And—'

'What was that?'

A short pause. 'I – I was just saying, do feel free to come without Jay. Or with him, of course. Or whatever you'd like. Whatever works. I'd also love it if you could maybe give me George and Helen Franklin's number? And Gabby's too, of course. I'm hoping for a sort of Sri Lanka reunion! Although there will be other people as well. We're just—'

'I'm sorry, Sophie, what was the date, again?' said Marianne, hurriedly filling in the gaps.

'Friday week. It's a bit short notice, I realise. But—'

'Friday week – that's the third, isn't it? The third of November. Me and Jay. Dinner at your place, did you say?'

'That's right.'

Telling Sophie that they'd love to come, Marianne scribbled the details on a notepad. She couldn't really answer for Jay – 'he tends to come and go at a moment's notice, I'm afraid' – but she was free and more than happy to give Sophie those other numbers she wanted. No problem. Did she have a pen?

Thanking her, Sophie wrote them down. 'Is there anything you can't eat?' she added. 'I'm sure that, being pregnant, there must be all kinds of things you're not supposed to—'

'God, no. Don't worry about that. I'm fine. I eat anything and everything.'

'But – but what about shellfish? Surely that's—'

'Love shellfish.'

Another pause. 'Please don't be polite, Marianne. I

119

want to give you something you can eat. I just need to know what it is. And also – while we're on the subject – I know you can't have alcohol and I was thinking that elderflower might be nice, but Paul tells me that some people hate elderflower so – so again, please just tell me what you like. It would be a *help*, Marianne. Truly. I'd like to know . . .'

It was too much. Full of sudden exhaustion – from her busy day, her tricky meetings, this new anxiety with the 'padparascha', and all of it weighed down still further by the constant struggle she faced over attitudes to pregnancy, Marianne capitulated. The assumption that she was merely being polite, Sophie's innocent interpretation of Marianne's intransigence on the whole invasive subject of pregnancy dos and don'ts – that it was simply to save Sophie the culinary trouble, that no one would actually be so selfish as to put their own baby at risk – the disarming absence of criticism in Sophie's voice (and the shock she'd no doubt feel if Marianne actually told her the truth) . . . Marianne couldn't fight it.

So, instead of confessing her fondness for brie and homemade mayonnaise, or admitting that alcohol was frankly the only way she could get through a dinner party these days, Marianne closed her eyes and dutifully trotted out the mantras. And as Sophie then rang off – full of gratitude and friendly words and excitement about the ring – Marianne was appalled to find herself suddenly, irrationally, close to tears. The cab was waiting outside. She could see the headlights. She could hear the diesel engine.

Checking the office line once more, just in case Jay had tried to call while Sophie had been on the line, she knew in her heart that he hadn't. Of course he hadn't.

And then, with tears streaming down her face, Marianne knew that – even if he had bothered to pick up the telephone – it wasn't really what she wanted from Jay tonight. It wasn't enough: a tired voice at the end of a line. She wanted him – needed him – here with her now. His body to lean on. His hands at the wheel.

Marianne wiped her eyes. She locked the little stone away, picked up her bag, switched off the lights, activated the security systems and, after closing the door behind her, walked up the cobbled mews towards the waiting cab.

Chapter Nine

Gabriella was humming. She was sitting on the floor of the showroom surrounded by a number of large brown delivery boxes, bubble wrap, tissue paper and Box Company ribbons . . . humming happily as she unpacked the contents. Marianne sat at the desk, eating a smoked salmon sandwich.

'You were right about the colour.' Holding out one of the fat bracelet cases, Gabby admired the grey-green sheen. 'And I love this velvet . . .' She opened the case and stroked the interior for a moment before turning her attention back to the cardboard delivery box. 'How many of these bracelet ones did we get?'

'Thirty.' Marianne finished her mouthful. 'We can always order more, Gab. I know they're pretty, but we won't sell more than thirty before Christmas and I'd like to see how it goes with this first order. Don't want to end up with hundreds of boxes sitting around, taking up storage space, when—'

'Sure, sure.'

Gabriella took a pile of them over to one of the lower cupboards, sat down with them, and, rearranging the ring boxes on to a different shelf, returned to the subject of her date last night. It had been a running subject between them that morning.

'What should I *do* . . .'

Marianne bit into the second half of her sandwich.

'Can't say I'm not tempted,' Gab went on, reaching deep into the cupboard. 'It would be nice to have someone like Dexter looking after me in New York. He seemed keen. I'm sure he'd take me somewhere fabulous –'

'And then?'

Gab re-emerged from the cupboard. She looked at Marianne, over the edge of its slim white door. 'He's got great contacts,' she said, apropos of nothing. 'He hadn't heard of Hoffmann Sawyer either, but he's promised to introduce to me to some woman from Barney's. He knows Vincent and Ali. He lives on the Upper East Side. Has a place in Aspen. Might even take me there, if I stay the full week –'

'And then?'

Gab rolled her eyes. 'And then . . . and then, and then . . . then I guess I'd really have to ask him up to see my tourmalines!' she said, giggling. 'Beautifully packaged, of course.'

Marianne was smiling. But, distracted by the mention of tourmalines, her thoughts were no longer on the subject of Gabby's new admirer and his superficial charms.

'Oh God,' she said. 'I'm sorry, Gab. I never told you. That ring – your tourmaline ring – the bigger one . . . it's not going to be ready until Thursday.'

Gab said nothing.

'I know you wanted Tuesday. I did ask him. But – I can't remember why, now – he can't do it until

123

Thursday. I didn't think you'd mind too much – you're not leaving until Friday, are you? And I did explain that you needed it for New York, so I'm sure he'll have it done by then – and I can easily pick it up for you if you're packing, Gab. Or busy. Or—'

'That's not the point.' Gabriella shoved a few more cases into the cupboard, slammed the little door, and got to her feet. 'He never does it on time, does he? Never. None of them do. Not Lee. Not Graham. Even Mike's started getting lazy. And' – she sighed – 'I'm sorry, Marianne. I know you like them. I know their work is good. But their timing . . . sometimes I wonder if we wouldn't be better off with a different workshop altogether. They should be *grateful* for our business. Not acting like they're doing us some sort of favour.'

Marianne looked at the remains of her sandwich, at the drying tips of smoked salmon poking out from the crust. She felt a little queasy.

'I know you tried.' Gab began putting on her coat. 'And I am grateful. But it's getting ridiculous, don't you think? It's because we're women. I'm sure of it. They take one look at us and think they can treat us any which way they fucking please. And I'm not standing for it, Marianne. I'm sorry. Enough's enough—'

The telephone started to ring. And Marianne, looking at it, was torn between a desire to pick it up and a desire to stop Gabby, who was already halfway through the door, car keys jangling, tongue wagging with indignation, off to Hatton Garden, bruising for a fight.

'Gab, wait,' she called, through the open door. 'Gab?'

But Gabby, pretending she couldn't hear – another train was rumbling underneath the building – strode off down the cobbles towards her car, designer hand-bag flapping at her arm.

Marianne let her go. She knew what would happen – it wouldn't be pretty, and Gab would almost certainly come off the worse for it. But Marianne no longer had the energy. She was bored of keeping the peace. Yes, Gabby's chances of taking that particular tourmaline to the guys at Hoffmann Sawyer would now be non-existent – and no doubt her ranting would sink Cooper Franklin's reputation yet further in the trade – but there was also a part of Marianne which felt it was time for Gabby to learn her lesson. Learn it the hard way, while there was still some margin to play with, while she – Marianne – was still in favour. For if it meant that Gabby finally understood that Lee's workshop had no need of Cooper Franklin's custom – that Lee was doing them a favour, taking on their pieces; that she needed to show more gratitude, more flexibility, more respect – then it might, just might, prove the right long-term decision.

She waited for the train to fade before picking up the telephone.

'Hello?'

'It's me,' said Jay's voice.

Marianne sat back in her chair, delighted. 'Darling!'

'What's all this about the pad being dodgy?'

Silence.

'I don't understand. We practically mined the thing ourselves, Smidge. It can't be dodgy.'

'Then I must be mistaken.'

'What's wrong with it?'

Marianne bit her lip. 'I don't know,' she said. 'It's a feeling. I'm taking it to Rogerson tomorrow to get a proper analysis – then we'll know for sure. But in the meantime, I – I just thought you'd want to know what's going on. It's—'

'Rogerson?'

'Clive Rogerson. He's the—'

'I know who Clive Rogerson is, Marianne.'

'Great. Then you'll also know that, apart from running the institute and co-curating every worth-while decorative arts exhibition this side of the Atlantic, Clive Rogerson also happens to specialise in padparaschas. He's the absolute authority. He wrote an excellent paper on them last year, which I'm sure you read, and I just think it would be wise to run this one by him and see what he thinks. It's a precaution. I don't want to start work on the designs without being sure that this stone is what we're claiming it is. You know the score. It—'

'Fine,' Jay snapped. 'Take it to him, then.'

Marianne fought the urge to snap back. She hated it when Jay got like this – hated that mad male pride, the way he took it so personally when all Marianne wanted was a second opinion.

'Only do me a favour,' he added, 'don't see him tomorrow. See him on Monday, or Tuesday, or some-time next week, can't you?'

'I don't see what difference that'll make. If you've got a problem with me taking it to Rogerson, then it's hardly going to—'

'Just twenty-four hours! Is that really so hard?'

'But what can you do in twenty-four hours?' She was laughing now. 'Either it's treated, or it's bona fide. You're not going to—'

'I need to speak to Tariq.'

Marianne frowned.

'I want to go back to Galle.' Jay spoke very slowly. 'And I want to speak to Tariq about it – face-to-face.'

'But your Bangkok meetings? Your rubies. They—'

'Not important.'

'They were important enough when you set them up. They—'

'Not as important as this, Marianne.'

'And what if I'm wrong?' she said, her tone softening. 'Darling, you can't go messing up your plans and flying this way and that across the globe all on a hunch . . . *my* hunch. Why don't you wait until Rogerson has seen it and *then* go to Tariq?'

'Because by then it'll be too late.' Jay lit a cigarette. She heard the click of his lighter. 'If you're right about this, Marianne, and I can't help thinking that you are, and if I can fix it with a quick visit to Tariq's workshop . . .'

'But what can Tariq—'

'He's done something, Marianne. I know he has. I'm sure your hunch is right. And I'm sure that Tariq's behind it. He's been odd for weeks – creeping around, avoiding me . . . I knew something was up – even my mother noticed it. Ever since he got it wrong with those Genda sapphires he's been itching to trip me up. It bugs the hell out of him that I'm the newcomer, the foreigner, and yet I'm the one getting it right these days. Especially when he's the one who taught me everything I know. It was okay when I was just the dealer and he was the rough-stone expert – the cutter. But now he's losing his touch and I . . . please, Marianne. Just wait until tomorrow, can't you?'

'All right,' she said, quietly.

'And don't tell anyone.'

'Of course I won't.'

'Not Paul and Sophie. Not Rogerson. And certainly not Gabby. She—'

'I won't, Jay. I promise you, I won't.'

'Thanks, Smidge.' Jay heaved a sigh of relief. 'Guess I'd better get going, then. It's a long flight back . . .'

Marianne thought of all the things she wanted to speak to him about – the baby stuff, especially – and then there was the whole subject of Paul and Sophie, the way Paul had made her feel, the weird fact that there were still people of their generation who regarded marriage as some sort of achievement.

'Marianne?'

'Still here. I – I was thinking about the baby.'

'I have to go, Smidge. I'm sorry. There's a flight at eleven. I need a ticket. You're okay, aren't you? You're not—'

'I'm fine.'

'Great. Love you.'

'Love you, too,' she murmured – but he was already gone.

Marianne replaced the receiver. She looked at what was left of her smoked salmon sandwich – half in, half out of its broken plastic wrapping. She looked at all the jewellery boxes scattered across the floor. She listened as another train went by. And she thought of Jay – standing at some airport booth on the other side of the world, buying his ticket back to Galle.

She'd never had a doubt. Ever since meeting him that chilly day the summer she and Gabriella left the institute, caught in the rain on their way back from lunch in Oxford Street . . . dressed in flimsy summer clothes and no umbrella . . . running up the steps of the old Bloomsbury house, waiting under the porch while Gabby searched for the keys . . . and then the door had opened unexpectedly from the inside. 'I saw you from the window,' he'd said, while Gab fell on him, kissing him delightedly. Then he'd looked over her shoulder at

Marianne. He'd smiled. And ever since that moment, it had always been so clear to her. So easy. When she remembered the muddled feelings she'd had for Paul – all the hesitations, the is-he-isn't-he questions she'd asked herself on an almost daily basis, it now seemed extraordinary that she'd ever found that state of affairs acceptable; that she'd even considered marriage.

It helped her, sometimes, to think back. Picking up the discarded jewellery boxes, and unpacking the rest – putting them all away in the cupboard, bagging up the packaging for the recycling cart – Marianne knew she couldn't expect perfection. She and Jay were bound to irritate one another from time to time. Of course there would be friction with that degree of intimacy. The tugging and dragging and bumping . . . like running three-legged. It was part of doing it – whatever it was – together. The important thing, she felt, was that first moment of clarity. Like seeing an unusual stone and knowing. Just knowing. Or a house you wanted to buy. Or a dress. A sense of things fitting – of rightness over perfection. A gut sense of 'mine'. Of course there would be irregularities – inclusions, cracks, stains, collisions. It wouldn't be human, otherwise. But if the partnership was right and true at its conception then Marianne was certain there would be deeper rhythms, bigger designs at work . . . the vast natural patterns of a large system, patterns that extended far beyond the regular day-to-day scope – like the long base note of a baroque dance holding on through passing upper discords. Her job was to trust that the clashes were part of the pattern – perhaps even enjoy the awkwardness, find beauty in the rougher, harder, uglier intervals . . . in the understanding that all would return to order again, that the music had direction, and wouldn't just disintegrate into senseless cacophony.

Chapter Ten

Ever since discovering that, at twenty-five weeks, Marianne still hadn't got round to arranging a proper antenatal scan, Patricia Cooper had made it her business to monitor her daughter's pregnancy. She'd taken Marianne to see a top gynaecologist that very afternoon, and had sat in the waiting room while Philip Dewberry gave Marianne a thorough examination and made an appointment for the scan. It was disgraceful that nobody at the clinic had insisted on it. The twenty-week scan was an essential part of modern obstetrics. And while of course she understood that Marianne and Jay had to watch what they spent – indeed, while she herself was barely in a position to afford Mr Dewberry's fees and would have to make considerable adjustments to fund this gesture – Patricia had, nonetheless, reached breaking point. She'd seen her daughter drinking and smoking, and had even – on one occasion – caught her eating scallops. She knew Marianne skipped check-ups from time to time. And, understanding that it would only be counterproductive if, as her mother, she began telling

Marianne what she could and couldn't do in her condition, Patricia was still optimistic that the girl might pay more attention to the advice of a professional.

She decided to wait until the day of the scan appointment. With Jay still abroad, still roving, still free, Patricia had been able to seize the opportunity his absence offered and point out the necessity of having someone else, preferably a mother, holding Marianne's hand instead. Marianne had agreed – it would have been churlish of her not to, given that Patricia was paying for the procedure. And so, with Jay comfortably out of the way and Marianne somewhat indebted to her . . . the circumstances now seemed ideal for raising the whole subject of sustained antenatal care.

Having suggested – casually – that they meet for lunch somewhere near the clinic, Patricia now had her daughter captive that Monday afternoon. Fixing her eyes on Marianne's, she ran through the advantages of going private: total control over appointment times, less hanging about, better facilities, more attention . . . and while, of course, it was Marianne's decision, Patricia couldn't help thinking that going private made real sense for a girl in Marianne's position, a girl with a business to run.

Marianne smiled. 'Except I'm not made of money, Mum. Not everyone can afford private treatment. And I'm sorry to have to tell you this, but Jay and I now fall into the – er . . . the rather less fortunate category these days. We're not—'

'Then let me pay. Please, darling. Let me arrange for you to have proper care – so that you can go on seeing Dewberry, and find a decent hospital for the birth instead of some half-baked midwifery clinic. They say the private wing at St Mary's Paddington is excellent –'

'I'm sure it is – if you're willing to part with five or six grand.'

'I have the money.'

Marianne gave her mother a searching look.

'I have it,' Patricia insisted. 'I have enough savings – and I'd like to spend it on you, Marianne. And the health of my future grandchild.'

Patricia looked at her daughter for a moment, assessing the level of receptivity. It wasn't bad. She hadn't said 'no'. Not yet.

'It's what your father would have wanted,' she added, shamelessly. 'And – and what I'd really love, Marianne, is to arrange for you to have a maternity nurse. Would you let me do that? Just for the first month or so? Just in case . . .' she swallowed, and tried again. 'Just in case Jay isn't . . .'

Marianne didn't help her.

'I'm sure he's *planning* to be with you, darling. I just . . .'

Marianne sipped her coffee.

'I know you'd hate to have me there, darling. I'm not even suggesting that. But – but a professional nurse . . . someone who could really support you. Especially with the exhibition in March. You'll be frantic, Marianne. Even if you do manage to persuade Jay to stick around, there are things . . . things that – as the mother, as a woman – only you can really . . . Bethany Williams had a fantastic one. She cried, apparently, when the woman left. I'm sure I could get the name, if you were interested. And if you didn't like her, you could always send her away. It would only be as back-up.'

Their eyes met. Marianne noticed, to her discomfort, that her mother was close to tears.

'I'm worried about you. Having a baby isn't always straightforward. You need proper care, Marianne. There can be complications . . .' Patricia looked at the little espresso that her daughter was drinking, at the empty glass of wine by her fork, at the fresh packet of Silk Cut waiting on the table. She looked, too, at the purple-and-black-striped stretch-dress, and the wild orange scarf; at the dangly mismatched earrings and the giant patchwork bag; at the black nail polish, and the smudged eye make-up that could have been left over from the night before. Marianne had never been interested in looking wholesome or healthy. And while Patricia understood that her daughter was never going to embrace the natural preppy clear-eyed look that she herself had spent a lifetime cultivating, while she'd long abandoned any hope of influencing the girl away from the darker, rougher, more sub-versive looks that Marianne admired – understood that it was only 'dressing', that there were other more important things for her to worry about . . . Patricia was still disturbed by the pirate look now that Marianne was visibly pregnant. Nothing about her seemed ready for the job. 'Sometimes I wonder if you quite realise what's involved.'

Marianne looked away. She knew her mother meant well. It wasn't often that Patricia came to London – she didn't like the traffic, she found the pace distressing. It was only because she wanted to be there with her daughter for this all-important scan that Patricia had braved the journey at all. She didn't like upsets. She needed routine and quietness in her life. And while it was precisely this element of her mother that had had such a profound effect on Marianne – while it had sparked in her a craving for the exact opposite, for risk-taking, rule-breaking, convention-flouting freedom – she had learnt to understand her mother's nature. Safety was everything to Patricia.

But that didn't give her the right to impose this exaggerated sense of caution on others – not even her adult daughter, who was now feeling close to allergic to this particular side of her mother. In truth, Marianne wasn't entirely averse to the idea of transferring her antenatal treatment to Philip Dewberry – especially if it was to be at Patricia's expense. The idea of controlling her appointment times was certainly tempting. But the offer of a maternity nurse appalled her. What did Marianne want with some strange woman invading the few precious post-birth days and weeks she imagined she and Jay would share? Or telling her how to breastfeed, or bottlefeed, or whatever it was . . . or when to let the baby sleep, when to take it out in the pram, and so on – what weird kind of environment did that present as a first introduction to the world?

'Shall we get the bill?'

Patricia reached across the table. She put a hand on Marianne's. 'Please, darling. At least think about it, can't you?'

Marianne resisted the urge to pull away. But her hand sat oddly in her mother's, and in the end Patricia was the one to retreat.

'Well, I can't force you,' she said, sadly. 'But the offer still stands, darling. So if you do change your mind . . .'

'Sure. Thanks, Mum.'

Philip Dewberry's waiting room was on the ground floor of what once would have been the dining room of a traditional house in Harley Street, and still retained the essence of those former days. For, in spite of the water-cooler in one corner and the sofas and armchairs pushed sensibly against the walls, there were other elements to the room – such as its dark green colour scheme, its grey marble mantelpiece with the pastoral Landseer print above, the grandfather clock, and the large mahogany table in the centre of the room – elements that sent a different message. No matter that the table was covered with magazines or that the dominant smell was more disinfectant than roasting beef, there was an unmistakeable air of establishment, of imperial formality, in the style of the building and in the singularly inappropriate mood it conveyed – more gentleman's club than woman's doctor . . . an air that wasn't lost on Marianne.

She sat in one of the leather armchairs while her mother stood at the table, searching for a magazine. In the end, Patricia found two. Taking a seat beside Marianne, she handed one over (it was dedicated to expectant mothers, with special features on nutrition, and tips on how best to prepare for Christmas with a baby on the way) and began reading the other. Marianne didn't open hers. She sat looking at the cover – at the pretty model, with her pretty smile and pretty bump – while she listened to the ticking of the clock.

'He won't be long,' said the PA, putting her head around the door.

Marianne nodded.

'And – just so we're clear – will you be wanting to know what sex the baby is, Miss Cooper? Or—'

'God, no. Definitely not.'

'Of course.' Smiling at them both, the PA disappeared back down the corridor to her office – shoes tapping neatly on the cool stone. They heard her calling the scan room nurse, and relaying Marianne's instruction.

Patricia put the magazine aside. 'Are you sure you don't want to know, darling?'

Marianne looked at her.

'All right. All right . . .'

Patricia's magazine was open again and, for a moment, the pair of them sat in resumed silence before Marianne, irritated, said, 'Why would I want to know?'

Patricia shrugged. 'Why wouldn't you? I wish I'd had that option when you were on the way – imagine how much easier it would have been for me, when I was buying your clothes and your cot and a pram, and deciding how to decorate your bedroom . . . not to mention the whole subject of choosing your name. Why complicate it with fussing what to do *if* it's a boy . . . *if* it's a girl . . . why not just know, and get on with it? Seems to me you—'

And then Patricia broke off, turning suddenly. There was a commotion at the door to the street – someone was shouting – and then the same tidy footsteps, tapping past. Then a metallic click as the door opened, and more voices.

'I'm sorry, sir. But unless we have specific instructions from the patient, we can't just admit anyone claiming to be the—'

'Fine. Check with her if you must. I'm only asking that you—'

The man was admitted into the hallway. The door closed. The street sounds faded. 'If you could just wait here, Mr Franklin. I'll see if she—'

The PA's head appeared at the door. 'I'm sorry, Miss Cooper. But this gentleman is insisting—'

'Marianne!'

Abandoning his suitcase in the hall, Jay pushed past the PA into the waiting room. It was clear he'd come

136

straight from the airport. He was crumpled and unshaven and had that particular look of long-suffering that could only be achieved by twelve or so hours of economy travel.

Grinning broadly, Marianne got to her feet.

'Smidge . . .'

Jay kissed her. Ignoring the neat PA – hesitating in the doorway – and the equally neat Patricia, whose dutiful smile was comprehensively failing to involve the upper part of her face – he pressed his lips on Marianne's and held her as close as the baby bump allowed. And Marianne kissed back. It wasn't entirely comfortable. He was scratchy. He smelt of airline food. He seemed to have forgotten that she was bigger now, that pulling her in by the waist probably wasn't the best idea, but none of those things really mattered. The important thing was that he'd come, that he was here, and that her mother could see that he cared.

God only knew how he'd found her. So far as Marianne was concerned, Jay was meant to be in Galle that day, putting the wind up Tariq Ibrahim. There had been one message from him since their last conversation, a short message telling her that he'd seen Tariq, that their hunches had been right, but that – with a bit of time and sensitivity – there was nothing that couldn't be fixed. All Marianne had to do was hold on to the stone that Paul had given her until Jay got to London. He'd explain it all properly when he saw her . . . but she hadn't expected it to be today! Or even that week. For all she knew, Jay was set to return to Thailand and complete his original itinerary as planned. Instead, he was here in London. Here, with her, in time for the scan. And there was something so typical about it, a sort of brilliance in the uselessness: unpredictable, yet perfectly on time; chaotic, yet oddly focussed and determined . . . for, with Marianne unobtainable that afternoon – not at the showroom, nor at her flat, and her mobile on mute, and her attention elsewhere – he must have had to call Gabby, and then make his own additional enquiries, to find out what she was doing that day, and exactly where she'd be. He was brilliant. She loved him beyond measure.

So it was Jay who went in with her for the scan. It was Jay who first discovered that he and Marianne were expecting a daughter – for of course he wanted to know the sex.

'Quick, quick!' Jay clutched her hand. The sensor moved over her skin – pressing into the gel, as Philip Dewberry got a better angle. He twisted the screen so that they could both see – and pointed out the relevant bits of their baby's anatomy.

'It's incredible,' breathed Jay. '*She*'s incredible!'

. . . while Patricia sat in the waiting room – with Jay's suitcase beside her, and the same magazine on her lap.

The scan was entirely normal. Combined with the equally normal results from the blood tests that Philip Dewberry had conducted at her last visit, there was nothing for them to worry about. Marianne's blood pressure was marginally high, but that was all. Certainly no need for an amniocentesis. Getting up from his chair, Dewberry gave Marianne a wide smile and advised her to continue doing exactly what she was doing – eat well, of course; get lots of rest – but, in general, her baby was thriving. All she needed to do was make a date with his PA to see him again at the end of November and try, so far as was possible, to enjoy this last trimester of her term.

'I will, Mr Dewberry! Thank you!'

And it all was fine – except that Mr Dewberry hadn't the faintest idea that this new patient of his was drinking and smoking as freely as ever. He didn't know that her approach to food was almost as cavalier. He'd assumed – as the midwives from Marianne's previous clinic had assumed, and Sophie Mostyn had assumed, and anyone less intimate with Marianne who bothered to concern themselves with the subject – that the girl had done her research and accepted the general mores of pregnancy. And Patricia, realising this, realising that the chance she might have had to prompt him to emphasise to Marianne the risks she was taking was all but gone, found it hard to forgive Jay for turning up that day, for taking her place at Marianne's side, for failing to ensure that the girl was given the right advice. And while she was glad to see that Marianne had liked Dewberry – glad, that at least she would indeed be taking up her mother's offer on that front – Patricia still felt full of concern as she bid the pair of them goodbye.

'What's wrong with Patty?' said Jay, standing with Marianne on the stretch of pavement by Dewberry's practice as Patricia walked away from them – upright and restrained – in the direction of the Underground.

'She's worrying again.'

Jay hailed a taxi. 'Should she be?' he said, opening the door for Marianne.

The enquiry was sincere. But Marianne, struck afresh by the exclusivity of Jay's attention, by the dizzying knowledge that they were finally alone after weeks of separation . . . Marianne wasn't interested in talking about her health. There was nothing to worry about. Dewberry had said as much. He'd confirmed everything that Marianne had already believed. All that mattered now was a proper reunion with Jay . . . who was equally up for it, once the small matter of the padparascha stone was put to bed.

'Darling –'

'It won't take a second. I just have to see if it's a decent match.'

'But you can do that any time! Come on! It's—'

Kissing her quiet. 'I won't be able to concentrate, Marianne. Half an hour at your smart new showroom – that's all I need. I promise . . .'

It hadn't taken long for Jay to extract the truth from Tariq. Catching him at his workshop just as Tariq was locking up for the day, Jay had made him reopen the doors and the pair of them had gone back inside.

'You know what this is about, don't you?'

Tariq nodded. Without Jay needing to say another word, he went to the back of the room, squatted down, and produced – from a hole in the floor – a small cloth package containing the rough padparascha. Silently, he handed it over.

Jay took the stone out. Helping himself to a torch from Tariq's workbench, he shone a beam of light into the heart of the stone and – recognising it instantly – returned it to the package, and put it straight into his pocket. Then he turned to Tariq again, and looked at him with the same disenchanted expression that he might have had when looking at a stone that didn't measure up.

Tariq squirmed. 'Come on man,' he urged. 'Come *on*, Jay. It was a joke. A joke! You remember those diffused pinks we got from Uncle Mohan before he married

Jeevitha? The job lot from Thailand that everyone knew was worthless and we all had to pretend to be grateful and . . . oh, the *fuss* he made! And – and suddenly there were damn "padparaschas" everywhere, remember? So I never got round to trading mine. They just sat here in this drawer. And – and then there you were, Jay, putting so much pressure on me to do the cutting and all that – and I just saw it, and I thought I *bet* he won't notice it! I *bet* he won't remember! He'll be thinking about his rich client and his rich friends and – and all that . . . it would be such a joke to catch him out!'

Jay sighed.

'. . . only you didn't show, man! You just left us! And of course I couldn't start exchanging the stones there and then, at the New Oriental, with those peacock waiters staring at me, and . . . that sister of yours . . . I couldn't . . .' He trailed off.

Still, Jay said nothing. It was warm in the workshop with the fans inactive. Both men were sweating. And as the silence pressed on them, Jay reached into the pocket of his trousers and took the package out again.

'Okay, Tariq,' he said. 'Let's drop it, shall we?'

Tariq's expression transformed. 'Yes – yes.'

'If you could just do one small thing for me?'

'Of course, Jay. Of course I will. Anything at all. Just tell me what it is, Jay, and I'll—'

'Good.' Jay put the stone back down on Tariq's workbench and the pair of them looked at it. 'Now,' he said. 'I imagine you can recall what that first treated pink looked like – yes? How it was cut and so on?'

'I can do better than that.' Tariq opened a low, thin drawer beneath his worktop. 'See? I still have the others. And they were all the same, Jay. Totally identical. They—'

'Let's have a look.'

Jay held out his hand and a packet containing six perfectly matched stones was placed into its palm. Again, the torch came out. Jay sat on Tariq's old stool. And, once again, the torch was shone into the heart of each pink drop. Tariq stood silently watching. And as he watched he began to understand what Jay was going to ask of him. He reached for the padparascha – but Jay's hand was there first.

'Jay! Come on! I was only . . .'

Jay examined the rough stone. It was hard to know, for sure, if a copy could be made. There was a hefty inclusion across one corner, a smaller spot towards the other diagonal, and something cloudy further round. He wasn't an expert. He couldn't tell. Indeed, he wasn't sure that the thing *was* even a padparascha. What if – as was more than likely to be the case – it was just a pink sapphire? What the hell would they do then?

Telling himself that there was no use fretting about that until the thing was cut, he handed it back to Tariq, together with the torch.

'You think you can do it?' he said.

Tariq nodded.

'You sure you can do it?'

Again, Tariq nodded.

'I don't believe you.'

And Tariq, grinning now – that old Tariq-happy wily grin – put down the torch, returned the stone to Jay and said he was more than welcome to take it elsewhere. Or do it himself. Or whatever. He could even take one of the pinks to copy if he liked. And Jay knew – and Tariq knew – that in truth there was only one person with the skills, the experience, the precision

142

. . . the flair to pull it off. And that one person was Tariq Ibrahim.

Tariq didn't disappoint. Within twenty-four hours, the new stone had been cut – and it was perfect. Even to Jay's eye. More than perfect, if that was possible. For it was now abundantly clear to both men that it was indeed a padparascha . . . and that Paul and Sophie owned a stone that was worth five or six times the sum they'd originally paid for it. Not only was it the true padparascha that Jay had always believed it to be. No question. It was more that – somehow – Tariq had been able to find a way of cutting the thing so that no trace of an inclusion remained. It was stunning – a perfect copy of the fake little pink, and yet with some intangible extra quality of truth about it. The idea of swapping it for another of those all-but-worthless pinks stuck hard in Jay's throat. He'd do it. He had to do it. But the thought of a stone of this beauty and rarity on the finger of a plain little ignorant Englishwoman was more than he could bear. He had to get it to London before he was tempted. Had to make the checks and make the swap, in a way that was as quick and emotionless as possible. And nothing – not even the imminent prospect of making love to his beautiful Marianne – was going to get in his way.

Chapter Eleven

The stones were matched to Jay's satisfaction. Locking both of them back in the showroom safe, Marianne was still at the door – still twiddling the dials – when she felt a hand at her arm, another at her waist, and Jay's stubble tickling at her neck. She turned, smiling.

And, five hours later, with Jay still unshaven and Marianne still in the stretchy purple and black stripes – although her face was more flushed, more naked, more invigorated than before – the pair of them went out for dinner. They sat side by side at a table for four. They ate a lot of pasta, drank a lot of wine, and smoked a good number of cigarettes. They kissed and laughed and went to bed early.

And, work aside, that was how it was for the next few days.

Jay would go off for occasional meetings in Hatton Garden. He made an appointment with a jeweller in Burlington Arcade who was sounding close to desperate for Colombian emeralds – his client had a new mistress, a woman with green eyes, and he wanted those emeralds. He needed them. How soon could Jay come over? And then, as the trade began to realise he was in town, so the calls to Jay's mobile increased. He was asked to view an unusual brown diamond that a South African contact thought he should see . . . might Jay know a buyer? What did Jay think? His opinion was sought on the value of an Edwardian necklace of sapphires that was shortly to be up for sale at Sotheby's. There was some rumour about a rival dealer going under – with stock to pick up on the cheap, if he could raise the cash. It was certainly worth looking at. Jay cherry-picked the calls he liked, and ignored the ones he didn't – not necessarily even bothering to return the call if he wasn't interested. And nobody minded very much, or was even particularly insulted. They all knew that Jay had a take-it-or-leave-it approach. He needed to come and go at a moment's notice. And there was nothing to be gained from taking it personally. You never knew when he'd next be in town with something special to sell.

And while Marianne had no client appointments that week, there was still the usual ferrying about and chivvying with various works-in-progress to be done. There was paperwork to complete. And of course there were her designs for the exhibition she and Gab were planning – although, with so much due to happen before that time, and with the daily pleasure of finding Jay's beautiful warm body back in her bed, it became increasingly hard for her to get out of it in the morning, or the afternoon, or whenever it was, when there was really very little that couldn't be left for another day.

He wouldn't stay for ever – she knew that. Apart from anything else, he still had those commitments in Thailand and Colombia to honour. But when Marianne came back from the bathroom one morning – the

145

morning of Sophie and Paul's dinner party – to find an open suitcase on the bed, and Jay bending over it with a passport and travel documents stuffed into the back pocket of his jeans, it was still a hard sight to accept. Biting her lip, she found that she was suddenly fussing about the effect Jay's sudden absence might have on the party they were due to attend that night. It seemed easier, somehow, to object on Sophie's behalf, rather than for herself.

'I told them you were coming, Jay. You said—'

'I know I did.' He shut the suitcase. 'But you got me at a weak moment, Smidge – and you know it's not my scene. It really isn't . . .'

'So that's why you're leaving?'

Jay smiled. 'Well, it's not exactly keeping me here,' he said, 'if that's what you mean. I've got better things to do than to make conversation with Sophie about worthy post-tsunami projects, or – or think of something half-civilised to say to your old boyfriend . . .'

Marianne turned from him. She began drying her body – her stupid, top-heavy, blown-up body – and wished, fervently, that she had the old one back. The old one she could have used. The old one might have tempted him to stay. But *this*? This lumpen swollen uterus-on-legs that she'd become . . . Marianne glimpsed it in the mirror. No wonder he was off.

Sensing he'd overstepped the mark, Jay came round to her side of the bed. He sat on the edge and continued, more gently, 'I'm running out of time on those rubies. You know I am. If I'm not in Bangkok by the end of the month—'

'I know. I know.'

'There's a lot to do before Christmas –'

Silence.

146

Jay reached for her hand. 'I thought we'd talked about this,' he said wearily. 'I thought we'd agreed. I'm working now, so that I can be with you in January. I'm sorry it has to be this way, but—'

'You have to travel. I know.'

She let him pull her down beside him on the bed. Wrapping the wet towel over her breasts, her stomach, her thighs, she tucked its corner under her shoulder and – black curls dripping – looked down at her black fingernails. And at Jay's hand – warm and concerned – resting over her own.

Was this really it? Had she really become the nagging home-bound woman she swore she'd never be? Was she really now that matronly figure of sense and restraint, of rules and obligations and duty? How had it happened? How had she changed? Who was occupying this body of hers? It was as if, along with the baby, an ugly clinging personality was now in possession of her flesh and blood and Marianne – the old Marianne whom Jay had fallen in love with – had all but vanished.

She smiled at him, willing her old self back again. And if she couldn't be that person any more, then – teeth gritted behind the lips – she'd damn well fake it. She wasn't going under. Wasn't going to surrender to this new invader, not without a fight. She could still be the person she chose to be. She might have other feelings, feelings she couldn't quite explain – with strange settling inclinations, and a foot twitching over the brake pedal – but that didn't mean she had to indulge them. She could still be that free spirit, that light-handed sort of woman who could watch her lover take a plane as easily as watch him walk into the next room. She would be that slim, airy girl – who'd never cling, or ask too much. She *would*.

She pushed aside all the arguments she'd wanted to throw at him. Why didn't you tell me you were going today? You've got your ticket, you must have booked the flight, why not extend me the courtesy of informing me of your movements? Is it really too much to ask? How would you like it if I messed you around like this? How would you like to have to suddenly go to a party alone and have to explain *my* absence? How would you like it, trailing around Mothercare on your own, or dealing with the pitying glances from ignorant people who assume you'd been insulted by the lack of a wedding ring? On and on, it kept on coming, this muddy flood of rage – a flood that seemed to sweep with it every petty, polluting little gripe – towards the man she loved who was simply being himself. It didn't make sense. Why did the very thing she loved most about Jay now fill her with such fury? With a supreme surge of effort, Marianne directed her will against the flow of emotion and – smilingly, flirtingly even – wriggled her hand free of his, and stood up. Something about the gesture restored her pride, as if she were the one needing space. Not him.

'I'd stay if I could,' he said, miserably. 'It's not that I want to leave.'

'Don't you?'

Jay despaired.

'*I* would,' she went on, giving her hair a final rub down. He couldn't see her face. Then she dropped the towel. She pushed back her hair and faced him.

'Oh, Jay, Jay . . . don't look so worried! It's okay!' – laughing now – 'I'm just envious. I'd love to skip tonight's party and jet off to Bangkok and Bogotá! I'd love to be concerning myself with flight schedules and currency exchange rates, instead of blood sugar levels and cot mattresses. You're a lucky bastard –'

Jay smiled. 'I'm a man.'

They didn't talk about it again. She still went with him to the airport that afternoon. She kissed him goodbye – fondly as ever, on the lips. There was no resentment in the air. She made sure of it. No tension. No with-holding. But it was a quiet farewell. Their eyes weren't meeting, not as much as before. Their gestures seemed perfunctory; their words, routine. She waved him through the gate. He turned at the end of the corridor, blew a kiss at her and raised his hand – the picture of regret.

Except Marianne didn't buy it. And as she drove back into London, her thoughts returned to that morning; to the conversation by the bed – *I'm a man*.

It was a neat excuse. Of course he couldn't have the baby for her, of course he needed to continue to work . . . but it wasn't good enough. And somewhere, in the back of her mind, Marianne knew that it wasn't about duty – all this travelling, this coming and going at a moment's notice. Jay liked it that way. He was lying when he said he didn't want to leave. His display of regret was empty – or, if not exactly empty, then it was regret about something slightly different . . . something to do with a certain sadness that this change in Marianne was a problem he couldn't fix. Because they both knew he couldn't wait to be above the clouds. That thinner, lighter atmosphere was where he belonged. And, thinking of the way other men treated their wives and girlfriends – the animal propinquity they maintained, particularly when there was a baby in the offing – Marianne couldn't help wishing that the love Jay felt for her, a love she didn't doubt, meant that, naturally, he wanted to be here on the ground with her. Couldn't help wishing that she was his air, his element, his natural preference.

Chapter Twelve

Sophie and Paul's dinner party was being held in the sort of London terraced house that, in recent decades, had doubled in price and was now worth over a million pounds.

Charles and Victoria had bought it, as newlyweds, back in 1976 – when he was still a muddled account manager for an advertising company and hadn't yet found God. It had cost them about twenty thousand and, at the time, had seemed shockingly expensive. But over the years, as the Mostyns moved around the country from one church residence to the next, so the market value of their house in Ifield Road had only continued to rise, together with the income it afforded them in the form of rent. They had never quite been able to bring themselves to part with it. As the place of Sophie's birth and, more importantly, the place where – together, over a cheap bottle of rosé in the kitchen – they'd decided Charles would quit the rat-race of advertising and the pair of them would devote themselves to something so much more worthwhile, to a life of Christ, with all the joys and sacrifices that entailed, it held a special place in their hearts and gave their peripatetic existence a certain anchor. Recently, with Charles's current position at St John's, the couple had finally been able to move back to London – back into their proper home . . . a home that had once been relatively humble, but now had a rather higher status.

So high, in fact, that Charles and Victoria no longer felt comfortable living there. And so, with their daughter recently engaged and looking for somewhere to live – and then, with any luck, a brood of children to raise – it seemed almost inevitable that they should decide to give the place to Sophie as a wedding present. Paul didn't have much money. They knew it would be difficult for him and Sophie to get started. Sophie would, in any case, be inheriting the place one day . . . so why not fast-forward a few years, and perhaps reduce her inheritance tax liability in the process? Charles and Victoria didn't need a family house any more. They had enough, in savings, to provide for their retirement – and, until that point, church accommodation would be ample for their needs.

But they hadn't yet moved out – that wouldn't happen until Sophie and Paul returned from honeymoon – and, in the meantime, the idea was that Paul would continue to live in his little Earl's Court basement flat. At least until he and Sophie were married. There was no question of him moving in before then. And while this arrangement was what everybody wanted, it was also – in truth – starting to get a little tiresome. For Paul's current flat was charmless and dark. It had no outside space. He and Sophie invariably spent their evenings and weekends at Ifield Road, with Paul shuffling back to his cold little flat at midnight, and lying there in his dull empty bed, counting the days to his wedding. He couldn't wait to move on. And so, with Sophie's parents off to Norfolk on a retreat that week, it seemed to him the perfect time to hold a little dinner party at Ifield Road – and glimpse, for a moment, what it might be like to live there as a couple.

Marianne was last to arrive. This was partly due to her getting stuck in rush-hour traffic on the way back from Heathrow, but it wasn't helped by her subsequent resolve to look good that night, and not care how long the process took. Fight the heaviness of pregnancy. Prove to herself that the old appeal hadn't totally vanished; that there was still something desirable, bump notwithstanding. And as the hair was styled and the make-up applied, as she looked at the transformation in the mirror – at the freshly buffed and polished skin, at the colour in her cheeks and lips, the added drama in her eyes, the way it all seemed to glow and hum against the bright green neckline of her dress – Marianne couldn't help but be pleased.

And later, walking into the drawing room in Ifield Road, she was glad of the efforts she'd made. Of course it was annoying that the real target, Jay, wasn't there to appreciate the results, but there was certainly a degree of consolation in the way that Paul was looking at her.

Marianne basked in it for a moment. She thought of the way Paul had been at the showroom – his apparent indifference to her charms that day, the pitying look he'd bestowed upon her bump – and compared it to the moment of speechless admiration as he'd opened the door just now.

'You . . .' He'd laughed at his own reaction, at the way she'd taken him by surprise, at his inability to hide it. 'What can I say? You look *great*, Marianne!'

'Thank you, Paul.'

'Wphfff!' He'd shaken his head as she'd walked past into the hallway. 'Pregnancy definitely suits you.'

Marianne smiled. She couldn't help it. Paul's words seeped into her parched ego and – pride restored – she moved into the drawing room where Sophie, equally admiring, greeted her. 'Oh my goodness, look at you! Wow, Marianne, that's a beautiful dress. You . . . look at her!' She turned to Helen, standing by the sofa. 'How annoying is that? Marianne manages to look more beautiful than the rest of us put together and she's pregnant! Don't you just hate it?'

Helen never complimented other women, not unless she was lying. 'I loved being pregnant,' she said. 'It's nice when a woman can carry it . . .'

Amused, Marianne took a glass of wine from Paul and looked around at the other guests. She knew that Gabby – who would only have got back from New York on the red-eye that morning – had declined the invitation. Tame dinner parties were hardly her scene. She'd no intention of going. And with her tendency to jetlag – a tendency that wasn't helped by Gab's childish excitement at the little bottles of airline champagne . . . it was better all round that the girl had a night in. Marianne pictured her snoring peacefully on one of Helen's sofas, unpacked suitcase sitting in the hall.

And so, with Gabby absent, Marianne wasn't surprised to see that, aside from Helen, none of the other guests was familiar to her; none except for George Franklin who – somewhat predictably – was standing outside on the dark November balcony, overlooking the garden, glued to his mobile telephone. Not really at the party at all. She watched him through the glass of the French windows. His head was bent. His expression was blank. He was listening intently to whoever it was at the other end of the line as he stared at the smart black tips of his shoes. Marianne wondered for a moment what it was like for Helen, as his wife. At least when Jay was with her he was *with her*. George, on the other hand, was absent even when he was present.

The other guests were seated on sofas and chairs around a small fireplace, and talking amongst themselves. Sophie tried to introduce Marianne.

'This is my cousin Max. Max?' Max turned, gave Marianne the briefest of nods as Sophie explained who she was, and returned to the conversation he was having with the greying man on his left. Sophie's confidence left her. 'And that's Will he's talking to,' she said. 'Will Sanderson, who's quite heavily involved with a sister church of ours in the City, and manages to run a hedge fund business *and* compete in marathons *and* keep Maggs happy . . . Maggie, his wife – the one in the blue top? And she's talking to Dina. Dina Gimiligni – Max's girlfriend, and – oh my God, the chicken . . .'

Pushing her bowl of crisps into Marianne's free hand, Sophie darted out of the room. Marianne heard her running down the stairs. She heard the bang of an oven door, the hum of an extractor fan, the ferocious sizzling of fat. A smell of well-cooked chicken wafted up the stairs. And as she heard and smelled these things, Marianne – momentarily abandoned – put down the crisps, lit a cigarette, and looked again at the room she was in. The sofas were sunken, but prettily faded. The walls were covered with bookcases, and interesting family pictures. There was an upright piano in one corner, with dog-eared sheet music stuffed on to the stand – and smiling faces in photographs, arranged higgledy-piggledy along the top. The carpet was old, and covered with rugs. The tables and chairs were scruffy brown antiques. There were chipped cachepots filled with Christmas roses and cheap bright poinsettias – and a pile of yellowing newspapers by the fire. It wasn't glamorous. It wasn't smart. Marianne's mother would have been appalled at the state of the chairs, at the marks on the carpet, at the lack of co-ordination – the total absence of *scheme* in the arrangement of the room. Marianne herself could see that it was a wholly unimaginative, design free, traditional English interior. Traditional English – not because the occupants had chosen for it to be that way, but because it was quite impossible for them to carry any other sort of look.

But she was also aware that it was, quite overwhelmingly, a home. Seeing Paul occupied in that traditional male dinner-party role of opening another bottle of wine – corkscrew in hand, elbows bending, biceps straining, as he stood squarely at the drinks' table, which was a ludicrously outdated affair, with bottles of gin and vodka from the seventies, and a silver-plate cocktail shaker that was now turning brown from lack of use – Marianne read his future in a flash. She saw Paul and Sophie filling this house with children. She saw Paul going greyer and Sophie getting fatter . . . yet all the time their lives would be held together, bonded by a mishmash collage of tradition, by layer upon layer of exactly those familiar homely details and attitudes and day-to-day conventions that Marianne habitually rejected.

Only today – tonight – it all seemed rather

wonderful. She still suspected that Paul was merely following what the rules dictated – that his good behaviour was driven more by a need for tribal approval than any sort of passion for Sophie. But with Jay perpetually in the sky, and George perpetually beyond the glass, it struck Marianne that there was a lot to be said for the kind of man who stayed in the room, and opened the bottles, and made conversation, and helped hand round crisps, and actually wanted to be there. Even if his reasons weren't exactly poetic. Even if . . . Marianne wavered. Would she really have Jay on such terms? Was obedience to tribal rules the best she could hope for from a man? It was hardly flattering.

Paul pulled the cork from the bottle and, catching her looking at him, smiled. It was Paul in his comfort zone, Paul at his best. His faded corduroy look perfect in this shabby-English context. The brashness of his former days had mellowed into something far more subtle – more attractive, she had to admit it, now that he was on his own territory . . . he didn't look weak or reduced or inadequate tonight. He looked relaxed and happy. He had also shown himself big enough – mature enough, wise enough – to appreciate the look of pregnancy, instead of regretting it . . . and that in itself (after Jay) was enough to make Marianne warm to him. Paul was a good, kind man. She shouldn't have been so quick to judge. She shouldn't have been so critical. Touched by a moment of shame, she – gratefully – smiled back.

And then Sophie reappeared – coming up from the kitchen with a thin film of sweat across an overly pink face, a strand of damp hair clinging to her cheek, and a label poking out from the neck of her shirt. 'Dinner,' she gasped, 'finally!' and urged them all to come downstairs.

Helen and Dina went first – Helen giving the balcony window a short, sharp rap as she passed. Startled, George looked round. He said something into his mobile, apologised to the person at the other end of the line, and – switching it off – came back into the room with a gust of cold November air.

'Sorry about that.'

Paul chuckled. 'Don't be silly,' he said. 'To be honest, there's something rather satisfying – to me, at any rate, having left the City with everyone telling me I was mad . . . something almost reasurring, George, about the sight of you out there, still in your suit, getting all wet and blown about while some other bastard yanks your chain!'

George dredged up a lukewarm smile. Putting the mobile into his trouser pocket, he loosened his tie and stood aside for the women to go first.

Downstairs, they grouped at the door looking at the silvery candlelit table as they waited for Sophie to direct them to their seats from a scrap of paper in her hands. With Jay now absent and the numbers thrown, Marianne found herself between Dina Gimiligni and George. She took a final drag from her cigarette and looked around for an ashtray.

'Here you are,' said George, spying one in the middle of the table and reaching for it. And then, unable to resist it, he went on, 'Glad to see you're taking care of yourself these days, Marianne.'

Marianne deposited the end of her cigarette on to the ashtray and left it in his hand. *Here we go*, she thought to herself. *Dig, dig, dig; pick, pick, pick.*

'Oh George,' she murmured, sitting down. 'How kind of you to concern yourself with the state of my health.'

George put the ashtray on the mantelpiece. He sat beside her. 'It's not *your* health I'm worried about,' he replied, glancing at the bump.

Marianne was silent. She watched the others taking their places at the table, chatting and laughing in pairs and threes. She watched Paul filling fresh glasses with dark red wine and heard the chairs scraping in and out of position . . . while George, fired by a sense of duty, a sense that Marianne needed help even – help from herself – pressed on.

'And – and Jay's okay with it?' he said.

'Jay? Why shouldn't he be?'

'And your mother? Your doctor? You can't tell me your doctor's not concerned about the effects of this addiction on your unborn—'

'*Addiction?*' Marianne laughed. 'Christ. If anyone round here has an addiction – one that forces him out into the wind and the rain at a time of day when any sane person would be inside, enjoying a glass of wine . . . if anyone here has an addiction, George, it certainly isn't me.'

George heard the edge to her voice. Aware he'd touched a nerve, he glanced at Marianne uneasily – and scratched his head. 'I'm sorry,' he said. 'I was only—'

'Well, don't.'

'It's—'

'Just back off, can't you? Is it so much to ask?'

George raised both hands in surrender.

'. . . Gabriella might let you boss her around. And Helen, no doubt. And your poor minions at work. But it's my body we're talking about here. And – fine – the baby's too . . . but – but do you honestly think that a couple of cigarettes are going to hurt anyone?'

George sat back looking at Marianne, waiting for her to finish.

'And, when you think of the things our mothers were eating and drinking when they were carrying us . . . my mother smoked like a chimney – twenty a day—'

'My point exactly.'

Marianne looked at him. Her lips twitched. For a moment, it seemed she was going to laugh at his joke – laugh at herself as an example of the unfortunate kind of person who might result from a mother with a twenty-a-day habit, the kind of person you really wouldn't want to reproduce – as if the existence of Marianne herself, with all her faults, was reason enough to quit smoking . . . and then the moment passed.

'I'm sure you mean well,' she said primly. 'But if Jay doesn't have a problem with my approach, then I'm afraid I can't see what possible business it is of yours to—'

'Sure. Of course.'

'And—'

'I hear you, Marianne. I'm backing off.'

Sophie was sitting on George's left – fully occupied in a conversation with the man on her other side. She was fond of Will Sanderson and interested in everything he had to tell her about the Norfolk retreat that her parents were undertaking – a retreat he himself had often attended . . . and a full week was so much better than a weekend . . . that particular monastery was exceptional, truly exceptional – Sophie and Paul should try it . . .

Sophie nodded, she smiled, but she couldn't quite engage. Directly opposite – and not entirely visible to her, because of the flowers and candlelight – was Paul. She could hear him laughing with Maggie. She could sense his movements.

160

'You don't have to go as a couple,' Will was saying. 'In fact, there's a lot to be said for going solo from time to time, even after you get married. I went alone to a weekend in North Wales last year, and met a completely different sort of person – I'm sure of it – from being by myself . . .'

Perhaps not being able to see him made it worse. Perhaps if she could see Paul, she'd then feel reassured. Perhaps not. For if what she saw was another shared secret smile with Marianne – like the one she'd witnessed earlier – Sophie wasn't sure she could bear it.

When they'd met last week, she'd found Marianne approachable and appealing; unintimidating. She'd liked Marianne's smile, her natural manner, and the straightforward way she spoke. She was looking forward to having Marianne and Jay to dinner. She hoped they might become friends. Certainly, she was drawn to the idea of a social life that wasn't quite so centred on the Church. It was a relief, at times, to have a break from the Christian way of engaging – that impressive, if somewhat earnest, attitude of consistent kindness and forgiveness that her immediate circle couldn't help projecting . . . that very un-English love-on-the-surface that, in its directness, was hard some-times to absorb.

But in wanting to get to know her better, Sophie had been unprepared for this other side to Marianne – this shocking beauty that the latter was radiating as she sat, seemingly oblivious, at the table. Sophie could cope with the expensive glamour and skinny physiques of women like Helen and Dina. She knew that Paul was as unimpressed as she was – ultimately – with women whose good looks projected such shallow values.

161

The former so completely cancelled out the latter as – weakly enslaved to the gym, the salon, the dictates of fashion – Dina and Helen fought valiantly against the signs of fat and aging and whatever perceived financial restraints they struggled against . . . and failed to invest in anything more meaningful. They were objects of pity.

But Marianne's beauty tonight – which was all about colour, and health, and womanliness – it blew Sophie away. For Marianne wore her pregnancy not as something to hide – or regret, or disguise, or apologise for – but in such a way that any woman not pregnant longed instantly for that ripe curve to her stomach, that richness in her hair, her skin . . . and – oh – how much more understated and 'must-have' were velvet flat shoes with a chic little strap – how much more empowered and yet gentle did it look to be standing with a hand resting lightly on your innocent, unborn child? There was an effortlessness to it which, when combined with the messages of fertility and joy she gave out, made Marianne's beauty – unfairly, cruelly – real. Beside it, all other women seemed over-ripe, under-ripe, or genetically modified.

No wonder Paul looked at her the way he did. And no wonder big-boned Sophie – whose beauty, if beauty it was, had a masculine quality that was hard to work with . . . that looked ridiculous in a flowery dress, yet hopelessly unfeminine in jeans – poor Sophie, who'd always hated trying to look pretty, who'd never enjoyed dressing up, even at the age of six . . . no wonder she couldn't compete.

And shouldn't compete. It was ridiculous.

Putting aside her napkin, Sophie apologised to Will as she got up to clear away the first course and start serving the second. Will rose instantly to help her. And as the pair of them cleared the table – as Sophie saw afresh that Paul was happily conversing with Maggie – and no little smiles in Marianne's direction . . . and, equally, that Marianne was involved in a three-way conversation with George and Dina . . . so she began to chastise herself. She must put her jealousy aside and try to celebrate Marianne's astonishing beauty – celebrate it inside, the way she'd celebrated it on the outside when Marianne had first walked into the sitting room tonight. Sophie knew that this was the only credible way she could deal with it. For what possible advantage was it for Sophie not only to be the plain one, but also the mean-spirited, green-spirited, ugly-hearted one as well? She needed to see Marianne's beauty less as a threat, and more as an opportunity for her to show a bit of courage and spirit; a chance for Sophie to stretch her heart, test her generosity, own her flaws, as much as her assets. 'Beauty on the inside' was – she knew – a clichéd phrase but it was also, unfortunately, all she had to work with at the moment.

Yes, Paul and Marianne had once been 'friends' – and Sophie wasn't stupid. She could read between the lines. She'd already guessed that they'd shared some sort of romantic past long before Helen Franklin had 'accidentally' let it slip earlier that evening, before Marianne arrived . . .

'I must say, I think you're brilliantly calm,' she'd said, as the subject of the padparascha came up again, 'letting an ex of Paul's make your engagement ring . . .'

And Sophie, taking a quick breath, merely said how much she liked and admired Marianne's work before adding, with a light laugh, that so long as Marianne

163

remained an ex, there was surely nothing to worry about!

And she was right, wasn't she? There was nothing to worry about. And yes, okay, it had been easier for her to present an attitude of indifference to the subject *before* seeing just how beautiful Marianne could be (and thank God for that, for Marianne's late arrival, for allowing Sophie the ignorance that had made it possible for her to give Helen the impression she genuinely didn't feel threatened). And yes, okay, it was a little odd of Paul not to have been more upfront about his relationship with Marianne . . . but then, Paul often did things that way. He liked to look after Sophie. He liked to protect her from the world – financial worries, tricky people, problems at work . . . it didn't come naturally to Paul, to share the load. He preferred to carry it alone. And while there were times when she found it frustrating, there was also a part of Sophie that felt touched by this side of her fiancé. It was Paul's way of loving her. And if it meant being shielded from certain awkward aspects of his past, was that really so bad?

In any case, such matters aside, Marianne was still with Jay – very much with Jay – and Paul was with Sophie. Paul had asked Sophie to marry him. He loved Sophie. What's more, she knew he loved her. He needed her – and not just her, but her family, her parents, her religion, her whole world and belief system was something he wanted and loved and embraced. It had resulted in a complete change of direction for Paul: a change of job, of image, of clothes, of life. He was, in every sense, reborn; and reborn into all that Sophie embodied and stood for. It was unthinkable – quite unthinkable – for him to go back to the old world and the old ways.

'So,' said George, to Sophie, as they moved into the main course and – politely, correctly – both he and William turned to speak to the women on their respective other sides. 'What did you make of Galle?'

Sophie gave the matter some thought before replying, 'I loved it, George. I absolutely loved it. That coastline – and that beautiful town, saved by its old fort walls . . . what kind of miracle was that?'

George smiled.

Sophie smiled too. 'I know, I know . . . it's hard for me to be objective when Paul proposed to me there! But I think I would have loved it anyway. There's something about a place – or a person – who has gone through something truly terrible, and then gets back up on to his or her or its feet and – and starts to walk again . . .'

George nodded. 'I've been hearing about your online gallery project,' he said.

Sophie looked embarrassed. 'It's hardly—'

'My stepmother has a friend with a daughter at the Fort School – and, according to her, they think it's a great idea. Apparently, they've all been frantically drawing pictures of their families, and borrowing Anusha's camera so that they can get theirs on to the website! Sounds to me like it's doing rather well . . .'

'I wish more of them had access, though. It seems so unfair.'

'It's better than nothing, surely. There's a computer at the library. There's another one at the Galle Foundation that they seem happy to lend . . . it's giving them so much confidence, and teaching them great computer skills at the same time. Anusha's been full of praise for you and your mother – you should see the email she sent last week!'

'Well, it's certainly working this end,' said Sophie. 'It's been a fantastic way to expose our unruly lot to what's been happening in Sri Lanka – make them realise how lucky they are to be living in such comfort, and – and just thinking about what other children have to live with, or without. Personal stories make it real, somehow. We did it in Bucharest a few years ago – Mum and Dad have friends there. And I have another project up and running with a school in Soweto. We're hoping to get going on pen friends in the new year . . . I think that'll be even better – and so much easier and more interesting now that they can email, don't you think? Paul's been looking into fundraising, so that we can maybe help them buy a few more computers . . .'

She spoke on. And George, watching her animated face, was struck by how different Sophie was when talking about her work. The meek, deferential woman who'd met him at the door – the woman who clearly hated the way she looked, whose body language spoke of someone who saw herself as easily the most inferior person in the room . . . this same woman was now speaking with all the strength and confidence of a leader. He could see how much she loved it, and fell to wondering what she'd do when she had children of her own. Would she be like Helen, and quit work to become a full-time mother? And what about her aid work abroad? Would she continue to travel to these far-flung destinations and go on setting up projects? Or would she settle down?

Sophie hesitated. 'I couldn't stop working altogether,' she admitted, finally. 'Just couldn't. But,' – sighing – 'nor would I be able to travel so much, of course. It's a pity, as there's so much that I still want to do. Especially in places like Galle, where the local response is so encouraging. But, assuming Paul and I are lucky enough to have a family,' she smiled at George, 'and, believe me, we're extremely keen to get going! . . . but I'd have to make changes then, don't you think? And if that means letting a few projects go – the overseas ones, certainly – I suppose I just have to accept that. It's already different for me, simply being engaged. And as for having a baby . . . well, that's something else entirely, right? I couldn't simply expect to carry on as before . . .'

George nodded. And then, aware that, beside him, Marianne and Dina seemed to have run out of things to say to each other – aware that both were listening to what Sophie had just been saying – he couldn't resist catching Marianne's eye.

Irritated, Marianne turned away. She read what George was saying in that glance. She knew that, next to the enormous sacrifices that Sophie was prepared to make in order to be a good mother and wife, her own refusal to quit drinking and smoking looked suddenly selfish, not to mention immature. But the comparison was false. Sophie wasn't pregnant. Not yet. There was a world of difference between the person one might want to be and the person one actually was . . . who knew what saintly Sophie would really do in such circumstances? And anyway, was it really so sinful to indulge in a quick fag or drink from time to time?

Full of renewed antipathy towards him, Marianne wished she could think of something smart to say to Dina. Or, indeed, anything . . . for Dina had long given up on Marianne, and had turned her back on that end of the table in favour of a three-way conversation with Paul and Maggie. Annoyed to find herself sitting next to another woman, especially the same woman whose 'fault' it was that the numbers were uneven in the first place, a pregnant woman to boot; pregnant and unmarried with designs, no doubt, on Dina's precious boyfriend – for Sophie's cousin Max was from an important Bavarian family with riches and titles to bestow on any woman he deemed lucky enough to be his wife, and Dina wasn't letting go of such a prospect, not without a fight, and certainly not to a woman carrying another man's child . . . Dina had no interest in bonding with the enemy. On the contrary, her priority tonight was to keep the woman at arm's length and to ensure that she and Max had minimal contact. And, while it afforded Dina little pleasure to look across the table and see Max flirting with Helen Franklin, at least Helen Franklin was married.

So Marianne sat there, beautiful and ignored. Noticing the situation, Paul tried to steer the conversation in her favour – but Dina was having none of it.

'No, Paul! No!' she said, playfully wagging a finger at him. 'I want to hear what *you* think!'

'But I don't know what I think, Dina! I've never lived in Barnes. It . . . Marianne, what do you think? Would you live there?'

Marianne smiled. She opened her mouth. But before any words emerged, Dina had grabbed the conversation once more. She swiftly intercepted the line Paul had thrown to Marianne.

'Ah, ah, ah – you're avoiding the question!'

Paul looked at her.

'. . . and I'm afraid that leads me to conclude that it must be because you don't like Barnes.'

Embarrassed, Paul started laughing. 'Not entirely, Dina. You're—'

'It's okay. I'm right with you. I've no idea what Max sees in Barnes, or why he'd ever want to leave South Ken . . .'

Marianne and Paul gave up – but not before they'd shared another smile.

Paul felt a blood-rush of desire. He shouldn't be doing it, of course he shouldn't. Marianne was history. In all but name, she was another's man's wife. And he, Paul, was committed to Sophie, to Christ, to all the new and wonderful things he'd discovered in recent years.

Paul took these new commitments extremely seriously. He wasn't about to quit. But there was no escaping the fact that, however worthy they were, and good and right and absolutely what he wanted for himself, they weren't always thrilling. They were loving, and stable, and reliable, and admirable, and so on – and there was no denying the fact that, at times, during the past few years, Paul had felt truly uplifted and inspired by these new influences in his life – but there were also times when it was all, dare he say it, a little bit dull. When he'd first discovered God, it had been so exciting. Lying in bed at night, or resting on his knees in church, or wherever it was – at work, in the car, on the underground – he'd regularly found himself overwhelmed by a powerful, almost intoxicating, sense of God *everywhere*.

But, oddly, in the weeks that had passed since he and Sophie had returned from Sri Lanka and had started discussing their future – Paul couldn't help it . . . but somewhere along the line he seemed to have lost that dizzying sense of God's presence in his life. His honeymoon period with Christianity was over. And while they'd warned him this could happen – Sophie's father, in particular, had explained that that was one of the main reasons for going on regular retreats such as the one he and Victoria were attending that weekend to refresh themselves, to *rediscover* – Paul nonetheless felt flat, distinctly flat, when it came to matters of the spirit.

While, all the time, matters of the flesh – Paul's flesh, Marianne's flesh – played on in the forefront of his mind. Perhaps it was the lack of activity with Sophie in that area. Perhaps it was the fact that the last woman he'd known in any significant way was Marianne herself. Taken with the relative secrecy of their shared past, which was something private, something exclusive to Paul and Marianne, something slightly naughty – in the context of this decision not to tell Sophie – it was as if they were already guilty. And there she was now, smiling at him in the way she might have smiled when they'd last made love. Paul remembered it all in great detail. He remembered her looking down at him; remembered the movement, the tension in the sheets, his hand pressing against the wall and Marianne's dark hair spiralling across her face.

As soon as dinner was over, Marianne made her excuses and left. Being pregnant, she had less energy than normal. She needed her sleep.

'Of course,' said Sophie, full of sympathy. 'You want Paul to help you find a cab?'

Marianne hesitated.

'We'll give her a lift,' said George, getting to his feet. 'Helen –'

Helen turned reluctantly from a gossipy story Max was telling her – a thrilling 'insider' sort of story, the kind that made her own life seem suddenly rather provincial. Why didn't George have glamorous friends

170

like these? Why didn't George shoot wild boar in the Black Forest? Frowning, she looked at her watch. It wasn't even eleven.

George sighed. 'I'm thinking of Marianne, darling. She needs a lift home. She's tired. As, I'm afraid, am I . . .' He put a hand on the back of her chair. 'I'm sorry, angel. Would you mind?'

Helen was about to say that yes, actually, she minded quite a bit, when Max himself stood up. Executing a short bow, accompanied by a brisk little clip of his heels, he bid Helen a flirtatious farewell and stood aside for her to pass.

Meanwhile, Paul was following Marianne up the stairs. He found her coat and helped her into it – neither of them saying a word.

'Did you bring a bag?'

'I've got it.'

She looked at him now. It felt oddly intimate: the two of them together in the dark hallway – which was lit only from the floor above and the floor below. The main light by the front door remained off. The others were still downstairs, still saying their goodbyes.

And then they both spoke at once.

'That was—'

'So you're—'

Both stopped.

'You go,' she said, laughing. 'So, I'm . . . what?'

Paul pulled himself together. 'I was only going to say I'm hoping you're still on for our meeting next week.'

'Absolutely.' Marianne took a diary from her handbag and flicked through to November. She and Sophie had spoken a few days ago – and arranged a provisional time for Paul to come over and approve the

171

drawings. 'It's Friday, isn't it? Friday the tenth, at five p.m.? Sophie was pretty sure you could make it from work by then . . .'

'Come on, darling,' said George, his voice getting louder as he thumped up the stairs. He was switching on his mobile as he turned the corner. Giving Marianne and Paul a weary smile, he fumbled through the coats on the pegs by the door, switched on the light for a better view, and unhooked his coat – and his wife's. 'Helen?'

'All right, all right.'

Marianne and Paul looked at each other in the bright yellow overhead light. He opened the door. 'Friday, five p.m.,' he confirmed, almost in a whisper – as she passed him, out into the street. 'See you then.'

Moments later, Marianne was shuffling along the back seat of George and Helen's car with a strange, fluttering sense of guilt, as if there was something illicit – clandestine, even – about what had happened in the hallway just now. Reminding herself that he'd only arranged to view her drawings, that it was simply part of the process – absolutely above board, nothing to get fluttery or guilty about, that Sophie herself had fixed the meeting – Marianne was also aware of something beneath the surface. Nothing serious, nothing that was going to ruin anyone's life or change anything in any real sense. Just a small ripple of pleasure – a mild boost to her ego – entirely private, entirely safe.

It made her smile in the darkness.

George and Helen had planned to stay at Fitzroy Place that night. With Marianne also living north of Hyde Park, it was no trouble for them to go via Bayswater and drop her en route. Indeed, George was glad of an excuse to get going, glad of an early night, for there were things he needed to talk to Helen about – things that had happened at work that day – and, while there was never an ideal time to raise the subject of family finances, he knew that the sooner they discussed it the better. He wasn't like Paul. He didn't believe in concealing bad news, not when it involved money. In any case, there were decisions to be made about their future – decisions that needed Helen's approval – and there was certainly no advantage to be gained from hanging about. He waited until Marianne was out of the car. He waited while she found her keys, waved goodbye, let herself in . . . and then – pulling out into the road again, heading north to Bloomsbury with Helen at his side – he gently steered their conversation away from Max's marvellous sporting escapades, and on to the rather more mundane subject of his job.

George had been running his own investment management business for over fifteen years. After a brief stint at Goldman Sachs, learning the ropes, he'd joined up with a colleague, Nick Malloy, and created Franklin Asset Management – a specialist London-based outfit, providing services to private clients, charities and an increasingly wide range of institutional investors. They now employed over a hundred people, and managed close to £7 billion in funds. Much of their recent success and increasing high profile, however, was down to Nick Malloy bringing Kau Lung Banking into the picture. Back in the mid-1990s, Kau Lung had identified the need for a UK presence, and links with an outfit such as Franklin's – with its history of solid earnings and its mature client base – exactly fitted the profile. In exchange for 51 per cent of their equity and 75 per cent of the voting rights, George and Nick would enjoy the benefits of a huge rise in status and direct links to the rapidly expanding markets of the Far East.

And it was around this time that George had married Helen (who, having worked in the City herself, had made a point of conducting some thorough due diligence before signing up to that particular partnership). So when, a year or two ago, Kau Lung then offered George a dazzling renewed contract of employment, he barely thought twice about accepting. With a growing family and a wife with prodigious spending habits, the substantial rise in income – not to mention the promise of a serious lump-sum incentive – was exactly what he needed. And while, of course, it was to be an earn-out contract (so George would not be able to get his hands on all the money, all at once), that didn't bother him. He was happy to get some of it up front, and then wait for the balance when the five-year lock-in period was up. It was given business practice to handle such contracts in this way.

Recently, however, George had had an inkling that something wasn't right. The first was Nick Malloy's decision to move to Kau Lung's head office in Hong Kong – effectively leaving Franklin's, and London, for good. And then, that very morning, all had been made abundantly, horribly clear . . .

Kau Lung was wanting a bigger UK presence. It had – presumably with Nick's knowledge – secretly bought Franklin's main rival, and now wanted to amalgamate the two, pushing George out from his position as managing director of his own thriving business and into subservience to the team he'd always pitched against, a group of men and women whose methods and business practice he'd never much admired. And so, it seemed to George that the only course open to him now was to resign. Incur a breach of his five-year contract, pay the penalty, take the hit – not to mention the loss of the balance of his lump-sum incentive.

He'd been a fool. A stupid, trusting fool. He was ashamed of himself – more ashamed than Helen could possibly realise. He'd let her down. He'd never forgive himself. But – well . . . she'd be relieved to hear they weren't entirely ruined. As a result of following a sensible private investment policy, George wasn't penniless. Yes, it was true that the bulk of his estimated wealth would disappear, but he'd also made independent property investments – not least, the elegant Hampshire house that he and Helen now lived in – and held various tax-efficient lower-risk widespread portfolios of shares that ensured a degree of stability. He could apply for jobs elsewhere – at least, until another opportunity arose for creating his own business again. With his experience, and his work ethic, George was still highly employable. With his client base, he was confident he'd find a respectable position. And then, in a few years' time, he'd be able to start up another financial services business which – after the lessons he'd learnt recently – he'd know better than to throw away to the first bunch of wolves that came sniffing at the door.

It was the right way to go. He didn't want to waste any more time on a business he no longer believed in, a business he no longer controlled. He needed a fresh start. But he also needed to discuss it with Helen. He needed to decide how best to pay for his exit: whether it was wiser simply to sell the house in Hampshire and return the family to London (which would, of course, mean the older children changing schools, and no private swimming pool, and saying farewell to Helen's beloved new kitchen, and bathroom, and so on . . .), or whether he should cash in the ISAs and TESSAs (which would mean fewer treats for a couple of years – certainly no smart holidays, no new car, no redecorations, possibly no full-time nanny – but at least they'd keep the family house). He couldn't sell the house in London, not without Gabby's consent. George reached across the gearbox and took Helen's hand – what did she think?

'What do I *think*?' said Helen. Her hand felt like stone.

George pulled the car to one side, turned off the engine, and looked at his wife. But with her face in profile – and silhouetted against the dingy strip lighting of the 24-7 convenience store beyond – it was hard to see her properly.

'Darling one . . . I'm truly sorry.'

Helen laughed. 'Yes, George,' she said. 'I'm sure you're very sorry. But that's not going to change things, is it?'

George looked down.

'So – tell me. How long have you known about this?'

'A few hours. Just a few hours. I—'

'You suspected something.'

'Yes, darling. I suspected something. But nothing like this. How could I have imagined that they . . . that Nick . . .' He swallowed hard.

'I see. And now you want to run away, is that right?'

George stared at his wife.

'You made a mess of your precious business, you took your eye off the ball, and now you think it's okay to uproot the family – sell the house, switch schools, sack the nanny, make me take the bus, and God only knows what else – simply so that you don't have to deal with the daily humiliation of working for the people who wrecked your sad little life?'

'Please, Helen.'

'Sorry, *our* sad little lives.' She undid her seatbelt. 'You think that's the best course of action, then?'

George sighed. 'I don't know. I wanted to discuss it with you, darling. So if you can think of a better solution then please, *please* just tell me. The last thing I want is for you to feel deprived –'

'Then why not just stay on at Franklin? They pay a decent wage, don't they?'

'Decent enough. Except—'

'What's wrong with staying put, then? What's wrong with keeping the house, the shares, the children at their schools, and Dolores living in, and – and the hundreds of thousands of pounds it would take to extract yourself . . . keep all that, put up with three years or whatever it is of mild professional embarrassment?'

'Because it would break my heart.'

'And you'd rather break mine, instead?'

George closed his eyes.

'I'm sorry, George. I probably sound cruel. But can't you see? The man I married, he – he was someone who could take care of me, and our children, and our lives.' Helen put her head in her hands. 'I thought you were responsible. Dependable. You certainly know how to look after the rest of your family. Oh, yes. It's okay to make sacrifices for your dear mother, and darling Gabriella – can't uproot *them*, or let *them* do without, but your own wife and kids . . . oh no, that's obviously another matter entirely . . .'

George listened with growing horror to Helen's

tearful description of the man she thought she'd married, the man he no longer was – not, at least, in the eyes of the woman he still loved – and as he listened he realised that there was something far more unbearable, more heartbreaking, than working on in a shell of a business he'd once loved, employed by people he should never have trusted, working hard and late not because he loved it, but because they were forcing him to . . . and that was the bitter disappointment of a once-devoted wife. With a father who'd gone bankrupt when she was twelve, and a mother who'd spent most of her working life pulling pints in a pub, Helen had worked hard for her lift up the ladder. She wouldn't have considered – not for one moment – abandoning her own precious career in banking if she'd thought that the man she was doing it for would fail her in this way. George understood how much she minded – minded desperately – about material security. Selling the house, sacking the nanny . . . it probably *would* break her heart.

'I'll do it,' he said.

Helen bit her lip. 'You – you will?'

George nodded. 'I will,' he replied. 'I'll stay at Franklin – it's only a few more years . . . you're right, sweetheart. I can cope with that. And – and you're absolutely right about the kids' schools, and the house . . . of course I want you to feel stable and protected.'

He started the car. And as they continued on their way, Helen's hand crept over on to his. It was meek and warm – grateful, even. George squeezed it, and brought it to his lips.

He wanted – more than he'd wanted for some time – to make love to her that night. So, it seemed, did she. But it was clear to him, even before he parked the car, that that would not be possible.

'What is it?' said Helen.

George nodded in the direction of the house. And Helen, glancing round, saw – all too clearly in the automatic porch light – the sight of Gabby's well-dressed body slumped against the door.

'Oh God.'

Gabriella was conscious, but badly drunk – sitting in her own vomit. George sent Helen off to bed. 'I'll do it, darling.'

'But—'

'Please, Helen. It's the least I can do.'

Oblivious to the spread of sick from her clothes to his, George helped his sister inside and made her drink some water. Wiping away the worst of the mess with a sponge, he changed her into a fresh T-shirt and put her straight into bed. Then he found a mop, a bucket and a brush, and got to work on the steps of the house. Perhaps it was good that Gab had forgotten her keys – he didn't like to think of the state of Helen's precious carpet if she had managed access by herself.

It was almost three when he got into bed. George set his alarm for six. No matter that it was Saturday tomorrow, no matter that nothing would have given him greater pleasure than going back with Helen to Hampshire and the children . . . this would now be a working weekend. This was the new regime. He had a lot to do for Monday's meeting – especially now that the plans had changed.

George lay in the darkness, oddly at peace. He was glad of his decision – glad he was doing the right thing by his wife and family. How could he have considered anything else? With so much else in disarray, not least this latest development with Gabby – poor, weak, single, childless Gabby . . . George shivered when he thought of how close he'd been to losing his own precious family that night.

Just a few more years at Franklin – it was a tiny price to pay.

PART THREE – LONDON

Chapter Thirteen

Gabby wasn't well. At first, George thought it was merely another of her sporadic binges gone messy. It happened from time to time. There would be a trigger: a party she hadn't been invited to, a failed relationship, a slurred call from her mother, a loss of some sort . . . certainly, there had been a rash of binges after their father had died. Gab would then submerge her nerves in a sea of vodka, throw up, pass out, and crawl around complaining for a day or so before skipping off to an expensive spa in Somerset, picking herself up with a laugh and a facial, and going on as before. George hated this pattern. Even when his sister had been a student – when benders and hangovers were part of the deal – even then, he'd wished for more balance in her life. There were already far too many parallels with their broken mother for George not to fear that Gab, too, was susceptible to alcohol – to the habit of alcohol. For some time now, he'd felt uneasy about his sister's tendencies and what kind of impact they'd have on her future. But there was never any accompanying sense of urgency. Like his fears for global warming, or what might happen to him after he died, George's concern about Gab managed to be profoundly serious while never quite reaching the top of his list of priorities. For sure, it never occurred to him that the girl was in any sort of immediate danger.

However, as the weekend came and went with no sign of Gab making it out of her dressing gown, or into the shower – or barely out of her bedroom – it struck George that this particular nosedive was different. He could see that she was having real trouble moving into the 'up' stage of the cycle. It wasn't simply her lack of interest in getting dressed, or the grey tinge to her skin – neither of which was entirely out of character where Gabby post-bender was concerned. It was more that, on the rare occasions when she did manage an appearance upstairs in the main part of the house, it could hardly escape George's attention that his sister was constantly on the verge of tears. The smallest thing would set her off. She had no fight in her. None of the old energy. No sense of humour. No rage, either. Instead of the grumbling and groaning that usually followed one of her binges, the air around Gabby was oddly quiet. She dragged herself about the house like an invalid.

And by Monday, Marianne, too, was worried. She didn't expect a call the second Gab's plane touched down. She wasn't surprised by the lack of response to her voicemail messages over the weekend – Saturday night and all that, no doubt the girl was on the razzle. But when Gab failed to turn up for work, Marianne stopped making excuses for her friend and rang Fitzroy Place.

'George?' said her voice, into the answerphone. 'Helen? I'm calling about Gabby. She's not answering her mobile. She didn't come in today and I . . . I'm just checking she's all right.'

Picking up the message when he got home late that night, George stood frozen for a moment. His blood ran cold. *How could he have left her alone today? How could he have been so casual?* Dropping the telephone, George rushed down to Gabby's room, opened the door, and saw the shape of her body on the bed. Heart beating, he came closer – close enough to check she was still breathing – before quietly creeping out again. And while he felt a little foolish – over-dramatising, overreacting, he was also aware that the situation was real. His fears weren't wrong. Not if Marianne felt them too. And when the cleaner arrived the next day and told him she'd seen Gabby pouring vodka into her cup of coffee at eleven o'clock the previous morning, George decided to act.

Gab still listened to him. That child-like longing for her big brother's approval – the same longing that so irritated Marianne when it came to their business efforts – now stood strongly in Gabriella's favour. For when George came into her bedroom that Tuesday morning wearing a smart suit and a grave expression, and proceeded to switch off her garish TV cartoons with a quiet 'Sorry, Gab' before drawing back the curtains, opening the window, and telling her bluntly that he was worried: it was serious, he was taking her to his doctor . . . it didn't occur to her to refuse him.

George was relieved, but not entirely surprised, to find his sister so submissive. He was grateful that the clinic recommended by his doctor had had room for her, that the admittance procedure had been so comparatively straightforward, meaning that he was able to return to the office in good time (and well before the directors' meeting that had been scheduled to take place later that same day to discuss, amongst other things, his continued employment at Franklin's). But it was still a grim process – grim and oddly lonely.

For George couldn't trouble Helen with the matter, not after everything he'd put her through. He couldn't burden her with yet more problems. On the contrary, he should be whisking her off to Venice for the weekend, or skiing perhaps, or shopping in Paris . . . something to make her smile again, something positive and romantic; not telling her that Gab was now in rehab. Expensive rehab, at that.

And nor, for diverse reasons, could George look elsewhere. His mother was far too frail – both physically and mentally – to provide support to anyone, particularly support of this nature. She would only blame herself, perhaps even have a relapse. It wasn't worth the risk. And Jay was no good. Even if George were able to contact his brother, he knew what Jay would say. No need for *both* of them to be there, right? And – yeah, yeah . . . well done, George. Good job. What would we all do without you? But no offer to share the load. No real effort to engage. And as for calling a friend . . . well, that was a joke. With work and family taking up all his time in recent years, George had all but abandoned his social life. Certainly, any sort of functioning social life. Nick and Ange Malloy had been the only people he and Helen saw on a regular basis . . . and some friends they'd turned out to be. On the last occasion he'd rung a 'friend', George had found to his shame that he'd needed to specify which George it was on the other end of the line – 'George *Franklin*,' he'd said, embarrassed, and never did invite the man and his wife to accompany them to the opera. It had been easier – much easier – to give the tickets to a client.

So George battled on alone. With Helen deep in autumnal Hampshire, it would have been nice to go home to her at night. Sweep the leaves. Help a bit with the children. Be there for her. Enjoy a glass of wine before supper . . . remind himself, remind them both, what their lives were meant to be about. But that simply wasn't an option at the moment. With the hours he needed to be working – and with Gab so vulnerable – George had other responsibilities. He couldn't leave London. Helping Helen in a domestic way was a luxury he couldn't yet afford.

His job, which had once been such a source of self-esteem and security, rapidly became the reverse. Learning that George wasn't going to buy himself out of the business after all, that they had him for the next three years, seemingly on whatever terms they liked, his new lords and masters wasted little time in taking full advantage of the situation. George's PA was requisitioned elsewhere. He still had a private office, but it was relocated to a darker part of the building – and away from the main dealing area, effectively excluding him. And his desk – which, until recently, he'd made a point of clearing at the end of each day – now gathered far too much paperwork to make that principle practical. Within days, he had only a small A4-size square a space of wood between the front of the desk and his computer. The rest was a sea of paper and files.

He sat at it that Friday morning, thinking for a moment about his sister. Of course he was glad he'd acted, glad he'd been there for her, glad to the point of grateful tears that he hadn't been too late. She'd been breathing when he'd dashed down to her bedroom that night. She was alive. She was going to be okay. They had hope. Yet – in spite of those feelings – there was another part of George that blamed himself for letting it get to such a point. Why hadn't he acted sooner? He'd seen the signs, he'd made the link – and yet . . . and yet . . . he'd somehow got himself to a point of denial about the urgency of it all. It hadn't been *convenient*, and that was the bottom line. Work had come first. Work had blinded him. And the idea of making himself unpopular with Gabby and Helen and probably his mother as well, and no doubt Marianne, and Jay, and maybe even Anusha, too – of having to weather accusations of stuffiness and over-reaction and lack of belief in Gabby and all the rest of it . . . the prospect of inciting all that criticism, on top of the stress at work . . . it was simply too uncomfortable to contemplate. *Uncomfortable*. Jesus. So he'd put his head in the sand. And now? Now Gabby was in rehab. Might have died. And George – who'd been given the insight to notice the signs, but the lack of gumption to act on them – George knew himself to have contributed to his sister's collapse. Gab had needed him. Poor, frivolous, Butterfly Gab . . . she depended on George to say the things that needed to be said – even if it wasn't always what she wanted to hear. And in the final analysis, he'd failed her. So all George could do now was pray that she'd pull through – pray that his hopes would come good, that these feelings of remorse wouldn't haunt him for ever. Impotence pressed at him. Impotence and frustration. He longed for an instant result . . . except it was way too soon for that, of course. Just a few days in rehab: it was too soon even for the staff to give a prognosis. They'd only just finished the tests, only just started her on a programme.

Still. It was good to see that there had been no setbacks; good to see that Gabriella seemed to have accepted the authority of the clinic – the discipline of her programme, the iron timetable, the early nights. She showed no interest in putting up resistance. Far from grumbling about her new circumstances, Gab was full of praise for its doctors and therapists. Indeed, her main concern – perhaps it was a way of escaping her bigger troubles – was the business.

George had been quick to reassure her. He was on the case. He'd spoken to Marianne the same day that Gab had been admitted. There was nothing for Gab to worry about. And while, of course, it hadn't been quite that simple – it was, in essence, true.

George had explained the situation to Marianne. And after the ensuing discussion of Gab's health and state of mind, and whether she was allowed visitors and so on . . . he'd taken a deep breath and raised the tricky subject of their business. George was wary of Marianne – especially after their last conversation, the one at Paul and Sophie's dinner party when she'd told him to back off. He didn't want to interfere. But, as Gabby's representative, it was also George's responsibility to ensure that he and Marianne explore the necessary adjustments. Together. For a start – he hoped she wouldn't be too disappointed – but he did feel strongly the exhibition date must be put back. March was quite impossible. They were looking at the summer – June, at the very soonest. Ideally, later.

'I agree,' Marianne had said. Her voice was very clear. Her manner, surprisingly direct.

George allowed himself a long, deep breath. 'And

what about work in progress? I imagine there must be quite a backlog –'

'It's fine. We do need to follow up her trip to New York. I haven't heard anything from Hoffmann Sawyer, which makes me think they're trying to deal with her directly, and obviously that won't work. They'll need to speak with me. That aside, it's important we get those samples back here to the showroom – otherwise, they're not insured . . . You think you could speak to her for me? Ask her where she's put them?'

George assured her that he would.

'Great.' Marianne looked through the paperwork on her desk. 'She does have a number of outstanding matters with the silversmith, but that's okay. I'll liaise with the workshop and speak to the clients. But,' – switching tone – 'I know you're busy, George, but it would be a huge help if maybe you could drop round in the next week or so, so that we can go through the accounts and the projections, and so on. Gab and I have been talking for some time about hiring an accountant to help us with the books – we've got to have *someone* in place before the baby arrives. That side of things is just getting a bit much, even for me to handle . . .'

'And it's not exactly Gab's forte.'

Marianne smiled. 'So – so what with everything that's happened,' she went on, 'what with all the adjustments we'll be making, I just wondered . . . could you bear it?'

'Of course I can,' said George, his feelings of impotence fading.

It took a few minutes for them to find a mutually convenient time. Both were busy. Both had commitments. In the end, Marianne agreed he could come that Friday afternoon.

'Three-thirty?' George suggested.

'Three-thirty,' said Marianne, writing it into her diary. It wasn't ideal. She wouldn't be able to go to Hatton Garden now – not until the following week. And with Paul due at five, they'd be rushed to get through the figures. But at least it was soon and – bottom line – if George was doing her this favour, then Marianne couldn't be too fussy about when or where or how. She and Gab were lucky he was helping them at all.

Amused, George had written the time in his diary. He simply hadn't expected it of Marianne – that she should be so efficient, so professional, so easy to deal with in this way. For some reason, he'd always assumed she'd be more like Gabby: vague, artistic, with her mind on 'higher things' than profit and loss, or how to deal with the tax inspector. He'd always imagined Marianne as the sort of person who'd wait for someone else to raise any mundane questions of money and admin. He'd braced himself for a degree of resentment if anyone tried to get her to look at such things, picturing a showroom where, for all that beautiful jewellery on display – perfectly lit, with champagne flowing, and smiling faces – a completely different state of affairs was happening beneath the surface: printed envelopes left unopened and stuffed to the backs of drawers, forms unfilled, bills unpaid, inefficient banking arrangements, ugly red reminders falling on the doormat, and frantic January dashes to the Tax Office. He never once thought of Marianne – with her gypsy clothes, her wild hair, her pirate eyes, and total refusal to conform – never really thought of

her as properly competent. Instead, here she was –
handling it all with aplomb. No panic at this turn of
events, at Gabby's sudden departure. No fluster. No
silly expectations. Cool, calm, sound: entirely realistic
about the new exhibition date. From a professional
point of view, he couldn't fault her.

Chapter Fourteen

'. . . So if I don't hear from you by tomorrow, I guess I'll have to go ahead and book the woman.' Marianne sighed into the ether. 'I don't know what else to do, Jay. The general consensus is that Gab'll be out of the clinic by Christmas, but what if she's not? I can't risk it. We've only got a couple of months to go, and I – I'm going to need help when the baby arrives. And while of course I'd much rather it was you, darling, I'm just not sure how realistic we're being . . .'

She hated it – hating speaking to him like this, like some sort of weary schoolmistress. Putting down the telephone, Marianne turned to her computer once more, scrolled down to the maternity nurse's email, and looked at it unhappily. Yes, yes, the woman had all the right certificates and the right references and so on. She'd sounded very experienced when they'd spoken on the telephone that morning, and nice enough – if a little surprised to hear that Marianne was now in her third trimester.

'I wouldn't leave it too long,' she'd said, when Marianne explained she would need to speak to Jay before confirming. 'Most nurses – the good ones – get booked up months, sometimes years, in advance. If it weren't for Mrs Parker's miscarriage . . .'

'Sure. I'll confirm tomorrow, Fiona. Just give me another day.'

Fiona sounded grim. She was into rigid routines, 'controlled crying', and keeping the baby in its own room from the start – none of which sounded natural, kind, or right to a woman of Marianne's autonomous disposition. No doubt there were submissive new mothers out there who loved being told exactly what to do and when to do it, and who wanted just the same for their babies, but, to Marianne, the idea of having someone like that in her house at such a time – taking charge, bossing her around – it was quite intolerable. On the other hand, Fiona was also available, experienced, recommended, organised. And Marianne was desperate. She sent the email to the printer and reached for her cigarettes. There was time – just – for a quick one before George Franklin arrived.

Marianne wasn't looking forward to this meeting with George. Yes, she'd initiated it. Yes, the business would no doubt benefit from the man's financial experience. And with this latest Gabby crisis, Marianne didn't feel she had much choice in the matter. At some point or other, George Franklin was going to want to know what was happening to his sister's business – and Marianne was sure that it was better to invite him round now, than wait to be pushed into a meeting. Better to involve him in the accounts and the projections for next year while she was doing them, rather than wait for him to sneer at the finished product.

She didn't anticipate an easy afternoon. George might be useful to them from a financial point of view, but he was also critical and old-fashioned. His dislike of the enterprise was clear. And he would no doubt be shocked that, on top of the fags and booze, Marianne was also planning to keep working . . . on through pregnancy, into motherhood, with only the shortest of maternity leaves. No stay-at-home mothering for her. No sacrificing her career to be with her children as Helen had done (although, in truth, it was hard to think of the gesture as a sacrifice – not when Helen still had the services of a top live-in nanny, and would no more allow sticky jammy fingers any contact with her cashmere – 'I'll cuddle you when you're clean, darling' – than she would relinquish her smart gym membership). Marianne had no respect for women like Helen, no guilt about her own approach to mother-hood, but nor did she entirely relish the prospect of explaining herself to George.

She hoped poor Gabby was all right. Gab wasn't allowed any visitors at the moment, no outside contact at all – except, and to a very limited extent, with George. So Marianne was struggling to get a decent picture of what had happened to her friend and what, in particular, had triggered such a crisis. She knew Gab drank. She knew Gab wasn't stable. She'd seen her friend through this therapist and that therapist, to this spa and that spa – through Reiki and homoeopathy and antidepressants, and so on. Years and years of it. But that was part of Gab's nature. Her charm, even. Gab liked her highs, and she paid for them with her lows and, in a lesser way, Marianne herself had the same tendencies. She certainly didn't think it right to interfere with what she took to be her friend's personality. On the contrary, she relished the colour, the darks and lights, the ups and downs . . . Gab was fun. She took risks – accepting that extra drink, that strange invitation, that lift in the soft-top with a man she'd only just met. It was typical of Gab actually to have gone all the way to New York for a business meeting on the back of a couple of emails. Gab broke the rules on principle. She thrived on risk and instinct. In short, she was alive.

Only now . . . had Marianne been wrong? Should she – like George – have recognised that Gab needed help? Should she have seen it coming? Had she been a bad friend?

Not having spoken with Gabriella – not since her admittance to the clinic; not even, frustratingly, during the few hours that Gab had been back in the UK after her New York trip, the hours that had led up to her collapse – Marianne could only guess. But she still couldn't help thinking that while, of course, Gab's habits and her way of dealing with problems by escaping, not confronting would certainly have made things worse, something else had happened. Something in New York. Something – she couldn't help but wonder – involving that friend of George's . . . the one with the chalet in Aspen and those smart Manhattan friends.

Marianne toyed with the idea of raising the possibility with George that day – before it occurred to her that if Dexter Rawlinson was at the heart of the matter, then Gab would surely have understandable qualms about confiding in that direction. George wasn't the man to ask. It was better that Marianne wait – wait until Gab was allowed visitors, then ask her herself.

George closed the books.

'Well, I'm happy,' he said. 'Your cash flow is good. The projections seem realistic enough – especially now you've rescheduled the exhibition. July should be fine. Your outgoings aren't a problem, even with the new premises. I see you've handled the bank arrangements nicely. Compared to last year's pre-Christmas position – which wasn't at all bad – you've an impressive number of commissions. It all looks rather promising. And that's *after* we factor in those losses from New York . . .'

Marianne listened. Yes, he was being nice – and yes, it was good to hear that the accounts were healthy. But the reference to New York . . . the fact that George had not been able to bring Gab's New York samples with him to the showroom that day (that, indeed, all Gab could offer was the somewhat overdue confession that the samples were no longer in her possession, that Hoffmann Sawyer had been a set-up, that the man she'd been corresponding with had met her in some smart hotel and bought her dinner and persuaded her to leave the samples with him overnight so that he could show them to his partner and had then 'disappeared') . . . in all, it was enough to make Marianne weep: both at Gab's naïvety and her own failure to monitor the venture. Not so much from a financial point of view – the cost of the trip, the loss of the jewellery, several thousands down the drain – but nothing next to Gab's humiliation, the damage to her confidence, and the ensuing collapse it had triggered. Suddenly it all made sense. In some ways, Marianne rather wished the trigger had involved the now entirely blameless Dexter Rawlinson – at least, in that way, she wouldn't have felt so horribly responsible. Why hadn't she checked Hoffmann Sawyer herself? Why hadn't she seen this coming?

'. . . which in itself is quite an achievement,' George was saying. 'You should be proud.'

A short silence followed.

'But?' she prompted – knowing there was more to come.

George couldn't look back at her. 'I'm sorry,' he said. 'I'm sorry, Marianne – you're not going to like it – but my only real concern about this otherwise-flourishing enterprise is the fact that its future rests entirely on the shoulders of a heavily pregnant woman.'

'Less of the heavy, thank you. I'm not due for a while yet.'

George smiled in spite of himself. 'Whether you're due in a week or due next July, my point, Marianne, is that your whole world is about to change. As it is, we're looking at January and I'm sorry, but you really need to think through what will happen then. I mean, will you just shut up shop? Or get someone in to help? Or what?'

'I'm hoping Gab will be better by then. And if she isn't—'

'I don't think you should bank on Gabriella. Even if she does leave the clinic by Christmas, she'll hardly be strong enough to—'

'Fine,' Marianne snapped. She couldn't help herself. For while she knew George was being sensible – kind even, worrying about her workload, her health, her lack of domestic support . . . all things she longed for Jay to consider – she wasn't ready for an alternative. What did he want her to do? Wind up the business? Just like that? Just because of a baby?

'Fine, George. If she isn't out by then, or isn't strong enough, then I'll just have to come in myself.'

'What,' George laughed, 'with an infant at your breast?'

'If necessary. Although I will have Jay, and it's a quiet time of year, so—'

'You're counting on Jay?'

'And a maternity nurse. We're getting a maternity nurse.' Marianne bit her lip. 'Or trying to,' she added. 'It's harder than I realised to find one that's half decent. But, with any luck, she'll see me into March, and then I'll have to get a nanny, I suppose. Or find a day nursery. It's not ideal. But I will make it work, George. I'm not giving up on this business. Not now that we're doing so well . . .'

George fell silent. He looked at Marianne. In the course of the meeting, they'd both moved over to the sofas for more space – and she was now sitting with her legs pulled up, curled round, under her bottom. Her tights were woolly and stripey – black, purple, mustard, green. Her dress was an old black cotton one she'd found in a charity shop – worn peasant-style over a purple polo neck. A long chain of multicoloured semi-precious stones – all different sizes and with different degrees of shine – hung loosely from her neck. Her earrings were the same style, obviously a pair, but with different coloured stones. Her hair was its usual wiry mess, held together with a red pencil. She pulled the pencil free now, and – turning it in her fingers – looked back at George, waiting for his response.

Still, George hesitated. He wanted to explain that – business aside – he was worried, simply worried, about pregnant Marianne . . . about how she'd cope next year. Did she really think she'd be able to haul a baby about like that? Dragging the poor mite across London, to and from the showroom, and her flat, and Hatton Garden, while dealing with health visitors and taking the baby off for injections and registering the name and getting the birth certificate and . . . and . . .'

and . . . all the time trying to breastfeed and recover from the birth? And that was assuming it all went well. His heart had twisted at her reference to Jay – at the way both of them knew how unreliable he was, how employing a maternity nurse was an absolute necessity. He wished his brother were a sounder prospect. He wished he could do something to help. Marianne might think she was strong enough. Perhaps she was . . .

'What is it?'

George hesitated. He still hadn't replied when his mobile rang. Apologising, he pulled it from his pocket. He couldn't afford to ignore it these days.

'Helen –'

Marianne moved away from the sofas, discreetly back to the desk, as George held his wife's voice to his ear.

'I see.' He looked at his watch. 'So what time are we looking at?' He glanced at Marianne. 'Sure. No, I understand . . .'

Silence. Another glance at Marianne.

'All right. Hang on a second and I'll ask her.'

Embarrassed, George walked over to the desk. 'You couldn't do me a favour, could you?' he said to Marianne. 'Helen and I are driving out to Hampshire tonight. We'd arranged for her to meet me here – she's got the car – but she now tells me she's running late and we were hoping you might let me – er . . .'

'You want to wait on here for her?'

George sighed. 'Would you mind? She shouldn't be too long – I promise not to get in the way . . .'

Marianne smiled. 'Paul Farage is coming at five, so it would be great if you could maybe have gone by then, but—'

200

'Of course. Thank you.' Giving her a grateful smile, George put the mobile to his ear again. 'Helen? She says that's fine. But you have to be here by five, darling. Okay? See you later.'

Marianne could hardly refuse him – not when he'd been so helpful, and so generous with his time. She made George a cup of tea and left him sitting on the sofa reading a newspaper while she returned to the desk. And the pair of them sat in silence – surprisingly easy silence, from George's point of view. His overworked eyes wouldn't stick to the newsprint, but that didn't matter. Instead, his gaze drifted over the soothing beige of the showroom while his ears picked out the kinds of sound that usually passed under his radar: the gentle tap-tapping of an email being written, the shifting sound of cartridge paper being pulled from a drawer, the soft movement of Marianne's pencil – its fine point of lead making brush-brush marks on the page as she shaded a facet and marked out a new idea for the links of a platinum chain. George put aside the newspaper and the cooling cup of tea, and closed his eyes – giving himself over to the agreeable sensation of being the one at rest while another person worked.

He was asleep when Paul arrived – whistling, perky, pulling off his plastic helmet, hopping off his bike, pressing Marianne's doorbell with a brisk taut finger.

Startled, Marianne looked at the time. Christ. Five o'clock already. She glanced in the direction of the sofa to see George stirring – blinking, rubbing his shoulder, looking at his watch. Partly irritated that he was still there, but also amused to see that even the perfectly controlled George Franklin had his dozy moments,

Marianne crossed the room. She opened the door to see Paul on the step, flushed from cycling, smiling at her.

She smiled back.

'Come in,' she said, standing aside. 'George is here, I'm afraid – we've been going through the books – it's run on a bit . . .'

George. Great. Discarding his plastic helmet, Paul entered the showroom.

'. . . shouldn't be much longer now. We've finished our stuff. He's just waiting for Helen to pick him up.'

Inside, George was on his feet, stuffing his newspaper into his briefcase, gabbling apologies. 'I'm so sorry – I completely lost track of the time. But I'm out of your hair now, I promise. Just need to find that mobile . . .' – rummaging now in the sofa cushions . . . spotting it, grabbing it, checking it . . .

And then the three of them heard a car pulling into the mews.

Helen didn't bother to get out. Sitting at the wheel – coiffed and buffed and salon-perfect – she gave the others a perfunctory wave as George, still looking slightly dazed and tousled, got into the passenger seat.

Marianne followed Paul back into the showroom. She shut the door with a thud – it was impossible to do it softly – and in the silence that followed, she was acutely aware that they were now alone.

'Do sit down,' she said, not looking at him. 'You want a cup of tea?'

'Great.' Paul settled on a sofa.

Marianne disappeared to make the tea – glad of the separate kitchen, of the space it put between them. Insisting to herself that he was only there to check the drawings, that it was a perfectly innocent meeting –

there was nothing to feel awkward about . . . nothing on the surface, at any rate – she returned with the tea, composed, and set about showing him her work. Only there was something about the angle at which they were sitting – the low level of the sofas, the cushiony quality, the lack of support . . . it was having a strange effect on Marianne's balance. It wasn't so bad when she leant forward to point at something in the drawings laid out on the table between them, but the moment she sat back to take a sip of tea and listen to Paul's comments, a giddy sensation flooded her brain. She was blacking out. She—

'Christ.'

'Marianne?'

Marianne sat forward again – sharply forward, with her head between her knees.

'What can I do?' Paul was on his feet. 'Tell me! What's wrong, Marianne? Are you hurt? Are you—'

'It's okay,' she said, breathing deeply. 'It's okay.'

Marianne had suffered a few dizzy spells in the last week, but nothing as extreme as this, nothing close to fainting – and it took a moment for her to realise that this was part of the same pattern of episodes; a pattern she had no need to worry about. Philip Dewberry had already offered to see her about it but, in the end, Marianne hadn't thought it worth the effort of rearranged plans and a trip to Harley Street. Dewberry hadn't sounded concerned. It was up to Marianne, of course, but he didn't think it was anything serious. Women at a more advanced stage of pregnancy often suffered from bouts of dizziness. It was to do with the position of the baby, he explained. As Marianne's daughter grew larger, there was obviously less room for movement – making it perfectly possible for her to lie in such a way that Marianne's blood circulation was restricted . . . temporarily restricted. He understood that the experience might be alarming, but all Marianne had to do was sit or lie in a position that eased the flow again. It really was that simple.

'Are you sure?' said Paul, unconvinced. 'I could call someone for you, Marianne. Or—'

'No, no . . .'

Paul sat beside her on the sofa. He waited for a few more moments and then, putting a hand on her shoulder, persisted, 'It would be no bother. You don't seem at all well. I—'

'Really, Paul. It's fine.'

And then, as if to prove the point, Marianne sat up again. She tried to return to the subject of the drawings, but Paul was having none of it.

'Please,' he begged. 'You're white as a sheet. At least let me fetch you a glass of water.' He was on his feet again, walking over to the kitchen. 'It's in here – right?'

'Yes. Yes, but I . . .'

'Hang on.'

She heard him find a tumbler and turn the tap, heard the water hit the sink – heard him wait until it grew properly cold, before filling the glass.

'Here you are –'

Marianne took the glass. But it was getting harder and harder for her to meet Paul's gaze. And the kinder he was – the more attentive and concerned – the more Marianne struggled. It wasn't simply the contrast with Jay – the fact that Paul was just so much gentler, so much more willing to take care of her, so naturally inclined to provide comfort . . . all things she'd come to crave in recent weeks – it was the way she now knew – just *knew*, with sickening certainty, through the dizziness – that he still fancied her. Every time she looked at him, it was there in his eyes. And the combination was just too dangerous – too real, too awful, in terms of collateral damage – to exist as a happy daydream any more. With her new vulnerability, her longing for someone to lean on, and the way Paul seemed to meet that need, combined with the old desire that she sensed had never really left him, that had kept a small blue pilot light flickering deep down in the recesses of his nature, and was now an orange flare, Marianne realised she had to get him out of the showroom.

She couldn't claim to be surprised – not after Sophie's dinner party, not after that moment they'd shared in the hallway that evening. She wasn't innocent. She knew – had known, for days now – that the show of indifference he'd maintained for the entirety of that first interview they'd had here at the showroom – an indifference that had verged on the insulting – was, in truth, no more than that. A show. A good performance. No matter that he was now engaged to another woman, no matter that Marianne was pregnant by another man . . . Paul was, plainly, far from indifferent. And while Marianne's vanity had been comforted by this discovery – it was a relief to learn that her initial fears had been misguided . . . he hadn't seen her as sinful or dirty after all, she wasn't a source of shame to him, her charms hadn't faded – she also knew that there was something wrong about the level of admiration the man was now expressing. They'd reached that point – the point where what might pass as a pleasing mild aroma, a whiff of the exotic, something toxic, even, although entirely safe in small doses . . . the point where it becomes a clinging stench.

'I'm sorry, Paul –'

'Don't be.' Smiling, he sat beside her. 'I'm glad I was here.'

'No, I mean . . .' She swallowed some water. 'I mean, I think I'm not really up for having this meeting now. I hope you don't mind. It's just—'

'Of course I don't mind!'

'– such a waste of your time . . .'

Paul rolled his eyes. 'Honestly, Marianne!'

'It's probably best if I let you take the drawings away, and you can think about it – maybe discuss them with Sophie, and let me know? It would certainly be the quickest option. Of course, we could simply have another meeting – fix another time. It would take a little longer, though, and—'

'Let's do that,' said Paul. 'I don't mind waiting.'

They agreed to speak in a day or two, when they both had their diaries to hand. It wasn't ideal. But Marianne couldn't think quickly enough; couldn't find a neat way out. She'd have to deal with it later, when her mind was settled. For now, a quick exit was the only thing that mattered.

Paul hesitated in the doorway, the plastic helmet in his hands. 'I really don't like leaving you here like this,' he said. 'All by yourself . . . are you sure I can't find you a taxi? Or—'

Marianne shook her head.

And another train went by – great iron screeching, tearing through the stillness. Paul smiled, waiting for it to pass. And as he waited, he looked at Marianne – whose eyes fell to her woolly, shoeless feet. If she looked up, even for a second, she'd be gone. Stubbornly, desperately, she refused to lift her gaze.

Paul bent forward as the train passed on. He kissed her cheek – his skin on hers, his breath at her ear, his hand on her wrist. Close, unbearably close . . . and then nothing. Just a clickety-click of bicycle wheels, off into the night.

Chapter Fifteen

Paul hadn't intended to go to the church that evening – not consciously. There was nothing he needed to collect from the vestry office. No service to attend. No wedding matters to concern himself with – Victoria had it all in hand. But somewhere in the back of his mind he must have imagined going straight from Marianne to Ifield Road where he was due for dinner that night. Without thinking, forgetting that his plans had changed – that he now had an hour or two to kill – Paul was practically at his future in-laws' doorstep before he realised his mistake.

He stopped in the street and, still astride his bicycle, with one foot on a pedal, and one on the road, looked up at the windows and caught a glimpse of Victoria inside. She was talking to someone on the telephone as she closed the sitting-room curtains. And while he knew she would have let him in, might even have been pleased to see him early – the wedding plans gave them more than enough to talk about these days – there was something about the sight of her there, the private conversation, the curtains closing, that held Paul back.

In any case, he wasn't sure he could face two hours of wedding talk. Not after what had happened – or not happened – with Marianne. And so he cycled idly on, lost in thought, turning this way and that until, passing the church, he heard the choir at practice. It was only November, six weeks until Christmas, but the choir was hard at work, rehearsing an early carol. It was a girls' choir.

Lu-li-lu-la, they sang, *thou little tiny child . . .*

It was beautiful.

Paul slowed his bicycle to a standstill. He dismounted and wheeled it over to a nearby bench. And as he sat, he could hear – from inside the church – the rapping of a baton on a music stand. The choir stopped for their instructions, and then started again – this time just the soprano voices. They did the same line twice, before being joined by the rest of the choir again.

Paul sat on the bench and listened – thinking of his faith, and of how it squared with these new developments in his life. With that first flush of Christian fervour now settling into something more prosaic – more realistic, perhaps, in terms of what his personality could sustain over a lifetime . . . certain adjustments were taking place at the core of who Paul was. Unlike Sophie's conscience – so rock-hard, so incapable of bending, anchored to Christ through a benign combination of nature and nurture – Paul's had more pliability.

And so it seemed to him that while of course it mattered to be a Christian, it mattered even more to be Good. And his sense of what God wanted from him, his idea that salvation was something to be earned through striving to be good – as opposed to something

divinely bestowed, regardless of goodness or badness
. . . that idea was infinitely more motivating, to a man
of Paul's disposition, than one that rested on faith
alone.

And so, telling himself that all he wanted to be – all
he'd ever wanted to be . . . he knew it now – was a
Good Person (that, indeed, such a longing lay at the
heart of what good Christians such as Sophie and her
family wanted as well – they just didn't like to express
it in that way) Paul fell to pondering how best to
achieve that end in the context of this new dilemma.
Believing himself to be as Christian as ever, he did not
realise the deeper implications of this shifting
perspective, this change of goal to the rather more
nebulous 'Good' – did not understand that, far from
clarifying his direction through the moral landscape
ahead, he'd effectively dismissed the guide. Or
perhaps, more precisely, demoted that same Guide to
a role that was more consultative than authoritative.

So what did a Good Person do – Paul wondered . . .
in a situation such as this? Would a Good Person stick
to his word and stick with Sophie no matter what?
Even if he now had doubts about his God and his
religion; even if he had feelings – overwhelming
feelings – for another woman; even if he thought he
might have got it wrong . . . would a Good Person still
go through with the marriage? Would a Good Person
be so dishonest to himself?

On the other hand, would a Good Person simply
abandon a family and a woman he loved? For Paul was
in no doubt that he loved Sophie; it was just that the
love lacked fire. Would he leave all that decency
behind him, all for a shot of lust – or whatever twisted
version of lust it was when the object of his desire was

heavily pregnant by another man (which, of course, was a whole other moral minefield he'd yet to navigate)? Could Paul live with himself if he publicly humiliated Sophie in this way? For that was absolutely what it would be. And to a man like Paul, public humiliation was about as cruel as it got. Could he – as a Good Person – really be responsible for inflicting that particular torture on someone as innocent and loving as Sophie?

Paul sat there – wretched, in the fading light – while the choir sang on. He sat there, agonising, as seven o'clock came and went and the rehearsal drew to a close . . . the girls trooping out in twos and threes, and one or two by themselves, some laughing, some texting on their mobiles, some hurrying out with serious expressions – looking at their watches, running for the bus – followed, finally, by their choirmaster. The lights in the main part of the church went off. The great, heavy doors were shut and locked. The man walked across the flagstone area that led through a small gateway, out into the street. His footsteps were precise.

Paul watched him cross the road. He watched as the man got into a small car and drove off into the night – leaving Paul in deeper, darker silence, with no answer to his dilemma. No help from God. No guidance. No sense of being loved, or forgiven, or accepted, or understood. He felt absolutely alone. And whatever he did – whatever decision he made – Paul had the horrible feeling he was going to get it wrong. He could either leave Sophie and be forever despised by the people whose good opinion mattered most to him. Or stay – and spend the rest of his life in the half-light. He—

'Paul?'

Paul looked round.

'Thought it was you,' said Charles Mostyn, coming round the side of the church towards him, smiling broadly. 'Recognised the helmet!'

Paul smiled back. He got to his feet.

'You waiting for someone?' Charles went on, sensing Paul's lack of direction – his helmet off, his bike to one side, his quietness. 'There's no one else inside, you know. Just me in the office, I'm afraid, and I've shut it all up now. The choir's gone home, but,' – jangling his keys – 'I can easily let you in again, if you like.'

Paul shook his head. 'It's all right,' he replied, lifting his bicycle to a standing position. 'I was just – sitting here . . . listening to the choir . . .'

It sounded lame. For a moment, Paul wondered what Charles would think – finding his future son-in-law sitting on a church bench at seven o'clock on a Friday evening. But Charles Mostyn was used to strange behaviour – much stranger behaviour than this. Indeed, he often sat on that bench himself for no particular reason. He liked listening to the choir as well. It seemed perfectly normal to him. In any case, the sight of Paul had put Charles in mind of other things.

'Must say, I'm delighted to catch you,' he said, as the pair of them walked away from the church – up the street again, back to Ifield Road, with the bicycle ticking at their heels. 'Been wanting to say how thrilled we are that you managed to fix the television. Quite brilliant of you.'

'Anyone could have done it, Charles. You only needed some new batteries in the remote control. It was hardly—'

'Well, you saved us the call-out charge,' Charles persisted. 'More importantly,' he went on, grinning now, 'you saved us from Vince having a go – which would surely have finished the thing off . . .'

Paul smiled back. Vince was a homeless man with a drug problem. Charles had picked him up in Brompton Cemetery a few weeks earlier – he'd found the man some accommodation and had put him in touch with the right help groups. Vince was much better, but he still came to Ifield Road from time to time for baths and food. Paul didn't like him. Vince had a sly smile and a disrespectful slouch. He was clearly using Charles and Victoria – although Paul, being Paul, would never dream of saying as much. It wasn't his style to criticise. Not openly, at any rate. Better to pretend – as the Mostyns seemed to do – that everyone was good.

'. . . and Victoria tells me you found her camera – in the vault, of all places! Can't imagine what it was doing down there – hate to think what else you must have found amongst all that junk . . . but so good of you to do that, Paul. So thoughtful . . .'

Paul said it was nothing. He took no overt credit and played it down – but there was something very sweet about the older man's approval. Paul liked being praised. He liked being told he was brilliant, and kind, and thoughtful, and modest. He liked it when other people thought he was a Good Person. Particularly people like Charles Mostyn. The experience was every bit as vital to Paul as the warmth of Marianne's skin against his.

That night, before he went back to his own little flat, Paul told Sophie all about his afternoon with Marianne

– except, of course, the important part. He told her he'd been to look at the designs. He told her that Marianne hadn't been well, that they'd decided to reschedule, that he might even call her tomorrow – just to make sure she was okay. Poor girl. It couldn't be easy, with Gabby in rehab and Jay away.

Paul was good at deception. Like all good deceivers, he had a knack of keeping as close as possible to the truth. And because he had such a clear style of speaking – precise, controlled, with lots of eye contact – it disguised any absence of clarity in the substance of what he was saying, which was invariably obscure, off-centre, incomplete. Paul liked using fancy words and long, elaborate sentences that drifted into the air so that others were obliged to fill in the gaps. It was a useful trick, with the added advantage that Paul often ended up deluding himself as well as everyone else. He could find himself quite moral, quite acceptable, in a staged world of half-truths – a world that allowed him Sophie, and allowed him Marianne – in a way that simply wasn't possible when the curtains were open, when daylight spoiled the effect.

Paul was a compulsive spinner. He found it very easy to perform what he perceived to be the Christian routine of seeing the best in people, or of appearing to do so . . . even about himself. With the right angle, in the right light, anything could look good. He was, in short, that dangerous combination of cleverness without wisdom; wisdom to see that – when immersed in the business of creating wonderful effects – it was harder than usual to keep an eye on what was bad.

It wasn't that Paul turned a blind eye to the truth. It was more that he embellished it – relighting, rearranging . . . fiddling about until the thing looked

214

right. He knew that his feelings for Marianne were morally incompatible with being engaged to Sophie. He knew that there was a clash. He agonised. But he did so with a sense of it all being out of his control – as if the impossible situation in which he now found himself was absolutely not his fault; as if God was somehow to blame. Certainly God had been shockingly neglectful of late, and if He wasn't responsible for putting Paul in this mess, He was certainly doing nothing to help him out of it. Indeed, when Paul thought of God these days, it was more with a sense of disappointment than one of gratitude or praise. And the more Paul fretted, the more inclined he was to interpret his circumstances in such a way that he emerged as the victim of them – as opposed to the perpetrator. He was a Good Person, trying to do his best against quite impossible odds.

And Sophie – loving Paul – was all too willing to buy this nobler version. Paul was simply being kind to Marianne. Any feelings of unease were down to jealousy – Sophie's jealousy – and needed to be stifled. Why shouldn't Paul be worried for his friend? Why shouldn't he call her from time to time when the poor girl was clearly struggling? And if he wanted to run the occasional errand for Marianne, or offer to collect some things for her from the workshop in Hatton Garden while Marianne went for a check-up, who was Sophie to stand in his way? Why shouldn't Paul put himself out? He was always doing that sort of thing for Sophie and her parents. Why not Marianne, too?

So Paul rang Marianne with a conscience that was not only clear but also – in the end – positively humming with a sense of selfless duty and concern. He called a number of times to make sure she was okay: had she seen the doctor? Why not? Was there anything he could do? And Marianne – touched that he'd noticed, touched that he cared . . . Marianne had melted. With Paul at a more comfortable distance – safe at the end of a telephone line, ostensibly offering nothing more than friendship – her previous qualms were all too easy to forget.

She was also getting very tired these days. With her baby getting bigger – pressing against her bladder and her lungs, squeezing the rest of her organs into a tighter and tighter space – so the demands of Christmas business began to press at her as well. It was very quiet at the showroom these days . . . and while, in many ways, Gabriella's absence was a blessing (certainly, it was simpler working on her own, without Gab's constant interruptions or having to clear up the mess of ill feelings she invariably left in her wake), Marianne missed her friend. Professional standards aside, she missed the basic companionship, the sense of a load shared – even if the burden was unequal. Gab's chatter was distracting, but perhaps the occasional diversion – having a longer lunch in a local restaurant instead of another sandwich at her desk, or giggling about the dustmen, or smiling at the latest rant . . . perhaps such moments would have provided some release for the internal tension that was building in Marianne. Instead, the silent focus of her daily life held its own particular strain, and Paul's kind voice at the end of the telephone – his willingness to help, his offer to come over – was comforting.

'I've got the address,' he'd said, yesterday, into her answering machine. 'And I've spoken to . . .' there was a rustle of paper – 'to Lee. I'm picking it all up tomorrow afternoon, I'll be bringing it over sometime around five – and I can OK those drawings at the same time. No need to call me back, Marianne. Not unless I've got it wrong, or you're out or something, okay? Now go home and get some sleep. I'll see you tomorrow.'

His words touched the exact part of her that most craved relief – and Marianne had listened in tears.

Today she was feeling a little better. There had been no more fainting, and no more whopping kicks. For once, her baby – who'd clearly been as stressed as Marianne by the late nights and increased workload – was quiet. Quiet and calm. Sleeping. And Marianne was full of gratitude for Paul's friendship. And with him now collecting those pieces from Lee, she'd been able to spend the entire afternoon at her desk. Had even managed a nap. She was bright and refreshed when he arrived – sitting at her desk with the radio on (it was the next best thing to Gabby), listening to the news.

Leaving the radio playing, she went to answer the door – greeting Paul with a social kiss. Then she took the Hatton Garden packets he'd brought and gladly ushered him in.

'You're a lifesaver, Paul. A total lifesaver.' Closing the door behind him, she went over to the desk and opened the packets to check the contents: all there, all perfect. She smiled at Paul – a smile of such gratitude it made him reel – before directing him over to the sofas. 'I've put out your drawings,' she said, taking the packets over to the safe, punching in the security code. 'Do have a look. I'll just put this lot away . . .'

Paul did as he was told. He flicked through the series of drawings that made up Marianne's proposed design

217

– it looked beautiful – while she opened the safe and chattered on.

'I can't tell you what a difference it's made – not having to go in today. I've returned all my calls. I've caught up with my correspondence – including my tax return. I've finished the drawings for another job. I've spoken to my mother – even found time for a quick snooze. In fact, I feel amazing – and it's all down to you . . .'

Paul shook his head. 'It was nothing,' he said. 'You know I had that other stuff to do in Farringdon – it couldn't have been easier. And if I can help you out in the process, so much the better.'

'Well, you certainly did that,' said Marianne, leaving the safe open for a moment as she went over to the radio and switched it off. The programme had ended, and the series of commercials that followed were all accompanied by tinny seasonal music.

Marianne rolled her eyes. 'Damn carols. They might wait until December, don't you think? Before ramming them down our necks . . .' And then, remembering Paul's Christianity, she ground to a halt. She bit her lip. 'At least . . .' – swallowing now – 'I'm sorry, Paul. I didn't mean –'

Paul shrugged. 'It's all right,' he said, amused. 'I don't particularly like them myself, to be honest.'

He just couldn't help it. It wasn't a lie. Indeed, he probably meant it – in that moment, that very second, with Marianne there, and the bad quality of the recording and the cheap, gaudy commercial . . . it wasn't the same as the carol he and Charles Mostyn had been listening to last week, outside the church. Perfectly valid to like one, and dislike the other. But it was also perfectly typical of Paul: that compulsion to

218

agree, to seem to agree, to create – within himself – a new person with new tastes and new priorities to suit each and every circumstance.

Marianne grinned. 'Glad to see you haven't *completely* changed . . .' she said.

And Paul's expression shifted. He got to his feet. 'I haven't changed at all,' he replied, rather too seriously. 'In fact—'

'Great!' she gulped, hurrying back to the open safe. *Oh God.* Where did harmless flirting end and hardcore teasing begin? Had she really given him a cue?

'Now,' she went on, in a let's-get-down-to-work sort of way – not looking at Paul as he came towards her; hoping, desperately, that an air of apparent obliviousness to his hint would make him hold back. 'While I've got this thing open, would you like to see your stone again? In fact, we should definitely get it out. It'll help when you look at the designs. It—' Marianne leant further in, searching down the rows of packets that were arranged alphabetically at the back. 'Chester-Brown,' she muttered – anything to fill the silence – 'Crechy . . . Czutskaya . . . D – Driver . . . E . . . F . . . Farage! Here we are!'

Thinking only about Paul, about keeping him at arm's length – not because she wasn't attracted to him, but because of the reverse, because she was scared of what she might do if he got too close . . . she couldn't trust herself, not at the moment, not with everything so messy and muddled and strained . . . her moral compass needle spinning madly, Marianne whisked the Farage packet over to the desk. Protected – as much from herself as from Paul – by the position of that bastion of good sense and traditional values, sheltering behind its crafted drawers, its tooled leather surface, its solid mahogany, she opened the packet carefully to reveal two stones in the folds.

The room felt very silent. Marianne's heart lurched as she realised her mistake. How could she have forgotten about that other stone? How could she have been so stupid? Yes, Paul's presence was distracting her, yes, she had other things on her mind . . . but still. Kicking herself, she knew it was now too late. She'd have to brazen it out.

'Two?' said Paul.

Marianne looked at him.

Paul looked back. 'What's going on?'

She had to tell him. In a way, it was a relief to have a genuine change of subject. And while she found it was mildly embarrassing to find herself explaining – in detail – what had happened with Jay and Tariq, having to convince Paul how extremely difficult it was to spot this sort of fake, to be caught with both stones there, as if she were still considering using the lesser one . . . but the embarrassment didn't last. For Paul – of course – was very kind about it, and very understanding. He seemed more intrigued than put out. Even amused. When she finished explaining, he asked her to show him – exactly – how to spot the difference between the stones, and Marianne was more than happy to oblige.

Or at least have a go. Her gemmology equipment was fine for a showroom, but it wasn't the same as in a proper laboratory. Without proper laser testing equipment, proper microscopes, proper lighting, there was only a certain distance they could go. And with only the naked eye to work with, it was more about a feel for the thing . . . and not everybody had the instinct. Gabby had missed it when she'd checked the stone back in Galle. And Marianne herself had missed it too – when Paul had first brought it in, at that preliminary meeting when Sophie had been there as well, when they'd had so much to discuss. In any case, such fakes were notoriously difficult to spot. A layman such as Paul, who hadn't studied gemmology, who hadn't spent decades working with stones, wouldn't stand a chance.

But Paul still wanted to try – so Marianne took the stones outside, into the empty mews. The day was fading, but she still felt that natural light would be best. Paul followed her out. He sat beside her on the showroom steps – holding the little velvet tray with the two stones rolling around in it, while Marianne searched her handbag for the old magnifying loupe she always carried, and a small battered torch. He watched as she took these items out, wiped them, and then, picking the genuine padparascha from the tray, held it out and low, keeping the light on its surface as even as possible, and the loupe just above. To Marianne, it was easy now that the stones were together. The good one had a particular softness – a soul . . .

Paul stared hard into the cushion-cut depths. Reading his silence, Marianne reached for the torch. She held it, with a tissue pulled over its head, and the stone against the tissue – held it so that both of them could see, and handed Paul the loupe. 'See? There!'

Paul squinted stupidly through it.

'Let me find the other stone. We can look at them together. It . . .' The effort of explaining the difference was written across Marianne's face. 'There's something unique in the balance of orange and pink . . . something that's lost in the fake. It . . .' Marianne's face softened as the beauty of the good stone struck her naked eye afresh. 'It's amazing, Paul . . . there's some-

221

thing *unresolved* at the heart of it . . . something you can't stop looking at – something alive.'

But Paul couldn't see it. And after a while he stopped looking, because it wasn't nearly as interesting, or as beautiful, or alive, as the sight of Marianne's excited face – her look of total wonder as she marvelled afresh at the subtle properties of the true padparascha against the dreary fake.

He smiled as she finished. And Marianne – aware that his smile suggested more amusement than agreement – looked down, embarrassed. 'I'm sorry,' she said, putting the loupe back into her bag, together with the tray and the stones, pausing for a final look at the good one. 'I do get carried away sometimes. But it's only because your stone is so exceptional.'

Paul took it from her. 'I wish I could see what you see.'

'Oh, you will. When you get to know it a little better . . . when you've lived with it for a few months, you'll understand exactly what I'm talking about. Sophie certainly will – having it on her finger every day. She—'

'That's assuming she does,' he muttered.

Marianne looked at him.

'I know she said she'd wear it every day,' Paul went on. 'I know she agreed to a simpler design – and I think you've done a brilliant job with those drawings, Marianne, absolutely perfect. You mustn't change a thing. But . . .' – sighing now – 'I don't know . . . even with your discreet setting, can you really see this beautiful thing flashing on her finger while she hands out soup to the homeless? Do you really think she'll take the school register with it sparkling against the margin of her book?' Holding the stone to the sky now, he quietly shook his head. 'It's wasted on Sophie. Completely wasted . . .'

Marianne sat silently – unable to disagree.

'And – and when I *think* of that stupid diamond I gave you,' Paul went on, his voice rising. 'You – of all people! I mean . . . how could I have done that? How could I have been so *blind*?' he cried. 'So unthinking? So completely and utterly arrogant? What must you have thought of me?'

Marianne sighed. 'You weren't to know. In any case, it was a very nice ring. And extremely generous. I just wasn't—'

'But what would you have done,' he went on, 'what would you have said, if I'd given you something like this instead?'

Marianne hesitated.

'You'd have said yes, wouldn't you?'

Still, she hesitated.

'Oh, God.' Paul felt sick. 'You'd have said yes . . . you'd have – you bloody would. And we'd be married now, it would be *my* child you'd be carrying, and—'

'It wasn't just the ring, Paul. And it was a long time ago. Who knows what I'd have said or done?'

But Paul wasn't listening. Overcome, he turned to face Marianne – still sitting beside him on the little step – and, taking her hand in his, he pressed the real stone back into its palm. 'You have it,' he begged. 'I know it's too late for anything more – we can't turn back, can't . . . can't change what's done. But – oh Marianne, please – *please* let me do this. At least let me give you the stone you always should have had. It's wasted on Sophie. Let her have the fake one – she'll never know . . .'

Marianne shook her head, unable to speak.

'. . . and you can have this real one – this tiny thing I don't begin to understand . . . except – except that it makes you so thrilled and excited . . . and remember that I gave it to you, that I wanted you to have it. You – please, Marianne?'

She could feel the emotion welling, brimming and spilling . . .

'Marianne?'

She looked at him. Looked up at his frantic face – swimming before her, through the tears – and knew herself to be lost. She let him kiss her, and she kissed him back – barely feeling the small, hard stone as he pressed it, harder and harder, into the soft palm of her hand. And it was only the flash of headlights, and the approach of a familiar-looking car coming towards them, bumping over the cobbles, right up to the showroom door, that brought her to her senses.

She knew, even before he got out, that it was George. It wasn't so much the car as the sheer sod's law of it all. It had to be George . . . and it was.

Paul got to his feet. 'George.'

'Paul.'

Paul watched him get out of the car. 'I can explain—'

'I'm not sure you can,' came the cool reply, as George slammed the car door shut and walked the final yards. 'And even if you could, Paul, I'm really not sure I want to hear it. Certainly not from you.' He was looking now at Marianne. 'In fact, why don't you just piss off?'

Paul was shocked. 'I hardly think—'

'I don't care what you think. Just bugger off. Sayonara. On your bike . . .' which, unfortunately, happened to be propped within George's reach. He grasped it with a hand that was shaking with rage and threw it at Paul's feet. 'Go home to Sophie. God knows, she deserves something better than a squirt like you but . . . *go on*, man. *Go.*'

Blindly, Paul gathered his things and went, shakily mounting his battered bike, wobbling this way and that as he rode it over the cobbles and out, through the mews gates, into the street.

George looked at Marianne, standing on the doorstep – her face very pale, her legs very slim, her baby very evident – and found his anger leaving him as instantly as it had arrived. And with the conviction of rage no longer in his sails, George sat dead in the water – all momentum lost. How could he remain cross with her, knowing what he did about Jay's neglect, and all the pressure she was facing at work? How could he blame her for succumbing to the charms of a man like Paul?

Marianne knew he was looking at her, but she couldn't lift her eyes from the bumpy cobbles, couldn't bring herself to face his disdain. For all the outrage she felt towards George – for humiliating Paul like that, for taking it upon himself to judge a situation he couldn't possibly understand . . . for all that, she was also shot through with shame, and overcome by a sense that there was no explanation, no justification, nothing that she could say to him now that would make things better. George had caught her betraying Jay, and betraying their child. She might have been able to defend the smoking and the drinking, but – but this . . .? Under his gaze, Marianne saw herself as a man like George might see her: as wholly unfit to be a mother – she knew that now – and the poor baby wasn't even born.

'I was dropping this in,' he said, passing her an envelope. 'It's addressed to the business, but it came to Fitzroy Place. Someone can't have realised you've moved . . .'

'Thanks.' Marianne took the envelope with a shaky hand and put it into her bag. 'Anything else?'

'No.'

She turned and went back in. She closed the door, and leant against it from the inside – dizzy with emotion. Dropping the bag, she slid to a squat and put her head in her hands.

George went back to his car. There was a moment of silence before she heard the engine, and another moment before she heard it rumbling back up the mews – fading, fading, until there was nothing left. Marianne felt faint. But it was only when she tried to get up from her squat position that she realised just how weak she was. She needed to sit down. She needed to . . . Christ. What was wrong? Her whole body was sweating. Her legs wouldn't hold. And her last sensation – before she passed out on the doormat – was the thick warmth of sudden blood against the insides of her thighs . . . a slippery sensation between clothes and skin as her knees crumpled beneath her.

Chapter Sixteen

She woke the following morning – alone, in a hospital bedroom. There was tape on her arm, and a thin red tube that led to a drip. There was soft, dry padding between her legs. A plastic tag had been put round her wrist, and she was wearing a backless hospital tunic. They must have given her a lot of drugs. She felt warm and woozy – certainly she was in no pain – and apart from a ferocious thirst, she was really very comfortable. She could have lain there all day, drifting in and out of sleep.

Even when a female doctor came and told her that the baby had died, Marianne didn't feel so bad. Couldn't, in truth, feel anything. A combination of shock and drugs had numbed her, completely. And it was only when the woman explained that, due to the advanced state of Marianne's pregnancy, she was still going to have to give birth . . . only then, did Marianne begin to realise – in a dull, flat, grey sort of way – the truth of what was happening: her first reaction being really more one of exhaustion at the prospect, than one that was maddened or tortured with grief.

The doctor looked at Marianne's papers for a moment. And then, with a quick apology, pressed on – with headmistressy orderliness – down the list of questions, wanting to know if Marianne preferred to be induced, or wait for a natural birth. After listening to the various repercussions that went with each option, Marianne went for the former. Just wanted it to be over. As soon as possible. The doctor put a tick in the induction column, and turned to the list of operating times at the back of her notes. Yes, that would be fine. Marianne could have it this afternoon if that was what she wanted.

Marianne nodded.

And what about an autopsy?

Marianne's raw, unadorned eyes met the doctor's – which were clear, blue, professional, with a light cosmetic glimmer on the lids and a touch of mascara on the lashes. The doctor looked away. 'The advantage of an autopsy', she explained, 'is that you do get answers. It won't always reveal exactly what went wrong, but it will rule out certain possibilities. It can be a real help, particularly when it comes to avoiding the same thing happening again,' – sighing now – 'but I'd be lying if I told you it was easy.'

Again, their eyes met.

'The main problem', the doctor went on, 'is that autopsies can take weeks, which often means postponing the burial – which of course makes for a horrible time while you wait. For some parents – quite understandably – the idea of their baby in a pathologist's laboratory is simply too much.' She put a hand on Marianne's. 'A lot rests on how strong you feel you are; and how important it will be to you in the months to come to feel that you did all you could to get to the bottom of what happened.'

At the moment, the doctor couldn't say for sure what had caused Marianne to lose her baby. With that kind of blood loss, it was almost certain that the problem would have been the placenta – detaching itself from the wall of the womb. *Abrupting* was the term. And while placental abruption didn't always result in a stillbirth, it clearly had in Marianne's case. But as for what might have caused her placenta to abrupt in the first place, there could be all kinds of reasons – from an inherent genetic fault to some aspect of the mother's lifestyle.

'Like smoking?'

The doctor nodded. 'Possibly,' she said. 'Or excessive drinking. Or drugs. There's certainly evidence of a connection between things like that in the mother's system, and placental abnormalities – absolutely.' Marianne looked stricken. 'But there may be some other reason entirely,' the doctor added, hurriedly. 'Something you could have done nothing about, Marianne – some blood condition, some irregularity with the umbilical cord. At this stage – I'm very sorry – it's simply impossible to tell.'

Marianne sat back in bed – staring at the ceiling as the doctor explained they'd know a bit more after the labour, but not everything. An autopsy would certainly provide more a definite conclusion, if that was what Marianne wanted – although, of course, that decision was ultimately up to her.

Marianne closed her eyes.

'Not that you need to decide just yet,' said the doctor, quickly. 'It's only in situations where parents are positive they want a quick burial that it helps if we—'

'I'll decide it later, then, shall I?'

'Sure.'

229

Marianne was left with her thoughts. From time to time, someone would come in and take her blood pressure, or change her drinking water, or ask what she wanted for lunch. She ate and drank. She used the bathroom. She answered questions, filled out forms, submitted to preparation for induction . . . and was, in general, a perfectly functioning human being . . . except that she couldn't cry.

She stared out of the window, waiting for it to happen. She closed her eyes – letting her imagination edge forward, little by little, into more sensitive places . . . and then, when she still felt nothing, Marianne quit 'edging' and thought instead, in forced and vicious detail, of what now lay within that mocking bump – the abrupted placenta, the floating lifeless child. She thought of the moment of telling Jay the bad news, of telling her parents, her friends. She allowed herself to imagine holding a vigorous newborn baby – heard, inside her head, those first, wide, healthy cries that, far from passing distress into a loving post-birth mother, merely put her mind at rest. And contrasted it with the disturbing silence that enveloped her now. She imagined the beauty of breastfeeding, and Jay opening the door and smiling at them. She imagined her daughter growing – first steps, first words, first uniform, first boyfriend . . . ramming home the extent of her loss. Not just a baby . . . a child, a teenager, a woman, who might one day have carried her own children . . . and on, and on . . . an army of descendants sloshed away with a rush of blood down the insides of her thighs.

And still she couldn't cry. Perhaps it was the drugs. Or her body's natural reaction to trauma. Perhaps she couldn't expect to feel much. But even so – in a different way – the failure of proper expression tortured her. So she turned to other things. And little by little – as the day progressed – she discovered more about how she'd made it into hospital at all.

She learnt that George had found her. She'd no idea why he would have come back to the showroom that night but, guessing it was something to do with Gabby – and guessing that Gabby must have given him her keys – Marianne assumed he must have let himself in and found her there on the floor. Certainly, it was George who'd called the ambulance. The nurses were clear about that. Apparently, he'd even come to the hospital with her and stayed for an hour or two – waiting while the preliminary examinations took place, and then fighting for Marianne to have her own private room before finally leaving in the small hours of the morning.

She was glad that it had been George. He might disapprove of Marianne, but at least he was reliable, competent . . . capable of acting when action was required. He wouldn't have been squeamish, not after witnessing the births of his own three children. He'd have balanced the need for quick, clear decisions – a right sense of emergency – with no unnecessary fuss. Indeed, the more Marianne thought about it, the more she could see that the very things she'd once despised about George Franklin – his particular adherence to rules, his emotional detachment – such things had their uses at a time like this. Why, it seemed he'd even had the presence of mind to remember her handbag! With her keys and her purse and so on . . . and all kinds of useful cards and numbers, her mobile, her lip-balm . . . Marianne looked into it now. Yes. Everything was there, including her old loupe and – yes, there they still were, thank God. Paul's stones – the good one and the bad . . .

Marianne bit her lip. She needed to get them out of here. Certainly, the good one. She needed to make it secure. For a moment, she considered trusting it to one of the nurses, or asking for it to be put in the hospital safe – if indeed there was one. But the more she thought about it, the wiser it seemed just to keep the thing to hand – not draw attention to the situation – and quietly send it away with a visitor she could trust.

Induction took place. Marianne didn't have anyone with her – didn't want anyone with her. Even if Jay had been able to make it, she wasn't sure that having him by her side was something she could have borne – not after she'd imagined him with her in such very different circumstances. And the idea of her mother's pity was even less tolerable. It was easier to keep it clinical. Easier to bear, with emotion reduced to an absolute minimum. Easier to see herself as a body – just a body – as the medics no doubt did. Not speak to anyone, in fact – no one who knew her properly – until the thing was done.

Thankfully, the labour was quick. After being induced via a drip, with the induction hormone being administered intravenously so that the rate of the drug could be adjusted to control the contractions and minimise the pain . . . the process was relatively straightforward. It was still painful – more painful than she could possibly have imagined. But short. And after four hours, Marianne was back in her room again. All she had to do now was sleep – rest her body, recover her strength. At some point, she would need to decide about the autopsy, but that could wait for now. In any case, it was something she was keen to consult Jay about before reaching any final decision.

Except that Jay remained elusive as ever. According to the nurse, George had been constantly trying to contact him that first night. He'd even left a note for Marianne explaining he was on the case and not to worry about trying to reach him herself . . . not unless she wanted to have a go, of course. Let George handle the matter. And she didn't need to concern herself with hospital rules about mobile telephones, and whether to leave hers on (that's if the hospital would let her, which in itself was debatable) or whether it was running out of battery, and so on and so forth. He'd make sure that Jay had the hospital number.

So Marianne lay waiting – dozing intermittently, but unable to give herself over to the deep healing sort of sleep she needed. From time to time, she'd try Jay's number . . . but to no avail. And as the hours slipped by, through another night and into Sunday morning, she felt increasingly alone – and increasingly desperate to speak to Paul.

She probably should have rung her mother. She was going to have to do it at some point. But then she thought of Patricia's open pain at her hidden pain, and then the memory of her father, so safe and dependable – both of them good, proper, responsible, caring parents. And then there was the whole sense of defeat, the sense that she'd failed them somehow – that losing this baby was some sort of punishment for doing things her way instead of theirs – it still wasn't something she could face.

Paul, on the other hand . . .

Perhaps it was simply because he didn't know her so

well. Or perhaps because of that cooperative facility he had for transforming himself into the person others wanted him to be, for saying what they wanted to hear, constantly throwing back a flattering reflection . . . whatever it was, it was Paul she wanted. Paul she needed. Aware of the intensity of his attraction to her, his admiration of her – the sense that he was, absolutely, on her side, that he had always been on her side – Marianne craved Paul's warm, uncritical presence. And when she realised that he wouldn't even know what had happened – that, after his encounter with George on the mews cobbles, he was probably waiting for Marianne to call and wondering why she didn't, and drawing the worst of all possible conclusions – Marianne couldn't bear it. She reached for her bag, took out her mobile, and dialled Paul's number.

The mobile buzzed, and buzzed again. And Sophie, hearing the vibrations coming from underneath a cushion at the far end of the sofa, put aside the pile of homework she was marking and retrieved Paul's mobile from where he'd left it the night before. She looked at the display panel.

'Marianne?'

Marianne's heart sank. She tried to keep it business-like – hoped Sophie didn't mind, but she really needed to speak to Paul. She knew it was a bit of an imposition – especially on a Sunday – and she wouldn't ordinarily ask, but – but . . . well . . . the thing was, she'd had an accident the other night – nothing serious, she was fine, but it would be a great help to her if Paul might help out with a slightly embarrassing situation to do with their padparascha, which she'd been working on at the time of the accident, and which had somehow ended up in her handbag and come with her to the hospital and – and really needed to be taken somewhere more secure. She—

'Hospital?'

'It's fine. I'm fine. I just—'

'And the baby?'

Silence.

'Marianne?'

More silence.

'Marianne, are you okay?'

'I – I'm sorry ... it's ...'

'Is anyone with you? Which hospital are you in?'

Silence, again.

'Paddington? Chelsea and Westminster?'

Marianne told her.

'Right,' said Sophie, shuffling her feet into their shoes and reaching for her bag. 'I'm coming over.'

'But—'

'I'll leave a quick message for Paul – he forgot to take his mobile home last night, the idiot. But I can leave a note for him on the hall table – let him know where you are – and he'll see it when he gets back from church. It shouldn't be too long. He's due here for lunch with my parents, so he won't miss it. I promise. And I'll come over myself until he gets there. You can always send me away, Marianne, but I can certainly deal with the padparascha – which is the *last* thing you should be worrying about at a time like this ... and – and if there's anything else I can do to help you, please say. And ... and ... I'm sorry, I'm rambling ... but I'm off now, okay? I'll see you soon.'

So Sophie came – clutching grapes and magazines, which she'd bought in the hospital shop downstairs.

Privately she hoped Paul wouldn't mind. He was already slightly annoyed with her for going to the quick, early service that morning – so that she could catch up with her marking – instead of attending the longer ten o'clock one with him . . . but she was sure he'd understand. Marianne couldn't be alone at a time like this – and Paul was very fond of her. For sure, he'd have wanted Sophie to help.

She sat on the chair by Marianne's bed and, the situation being what it was, had only to say, 'You don't have to talk about it, if you don't want to', and Marianne was off. And once she'd given Sophie a quick account of how she'd ended up in hospital and what – briefly – had happened, it became apparent that Marianne's main source of distress was the question of *why*.

She thrashed around the subject. They . . . well, they did know it was the placenta – that it had broken away completely from the wall of her uterus, and that, because Marianne had fainted, because she hadn't been able to get straight to hospital in time, she'd lost the baby. But they still didn't know why the placenta had done that – at least, they weren't telling her if they did. Not that it really mattered, of course. Marianne already knew it was because she'd been smoking. Smoking and drinking—

Sophie frowned. 'You're certain it was that?'

Marianne shrugged.

'They told you so?'

Marianne was silent for a moment – before conceding that nothing specific had been said to her on the subject . . . but that was only because she hadn't spoken to a doctor since Maya had been born.

'I – I called her Maya.' She looked at Sophie. 'They

said it was a good idea to give her a name. They said it would help. I wasn't sure what to go for. I hope it's all right.'

'It's a lovely name.'

Marianne's eyes slid towards the window. 'She was so tiny, Sophie. So incredibly small . . .' She held her hands apart. 'Just this big. And I held her. They said I should. They said . . .'

'I'm sure that was the right thing to do.'

But Marianne wasn't ready to be consoled. She looked back at Sophie.

'I killed her . . .'

Sophie shook her head. 'Rubbish,' she said. 'You might have been a bit slack when it came to drinking and smoking – but you weren't crazy. You were never blind drunk, were you? No. Exactly. You had a couple of glasses from time to time, and the occasional cigarette – which they'd probably *recommend* in France!'

Marianne smiled weakly.

Sophie smiled back. 'And – it really couldn't have been anything else?' she pressed.

'Well, sure – theoretically, it could have been some-thing genetic. Apparently. And there is a condition some babies have – involving a short umbilical cord that tugs the placenta away, but . . .'

Sophie nodded. 'And have they told you how long your cord was?'

Marianne shook her head.

'You want me to ask?'

'Don't worry.' Marianne sighed. 'I can ask them myself. But I think we can assume it isn't that, or they'd have told me – right?'

Sophie didn't know.

Marianne looked at her, sadly. 'The thing is, Sophie – even if it does turn out to be something like that, something that isn't my fault at all, I . . . I should still never have taken those risks.'

'We all take risks. All the time.'

'Not with our children, we don't. At least, no decent person would. But me – with my stupid pride and my refusal to listen or take advice . . . I – I just can't stop thinking that I deserved to lose her.'

'Marianne.' Silence. 'Marianne, you can't think like that. You—'

'I wasn't a fit mother. That's the bottom line.'

Sophie didn't speak for a moment. Not because she agreed with Marianne, but because she knew that Marianne wasn't ready to listen to alternatives. And anyway, it was pointless to speculate. What Marianne needed was concrete information. She needed a proper post-labour debriefing. It was outrageous that the doctor hadn't done that yet. Sophie didn't care it was Sunday . . . completely irrelevant . . . that doctor of hers was a *disgrace* . . .

Marianne looked at Sophie in surprise – amusement, even. She'd no idea the girl could get that angry.

'And how dare they torture you with questions about whether or not to have an autopsy, and when you might be allowed to bury Maya, and so on, when they haven't even bothered to tell you what they might – or might not – have deduced from observing the labour? How dare they leave you in this state? Look at you – agonising over all the things you might have done to kill your child – crucifying yourself – when it might have been something completely beyond your control. I'm sorry, Marianne, but . . .' Sophie was on her feet. 'Would you mind if I spoke to

238

a nurse about it? At least we could find out when they're planning to see you.'

Marianne gave a weary shrug, and Sophie knew better than to wait for confirmation. She darted into the passage. Through the open door, Marianne could hear voices at the desk: Sophie speaking very politely to one of the nurses . . . and then rather less politely . . . no, they'd waited long enough. She was sorry, but with twenty-four hours having passed since the induction it was hardly . . . Sophie didn't care if it was Sunday, she wasn't going to drop the subject until somebody rang the consultant and found out when Ms Cooper might expect a visit from the consultant. Tonight would be good. In fact, in the circumstances, it was really the very least they should be doing. It was . . . well, call the home number, then. Or page the woman. Or – oh, for God's sake, let Sophie do it herself, if they were too damn scared . . .

Reappearing a few minutes later – a little flushed, but smiling – Sophie was able to inform Marianne that the consultant would indeed be coming to see her that evening.

'Seven o'clock, apparently. I hope that's okay?'

And Marianne, filled with a new sense of warmth towards Sophie, whispered, 'Thank you,' and sat back in bed, her eyes brimming with tears.

Sophie looked down at her, equally tearful. 'I'm sorry,' she said, wiping her own tears away. 'Don't know why *I*'m crying! It's pathetic.'

And Marianne was about to say that of course it wasn't pathetic – Sophie was strong, she was right, she was wonderful, and Paul was the luckiest man on the planet – when the telephone rang in her handbag.

It was Paul. He'd just got Sophie's note. He was on

his way . . . but – but what had happened? Was Marianne okay? What could he do? What could he bring? For a brief moment, Marianne sat listening to his voice – drinking in the special, soft, personal tone Paul kept for her these days. She longed for him to be with her – here, now. Longed for him to hold her and support her, the way she knew he would – gently, carefully, naturally. Longed for him to tell her that everything would be all right; that he'd look after her; that she, Marianne, would have been a good mother to Maya . . . the best mother; that nothing was her fault; that he loved her, more than ever. And were it not for Sophie – poor, awkward Sophie, standing now at the window, looking out, trying to be unobtrusive – Marianne wasn't sure she'd have been able to stop herself from expressing some of these thoughts.

But Sophie *was* there: with her, in the room. A new Sophie, in Marianne's eyes. Oh, she still loved Paul – loved his thoughtfulness, loved what he stood for. It had been growing for weeks, of course – growing and strengthening – but it was really only now, having lost Maya, that Marianne finally realised the kind of man she wanted in her life. Deeply, she regretted turning Paul down. Regretted, more precisely, that it had taken her so very long to understand her own needs as a mature woman – for a man who cared, a man whose love involved being there for her, a man who knew what it was to give unconditional support. When she thought, now, of that romantic figure she'd once found so compelling, that wandering hero, that wild, unpredictable alpha male who would talk tough, act tougher, keep her on her toes, and make her life a misery . . . it was like remembering that she'd once enjoyed wearing a tutu of sugary pink.

And yet, glancing over at Sophie again, Marianne was also aware that there was another, sterner part of her, a part that would find no solace, no relief, no peace of mind from leaning on Paul. Not now.

And so – after giving him the barest facts and reassuring him that she was doing well, she was going to be fine, Marianne then told him that a visit today was going to be too much. Some other day, perhaps. It was just that she was still very weak. She could barely sit up. 'I'm sorry, Paul. It's sweet of you to offer. I'm just . . . you could come tomorrow, if you like –'

'Marianne,' he whispered. 'Darling – *please*. Let me come now.'

Marianne couldn't speak.

'Is it Sophie? Has she said something? Please, Marianne . . .'

Marianne glanced quickly again at Sophie, who hadn't moved a muscle since the conversation began. In a slightly stronger voice than before, she said, 'Do come tomorrow, Paul – if that works for you. Three o'clock is good. Or else sometime around seven, after I've had supper.'

'That's really what you want?'

'Perfect. Great – I'll see you at seven, then. Seven, tomorrow.'

Marianne looked round at Sophie, still standing at the window, still looking down at the London traffic. 'I hope he doesn't mind,' she said, reaching for her bag to replace the mobile, 'me putting him off . . .'

Sophie turned from the window. 'You're exhausted.'

'It's odd. I didn't feel tired a moment ago . . .'

'You sleep.'

Sophie reached for her coat. She slung it briskly over her arm, and was just pulling the rest of her things together when Marianne spotted the padparascha. It was sitting on her bedside table – wrapped in tissue paper – ready for Sophie to take away. She held it out.

'I'm so sorry. Can't quite think how it managed to come here with me. I was meaning to take it to the workshop on Friday but . . . well, it's here now – which isn't ideal. It needs to be properly locked away and – and probably best all round if you just take it home with you. Just keep it until I'm up and running again – can you do that?'

'Of course.' Sophie put it carefully into her purse – in with the rest of her coins, and an old button and a couple of paperclips. It seemed very small and insignificant. 'Hope I don't forget about it,' she said, laughing, as she did up the zip.

Marianne touched her arm. 'Thank you,' she said.

Sophie smiled. 'It's nothing.'

'I mean—'

'I know what you mean.'

That evening, earlier than promised, Marianne received a visit from the doctor – who told her that, from the new information they now had following Maya's birth, information gained from looking at the placenta and the umbilical cord and the state of Marianne's uterus – they could now say with some certainty that there was very little chance that her baby could ever have survived to full term, no matter how many cigarettes Marianne had or hadn't smoked. The umbilical cord had been dangerously – freakishly – short. It was a recognised, but nonetheless extremely rare, condition. The chances of it happening were tiny: one in thousands, hundreds of thousands. It was rotten luck – and there was nothing that Marianne could have done to prevent what would have been an inevitable and total abruption of the placenta. The cord was simply too short to tolerate the degree of movement that a healthy baby would naturally create. Indeed, given the baby's good size, and the amount of kicking and squirming that Marianne had reported to her obstetrician in the last month or so, it was astonishing that Maya had survived for as long as she had.

Marianne listened with a combination of sadness and relief. She was glad that at least she'd had a fighter – proud of Maya for hanging on so long. And while she was still full of remorse – still knew, in her heart, that the loss of Maya would always be connected to her own carelessness, whatever the science – it was certainly better to hear that it was the cord, and not the cigarettes, that had proved the ultimate trigger.

It felt very quiet when the doctor left. Too quiet. Yes – Marianne had been glad at first of the privacy, glad to be able to shut the rest of the world away from the series of tearful fits that now assailed her (for Sophie, with her wonderful show of practical help – her willingness to fight for Marianne, somehow giving the latter permission to be sad ... Sophie had cleared that particular emotional blockage). Marianne wept freely now. But when the tears finally subsided, so, too, did her interest in privacy. And as she sank into a duller mood, it struck Marianne that perhaps a regular ward would have been preferable. She'd have enjoyed the distraction of the other patients getting in and out of bed, complaining of this and that, the general movement of the nurses. Messy, noisy open life, with all its uncomfortable comings and goings, would – paradoxically – have left her with a quieter cleaner mind than the sealed silence of a smart, private room, where dark thoughts could flourish – uninterrupted – with all the furtive excitement of bacteria in a Petri dish. It was only ten past six, and the coming night stretched out ahead with agonising slowness. Briefly, Marianne wished she hadn't said 'no' to Paul about coming to visit that evening – any company would have been welcome to her – and Paul, more than anyone, with his easy manner and his kind words and – and all the rest of it . . .

But the thought was swiftly stifled. Reaching for the remote control to her television, Marianne pressed the buttons, raised the volume, and fixed her eyes on the screen. That part of her life was over now. Over for good.

Something strange had happened in the hour or so that the doctor had just spent in her room. Something fundamental had changed in Marianne; changed for ever. For the overwhelming sense of a reprieve, in terms of conscience, that the doctor's news had brought . . . that sense of reprieve now made Marianne determined that she would never again make the same sort of mistake. Never would she be so irresponsible, so careless, so dismissive of the rules. It was a fallacy – misleadingly neat, but a fallacy all the same – to say that rules were there to be broken. They weren't. They were there for a reason. And whether those rules were about how to eat and drink during pregnancy, or whether they were about basic decency when it came to finding love, Marianne now subscribed, completely, to the code. To do anything else was selfish beyond measure and – quite simply – Marianne had had enough of hating herself. She wasn't about to steal another woman's fiancé. Certainly not Sophie's. Not now. Not ever. Even if that fiancé was Paul.

When he came to visit the following day, Marianne was tired but resolute, and perfectly prepared. She was

244

ready for his smile, his questions, his flowers. She knew, too, that at some point he would ask about the stone that Sophie had brought back with her . . . and knew, off pat, the answer she'd give him: that of course it was the good stone; that she couldn't, simply couldn't – from a professional point of view as much as a moral one – agree to a swap, however tempting.

It helped to have such a very clinical environment. Those clean, plastic surfaces, those bland furnishings, those ubiquitous mass-produced prints that were sealed off by glass . . . all helped Marianne in her attempt to present a neutral, two-dimensional, version of herself to Paul. So when he quietly took her hand and told her that he loved her, and that he *knew* now that she loved him back – *knew*, from how she'd kissed him on the steps . . . it was really much easier than she'd expected to tell him not to be so stupid. Paul didn't love her. She didn't love him. It was only a kiss. He had just been caught up in the moment – as, in truth, had she. Smiling, she said that she absolutely understood why he *thought* he was in love with her.

Paul didn't smile back. 'Except that I am, Marianne.'

She shook her head.

'I'm not deluded. You have to believe me. I – I still want to marry you, for God's sake.'

And okay, so she wasn't prepared for that. But it was easy enough to know what to say. Rigid in her resolve – if perhaps a little charmless, forgetting to prefix her rejection with a more considerate statement of how honoured and flattered she was, and all that guff – Marianne simply shook her head. She couldn't – wouldn't – accept his offer.

Paul stared at her. 'Don't tell me you're still in love with Jay,' he muttered scornfully. 'Don't palm me off

245

with that. You don't kiss me the way you did last Friday and expect me to believe—'

'I'm not saying that,' said Marianne, carefully. 'To be honest, Paul, I don't know what I want right now. Or who I love. I'm only—'

'I could understand you sticking with him while the baby . . . while you were still . . . while you might both have been parents. But that's not the case any more, Marianne! You're not tied to the man any more. You don't have to put up with being ignored and insulted and . . . surely you can see –'

'Yes, Paul. I do see. But just because Jay and I are having problems, that doesn't mean I'm prepared to rush up the aisle with you instead.'

Frustration crossed Paul's face. He had the obsessive expression of a teenage boy trying to fix a computer. Why wasn't it working? He bashed at a different set of buttons.

'Sure. Fine. I see what you're saying. I'm a bit premature with all this – I know I am, I can't help myself. But when you're better, Marianne, when you're out of hospital and – and thinking straight, you—'

'No, Paul.'

'But—'

'I won't do it.' She was staring at the glass-covered print, at the hospital room reflected in its surface. 'I won't find happiness in the wreckage of someone else's.'

At this, Paul's expression shifted. Encouraged by the discovery that guilt lay at the heart of this strange behaviour, that concern for Sophie was the main thing preventing Marianne from accepting him, and that this was an easy position to argue down – all he had to do was get Marianne to admit she loved him back – he almost looked victorious. Leaning forward across the bed, he took both her hands in his and said, 'Tell me you don't love me, then.'

'I don't love you.'

'Look at me and say it.'

She looked at him and said it. 'I don't love you, Paul. Please go.'

'Liar.'

'Go, Paul.' She pushed at him with her hands. 'Go.'

So Paul went. He didn't believe her but, still, he went – his shoes squeaking down the hospital corridor, the sound getting fainter and fainter and then disappearing altogether as he turned a corner, took the escalator back down to ground level, and followed the exit signs out into the street.

Listening, listening – long after there was nothing more to hear, Marianne ran her fingers over the wrapping of the flowers he'd brought . . . aware that, squeaking away from her, down that corridor, was the best chance of security and love she could possibly have hoped for.

The following morning, Marianne received a brief visit from George Franklin. He couldn't stay long. He was only dropping by to make sure she was okay, to find out if he could do anything for her, particularly with the business. He also felt he should let her know where he was at in his search for Jay.

The main problem had been Jay's mobile. Unreliable at the best of times, this mobile must finally have given out, and Jay – being Jay – would hardly have considered it a priority to have the thing mended . . . all of which had made George's job considerably harder.

But not impossible. He still hadn't managed to speak to his brother, but didn't think it would be long now. He'd spoken to Anusha. He'd spoken to Hassan. And with good information from the pair of them, together with certain brotherly assumptions, he'd been able to follow Jay's erratic trail from various remote locations in Thailand, to Tokyo, and finally on to New York. It had taken some time to find out where Jay was staying, but George had done it. He had the number with him, written out neatly on a slip of paper.

Marianne took it. 'So shall we dial it, then?'

'We could.' George glanced at his watch, and back at Marianne. 'Although it would be about four a.m. in New York . . .'

Marianne closed her eyes.

'. . . not that that's a problem,' he added. 'In fact, I'm sure we could get the hotel to wake him. It's not like you're calling for a chat. But—'

'It's okay,' she said, taking the number. 'I've waited so long . . . what's another couple of hours?'

For a moment, they sat in silence – and then George sighed.

'I'm so sorry,' he said.

Marianne shook her head.

'No – please. Please listen. Let me say this, Marianne. I should never have shouted at you like that. You and Paul . . . what business was it of mine? It must have been horrendous for you. Excruciating. And what with everything else you've had on your plate these past few weeks, so much to cope with: the business, and Gabriella, and Jay never around . . . I'm amazed you kept going for as long as you did.' His tone switched. 'And I can't help thinking that I – that my appalling outburst . . .'

'Stop it, George. You've nothing to apologise for. There's nothing to forgive. If anything, I should be *thanking* you. For coming back – for finding me in the first place.'

'Thank God I did.'

'You got me to hospital. You even got me this swanky room.'

They both smiled.

'I gather it was quite a battle . . .'

They chatted a little longer: about his fight for her hospital room, and then about Gabby – whom George and Helen had visited at the weekend.

'She's doing well,' he said brightly. And then, rather more awkwardly – and in a way that made Marianne suspect that she'd done nothing of the sort – added: 'She sent her love. Was so sad to hear what happened . . .'

Gab never sent love. It wasn't her style, and they both knew it.

George reached for his coat. 'Well – I'd better get on,' he said, standing up, putting it on. 'They're keeping tabs on me at work at the moment. Makes me feel like a schoolboy!' He kissed her cheek. 'Can I do anything? Open a window? Get you some water? Call someone?'

Marianne shook her head. She was fine. She had everything she needed, or could admit to needing – to George, at any rate.

'Not even your mother?' he said suddenly. 'You sure I can't call her for you?'

Marianne hesitated, newly aware that her instinct to refuse – to conceal, on principle, anything remotely significant from her mother – was, in fact, rather self-defeating. Immature. Something the old Marianne might have done. Patricia was hardly the enemy. And while she shrank from the idea of making the call herself, from explaining the complicated medical position, and the inevitable resurgence of pain that would come from the telling of the story to fresh ears, Marianne couldn't help but be taken with the idea of George doing it for her.

'You – you'd do that?'

'Of course.'

'Really?'

George smiled. 'Come on. Give me the number before I change my mind.'

Scribbling it down on a hospital envelope, Marianne passed the number over with a grateful smile.

And later – much later – when she recalled the brief conversation she eventually had with Jay (whose sadness had seemed somehow shallow – disengaged – against the New York background and his time in Thailand and Japan . . . he was distant, in every way), and the fact that Gabriella hadn't bothered to get in touch, or even send a message via George, Marianne couldn't help but feel ashamed of her own judgement; ashamed that meek Sophie Mostyn and Cityboy George Franklin had – at the critical moment – proved better friends to her than Gabby or Jay ever would.

Chapter Seventeen

Marianne was recovering – at least, her body was. The doctors were pleased with the progress she'd made. The onset of breast milk was heartbreaking, of course – how could it be otherwise? She felt emptied – emotionally and spiritually, as much as bodily – and while she couldn't see how the dreadful vacuum in her soul would ever be put right, at least her leaky body was doing what it was supposed to be doing. Yes, it would take another month or two for the old rhythms to settle – for everything to return completely to normal – but there was no real need for Marianne to remain in hospital any more. And no medical reason to think that – when the moment was right, and she felt ready – any future pregnancy would be similarly blighted. The doctors were most emphatic about that point. Their job was done. From a physical point of view, the trauma was over.

And so, with an autopsy no longer necessary, it seemed right to start thinking about laying little Maya to rest . . . a process that was, in truth, rather more complicated than it sounded for – in strict terms, and according to Church law – Maya was not deemed ever to have lived. There were, however, a number of ways around the problem – ways that Patricia's local vicar in Kent was more than happy to approve. A formal funeral might be out of the question but a blessing, words of comfort, that sort of thing . . . he'd be honoured to officiate. Marianne was hardly in the mood to quibble over matters of doctrine. Indeed, to her grieving ear, *words of comfort* sounded almost preferable to a funeral, and so the service was set for Friday, in Kent, at Patricia's local church. It just seemed so much simpler to do it down there, let Patricia liaise with her kind, accommodating vicar, sort out the details, host the wake.

Jay wouldn't like it. He'd never found Patricia easy, and her house was a source of mild torture for him. The extreme tidiness; the insistence that all meals – including breakfast – should be exactly on time; the immaculate sofas he couldn't put his feet up on; the pristine kitchen, the way Jay could never just wander in and help himself to something from the fridge . . . it amazed him that Marianne could tolerate it at all, that she hadn't 'flipped' – as he put it – years ago.

But Marianne had rather lost interest in keeping Jay happy. She didn't care what time his flight was due that evening; certainly didn't wait for him to collect her from the hospital. She was ready to go. Her mother – who, in any case, with her comfortable car and natural efficiency, would do a much better job of helping her leave the hospital – was all ready to pick her up and take her home to Kent.

Marianne sat in the passenger seat, looking out of the window at the rain-bespattered scenery: at fashionable London, where the wetness glistened; and at unfashionable London, where it was merely soggy.

'So what time do you think he'll arrive?' said her mother, stopping at a light.

Marianne had no idea.

'Before supper, do you think?'

'I don't know, Mum. He didn't give me a flight number. Just said he'd be arriving tonight sometime.'

'Tonight . . .' Patricia pondered. 'So that's too late for supper, then?'

'I guess so.'

Patricia sighed. 'It would help to know how many to cater for, darling. That's all. I was thinking lamb might be nice. There's enough at home for the two of us, but if Jay's coming, I'd need to make another trip to Waitrose this afternoon . . . which I'm more than happy to do. But there's no point in my going all that way –'

'I think you can assume he won't be here for supper,' said Marianne.

A dissatisfied silence filled the car.

'Or assume he *will* be here – I don't care, Mum; I really don't care. And throw it away if he's not. Does it matter?'

By the time Jay did get there – close to midnight, clutching a bottle of duty-free Scotch . . . a bottle he'd no intention of giving to Patricia – Marianne was almost ashamed by just how pleased she was to see him. The weary resentment she'd felt towards him that morning as she'd left the hospital had – in the intervening hours – evaporated, to be replaced by something oddly close to gratitude. It made her sad. She loved her mother. Respected her, admired her – knew her to be a good, kind woman – and yet . . . Jay might have been flawed – frustrating, unreliable, neglectful – but Marianne could see that there was also a wonderful simplicity about the

253

company of someone truly selfish. And, in the end, it was the very oppression of her mother's love that put Jay in such a favourable light. After a day spent on the receiving end of extreme hospitable concern, generated by Patricia's passionate need to be a good mother, good hostess, good housekeeper . . . after so much effort and fuss, Marianne found it a huge relief to be with Jay. He was an easy presence. Relaxed in his faults. Without lifting a finger – indeed, precisely because he wouldn't lift a finger – he gave more to Marianne that day than her poor, frazzled mother ever could.

Although there were certain other things that Patricia provided – not least, the pills she urged Marianne to take the morning of the church service – pills that could dull the pain. And while it meant that much of the service passed in a haze, perhaps that was no bad thing. She didn't break down, or collapse in floods of tears. And there was something about keeping an outward look of strength and dignity that affected how she felt on the inside. For sure, the pills helped – as did the sight of so many friends in the church that day. The keen sense of gratitude she felt towards them all, which was very real and very strong, was oddly effective when it came to keeping all those other emotions in check. She'd thought it would be a tiny congregation – just herself and Jay, her mother, a well-meaning uncle or two. Instead, the little church was almost full. And to see such a very big contingent from the workshop – Lee, Mike, Melinda, Kerry, Faith, all there, all wanting to support her – Marianne was touched to the core. Sophie was there too. Marianne spotted her standing, with typical self-effacement, in the least conspicuous part of the church.

And then, just as she was looking around for Jay, who'd been beside her in the pew a moment ago but was now no longer there . . . poor Jay, who hadn't slept at all last night, who'd been looking ghastly, who'd barely said a thing all morning, and hadn't touched his breakfast – she was worried about him . . . just at that moment, he reappeared with Anusha at his side and led her into Marianne's pew.

Anusha leant across her son. She squeezed Marianne's hand. And Marianne, squeezing back, was astonished at the sense of peace she felt. That so many people understood that this was so much more than a failed pregnancy: that a baby had been lost, that Maya was real, that Marianne's bereavement was valid, as valid as any other. The sense of recognition she gained from seeing all those people in church with her that day, and Anusha in particular . . . the relief, for Marianne, was physical. It was as if she'd spent the last week under water, holding her breath in a muffled world – as if all her proper, natural rhythms had been suspended – and it was only now that the air could flow again. She was back above the water. Oxygen flooded her system.

But Anusha did not stay long. After telling Marianne what a beautiful service it was, and how very glad she was to have made it; after insisting that Marianne come back out to Galle for a good long holiday – come as soon as possible – 'Just let me know when it suits, Marianne. Any time is good.' Anusha said her goodbyes. She was sorry to be leaving so soon, but she had a car waiting – the same car that had met her at the airport that morning; that had all her luggage in the boot – and she should really get going. Anusha wasn't worried about the expense of this car. It was simply that – having made the immense effort to be with Jay and Marianne in time for the service – she was now exhausted. She needed her hotel bed.

'You do know you can always stay here, don't you? My mother would love to have you – there's room enough . . .'

Anusha sighed. Tactfully but determinedly, she held to her original plan. The hotel was booked. The car had waited. There were things – boring but necessary things – that she needed to do in London tomorrow, people to see . . . it was really much easier this way. She hoped Marianne didn't mind too much.

'Of course not.' Marianne accompanied her out on to the gravel. There were tears in her eyes. 'How can I mind when you came all this way?'

Anusha paused at the car door. Saying nothing, she looked at Marianne for a moment – and then kissed her, squeezing Marianne's shoulder as she did so. It was the same gesture – wordless, yet infinitely articulate – as the one she'd made in church.

Marianne smiled.

But the smile was premature. For, moments later, there was a scraping sound . . . and Marianne turned to see Jay emerging from the house, dragging his old suitcase over the steps.

'Is there room?' he said, hauling it across the gravel and handing it to the driver. 'I don't mind having it beside me on the back seat, if that helps.'

'Jehan . . .'

'You can go in the front, can't you, Mum? It's only an hour to London. An hour at the most –'

'I'm thinking of Marianne.'

Jay couldn't quite look at Marianne. 'I'm sorry,

Smidge.' He sighed. 'I'm not good at funerals. Not good with your mother.'

Marianne looked at the sharp bright green of her mother's lawn, soaked in winter rain.

'I'm knackered, Smidge.'

'So am I.'

'Then it's probably best, don't you think? We can both get a quiet night. I'll take Mum back to London, and you can stay here – and maybe come up tomorrow?'

Marianne said nothing.

'Or whenever you're ready . . .'

She looked at the sky: grey, heavy, closing in. It was about to rain again.

'I'll call you tonight, shall I?'

Not waiting for Marianne to reply, Jay kissed her goodbye. Marianne stood very still, feeling the ghost of pressure that his lips had made upon her cheek. She thought of all the things she might have said to him – the rage she might have expressed, the disdain, the longing for more support. But she had no energy. No energy, and – perhaps more importantly – no faith that her needs would be met. Not in the way she wanted. And so, with a certain sleepwalking blankness of spirit, she let him go – as she'd let him go a thousand times before . . . watching the car ease off across the gravel, the little stones crunching under its wheels, the orange flash of the indicator at the gate, the smooth manoeuvre into the road.

She went back inside – opening the front door to find a group of people in the hallway: some just chatting, a couple on the verge of departure. Numb, she made her way through them – and it was only when she reached the far side of the room that she heard Sophie Mostyn's voice.

'Let *me* do that,' she was saying.

Marianne turned to see her sitting alone on the bottom step of the staircase, face to the wall, talking into a mobile as she fastened the buttons on her coat.

'Really, Paul. You've got more than enough to deal with at the moment. It's no trouble. I can easily . . .' Longer pause. 'I know. But . . . Okay, then – how lovely! And I'll get the wine! All right, darling. Love you . . .'

Marianne moved on unnoticed back into the sitting room, to where the rest of the party had dwindled to four or five.

'Here she is!' said her mother. 'Darling, where's Anusha? I was wondering if she wanted to stay on with us tonight? I'm sure she'd like to be with Jay, wouldn't she? Do ask her. It would be no trouble. There's fish pie in the freezer – I could easily defrost it in time . . .'

The house was quiet that night – with only two of them there, and neither inclined to talk. The sudden departure of Jay without even bothering to say goodbye to Patricia, or thank her, or anything . . . it was hard not to take it as a snub. Even when Marianne explained that it was only Jay and Anusha not wanting to break up the party, or interrupt things with their farewells, even that didn't really wash. Patricia wasn't impressed. And it was only when Marianne spotted a pile of mail on the kitchen table – mail addressed to her, at the showroom address – that a conversation of sorts took place.

'What's this?'

Her mother rinsed a saucepan. 'What's what, darling?' she said, with her back still to the room and the tap still running.

'This mail, Mum –'

The flow of water stopped. 'Oh God,' said Patricia, turning. 'I'm sorry, darling – I forgot to say. George left it. He seemed to think that with Gabby off work and you . . .' she hesitated – 'you off too – that somebody ought to drop by the showroom and make sure everything's okay . . . and it is, apparently. It's all fine. No break-ins. No disasters. But he brought your mail down. Wasn't sure when you'd next have a chance to go into work, what with—'

'George was here? George Franklin?'

Patricia nodded. 'For the church, at any rate. He couldn't make it here afterwards though. He had to get back to work, I think. But he did send his apologies, and gave your mail to Uncle David who, I have to say, thought he was charming . . .'

Marianne smiled – a small, tired smile. Why wasn't she surprised?

'. . . and full of praise for your business, apparently.'

Marianne picked up the small pile of envelopes and took them to her bedroom. She wished she'd seen George, wished she'd spoken to him. Thinking briefly of the old days, and the old George – smug, moneyed, patronising, detached – it amazed her how much he'd changed. Or she'd changed. Whichever it was, she'd never have had him down as the sort of man who'd go out of his way to attend the 'funeral' of an illegitimate, stillborn child of Marianne's. Certainly, she'd never have regretted missing him. It was kind, really kind of him, to have come; to have bothered to bring this mail for her; to have been so very nice about the business to her uncle.

Except that it was precisely this kindness – and the kindness she'd heard taking place between Paul and Sophie earlier, kindnesses that other people seemed to give out so easily, so willingly – that made the contrast with Jay so very hard to stomach. It wasn't that Jay was unkind. It wasn't that Jay didn't try. But nothing – *nothing* – ever happened in Jay's life on terms that weren't his own. Marianne couldn't imagine him actually refusing her. If she'd said, earlier, that she really wanted him to stay with her tonight, that she needed him with her . . . if she'd begged, then he probably would have taken that suitcase out of the car and heaved it back inside again – but she'd always have to ask. Directly. And, consequently, always feel indebted for the kinds of things that others got for free.

Sure, Jay had other qualities – but could those other qualities outweigh this fundamental lack of generosity? Marianne wasn't sure. A year ago, she'd have said 'yes!' without hesitation. Perhaps even last night, when she'd so embraced the lightness of his love, there was much to be said for it . . . that is, until the lightness grew so light that it was barely there at all – when, in all honesty, it felt more like neglect.

Sitting on her bed with her bag and her letters, Marianne looked at her mobile. There were three messages, none of them from Jay. Just one from Fiona the maternity nurse, sounding rather nice, saying she'd got Marianne's message and that she had no intention of keeping the deposit; she'd be sending it back next week . . . then a sales call; and the last – interestingly – from Gabriella.

'Marianne.' Pause. 'George told me, darling. I'm so sorry. Don't know what to say really – you must be feeling shit. I know I would be . . .' Long sigh. 'Anyway, I've left the clinic. They're a bit annoyed with me. Apparently, I should have stuck it for three months or something *completely grim* . . . which I couldn't help thinking was only in their interest when they're charging me five or six grand a week, or whatever it is. On that basis, they'd keep me there for good, don't you think?' Laughter. 'So I thought, fuck it – and left. And anyway, I'm better. Or kind of better. Not ready for work yet, of course, but . . . you know. On the mend. Except,' another sigh, 'I'm sorry, Marianne . . . I just think a funeral would have been a bit much. I hope you don't mind. After Dad's one, I swore I'd never go to a funeral again – and I think that's probably the right way to go. I'd be no good to you, that's for sure. And you've got everyone else, haven't you? You don't need me as well . . . so this call is just to let you know I'm thinking of you and all that. And do call me when you're back in London. I'm around this weekend . . . well, anyway – better go. Lots of love, Mazza. Big kiss –'

Marianne listened. She replayed the message, and listened again. And – after a third repeat – knew that, in those minutes, something about her view of Gabriella had changed for ever. She felt Gab's affection, and returned it. She knew that Gab was 'doing her best' – or what she believed to be her best – except, of course, it wasn't. It was merely typical of someone who was an utter joy to be with when life was going well, and utterly weak, utterly evasive, utterly lacking in substance when true friendship was actually required.

She put the mobile back into her bag, and turned to her unopened letters . . . more from a need for some distraction than any real interest in their contents. She could see that most of it was junk – leaflets and advertising guff, with plastic wrappings and bright pictures, and her name spelt slightly wrong. Amongst

261

this, there were a few bona fide envelopes: a bank statement, an invoice from the Box Company, a cheque from Lady Butterworth . . . all reassuringly normal. There was a sweet note from some bride whose ring she'd made last year – a woman who'd written, out of the blue, simply to say how much she still loved her ring. It gave her pleasure every day.

The last envelope was addressed in plain capital letters and had 'by hand' scrawled across the top in rather more familiar writing. She tore it open with a strange sort of tightness round her heart, and found inside a handwritten card from Paul with a small orange-pink stone taped roughly to the back.

I'm not sure when you'll get this, Marianne – but I don't really know what else to do. Of course I'd prefer to see you in person, but I'm pretty sure you wouldn't want that – and the last thing I want to do is upset you, not when you have so much else on your plate at the moment. So I'm dropping it round instead, and hoping – praying – you don't mind.

Please take it, Marianne. Make Sophie's ring with that other stone – it's perfectly nice and she'll be perfectly happy – and keep this one as your own. It's yours. It should always have been yours – you, who can really appreciate it; you, who truly understand what it means – not only in itself, but for what it says about my feelings for you (which, I'm afraid, will never change, although I do understand that yours have. Or maybe they were never what I took them to be? Who knows. But I do accept your decision. I won't be asking you again – not that, at any rate).

The thought that you might still keep this stone as a present from me; the thought that you might make it into something beautiful, something you can wear often, something that might, from time to time, remind you of my

*love . . . please, Marianne? . . . would mean so much to me
(and, I hope, in a way, to you too?) – for you to hold
something tangible and unique that can say you were once
adored; that, in truth, you always will be – albeit from a
distance.*

Forever – P

*ps – I'm sorry about Sophie coming to the service. I couldn't
really stop her – not without it sounding odd.*

Marianne looked at the poor, suffocated padparascha,
at the way it had been stuck to the stiff beige card,
bound and taped like some sort of hostage by someone
with no sense of its inherent beauty . . . someone who
saw it merely as a symbol of something else.

    Gently, lovingly, she eased it free and threw away
the tape.

Chapter Eighteen

With just a month to go until Christmas, Marianne was back at Hatton Garden, climbing the staircase to the workshop.

It was as if nothing had happened. The carpet was still grey, still threadbare, still emitting its stale old smell of coffee and fags mixed with something rather more toxic from the studios on the floor below. The light on the second floor still hadn't been fixed. Together with the familiar voices from the top level, voices that grew louder as she climbed – Kerry's misleadingly girlish one, giving out basic information about working hours to some random caller, and Mike's – further off – shouting for someone to bring him a cloth – it all, at some collective level, displayed an absolute indifference to Marianne's troubles, indifference that was simultaneously callous and reassuring – life's convoy rattling on, and taking Marianne with it. In many ways, it presented the swiftest ride out of her current sadness – so long as she could resist the urge to drop away at the side of the road, sit on her bags, and weep.

They were all very pleased to see her – Kerry smiling

through the tinsel-framed security porthole and making the other person stand aside so that she could let Marianne through to the inner sanctum; Melinda emerging from the office for no particular reason other than to say hello; Mike turning off his machinery, standing in the doorway, pretending to polish a silver goblet while he called out for Lee – hard at work in the next room with the radio at top volume . . .

'Oi, Leester. You've got a visitor.'

The radio fell silent. Mike winked at Marianne. 'It's all ready,' he said. 'Your stuff, at any rate. It's been mad this year. Been working evenings – all of us . . . it's a—'

'Hello, love,' said Lee, coming through, wiping his hands, heading straight for the safe. 'Right. I think we've got them all . . .' He took out a bunch of brown packets and read through the names, looking up at Marianne after each one to check he had it right.

'That last one got me,' he added, handing them over. 'Not sure I've ever worked with a –' squinting forward at the packet in Marianne's hands, at the description on the back, 'pad-pada-'

'Padparascha.'

Lee laughed.

'They're rare, Lee.'

'Well, that's a relief.' He grinned at her. 'Embarrassing for me if they weren't.'

Marianne smiled.

Lee was glad to see her smiling – the weight loss worried him, and that tight expression on her face he'd seen the other day as she'd hurried down the steps to the underground trains at Farringdon, lost in thought. He put a hand on her shoulder.

'You going away this Christmas?'

Marianne hesitated.

'You could do with a holiday, love. Know what I'm saying? It's all very well, you coming back to work – and we're right behind you, sweetheart; all of us – we think you're doing great. But a bit of time in the sun . . . it would do you no end of good, Marianne. It—'

'Little bird told me she's off to Sri Lanka in January,' said Melinda, coming in with two mugs of coffee.

Marianne thanked her. Taking the mug, she rested against a window frame. 'Well, that's the plan,' she conceded. 'Jay's taking me. But—'

'But nothing,' said Lee. 'You're going. End of.'

'Except it isn't that simple, Lee. I do have a business to run. I can't just up sticks and head off into the blue. It—'

'Yes, you can. Princess is back now, isn't she?'

Marianne hesitated. 'In a way . . .'

'Well, nothing new there, eh? She's never been exactly what you'd call full time.'

Marianne's lips twitched.

'Go on, love. She'd cope for a week or two, wouldn't she?'

He was right, of course. Gab was better now. She was out of the clinic, seemingly fine, returning to work with that combination of good company and dodgy professional standards that was uniquely Gab. More welcome than not . . . but only just. In any case, Gab could cope – especially in January, when business was dead. And it wasn't as if Marianne would be completely out of contact. She could always come home if it got too much. There was no real reason for her not to join Jay and Anusha. Except . . . except . . .

It wasn't really the business, of course. It was Jay, and Anusha, and the whole question of where Marianne

266

was going with her life. Having expected her world to be turned upside down by the arrival of a baby, it was now being turned upside down for precisely the opposite set of circumstances. Having geared herself up for a future of commitments and responsibility, for a certain loss of freedom, for a lifetime of parenting with Jay and the lot of a working mother – it was disconcerting to be facing a future where anything was possible again. She could go anywhere, do anything. That freedom she was so scared of losing – it was cruelly hers again.

But losing a baby shouldn't mean that Marianne had to lose everything else as well. Pale, silent, tiny Maya was never going to live, or cry, or laugh, or grow, or smile, or open her eyes . . . Marianne's little one was gone. And while she knew that there was a part of herself that would never quite get over the loss, Marianne also knew there was no need for the entire structure of her life to collapse because of it. Yet the inclination to drop the lot – and Jay in particular – it pressed at her. And because she knew that the inclination was distorted, because she felt that her relationship with Jay should stand or fall because of something inherent – something purely between themselves, their characters, or what they wanted from life – Marianne told herself it was something to resist. She'd chosen Jay first; and Maya had followed. It was that way round. So all the things that had drawn her to Jay in the first place still existed, Maya or no Maya. Remembering the way she'd felt when she'd seen him arrive at her mother's house – remembering how she longed for him when he was away; and, going further back now, to how *right* it had all felt at the beginning . . . she stayed with Jay. She accepted the invitation to

Galle. She stuck with the idea of them being together. Because to do anything else seemed, to Marianne, to be somehow letting the darkness spread.

And then, of course, there was Paul. But Marianne had made her decision where Paul was concerned – a decision that, for all the pain it brought her, was one she still believed in. She wouldn't take Paul from Sophie. Paul was out of the picture now. And the only question that remained for Marianne was, in feeling the way she'd felt about Paul, was it now right that she should coast along with Jay? For even though those feelings seemed to be fading, she guessed the answer was 'no'. In the context of Paul, she should really be ending it with Jay, shouldn't she? Or was that just rather foolish, given that Paul was no longer an option?

She didn't know . . . she didn't know . . .

The strands were tangled and knotted. Marianne could make no sense of it. All she knew, for sure, was that the idea of making further life-changing decisions was absolutely beyond her. And so she drifted on – accepting the invitation to Galle in the hazy belief that, one way or another, something would be decided vis-à-vis Jay. Certainly, it was better to make the decision with him close at hand, and not thousands of miles away at the end of a crackling line.

For Jay – back in New York again, completing his business there – was already embracing the old ways. He'd done his best with Marianne before he'd left. He'd given a whole extra week to her, making sure she was okay with the idea of him travelling again, making sure she was strong enough, and happy enough to go back to work herself – up and running, on the mend, tick, tick, tick – before, bit by bit, extracting himself and returning to his natural habitat – up above the clouds again: alone, nomadic, free.

And soon she would be joining him. Very soon she, too, would be on her way to Galle – stretching her body in the tropical heat, splashing in the waves, examining the latest hand of gemstones with him . . . all the old things they'd shared before could be hers again. Perhaps it wasn't all finished between them. Perhaps there was still hope.

Lee was right. She should go – go and rediscover.

It was cold in the showroom. The central heating wasn't working. On her first day back (and while Marianne had still been with her mother), Gabby had taken it upon herself to turn the system up full-blast . . . and the system couldn't cope. Having only been installed that summer as part of their renovation project, it had not been properly synchronised with the existing boiler – which, despite thorough testing back in August, had now crashed under the strain. And Gabby, being Gabby, had not felt equal to the task of calling in a plumber. Instead, she'd merely waited for Marianne's return, and it was only now that the matter was in hand. A plumber was due that afternoon.

Gab was sitting at the desk wearing a new camel coat, a scarf and gloves, and with an electric fire at her feet, when Marianne opened the door. She was on the telephone.

'One moment, Dex.' With the receiver in one hand, Gab reached towards Marianne for her attention. 'You don't mind if I go now, do you? No sign of your plumber, I'm afraid. But—'

'That's fine. Go.'

'You're sure?'

Marianne nodded. She didn't mind waiting. She had a full afternoon's work ahead of her, and – feeling the way she did about Gabby these days – it was probably better to have the place to herself.

It wasn't that Gab had changed. She was, in many ways, as funny and irreverent as ever – especially when it came to talking about the clinic, the staff, the other patients, and all the little rituals that they'd been made to perform. She was still entertaining, still happy to defer to Marianne on business matters. She was warm. She was bright and up-beat – unsettlingly so, sometimes, after what she'd been through – but that had to be better than doom and gloom. Indeed, on the surface, she seemed to have been entirely unscarred by what had happened. And Marianne, listening to the chatter, to Gab's thoughts on the whole issue of such places – her opinion that, by and large, her particular clinic had been a waste of time, that George had been wrong to take her there and, frankly, a little stupid to have paid those extortionate fees when two weeks at a spa in the Seychelles would have been infinitely preferable, cheaper, more effective . . . Marianne did begin to wonder if she had a point. Perhaps taking his sister to that clinic had been an overreaction on George's part. Perhaps there had been nothing wrong – not seriously wrong – with her at all . . .

Not that that negated what George had done for his sister, of course. The way he'd been there for her, stepping in and taking over, rising to the challenge . . . those actions seemed finally to have answered some half-formed question that had – Marianne suspected – been lurking at the heart of Gabriella's psyche ever since her father's death. She was still protected and valued. George did care, and had proved it –

comprehensively. So while it might have been true that, strictly speaking, Gab had had no need of the clinic – that the problem itself may not have been so bad – there was, nonetheless, something very healing about the way her brother had reacted, the display of concern, the willingness to support. It struck Marianne that 'overreaction' on George's part was exactly what Gab had craved.

Except a breakdown on that scale – a breakdown involving that degree of medical involvement, and George no fool . . . there was another part of Marianne that knew it must have been serious. Gab's struggle had been real – was, perhaps, still real. She just wasn't showing it, preferring to act happy, act positive, and pretend it had all been a storm in a teacup . . . hoping all the while to trick herself into genuine happiness; opening herself to possibilities that, previously, she might have discarded to the extent that she was even now dating the middle-aged American that George and Helen had introduced her to a couple of months ago.

Dexter. Poor maligned Dexter who, contrary to Marianne's suspicions, had plainly been exonerated from any sort of responsibility for Gabby's collapse – and, reportedly, was only sad not to have seen more of Gabby in New York back then, sad not to have been more help to her . . . this same Dexter was now in London again, and indulging Gabby wherever possible. Since leaving the clinic, she'd been taken out to dinner every night bar one – and had what looked like a whole new set of clothes. Rather more classic clothes, Marianne noted, than the ones she normally associated with her friend: a camel coat; a discreet pair of flats in chocolate leather with a sleek silver buckle; and a matching handbag that was so 'Helen' in its

271

conception, Marianne wondered for a moment if Gab was being ironic. Except, of course, she wasn't. She loved her new handbag. Marianne could tell – from the way it sat beside her on the desk, instead of at her feet; the way she put her mobile back into its special compartment, redoing the catch with a smile of the deepest satisfaction.

'And he's taking me to Paris,' Gabriella said, chuckling, breath visible in the chill.

Marianne raised her eyebrows.

'Tonight, can you believe it? We're going Eurostar. First class. We're staying at the Costes, where we're meeting some friends of his who have a retail business in . . . I don't remember exactly, it might be Colorado – and then we're going to do some Christmas shopping.' Still laughing, she gave Marianne a sidelong glance. 'You think he might propose?'

'Gabby . . .'

'Yes, yes. All right. But,' – brightening again – 'he might, mightn't he? I mean, he's not getting any younger, and he likes me. I know he likes me. He wants to settle down, he's told me as much –'

'What time's your train?'

'Five-thirty. There is a later one, but—'

'Better get a move-on, then.'

The lining of Gab's coat swished as she stood up. She grabbed her precious bag. 'Thanks, Mazza, wish me luck!'

The door swung shut. Marianne heard Gabby's footsteps tap-tapping down the mews and wondered, for a moment, what was really going on. Yes, Gab was being flippant. And yes, it seemed that she was far from sentimental about the situation with Dexter: happy to bang on about his money and his lifestyle, happy to cast herself in the role of ruthless pragmatist – gold-digger, even – almost going out of her way to emphasise the idea of herself as a predator. Because actually to care for someone, actually to be touched by the concern that Dexter was showing – filling the shoes left by Gab's father, a father she still clearly needed (for George, however supportive he'd been on this occasion, could only ever be a stopgap) . . . was Gab, in fact, infinitely more serious about this man than she could admit – even to herself? Noticing an uncharacteristic willingness to switch styles, prioritise differently, make that train on time, Marianne sensed something stirring in her friend. More had changed than Gab was letting on. A profound need – brought finally to the surface by her breakdown – combined with a possible solution . . . ? Put like that, the Gab-Dexter union seemed suddenly rather plausible. Desirable, even.

Smiling to herself as another train screeched past, Marianne returned to her afternoon workload.

It mainly involved informing her clients – those clients whose items she'd collected from Lee that day – that their pieces were now ready for collection. This she did by telephone and, aside from the designing itself, it was one of the most pleasurable parts of her job. The clients were always so excited. They also tended to be embarrassingly grateful – as if Marianne were doing the job for free, as if the money wasn't enough. And today would be particularly satisfactory. Most of the names on her list weren't expecting their pieces for at least a week. Some of them (the ones that didn't need a Christmas deadline) had even been warned that, because of Marianne's time in hospital, and then a backlog at the workshop throwing the scheduling awry, delivery of their pieces might be as late as February. So it was particularly sweet for Marianne to be giving good news for once; pleasing, to feel that she was on top of things again, to think that Lee and his boys had gone out of their way to prioritise her items, that they'd thought her worth the trouble.

Of the nine pieces she'd carried back from Hatton Garden that day, only one did not involve such a telephone call. Paul and Sophie's ring – set, as directed, with the inferior stone; the diffused pink sapphire from Thailand that had sat for so long in Tariq Ibrahim's old drawer and had only ever surfaced as part of a prank that had backfired . . . that ring was now also ready for delivery. But instead of calling to say that it was ready and to suggest that Paul come round to collect it, perhaps with Sophie – and, as was usual with such commisions, enjoy another glass of champagne – Marianne simply rang the courier company she used from time to time. These couriers were properly insured to carry priceless items of jewellery across London. They were also – more importantly – a means by which she could get round the inherent difficulties of a more personalised method of delivery.

The idea of calling Paul – of, perhaps, getting Sophie again by mistake . . . she simply couldn't do it. Not now. Not after the snippet of conversation she'd overheard at Maya's wake: Sophie on her mobile, so full of love and warmth. In many ways, it was this glimpse of their happiness – Sophie's happiness, in particular – that had driven Marianne's decision to accept the better stone. There was something about Sophie Mostyn that drove people to protect her – and Marianne was no exception. She liked Sophie. She wanted Sophie to be happy. She – hell – she'd laid aside her own needs so that Sophie could have hers: she'd given up Paul. And while it was a gesture that had, in the passing weeks, shown itself to be rather less painful than Marianne had expected, while there were moments when it felt less like sacrifice and more like relief . . . she still felt entitled to the stone; still didn't see why she shouldn't get to keep that exceptionally rare and beautiful crystal that only a handful of people in the world (a handful that included Marianne) could ever identify as being any different from the one in the box that was now addressed to Paul. It had been Paul's stone. He'd paid for it. And now he'd given it to Marianne. It was hers. Hers because she deserved it, recognised it, loved it. It was hers by right. Hers legally. Hers.

But it did involve deception – this keeping of the better stone. And Marianne's instinct to minimise the lie meant that it was only natural that she should prefer to deliver the lesser ring via courier, and so avoid any additional posturing that would come with a face-to-face handover.

Except there was no courier available. The operator was very sorry – she knew that Cooper Franklin were good clients, she wished she could help – but . . . what with the request being so last-minute, and it being a Friday afternoon, there was nothing she could do at this late stage. No courier was free until the following morning . . . and so – desperate, now, for a conclusion to the matter – Marianne resolved to drop it round herself, by hand, that very afternoon. It was still early. Both Paul and Sophie were sure to be at work. She could simply post it through Paul's Earl's Court letterbox with a short handwritten note, and be done. There was a degree of risk, of course: if anything went wrong, if the package failed to reach Paul's hands, she wouldn't be covered by the insurance. But Marianne was past caring about such matters. The value of the lesser stone was barely worth the cover, the chances of it going astray were – in any case – tiny, and the benefits of being able to draw a line under the whole affair, of not having to think about it any more, of things being finalised . . . all the benefits of a quick hand-delivery seemed suddenly compelling.

It wasn't far to Paul's little flat. With the money she'd be saving from not booking a courier, Marianne took a taxi. She asked it to wait as she ran down to the basement and – glad to see that his letterbox was big enough – swiftly lifted the flap and dropped the package in. It fell to the floor on the other side with a certain muted finality, a brief rustling roll . . . and then silence. Done.

Marianne returned to the showroom, feeling oddly empty. She paid the cab driver and went back inside, back to work. She let in the plumber, and made her other calls – the calls that should have made her happy, the calls she'd so looked forward to making – only . . . why were they suddenly so joyless? Why did she feel so flat, worse than flat, so full of a certain swelling and surging, a certain restless, sickening sensation she hadn't felt for years, not since her gem school exams, when a desperate-looking Gab – with a swift jerk of the chin – had persuaded Marianne to lift her arm aside from the paper so that she could see the answers.

She thought of the little brown package, sitting – out of reach – on the other side of Paul's letterbox . . . and, opening the safe once more she took the good stone out. She looked at it in the icy air, at the way the grey wintry light became transformed within its facets. Animated – warmed, seemingly from nowhere. But instead of marvelling at the quiet steady glow, instead of the sense of wonder it usually inspired in her, all Marianne felt was that same queasy sensation. And she knew, too, that every time she saw that subtle rosy beauty – in whatever capacity, down the line of her life – the feeling would only be the same. It wasn't hers. It was Sophie's. Sophie, who already had so much . . . but that, of course, was irrelevant.

Calling the workshop, she asked for Lee and explained she needed a replica.

'Sure,' said Lee, over the screech of Mike's machinery. 'We'll have to talk details some other time, love. It's all a bit tight here at the moment, as you know, but of course we can do a replica, so long as you have a suitable stone. And so long as your clients don't mind hanging on till January . . .'

January. Marianne's brain moved rapidly. Did it really matter, a few months' delay? Paul could easily make the swap. Sophie would never notice. It would all be fine. No need to upset the apple cart with Lee, who'd already done her so many favours. She wouldn't rest until the good stone was back where it belonged – it wouldn't be a comfortable time – but she could do it. The risk of discovery was tiny.

'All right,' she said, at last.

'You don't sound all right.'

'I'm fine, Lee. Honestly. January won't be a problem. I'll bring the new stone over, just in case you find the time . . . but – absolutely. Whenever suits. You've been such a star with all those other jobs – my clients love me – and it's much more important that *you* do the work.'

'Flattery . . .'

Marianne smiled.

Lee said he'd see what he could do – he'd let her know – and rang off, leaving Marianne alone again; alone in an empty showroom that, with a tick-tick-tick of radiator pipes, was slowly getting warmer again.

PART IV – SRI LANKA

Chapter Nineteen

It was raining the day Marianne left for Sri Lanka. Her Gatwick Express train, with its orange interior and smooth international announcements in every imaginable language, shot through the damp suburban landscape, and Marianne looked on with relief. Christmas with her mother, followed by two bleak weeks in London, had – perhaps predictably – converted that weary decision to accept Jay's invitation into something rather more positive. For time spent with her mother invariably made Marianne crave the opposite – an opposite that was embodied in Jay. She couldn't wait to be gone. And there was something about the sensation of speed that the train was giving her, together with the knowledge that everything she needed was packed away in two easy bags, that all the little pre-departure chores and tasks were done (or else it was simply too late and, frankly, did she care?), the brightness, the speed, the dank world flitting by and her detachment from it, the anonymity, the gaudy seats, the refreshments trolley with its miniature spirits bottles – something about all these things together that made Marianne feel very light. Almost her old self. If the carriage hadn't been full of people, she'd have lit a cigarette – blow the law, blow the consequences. It was that sort of moment.

For the process of packing up had, on a deeper level, encompassed rather more than Marianne's suitcase. And the feeling of lightness – it wasn't just about being on the road. It was about a conscience cleared, a wrong righted, a life in order again. And while there was a degree of wistfulness where Paul was concerned – of what might have been . . . if only this, if only that – Marianne was glad that the chapter was closed. Glad to be moving on. Settling back in her orange seat, turning her head to the window, she looked out at the dark January afternoon, through glass that was spattered with diagonal trails of rain, and recalled the events of the past fortnight with a pleasant sense of detachment.

With a few white lies and judiciously timed messages, she'd managed to avoid the wedding. She knew that Sophie would have been disappointed, especially when the latter had gone out of her way to come to Maya's service. She could see that the absence of a reciprocal gesture would, on the surface, have come across as ungenerous. But what else could she have done? Marianne refused to feel bad. Quite apart from the situation with Paul, which would have made attending infinitely worse, she couldn't help but think that the date Sophie had chosen – a Saturday between Christmas and New Year when most sensible people were either holed up with their families or, like Gabby, off on fancy skiing holidays with their lovers – hardly indicated a desire for hundreds of guests. As it was, the combination of bad weather and a nasty virus that was doing the rounds meant that Marianne was spoilt for choice when it came to finding a last-minute excuse to pull out.

Although, in truth, she was slightly baffled that she needed to pull out at all – that Paul himself hadn't found the courage to call a halt to the whole charade. It wasn't that Marianne expected him to continue pursuing her – not now: two knock-backs were clearly enough for any man – but nor could she quite believe what he was doing to poor Sophie. How could anyone claim to love one person and marry another? It shocked Marianne – the hardness of it, the apparent lack of sincerity. It seemed so uncharacteristic for a man like Paul, who was always so kind, so willing to put himself out for others, that his approach to marriage should, ultimately, be so casual. In his position, Marianne would certainly have called off the wedding, if not the entire relationship. And while she was aware that there were disconcertingly similar elements when it came to her own decision to drift on with Jay – a certain sort of weariness, a sense of being driven by habit rather than desire – she was also confident of the differences. Marianne wasn't about to walk up the aisle with Jay. She wasn't even sure that she would stay with Jay. She was going to Galle to see what – if anything – could be salvaged. And if Jay had ever shown a drop of the kind of love that Paul was offering, if Jay had been willing to give the way Paul had been willing to give, she'd never have looked elsewhere. Certainly not in Paul's direction. It was – and she was really only now just starting to understand this – it was Paul's love for her, not hers for him, that had made Marianne crave his company. Indeed, it was only because Jay had cared so little that she'd been susceptible to Paul's interest at all.

And so, for all her residual sense of sacrifice regarding Paul – her sense of having given up the one person who'd really loved her, someone she'd felt really knew (unlike Jay) what it was to love, someone who understood about *being there* – Marianne was also now starting to ask herself what kind of man Paul really was. For when she thought of the fast-track banker she'd first met, and then the ex who'd suddenly come back into her life – so low-key, with his corduroys and his bicycle and his church – and now this altogether shiftier character who seemed quite happy to say one thing and do another, Marianne couldn't help wondering if, in trying to do right by poor Sophie Mostyn, she'd in fact done the absolute opposite: that, far from having made a great deep sacrifice, she'd simply had a lucky escape.

One thing, however, was certain in all of this: she had to get that ring, that real ring, over to them as quickly as possible. Marianne knew that Sophie and Paul were taking a fortnight for their honeymoon – they'd be home the second weekend in January, just before she left for Sri Lanka – and she was determined to catch the moment. Lee had done his bit: the replica setting was perfect, the padparascha radiated authenticity. She could have arranged for it to be delivered straight to Paul's office the very same day she collected it from Hatton Garden. And it was only a sense that Paul might try to return it, or see her, or create some sort of fuss, that caused Marianne to wait until the last possible moment. If she was on an aeroplane to Colombo when he opened the packet, there really wasn't much he could do. He could try calling her at the showroom, but he would only get Gabby. He could try her mobile, but it wouldn't be switched on. And with any luck, by the time she did get back to London, Paul would have accepted her decision, switched the rings, and found some way to dispose of the lesser one.

It was certainly her best chance of closing off the whole unfortunate business. For Marianne was only too aware that, in ridding the showroom safe of its guilty secret package at the back, she was also clearing her conscience. Of course, it would have been thrilling to have had a padparascha of that quality slung around her neck or dangling from her wrist. It was stunning. She loved it, she'd wanted it, but not as a memento of Paul. Certainly not as a memento of the truer – lesser – Paul whom she'd glimpsed recently. And particularly not as a memento of the shameful person that she herself had become from spending time in his company. Because however much she disliked the idea of a stone that was so particularly beautiful in its own right being a symbol of something else – however much she found that traditional approach to jewellery so limiting, so ignorant – it wasn't something that, in this case, Marianne could ignore. More like a medal, the 'meaning' it now carried, the set of associations, the emotional context, the sense of right possession, the provenance, the *story*, had become so much more important to Marianne than the tangible stand-alone crystal. And for the sanity of all three people involved, that stone needed to be restored to its rightful place: on the large fourth finger of Sophie's freckled hand.

So the morning of Marianne's departure – which had mainly been set aside to spend with Gabby at the showroom, handing over the reins, making sure Gab understood the basics – that same morning also involved co-ordinating this all-important delivery. The courier arrived at eleven. And by five past, both he and Marianne had left the premises . . . the little ring, closeted in the security box on the back of the courier's bike, weaving this way and that in the wet London traffic, closer and closer to Paul's offices while Marianne sat in a taxi with her bags and her passport, heading in the opposite direction.

Galle was full of tourists, tourists of every variety: backpackers, culture-seekers, spa-addicts, sun-worshippers – together with certain migratory birds of privilege whose tax position and tendency to boredom kept them in a state of constant high-season, no matter what month it was. By February, they'd be off to their Alpine chalets, but now was prime time for Galle. Lower tides, wider beaches, balmy temperatures . . . it wasn't hard to see the attraction. And Helen, who'd suffered so deeply in recent months, with George threatening to leave his job and making her feel guilty every time she had her hair cut, poor put-upon Helen, wasn't going to miss out on this annual opportunity to see herself on equal terms with such people. Long before it had grown fashionable, Galle had been George's second home. First home, even. For – boarding schools aside – he and Gabby had spent the bulk of their childhood here in the sun at Anusha's *walawe*, keeping time in Basingstoke to a minimum. With their mother so fragile and their father so robust – and so ably supported by Anusha – it was an arrangement that, at the time, had suited all parties. And while, of course, since the death of her husband, Anusha now reigned supreme in her family house – while Helen couldn't treat the place as hers, exactly . . . nor did she hold back. She'd emailed Anusha in good time to let her know what dates they were looking at in the coming year and Anusha – ever courteous – professed herself delighted at the prospect of a visit from her stepson and his family.

So when Jay rang in mid-December to say that he and Marianne would also be coming home in January for a week or two of quiet recuperation, Anusha knew there'd be trouble. She couldn't cancel George and Helen. Nor could she mislead Jay, much as she longed to see him. Regretfully, she warned him that the quiet sanctuary that he and Marianne were hoping for would, in fact, be full of noisy Franklin children and competitive poolside dressing – it would hardly be ideal, especially with Marianne having just lost her baby . . .

But Jay wasn't put off by this. If anything, it made him more determined. He wasn't going to let Helen push him from the nest at the prime time of the year. He'd check with Marianne, of course, but they were coming home.

'And we're having the white bedroom, Mother.'

Anusha said nothing.

'Mother?'

'Yes, darling. I'm just a little concerned that they—'

'What's wrong with giving them the blue? It's perfectly nice. The children can go at the end of the passage.'

'And what about the nanny?'

'What about her? She can go in Gab's old room. Or the one by the laundry cupboard or – or anywhere, frankly. She's the god-damn *nanny* . . .'

Safe at the end of the telephone line, Anusha rolled her eyes. Jay already had his own bedroom and bathroom at the house. There was plenty of space, and a double bed. He and Marianne had never objected before. The White Room, meanwhile – with its position at the far end of the house, and two adjoining bedrooms and smaller box room – was the obvious place for a family and a nanny. The fact that it also had a giant four-poster, and an outside shower, and its own special path down to the pool, that it was private, luxurious, and beautifully finished – such things should have been irrelevant . . . but weren't, and Anusha wasn't blind to what was really going on. She understood completely why Jay was insisting on this superior room over the others. It wasn't about bedrooms at all. And for all Jay's playing up, Anusha knew he had a point.

Which was why, on arrival, Marianne found herself unexpectedly elevated. She'd been to Anusha's house before, of course – a number of times – but had never been honoured with the White Room, and was touched by what she took to be Anusha's concern for her comfort.

Jay had said nothing about it in the car. Combining the trip to Colombo airport with a few business matters in town, he'd then collected Marianne and the pair of them had journeyed together down to Galle. But instead of addressing the subject of sleeping arrangements, he preferred to talk of his progress at work: the new emporium that was opening in Pettah and the dealing opportunities it presented. It was an easy subject for them both, and Marianne – whose excitement about leaving England had somewhat obscured the problem of Jay and whether they had a future . . . Marianne had been glad of the neutrality. He'd kissed her at the airport – kissed her on the mouth as if nothing had changed – but she'd found it oddly difficult to respond. She'd turned for her suitcase a little too quickly. She'd disappeared into a restroom for a moment, hoping that it was only tiredness. Sleep and sunshine – that was what she needed. She was glad that Jay didn't seem to have noticed. With his attention now held by the road, he was more than happy to talk shop or amuse Marianne with tales of Helen and the children, who'd arrived three days ago and had taken over the house . . .

George had been delayed. With Helen refusing to spend Christmas with his mother, and Gabby out of the country, he'd gone by himself to Basingstoke for a few days – days he should have spent at the office – and taken the inevitable hit: returning to work to find two new business development projects on his desk (new to him, at any rate), and meetings agreed in his absence . . . meetings that conflicted, absolutely, with his scheduled fortnight in Sri Lanka. The first week was lost. But the second was still salvageable and George, who was only too aware of Helen's feelings on the matter, had sworn that he would be joining her by the weekend.

Only Helen wasn't to be mollified. Full of contrition, George made special arrangements for his wife to fly business class – but it was all, in her view, woefully inadequate; especially when the soothing benefits of the upgrade were comprehensively shattered by the helter-skelter taxi-ride to Galle. Helen had stalked up the steps, leaving the nanny and the driver to deal with bags and children, and her mood did not improve when she saw where they'd be sleeping. She made no direct objection but the irritation was plain as she fussed about with the nanny as they unpacked, and ordered Anusha's staff about.

'I think we'll have to put the children all in one room.

Claudie's not sleeping well at the moment, and if they can't be near me at night – and what with Dolores down at the other end of the house – I'm sure they'd feel happier together. You can move another bed in here, can't you?'

Helen wouldn't drop it. Later that evening, with Anusha and Jay, she playfully nudged the latter and tried a different tack.

'So I see you've moved into our room, then!'

'*Our* room?' said Anusha, sharply, before Jay had a chance to speak. Anusha did not respond well to her staff being ordered around – especially poor old Sunitha, who'd once been Jay's ayah and could barely lift a pillow these days, let alone a bed. Sunitha was part of the family. It would be like ordering Anusha's grandmother to do the job . . . and, etiquette aside, couldn't Helen see that the woman was frail?

Helen tittered. 'I know it isn't *strictly* our room, Anusha,' she said. 'But I've grown so fond of it over the years – and you've always put us there in the past . . . I was interested. That's all.'

Anusha smiled.

Jay didn't.

Neither of them said a word.

Helen took a sip of wine. 'Although our new room is wonderful, of course – so comfortable . . . such pretty walls. I couldn't be happier! Honestly . . .'

Jay lay naked on the large white bed. He was laughing as he related the story while Marianne – who was only half listening – paced about in her dressing gown, unpacking the last of her things. The room had a warm old-gold glow that came from a combination of sources: from a fine pair of low-watt lamps on a small dressing table in the corner and from a series of candles that flickered in the antique mirrored wall-brackets, flickers that were echoed and re-echoed in the grey-spotted glass and every finely bevelled edge – and everything reflected again in a free-standing full-length boudoir-style mirror beyond the bed. The overtly soft-focus quality of the light – gleaming through the lace-fine mosquito mesh that shrouded the four-poster bed, brushing the black Dutch paintings on the chalky walls, shifting rhythmically over the ceiling with the slow circling of a large colonial fan – that mellow atmosphere – combined with the sounds of the crickets outside, the warm air, and Jay sprawled at the heart of it all, so beautiful and dark, so easy with his bare body, chuckling away to himself . . . the mood, the scene – the direction it was prompting – it could not have been more blatant. Only Marianne, discordantly and sensibly unpacking, remained immune.

She put a final pair of shoes in the cupboard, took out her washbag, and – shutting the suitcase – pushed it under the bed.

'Would you mind if I had a quick bath?'

'Not at all.' Jay rolled on to his stomach. Laughter gone, he looked at her – saw the hand reach out for the washbag, saw the swing of the bathroom door. He heard the lock as she shut it, and the thunder of water on enamel.

Marianne didn't hurry. By the time she was out, he was sleeping – curled away from her under the sheet, all candles extinguished.

In the days that followed, nothing changed – although it did grow easier. For Jay, believing that Marianne's body was still recovering from her time in hospital –

that her reasons for stalling were purely physical – Jay had no interest in pushing it. His mother had already warned him that Marianne would be frail.

'Don't expect too much from the poor girl,' Anusha had said with a particular look in her eye. No matter that they'd only been talking about what Marianne might want to do while she was over – with Jay, being Jay, wondering if a little stone dealing in Ratnapura might have interested her, or even a trip to Kandy – no matter that Anusha herself may not even have intended the comment to extend to the bedroom, Jay found himself recalling it that night. And again the next day: catching sight of Marianne in the outside shower – slimmer . . . it was nice that she was sexy again. He'd never much fancied the bump.

Don't expect too much.

Well, he wouldn't. He wasn't desperate – wasn't one of those men who couldn't function without sex. He could wait. She'd let him know when she was ready.

Except it was just too tempting for Marianne, whose body was fine and fully recovered, to leave him with that assumption and avoid the real issue . . . which was what, exactly? And that was part of the problem. For if Marianne herself didn't know, how could she begin to explain any of this to Jay? It wasn't as if Jay had changed. He was still the same man she'd fallen in love with back in London, when she'd stood with Gabby in the warm summer rain on the steps of the Bloomsbury house. It was Marianne who was different. Marianne who'd changed – emerging from the mess with Paul, a mess that had, nonetheless, opened her eyes to what was missing between herself and Jay. Marianne, no longer pregnant, no longer tied to Jay in that way, falling back on whatever it was that had drawn her to him in the first place . . . and wondering, all the time, if there was really anything left of their love. Or if, like Maya – for all that swelling and kicking, all that vigour . . . with so much promise of life – it was something never destined to last. For the same sense of *rightness* she'd had about Jay when she'd fallen pregnant – the sense that the natural world was conspiring in their love, approving it and giving it fruit – all that had been turned upon its head. And it was hard for Marianne not to feel a *wrongness* – an emptiness, a certain sort of pointlessness – at the heart of what they now were.

She wished with all her might that Helen had won the battle of the bedrooms.

Chapter Twenty

'All right, then. Get down. Just . . . *leave* it, Lola.'

There was a sound of breaking glass, followed by silence, and then Helen's voice again.

'No, don't stand there. Or there. What's wrong with you? You're . . . *What did I just say?*'

Marianne hesitated at the kitchen door, wondering if it might be better to wait a moment before getting her own lunch.

It was now Saturday and, much to Helen's envy (for while Helen had managed to dispatch two of her children with the nanny to the beach for the day, she hadn't been able to shed the littlest), Marianne had spent most of the morning dozing by the pool. Jay was working, Anusha had a coffee morning, and the younger women had the place to themselves. And after a while, tiring of toddler DVDs, Helen had tried to join Marianne. She'd dressed little Lola in a cute frilly bikini and large pink hat and the pair of them had made the slow journey through the garden, down towards the pool. For five minutes, it had been idyllic – until Lola, who'd yet to discover the restful charm of lying silently on her back, grew bored. She wandered towards the edge of the pool and demanded to be taken in – when Helen, who'd washed her hair that morning, had no intention of going anywhere near the chlorine. Lola lost the top of Helen's suncream. She whined and pestered and eventually started crying – while Helen remained very quiet and still, behind her sunglasses, under her straw hat, turning the pages of a magazine.

Marianne couldn't bear it.

'Come on, darling,' she said at last. 'I'll take you in.'

Helen looked up from the magazine.

'You don't mind, do you?' said Marianne.

'No, no. You go ahead.'

But Lola wanted Mummy. Only Mummy would do.

'Jesus.' Stuffing the magazine crossly into a bag, Helen wriggled her feet back into their flip-flops, got up from her sun-lounger, tied a sarong round her hips and – pulling together Lola's bits and pieces – grabbed the little hand. 'If you can't behave, I'm taking you back inside.'

'Swimming, Mummy. Swimming!'

'No swimming.'

'Carry me?'

'No.'

'Mummy.'

Silence.

'Cuddle?' Lola couldn't say it properly. The word came out as 'Cuggle?'

Helen softened. Squatting down, she put aside the things she was holding and gave Lola the required embrace. And while there was something intrinsically uncuddly about the overslim arms and clunky jewellery, Marianne could also see a flash of what Helen might have been, in different circumstances, unspoiled by the values and priorities that had so corroded her general person. Helen – who must once, also, have been a toddler like Lola: cute and round, demanding hugs . . .

And then the moment passed. Catching Marianne looking at them, Helen rose quickly to her feet – a movement which, with Lola's podgy fingers still attached to the loosely tied sarong, caused the latter to fall away.

'Oh, for—'

'Cuddle! Cuddle!'

Her mouth tight, Helen snatched up the fallen sarong together with her child. 'It's tactics,' she muttered, carrying the thwarted Lola back towards the house. Marianne saw them disappear round a corner.

'I *love* you, Mummy . . .'

Marianne had assumed that Lola would have settled when, an hour or so later, she returned to the house. And for all her dislike of Helen, it was hard not to feel some pity for the woman – a woman who was always so controlled and smooth – when childish wailing and the sound of breaking glass rang through the building. Marianne opened the door.

'Can I help?' she said, looking at the kitchen carnage.

'It's all right.' With Lola in her arms, Helen jerked her head in the direction of the pantry where a maid was unloading the dishwasher. 'She'll do it. I'm taking this monster up now. Shouldn't be long – she's overtired . . . didn't sleep much last night, according to Dolores. I'll just settle her and maybe join you for lunch?'

'Great,' said Marianne, unable to stop herself from bending down and picking up the bigger bits of glass. 'You want a sandwich?'

'A drink would be better.'

Marianne smiled. 'Rosé?'

'Perfect.'

Twenty minutes later, the pair of them were sitting on the verandah in the shade with an open bottle of rosé on the table between them. Upstairs, in the room directly above them, Lola was now sleeping. Helen poured herself a second glass, sat back, and closed her eyes.

'Christ, I'm knackered.'

Marianne looked at her, surprised. Something seemed to have snapped.

'Two hours alone with that child . . . two paltry hours, and I'm a gibbering wreck. Can't think how other women manage – the ones that don't have help, I mean. The ones that do it all by themselves, day after day, week after week. And as for having more than one and – God forbid – no nanny. Or husband . . .' Helen shivered.

'George will be here soon,' said Marianne.

But Helen did not seem comforted by this idea. Indeed, it seemed to make things worse. 'Great,' she said, with a hollow laugh. 'Hooray. And what a relief *that* will be.' She glanced at Marianne's startled face, and drank some more wine. 'Oh, I know you all think he's devoted – and yes, I suppose he is. But it's easy to profess devotion for something you only see at weekends. It's easy to enjoy the cuteness when you've never changed a nappy in your life . . .'

Marianne watched the perfect fingers circling round the chilled wine glass and wondered how familiar they were with the process.

'Oh yes, he's more than happy to leave me to heave his kids across the globe and co-ordinate visits to *his* family and do all the heavy-duty crap, all the packing and checking and lugging about and have-you-been-to-the-loo? and are-we-nearly-there? and where's-your-wretched-passport? and where's-that-Dolores when you need her? and put up with all the evil looks from the other passengers on the flight and so on and so on, while he hides away in his office and then breezes over at his own convenience and expects us all to say what a wonderful job he's doing and – oh what a saint George is, working so hard for his family, sacrificing his holiday . . . it's a bloody joke.' Helen refilled her glass again. 'Don't you get any of this with Jay?'

Marianne hesitated.

'Of course you don't. You just have each other, you lucky things . . . I can barely remember what life was like with George before those horrors came along.'

Helen shifted in her chair and put her pretty feet up on the balustrade, plainly oblivious to what it was she'd just said, forgetting Marianne's loss – or dismissing it, maybe? 'Just' a stillbirth? A form of Tourettes? Inverted bragging? Marianne couldn't say. Hardening a little – what else could one expect from a woman like Helen? – she watched the latter's feet find their grip against the stone.

'. . . I suppose it would be all right if his precious work brought in a proper amount of dough, but it doesn't. Or won't – at any rate – when his contract expires . . . which will exactly coincide with Fred going to prep school.'

'You'll still be comfortable, won't you? It's—'

'Hardly. I've seen the figures, Marianne. I'm telling you – it's not a pretty sight.'

Marianne looked away.

'You don't believe it? Fair enough. Didn't believe it

myself at the beginning – which is why I thought it wouldn't do any harm to discuss it with my lawyer – get a second opinion, and . . .' Helen sighed. 'I can't totally blame him,' she said, sadly. 'Poor George. He was royally shafted. He was targeted. He was stupid and naïve. He wasn't paying attention. He trusted the wrong people and now they've sucked him dry,' Helen refilled both glasses, 'which *again* might be bearable were it not for his ludicrous attitude to money in the first place.'

'He spends too much?'

'If only . . .' Helen's laugh was bitter. 'If *only*. No, not spends, darling. *Gives*. George likes to *give it away*. He *gives* our family money away. And not to some grateful charity or other, or in some way that he might get any credit for it, oh no, that's much too straightforward. Oh no, George would rather pour the whole damn lot – or as good as the whole damn lot – into the current accounts of his mother and sister, and pretend it was theirs all along.'

Marianne was stunned. She recalled the blithe way she'd dismissed George in the early days, thinking him smug and uncaring; a bad brother to Gabriella; stingy and selfish; dominating a house that in fact was only ever his; addicted to his work, at the expense of his poor wife and children – thinking only about his pay packet, his fancy car, his trophy wife, his smart lifestyle . . . when all the time he was only protecting his sister and mother, while trying to keep his wife happy, too. It made her sick to the core.

'It's true. He feels guilty because his father left everything to him. He couldn't bear for his mother and Gab ever to know that they were totally cut out – not that there was much in the first place. Much less than we all thought – which was why I was so relieved that his father decided to leave it all to us. Such a load off my mind to know we'd be secure and – hell – George deserved it! Unlike the others – even your precious Jay,' Helen fixed her eye on Marianne, 'who, I understand, has his own private income from Anusha – that's right, isn't it?'

Marianne looked back – blank, lost in remorse. She was barely listening.

'Well, anyway, the thing about George is that, unlike the others, he's responsible. He'd invest it. He'd add to it. He'd protect it. Only George being George, he just decided that, after everything else, the snub would destroy his mother. And as for Gab . . . God. Let's not go there. I get so *upset* when I think about it – when I think of where we might be now if he'd just honoured his father's wishes and kept the wretched cash instead of handing virtually all of it over to that pair of hopeless causes.'

With a shaking hand, Helen emptied the remains of the rosé into her glass.

'I suppose, because of his job, he thought we'd always be all right,' she said. 'And perhaps we will. He seems to think he can start again when he leaves Franklin's in 2010 – but he's nearly forty, Marianne. I don't think it's possible. You can't make two fortunes in a lifetime, can you?'

But do you really need a fortune? The words were on the tip of Marianne's tongue – and then she checked herself. The sad truth was all too obvious.

'. . . two fortunes – from scratch? What's the likelihood of that? It – no, don't tell me. I don't want to know. It'll never happen . . . and then we'll have to let Dolores go – I know we will, I can feel it coming . . . and all my days will be like today, and the children will end up in the kind of schools one's never heard of – the kind I went to – and don't I know what a handicap that is. And we'll live in smaller and smaller houses, and . . . oh, *God*. The more I think about it, the more I realise I'm just not cut out for the kind of life George thinks we can live.'

Marianne listened – appalled. For Helen, undone by alcohol and the mistaken sense that she had an ally in Marianne – *you know what I'm saying . . . you understand . . . these Franklin men . . . us girls* – Helen was coming apart. And the sudden freedom to talk about things she'd only ever thought about at night, the things she should never say, the sudden unblocking of months of pent-up anger, it was getting out of control. The words were out and Marianne had the awful sensation that, by giving air to these dark thoughts and doubts about George – dear devoted George, who'd clearly done nothing to deserve such treatment – Helen was somehow giving them substance. Merely by listening to this talk of leaving, of getting a divorce, of doing it sooner rather than later, while the man still had some assets to split . . . Marianne felt herself to be colluding. She had to get away. Find a diversion –

And then, as if on cue, a wail came from the upper window.

'Christ,' said Helen, clutching her head. 'That's all I need.'

'Mummmmeeee . . .' Lola was shrieking.

'I'm coming.' Helen put the glass aside and got to her feet. For a moment, she looked down at Marianne, still sitting in her chair. 'Enjoy it while you can,' she said, with a bitter expression. 'You don't know how lucky you are.'

Lucky? Marianne looked back – aware that the experience she'd been through with Maya wasn't something she could expect a woman like Helen to understand. It was as if Helen herself was a toddler, with limited perception and a need to be treated as somehow not quite equal. More leeway was required. More patience. More kindness. Marianne's heart surged with pity and dislike. She felt too complicated to speak.

George arrived that night, earlier than scheduled. They were still at the table when his car pulled up.

'Is that him?' said Marianne, first to hear the wheels outside.

The others stopped and listened.

'He's early!' said Anusha, glancing round at Helen . . . who showed no sign of sharing her enthusiasm, and made no attempt to leave the table. Instead, she took another mouthful of fish and – turning to Jay – prompted him back to their former conversation.

So Anusha went. Discreetly, she excused herself and – after a short moment – returned with George to the dining room. George stood in the doorway, his eyes adjusting to the candlelight.

'Hello, darling,' said Helen, wiping her mouth with her napkin. 'Good journey?'

Marianne looked from one to the other, noticing the way George rushed round to greet his wife with an expression that was openly loving – and slightly disconcerting, coming as it did from an experienced man of business. It made him so exposed, so vulnerable, so – so unlike himself. And Marianne was riveted, as much by the transparency as by the emotions themselves.

Helen's face, on the other hand, was harder to read. She was smiling. She seemed quite happy – pulling up another chair, pouring him some wine – but there was an air of detachment about her. Next to George, whose joy at being reunited with his wife had an almost childish fervour, Helen seemed less vital, less engaged. Perfectly in control. And Marianne – with everything she'd learnt that day on the verandah – could not fail to notice the disparity. She was glad that George was oblivious, that his own excitement was blinding him from lack of the same from his wife.

And in the days that followed, it seemed almost as if Helen were looking for reasons to justify continuing the detachment. She wanted the distance, she wanted the estrangement, and – most of all – she wanted it to be George's fault. Certainly, he could never get it right. If he wasn't to blame for taking all the children off and having fun without her, then he wasn't helping out enough. And why in God's name did he have to keep taking those calls from work?

Waking, dozy, from an afternoon nap in the library, Marianne heard them coming down the stairs.

'. . . already over a week later than you said you'd be,' Helen was muttering. 'How do you think that makes me feel? And then you don't even have the decency to switch your BlackBerry off at lunch – and that's after everything I've already said . . . a million times . . . It's as if you get some sort of kick out of—'

'I forgot, darling. I'm sorry. It wasn't deliberate—'

'And you think that makes it better? You think that's okay? You put yourself in my position, George. Just for a moment. And imagine what it's like to have a husband who behaves like this. No wonder no one invites us to join them on holiday!' Her voice was rising. 'No wonder we're—'

'Please, Helen.'

'*Please, Helen?*'

George sighed. 'I don't know what else I can say, my darling. I've apologised. I didn't mean to leave it on. I just—'

'That still doesn't explain why you answered it.'

Silence.

'And don't give me all that bullshit about being available twenty-four-seven, or they'll find someone who is. You're not some minion with—'

'Nor am I the boss.'

'Hmm.'

'And – and anyway,' George went on, 'it isn't so much my colleagues. It's my clients. They need to be able to reach me. They—'

'*They* need to reach you? Holy Jesus! What about me? What about your children?'

And then, before George could answer her, the same BlackBerry beeped and vibrated from where it had been left, on the library desk, mere feet from Marianne's chair. She could have reached out and picked it up herself.

Helen was spitting now. 'Don't – don't – don't you . . .'

The beeping persisted.

'George. Don't even *think*—'

'I'm not! I'm not!' Through a crack in door, Marianne saw George backing away – both hands raised in a gesture of innocence.

The beeping stopped. The machine went through to answer.

'There.' Helen's voice was silken. 'See? That wasn't so difficult, now – was it?'

George didn't reply.

'Well?'

'Sure.' His eyes were closed. He sat at the foot of the stairs – head in his hands, defeated.

'Now,' said Helen, with a calculated adjustment of tone. 'When did Dolores say she'd be back?'

George looked at his watch, grateful – as she knew he'd be – for the change of subject.

'Four,' he said. He sounded tired. 'But don't you worry. You have a nice rest by the pool. I'll look after the children – maybe take them to the fort again – and come and find you later.'

'All right.' Detaching herself, Helen walked through the library – right past Marianne, quiet as a cushion in the shadows – and out on to the verandah, out towards the brightness of the pool.

'. . . but you'll need to keep an eye on them, George. Don't think you can speak to Kurt, or Tim, or whoever else it is on that thing, at the same time. In fact, why don't I just remove the temptation altogether?' Coming back into the library again, Helen reached for the mobile.

George was there first. 'I won't use it, darling.'

Helen gave him a penetrating look.

'Honestly. Look – see? All switched off. I won't touch it again until Monday. I promise I won't.'

And Helen, realising she couldn't physically grab the thing from him, decided to let it go. 'I'll hold you to that,' she said, ominously. 'And make sure you're back before five, darling. I don't want them late for their supper.'

He waited until she was gone, until the flip-flip of her flip-flops disappeared down the path, and the air was silent again. Just the whirr of an overhead fan, and distant staff voices from the kitchen. Then he came into the library and, resting against the side of the desk, turned the BlackBerry on again and held it to his ear.

305

'Tim. Sorry about that. I . . . sure . . . no, I definitely need to see it. You're quite right. Just send it out and I'll—fine. Except there's no fax here. Better to email and I'll print it out. Or, in fact, you could fax it to the New Oriental Hotel, I suppose. If that's better for you? Right. Okay. It's the New Oriental. Galle. G-A-L-L-E . . . that's right.' He found the number and reeled it off. 'I'll call them now – warn them it's coming through – and pick it up just before six, if that's— great. Okay, Tim. Thanks. Speak later.'

And then he saw Marianne – sitting very still, watching him from the depths of her chair. They looked at each other for a moment, both sensing they'd been caught. Both looking distinctly sheepish . . . and then Marianne grinned.

'I won't tell if you won't,' she said.

George shook his head, unwilling to conspire. 'I hope you didn't . . . she's just a bit stressed, that's all. It's difficult for her, with the children and—'

'It's okay. You want me to collect that fax for you?'

George hesitated.

'It wouldn't be a problem.' Marianne reached for her sandals. 'I could drop in on Hassan at the same time, and—'

'Don't worry.' He was smiling now. 'It's all right. I can do it with the children on the way back from the fort. It's fine.' His hand lingered on the side of the door. 'Thanks,' he added, in a different voice, fingers tapping restlessly, as if he couldn't quite decide whether to sit down with her, or whether he should simply leave. Again, their eyes met. And then the voices from across the courtyard grew a little louder as someone emerged from the kitchen, and he came to his senses.

'Oh well . . .' still looking at her, still hesitating. 'Better call the Oriental.'

'Yes. Of course.'

George nodded. And with a smile that was brighter, and somehow less meaningful, he left Marianne to her book.

For all his occasional moments of mutiny – mutiny that only ever took place behind Helen's back – George wasn't interested in open resistance. Helen was his wife. And, as her husband, it seemed only natural to him to want to make her happy. He saw no purpose in pointing out that these work obligations were purely the result of Helen's own demands; that, given a free rein, he'd have left the business months ago. Nor could he see that much was to be gained from reminding her that it had always been his dream to be his own master again; that these interruptions were a consequence of her decision, not his; that a less selfish woman might be offering sympathy and support, instead of a stream of objections. Some ingrained reluctance to defend himself in that way, some sense that Helen must already know these things – that there was no advantage to be gained from spelling it out – meant that George simply kept silent, and clung to his sense of duty . . . which was as much about his own self-respect as it was about keeping others happy. He wanted to like himself. Wanted to think of himself as a certain sort of person – dependable, straight-dealing . . . an upright citizen, a good strong link in the chain, a contributor, a man who pulled his weight. The giant creaking systems of family and work . . . they weren't perfect, George knew that, but they were still things he believed in. Or wanted to believe in. And he wasn't about to discard that faith simply because of a rough patch.

And Marianne watched him. She saw the effort he put into his children – the constant loving tone, the refusal to lose his temper no matter how exasperating they became. She saw him carry Lola back home along an entire stretch of beach. She saw him teaching Fred how to ride a bicycle. She heard him giving them their bath – his outraged laughter when they splashed him. She saw him helping Claudia make hibiscus chains for her mother – the pair of them walking through the garden, with Claudia saying which flowers she wanted and George obediently picking them.

And she saw exactly the same degree of patience and effort going on when it came to handling Helen. The same calm voice. The same refusal to snap. His love for Helen – like the love of a parent – was being tested and challenged all the time.

It made Marianne uneasy. Because, for all its impressive self denial, it struck her that there was also something deeply wrong about the sight of a man directing so much effort and love towards something so mean-hearted, so incapable of giving back. At least, with the children, it was supposed to be like that – and, in fact, George did get a return: it was Daddy they ran to when they hurt themselves, it was Daddy they cuddled up to for their evening stories. But those dodgy colleagues at work, and his irritable wife . . . were dignity and patience really the answer? It was all very well to subscribe to the rules, to honour your contract, to be a man of your word – and after the loss of her baby, Marianne had certainly acquired a new respect for the system. She no longer despised George for believing in it. She admired the decency at the heart of it all, the sense that there was something more important to George than his own selfish ends. But she also worried about him. For a man so au fait with business life, it seemed oddly naïve. And watching him that holiday, seeing the blindness of his faith in the system, the way he clung to the old structures no matter what – even when those same structures were hijacked by people who no longer deserved his loyalty – Marianne couldn't help feeling that George's precious rules would ultimately let him down.

Although for all her resentment, on George's behalf, that he was being used, that bad, selfish people were taking advantage, that he needed to stand up for himself a little more – Marianne couldn't help but appreciate it when she herself was the beneficiary of his good nature.

To have him miss his own bath one evening before dinner so that he could show her how to use his computer – pick up her emails, and send a few back – she could see how Helen might have grown rather too accustomed to such treatment, how it might be easy to start taking it for granted. Expect it, even. To then have George mix her a mojito and bring it over to the desk while she did a quick price-check on his Internet connection – looking up the current exchange rate to see if the gemstones she was considering buying from Hassan were really such good value, making pencil calculations to incorporate the tax position . . . it was certainly very spoiling. And completely unlike Jay who, at that moment, was enjoying a quick drink or two with Tariq in town – an arrangement Marianne knew, without even asking, that she was absolutely excluded from.

Then George settled himself in the chair by the door – the large leather chair that she'd been sitting in when she'd overheard the thrashing he'd got from Helen the other day. He took a sip from his own mojito, and waited.

Marianne turned from the computer screen. 'God. Sorry,' she said. 'I'll only be a moment. Didn't realise you wanted . . . you must *say*, George! Don't be so nice all the time!'

'It's all right.' George took another sip. There was sand in his fingernails. He was still in his beach shorts. His hair was salty from the sea. A rare – and not entirely unattractive – shadow of stubble had appeared on his jaw and chin. 'I'm in no hurry . . .'

Marianne smiled.

'In fact, it's rather nice,' he went on. 'Nice, to see someone else working for a change. Although . . .' Leaning forward, and then standing, to get a better look at the figures on the screen, he sighed. 'Shit. Is that sterling?'

'I'm afraid so,' said Marianne, clicking on a news item that went into more depth about another slump in the UK market. George stood, looking over her shoulder, as they read the article in silence – save for the occasional crack of ice in their mojitos. She could smell the warmth of the day on him. Then – sitting back down in his chair again – he waited for Marianne to finish her pencil jottings and log out of her email account before observing, with a chuckle, 'Well, well. Never thought I'd see you logged on to the *FT* website.'

Marianne reached for her drink. 'Someone's got to do it.'

George grinned. 'And it won't be Gabriella . . .'

'Appalling,' muttered Jay, turning on the engine of his jeep. 'Completely appalling.'

Marianne glanced at the wing mirror on her side of the vehicle and saw – in its distorting reflection – a lost-looking Helen on the steps of the house as the pair of

310

them sped down the driveway and out of the gates.

She'd wanted to come with them that day. Hearing their plans – which were to go up into Ratnapura that morning, work the market, drop something off for Hassan, and perhaps even go to an auction that Jay had heard about – poor Helen's envy had proved too much. She wanted adult time. She wanted to look at pretty jewellery. She wanted a jaunt to the hills. There was room enough in the back of the car. She wouldn't get in the way. She was merely interested . . . was it really so much to ask?

'Yes,' Jay had said, getting up from the breakfast table.

The tone was final, and Marianne was glad of it. She didn't want Helen in the back of the car any more than Jay did. She needed this trip with him alone – as much from a personal as professional point of view. She couldn't go on drifting when it came to their relationship, tempting as it was, what with his charming family, his beautiful country, his love of stones . . . it was all too easy for Marianne to let these peripheral things cloud her judgement. She needed to make a decision about Jay himself – not the world he offered her. And it struck Marianne that spending time alone with him on the road was as good a test as any . . . and Helen's presence, for sure, would have wrecked it.

'How dare she?' Jay spat, hurtling over a round-about and narrowly missing a dog.

Marianne glanced at him. 'She's frustrated. You know how much she hates being tied to the children. The idea of us making an impromptu road trip was obviously—'

'So she thought she'd spoil our fun?'

'I think it's less about us, and more that she's just

311

desperate to get away. It's those children. She's got some sort of bee in her bonnet—'

'What about Dolores? I'd assumed that George had forked out thousands of pounds to bring a nanny *precisely* so that Helen would get a proper holiday. It's not as if she and George couldn't do something alone together too. I don't understand what the problem is – or why she needs to bother us with it. Unless' – indicating right, Jay waited for a break in the flow of traffic – 'you think George has done something we don't know about?'

Marianne hesitated. Seeing a gap in the traffic, she nudged Jay – who took the gap and crossed the road – but her first hesitation wasn't lost on him. Sensing that Marianne knew something he didn't, Jay turned to her.

'What is it?'

'Nothing.'

'What's he done?'

'Nothing!' she insisted. 'At least, he missed their first week, of course – I don't think she was overjoyed about that.'

'But?'

Again, Marianne hesitated. Part of her was tempted to tell him what Helen had said that afternoon on the verandah – it would be useful to hear Jay's thoughts on the matter, and whether he thought George should be told. But another part of her didn't like to spread the idea any further – as if, by telling even Jay, by letting it further into the open, she was somehow colluding.

'Well, it's obvious they're not happy,' Jay went on. 'I know he's having problems at work. And I can see it's pissing her off –'

'I think she wants a divorce.'

Jay stopped the car. And as Marianne told him of

Helen's plans – of her bitterness towards George, over the way he'd handled his inheritance, and the way it was eating away at her, now that the business was in trouble; of the way she'd lost faith in George as a provider, and how important that was to her . . . Jay listened with growing fury.

'Jesus,' he spluttered. 'George should be the one doing the divorcing! George is the one who's been used and wronged! Isn't he? I mean—'

'He loves her.'

'More fool him.'

They sat in silence.

'So do you think we should tell him?' said Marianne, finally.

'No,' came the firm reply. 'Definitely not. I suspect he knows already. He must know. He's probably thought about the children and the expense of splitting up and so on . . . and – as you say – he loves her. I expect he thinks he can still win her back – it would certainly explain why he's being so fucking nice to her . . . and maybe it'll come good. George isn't stupid.'

'He is where Helen's concerned.'

Jay shook his head. 'It isn't our business, Smidge.'

'Even if she's talking to her lawyer and everything, don't you think it would help him, at least to know what he's dealing with? At least be prepared? It's—'

'No,' Jay said again.

Marianne let it go.

Chapter Twenty-One

In spite of the several trips to Galle that she'd enjoyed with Jay, over the years, Marianne had never made the inland journey to Ratnapura. It wasn't that Jay had refused to take her, exactly. But his attitude towards the idea of including his girlfriend on what amounted to a business trip had only ever been, at best, ambivalent. Marianne had heard, at length, about the frustrating time he'd had with Gabby: his affectionate efforts to educate a sister who declared herself keen and yet seemed unable to take it seriously . . . refusing to bend to what she perceived as sexist local customs; falling asleep at stone auctions; taking calls on her mobile while something was being explained to her; passing up on the opportunity of witnessing the cutting of one of the year's best sapphires because she wanted a facial at the New Oriental. It was easy to see why Jay was now averse to having anyone in tow, particularly a woman who mattered to him. He'd heard the mutterings of some of the other dealers. It was bad enough having such comments – however fair they might have been – directed at his oblivious sister, who was never going to bother to learn Sinhalese, and he wasn't about to risk the same with his girlfriend. Marianne understood all this. She was acutely aware of Ratnapura's importance in Jay's life – both as a source of stones, and as the initial inspiration behind his decision to become a dealer at all. She didn't want to invade his home territory. And so, in spite of the personal complications, she was touched that he'd pressed her to come with him this time.

Jay and Ratnapura . . . they went a long way back. As a six-year-old, Jay had been taken by his parents to visit friends in the region – family friends with mining interests, who happened to have struck gold, so to speak, while the Franklins had been staying. Jay had never forgotten the atmosphere, the air of excitement as the adults discussed a haul of sapphires that had been found that week – from deep down, in one of the many mining networks that spread out for miles under the surrounding paddy fields. He never forgot those first rough stones – being allowed to hold them, and play with them, and roll them across the floor like marbles . . . He remembered his host: a wrinkled man, with misty green eyes and a house the size of a palace, remembered the glinting smile and the sudden moment of attention – 'So, Jehan, will you own a mine one day? Will you make your fortune from sapphires like these?'

'Oh stop it!' Anusha had said, laughing. 'Don't give the boy ideas.'

Marianne had heard the story. She'd heard about the palace in the hills – a palace that subsequently fell into ruin when the old man had died, millions of rupees in debt . . . not that that seemed to have put Jay off. If anything, it had made him hungrier. He thrived off the extremes – the all-or-nothing element, the palaces and the shacks, the glamour of the stones and the women who wore them, beside the squalor of the mines and the all-but-naked labourers who were paid a pittance to clamber in and out of them, and risk their health in the process.

But he also loved the more prosaic market – loved working it, loved striding through all the haggling and dealing, dipping in and out, glancing at this or that little packetful of stones . . . knowing all the time that he was the one in control. He loved the sense that there could always be something special around the corner and that he, Jay, would be the one to spot it. Loved knowing he was good.

Marianne knew she'd be conspicuous that day. Even with the neutral colours she was wearing, and her head covered, and her dark glasses, even then – as the only woman in the market, and the only Caucasian – she attracted a degree of interest that made it impossible to do business. So she didn't try. She merely tagged along with Jay – strolling with him down the lane set aside for rough-stone dealing; drinking tea with his friends, who hurriedly found a chair for her to sit on and persisted in treating her more like a wife than someone in the trade, no matter how often Jay tried to correct them. And as the men did their business in a language she couldn't follow, she watched – across the street – the rows of artisan cutters and polishers, holed away in their tiny stalls, bent over their ancient faceters – spinning, cutting, adjusting, perfecting, like their fathers and forefathers before them. She inhaled the market air – the tea, the dust, the chemicals they used on the stones. And when, after a while, Jay got to his feet and moved on, so, like a meek, obedient wife, did Marianne – into the other lane where the cut-stone dealers touted their wares, where – here and there – Jay was stopped by random local dealers and wannabe dealers and asked to view yet another cluster of stones – glittering in the sun. Marianne glanced at them with him, and noticed when he chose to give someone his attention and when he breezed on by. Jay had a certain swagger, a certain way of walking, of holding his head, of firing questions, that gave him an extra degree of authority. He was easily the tallest man there. He was rich – comparatively. Here, in the Ratnapura gem market, Jay Franklin had reputation and power. He had a mafia-style cool – and, for a moment, Marianne remembered what she'd first found attractive about him.

She remembered, and then marvelled, at how different things now were. It was always easy being with Jay in a working context. They had an under-standing. And even in an environment such as this – with Marianne somewhat marginalised on account of both her sex and her newness to Ratnapura – each knew what the other's role would be. Marianne felt no need to prove anything. She was here to learn, to see, to build up some experience of dealing. Unlike Gabby, she understood that Jay was doing her a favour just by letting her be there with him. Had she been a man, her place that day would not have differed. She was there to shut up and listen. And Jay, aware that Marianne understood all this, that she could be trusted not to embarrass him, was glad to find himself in the role of teacher and guide. He liked the sense of authority.

But this good mutual understanding, this profes-sional respect, this shared pleasure in stones . . . it was oddly mild, oddly neutral – a neutrality that was only made more apparent by the market assumption that she was his wife. For Marianne was only too aware that there had been a time, not so long ago, when she would have given much to be treated in this way, yet, in spite of this – or perhaps because of it – she knew now, with absolute certainty, that they would never marry. The market was mistaken in its assumption. She and Jay were colleagues. Just colleagues. Their hands would brush as he passed her a stone, but the sensation of flesh on flesh was completely neutral. And while Marianne found it sad – that the charge between them was gone – she also felt a degree of relief that something else could be salvaged. She had a sudden sense of their future: in the form of a friendship made all the more easy precisely because they'd taken the sexual route for a while . . . tried it, tested it, enjoyed it, and moved on . . . effectively defusing any tension. She was glad she'd come with him that day. She was glad she'd travelled to Sri Lanka. And while, perhaps, it wasn't the result she'd hoped for when she'd accepted Jay's original invitation – while it was now clear that things with him were over, really over – this new resolution, this future path made clear, it was worth coming with him, if only to understand what it was that she now wanted. There was relief in the clarity – and also, in the back of her mind, relief that their lost child would be spared the inevitable break-up. None of this was meant to be.

So they worked the market. And after a while, with Jay vaguely dissatisfied, having found nothing of interest, they decided to move on. Returning to the jeep, they got back in and headed out of town again – following the main road back for a few minutes, and then turning sharp right, onto an uneven dusty track that led out and down to the paddy fields, and one of the many makeshift mines dotted across the landscape. Jay had some business there: a few new stones to look at. He also, as a favour to Tariq, whose deals were never straightforward, needed to drop off a stereo system and a bottle of Scotch. They pulled up beside a small new bungalow and a portly man emerged. While he was only wearing an amude loin cloth and sandals, it was clear – from his thick well-cut hair with its silvery streaks and his well-nourished body, together with a certain air of confidence he displayed as he and Jay shook hands – clear, that Lal Senkada was no humble labourer. Yet nor was he completely sophisticated. His English was minimal, and there was something about the way he looked at Marianne as Jay introduced them . . . something told her that the presence of a woman here at the mine – here, where men sweated and toiled and often did so naked on account of the heat and dirt, here, where they drank and swore and made their living . . . it wasn't a situation he liked. They stood for a while in the sun – with Jay and Lal talking together in Sinhalese while a skinny boy emerged silently from a side door and heaved the stereo box into the bungalow.

Marianne waited. The stereo was in. The whisky handed over. Jay had been shown a handful of stones – three of which he liked – but the talking showed no sign of drawing to a close. Indeed, it seemed to be getting more entrenched. Lal was explaining some- thing – something to do with the mine. From time to time he gestured out in its direction and then seemed to push his hand on, further. And Jay, plainly fascinated, was listening. He was nodding. He was asking questions, and then, suddenly, they were both looking at Marianne.

'You want to come with us?' said Jay. 'Or stay in the car? They've been having a run of luck with this mine, apparently. Lal's been telling me . . . they've found a much larger proportion of gemstones than they usually do, so they've been expanding one of the tunnels right down to the left, there. He says I can go down . . .'

'Both go down!' said Lal – somewhat surprisingly, until Marianne realised that he was glancing at her with the look of a naughty boy who thinks he's being clever. It was as if he believed he was insulting her by suggesting it.

'What, Marianne?' said Jay. 'Down the mine?'

Lal laughed. 'Why not?' he said. 'Modern women – they'll do anything these days . . .'

Marianne wasn't going to stay in the car. She followed them round the side of Lal's bungalow, over a small bridge – and on, to the mine itself. Like all the others in the area, the mine was little more than a hole in the ground – a couple of yards in diameter, looking more like a well than a quarry – with a wooden framework round the sides and a long drop of fifty or sixty yards . . . down, to where the *illama* soil held something more interesting than pebbles. At that point, it branched out in a series of small lateral tunnels, supported by wooden beams, that led some distance from the original drop . . . tunnels that were interspersed with larger chambers, where the painstaking scraping was done; tunnels that looked more like the sort of thing that an escaping prisoner might build in secret – low, small, uncivilised, unsafe . . . and quite intolerably hot.

Above the mine, a rough-and-ready shelter of palm leaves had been erected – and Marianne stood in its shade, looking down over the edge of the hole, into the abyss. A low candle flickered on a small shrine-like affair to her left, lit in the hope that it would bring good omens to the venture. It seemed oddly sensitive, oddly vulnerable, in such a macho context. Six or seven men – all dressed in amudé loin cloths, all filthy from the dust – stood watching, amused, while Jay stripped to his underpants and stepped boldly over the edge.

'You coming?'

Marianne smiled, and waved him on.

Grinning back, Jay lowered himself in – there was no ladder to take him down. Just the wooden framework of the mine itself. He adjusted his grip as he went, searching for decent footing.

'See you later,' he said, cheerfully.

Down he went – down and down, getting smaller and darker, until he was suddenly at the bottom and heading off, under Lal's instructions, crawling down one of the lateral tunnels. Marianne saw him go. Head, torso, bottom, legs, until there was just one final foot visible from the top . . . and then that, too, disappeared from view, and Jay was gone.

Marianne looked up to see Lal smiling at her from the other side of the hole, surrounded by his workers, all of them smiling too. She suddenly felt glad of the scarf over her head; glad that she was properly covered.

'He will be okay, won't he?'

'Yes yes! No problem! Chaminda will look after him.'

Marianne nodded uneasily. She looked down again into the empty hole. She thought of the dangers she'd read about, the accidents down the mines – the way they were rarely reported, the risks the owners took with the construction of their tunnels – the lack of health and safety . . .

Health and Safety. How she loathed all that rubbish when it came to her own secure little English life – the obligation to have fire extinguishers at the showroom, and smoke alarms, and all the rest of it; and poor Lee and his team at the workshop, with ever-more stringent requirements – especially when it came to using any sort of chemical. And yet – and yet . . .

And the longer she waited, she more anxious she became. The candle flickered in its shrine. It seemed hopelessly inadequate. Where the hell was he? What would she do if he didn't reappear? Who was Chaminda? How new was this new tunnel? How long should she wait before raising the alarm? He— *Damn it, Jay. Where are you?*

Twenty minutes passed. Another twenty. An hour . . .

'Tea?'

'No thanks.' Marianne looked at her watch. 'We really need to get going, Lal. I'm just not sure he's realised how long he's been –'

'I send someone?'

'Would you?'

It was unpleasant to find herself dependent on a man like Lal, but Marianne was done with pride. Hearing Lal make the order, and watching one of his men leap over the edge of the mine, she couldn't hide her relief . . . or, indeed, her gratitude as, within ten minutes, Jay was climbing up again – covered in dirt, his face radiant.

'We found a vein!' he cried. 'A great long red one, Lal – yards and yards. I thought I'd wait until they reached the limit, but it's just going on and on and on! They're bringing up the first bucket now – you think

322

you'll be able to sieve it through before I leave? I'd love to see what you've got . . .'

And he was off, in Sinhalese now, gabbling excitedly to his friend as he picked up his clothes.

He barely noticed Marianne, sitting on the bank with a stony expression.

Sieving through the buckets of soil, fishing out the good, rough gems, was never a simple process. They would have to wait for an auspicious time, which could be anything within the next twenty-four hours. Only then, and in the proper presence of an armed security guard, would the painstaking sifting begin. And that, too, could take hours. Perhaps days. From Jay's description of the vein they'd found, it could take the best part of a week. And then there'd be all the haggling, and all the squinting at stone after stone – some the size of olives – with torches and loupes and all the rest of it, rubbing each stone against the sweat of their brows, to give the surface a sheen, to see how best to cut it, but never really knowing, because you never really did. Not when the stones were rough. It was all about instinct, and feel – which only made it all the more fascinating, and all the more addictive. Particularly to a personality such as Jay's.

They drove home in silence – both annoyed, both keen for the journey to be over. For while Jay had been desperate to stay on at the bungalow overnight, drinking Tariq's whisky with Lal while they waited for dawn, when the sifting would begin, Marianne had no intention of complying. Nothing would induce her to agree to it. It wasn't just the bungalow, with its all-male occupants, and its far-from-comfortable all-male facilities, it was Lal, and the effect he had on Jay – the drinking and laughing, the talking in Sinhalese, the excluding of Marianne. She wanted to get back to Anusha's house and the cooler, coastal air. She wanted that beautiful white bedroom, and a long, soothing soak in the bath.

She was annoyed that Jay showed no contrition for having kept her waiting, annoyed that his obsession with gemstones was so all-encompassing. He didn't seem to care that, in taking so long down there, he'd scared her. All that bulldog bravado, that macho one-upmanship with Lal and his gang, the risk-taking, the showing off . . . there had once been a time when Marianne would have found it manly and sexy. Now, it just seemed immature.

Jay drove very fast – which, again, might once have excited her . . . but not now. She wondered whether to ask him to slow down but, given his mood, she knew he'd never oblige. It was bad enough that she'd made him leave, that she'd spoilt his chances of getting that ruby. He was damn well going to drive however he damn well pleased. It was his car. If she didn't like it, she could get the bus.

So she couldn't help smirking at the sight of the police car, with its siren and its lights flashing away at Jay to pull in to the side. Two policemen approached them – a large senior-looking one and his number two, who seemed, to Marianne, to have barely reached puberty. She made no attempt to hide her amusement as Jay was made to get out, and listened while they lectured him on the dangers of ignoring the police stop signs.

'Stop signs?'

The senior officer frowned. 'You didn't see them?'

'Yes, man, of course I saw them! I just didn't think they—'

'Applied to you?'

Jay shut his eyes. He'd forgotten about this new policy of random stops – set up primarily as a part of the anti-terrorism effort – and submitted, reluctantly, to the series of questions. What was his name? His address? His registration papers . . .

It was typical that there was a problem with the documents. For while Jay was able to produce the jeep's registration book and Vehicle Identity Card, there was no driving licence in his wallet. No proof of where he lived. Marianne waited while the paperwork was completed and then, noticing the glove compartment, it struck her that Jay's licence might be in there. Casually, she reached forward and opened it . . .

'Don't move,' said a voice, very close.

Marianne froze. In front of her, in Jay's glove compartment, was a small black pistol. It glinted in the torchlight. Without moving her head, she swivelled her eyes and saw the younger policeman – looking terrified as he pointed his gun at her. The gun wobbled slightly. She wondered if he'd ever used it.

'Get out of the car.'

Marianne got out.

Eight hours later – with the gun confiscated and the car impounded, and Jay bound over to produce the full paperwork and licences relating to each within twenty-four hours – George collected them from the police station. He paid off the officials, signed the release forms, and ushered them out across the yard.

'What happened?'

'He ran a stop.'

George opened the door for Marianne. 'I see,' he said. 'And what was with the handgun, Marianne? At what point did you think it advisable to pull a nine-millimetre Beretta on the proceedings?'

'I didn't—'

'She did,' Jay muttered, getting into the back seat. 'She opened the glove compartment –'

'I was looking for your licence, Jay! I was trying to help you! How was I to know you kept a pistol there?'

'It's got to go somewhere, Marianne. I happen to need a gun from time to time. It's the nature of the work I do. And the glove compartment – which, incidentally, is every bit as sacred as one of your handbags and should never *ever* be opened the way you just did—'

'You need a pistol?' said George, baffled.

Jay said nothing.

'Are you serious?'

'Of course I'm serious,' Jay replied. 'My work here – the people I do business with – isn't all pinstriped suits and jolly-good-chaps and let's shake hands and have another look at the balance sheet. It's tough out there. I'd be a fool not to have some sort of personal protection –'

'Have you used it?'

Silence.

And then George started laughing. 'Oh, come on! What is this? What in God's name makes you keep something like that in your car, Jay? Have you any idea how dangerous it is?'

'Of course I do. I'm hardly—'

'Fine,' George snapped. And Marianne realised that the laughter was edgy, that he was far from amused. His back was rigid. His hand shook as he put the keys in the ignition. 'So you're all right, Jack. Bully for you. And what about your passengers? Your mother? Your sister? You – Jesus, Jay. How would you have felt if things had gone wrong tonight? What if that police-man had shot Marianne?'

'He wasn't going to shoot her.'

'You want to take the risk?'

Silence.

'And what in God's name makes you buy one in the first place? A thing you've clearly never used, and are never going to use –'

'I didn't say—'

'So you have used it, then?'

Jay allowed himself a dignified pause. 'There are things,' he said, mysteriously, 'just . . . things you probably shouldn't know, George. All right? Things that are better kept quiet.'

'Oh *please*,' snorted George. 'Next thing you'll be telling me you're in league with drug tsars and guerrilla armies, that you regularly do business with terrorist groups, have multiple identities, and are, in fact, a secret agent with a penchant for vodka Martinis. You're a stone dealer, Jay! By all accounts, an extremely good stone dealer, but – I'm sorry to be the one to point it out to you – honestly, all you do is hawk a few crystals from one place to another and pick up a bit of pocket money on the way. It's hardly life and death or saving the planet. You're not Action Man. You can't possibly need a handgun!'

Jay didn't bother to reply. He merely looked out of the window as the car sped back to the house and stubbornly held his tongue. George was only guessing. George didn't know a thing about the work he did. There were plenty of men he knew – admittedly, more

327

in Colombia than here at home – men who carried pistols as a matter of course. Why shouldn't Jay have one too? It was his job, his life, his jeep, his glove compartment. Who was George to start telling him what he could or couldn't keep in there?

The house was dark when they arrived. Nobody was up. Nobody knew where George had gone. He'd made sure of that, giving the impression that the somewhat frantic person at the other end of his BlackBerry had something to do with work, that he needed to borrow Anusha's car to go into Galle to collect some papers that had been delivered to the wrong address. Jay's secret was perfectly safe.

George locked the car and followed the others in with an expression that was now more concerned than amused.

'Jay?'

'I'm going to bed.'

'Please, Jay –' George took his younger brother's arm. They moved into the next room and Marianne knew better than to follow. 'I'm sorry,' she heard George saying. 'I didn't mean to laugh like that. Bit shocked about the gun, but, seriously, Jay. I think what you do for a living is great. Wish I still loved my work the way you clearly love yours –'

'Why don't you do something about it, then?'

George gave an empty laugh. 'If only . . .'

The door closed. Marianne went upstairs.

Chapter Twenty-Two

Early the following morning, when only the nanny and Lola were up, Jay rang for a taxi. He found his papers, took them back to the police station, reclaimed his jeep and his gun, and then disappeared for a day or two.

Marianne wasn't worried. She knew where he'd gone. He was back at Lal Sendaka's mine, haggling for those rubies. She knew, too, that – while it was likely to take a couple of days for Jay to complete the transaction – he'd return before she left for London. He'd return with rubies in his pocket and self-respect restored: the same old Jay as before. Yet, instead of feeling rejected by this sudden absence and lack of explanation, instead of feeling slighted and snubbed and unhappy, or even indignant, all Marianne felt was the kind of affectionate pity she might have had for a kid brother or a pet.

Poor Jay. With the police treating him as some sort of criminal, and then the full force of his older brother's disdain – George shining a torch into his precious way of life, showing it up as some sort of schoolboy fantasy, and all in front of his girlfriend – it couldn't have been pleasant. Poor Jay, with all his macho accoutrements, having to give a meek account of himself to the kind of people he most despised; forced, finally, to submit to the rules and accept his place in the system. No wonder he felt the need for a bit of time out. Not giving an explanation to Marianne wasn't so much about wanting to be rude, it was more about needing to feel he didn't owe it to anyone. Didn't need anyone's permission. She understood that Jay, being Jay, would be desperate to re-establish a sense of himself as his own man. It was vital to his identity.

And afterwards? He'd carry on as before – she had no doubt of it. Indeed, she hoped he would. She didn't want Jay to change. She loved him just as he was. But it was the nostalgic love of a woman who'd moved on. In time, it would be nice to go back to an old home and see that nothing had been altered, it would be reassuring to walk down those old familiar corridors, turn those worn door handles, pull back those old outdated curtains and recognise a former world . . . but all that fondness would not include an accompanying desire to live there any more.

Marianne had to leave him, had to be the one to walk away – because she knew now that Jay never would. He didn't care that the spark had gone. Perhaps, for him, it had never really been there. He was clearly content to drift indefinitely, with Marianne more as background domestic colour than the main focus of his picture. Probably wouldn't even have been jealous about all that foolishness with Paul . . . which now seemed an eternity ago. And while she was pretty sure that Jay would never have looked elsewhere – he'd certainly never shown the slightest interest in other women – she understood, at last, that such apparent fidelity wasn't really so flattering. Because for Jay the romance, the love, the light of his life, wasn't sparked by women at all. It was only his work and his stones.

Anusha, on the other hand, despaired as – for the second evening in a row – they took their places for dinner and Jay's setting was removed.

'He's got some explaining—'

'He'll be back tomorrow,' said Marianne. 'I know he will.'

'So I should hope,' Anusha muttered. 'I don't know what happened between the two of you but, whatever it was, there's no excuse for this. When you've come all the way out here to stay with us, when I think of what you've been through, it—'

'Really, Anusha. I'm fine.'

'That's not the point. Jay invited you here. He's your host, and he should be looking after you – not abandoning you to a houseful of noisy children, a decrepit mother, and—'

'Hardly decrepit!'

'It's not the way we brought him up. And I'm sorry, but if he isn't here to take you to the airport tomorrow – *in person* – then I'm driving out to Ratnapura and I'm hauling him back myself.'

And then, with the same immaculate sense of timing that had brought him to the door of Philip Dewberry's clinic within seconds of Marianne's scan – the same timing that, for years, had tipped the balance back in his favour when she'd all but given up on him – Jay appeared in the doorway.

'Mother –' He was out of breath and deathly white. His eyes were feverish. He could barely speak. 'All of you . . .' He swallowed. He took another breath. 'We need to get out of here. *Now.*'

331

Anusha gave him a disparaging look. 'And hello to you too, Jehan. How nice of you to make an appearance, to dignify us with your presence after—'

'Stop it, Mother.' He looked at his watch. 'We've got less than an hour to get to higher ground – I'm thinking up by Lady Hill, maybe. Except that everyone else will be rushing in the same direction now, so the road might well be blocked . . .' More frantic swallowing. 'But we should still make it in time. And if—'

'Can you tell us what's happened?' said George, unmoved.

Jay turned to his brother. 'An earthquake, George. Another earthquake. And it's—'

'Here?'

'No, no – Sumatra.'

Hearing this, George's expression changed. The look of mild enquiry was replaced by one of reproach. 'Jay.'

'Like the one before! Don't you see? The one – the one . . .'

'I know. I get it. But you can't seriously be thinking that just because there's been another earthquake in Indonesia, it'll automatically trigger something here. Far less a tsunami on the scale of . . .'

Tsunami. Marianne felt a ripple of activity in her blood, a creeping sensation.

'Tsunami?' whispered Helen, unable to keep the horror from her voice – it sliced across the room. '*Tsunami?*'

George was with her. 'It's okay, darling. I didn't mean—'

'You might just as well have done,' said Jay, pointedly. 'Because there's one on the way right now.'

'Now?' Panic lapped at Helen's groomed perfection. Her chair scraped as she ran to the window, staring

332

wildly, through the grey lines of the frangipani branches, at the flat, faint sea beyond. It didn't seem possible. '*Now?*' she cried, muttering, jibbering. 'What do we *do*? The children . . . they – Christ . . . oh, Christ . . .'

Shushing her, George turned to his brother. 'Who told you?' he demanded. 'And how do they know? It's quite a jump from tremors in Sumatra to—'

'You don't believe me?'

'I—'

'Fine,' spat Jay. 'Stay here, for all I care. But anyone who wants to come up to Lady Hill with me, I'm going now.'

Instantly, Helen was at his side. But the others hesitated, all very still round the dining table in their tidy evening clothes. It didn't seem real. To Jay's feverish mind, their grouping had the look of a pre-war family snapshot – all of them decorated, elegant, civilised, all carrying that same tragic lack of awareness. Fading sepia. Dead already.

'What's wrong with you all?' Jay cried out, banging the table with such force that the silver clattered. 'What don't you understand? We're under a full-scale tsunami alert, and you're all sitting here like a bunch of—'

'Are you saying it's official?' said Anusha, taking a napkin from her lap.

'Of course it's fucking official! I heard it from Hassan, who heard it on the radio – they're going crazy in the town. There are tuk-tuks with loudspeakers telling everyone to evacuate . . . it's *real*, I tell you . . .' Jay grabbed the napkin from Anusha's hands and threw it on the table. 'Leave it, will you? We'll deal with whatever's left tomorrow. The important thing is to get away – now. Get into the cars . . . we've got mine – and,' – looking at his mother – 'and yours?'

'There's no petrol.'

'Okay.' Jay took a deep breath. 'Okay. So if you and Sunitha come with me and Marianne—'

'And Minnendra?'

'And Minnendra. Fine. And—'

'Deepak.'

'Deepak's still here?'

'Of course he's here, Jay. Who else do you think cooks your meals these days?'

'All right. All right. Well he'll have to go in the passenger seat, then – and the rest of you can squash in the back. In fact, Mother – as you know the way – you go with George and Helen in their hire-car and—'

'We didn't hire a car,' sobbed Helen. 'We came by taxis. We thought it would be . . . oh God – the children . . .'

And then the great wooden doors opened again – with Helen dashing out for her babies just as Minnendra and Deepak rushed in – hands moving wildly, eyes desperate, voices gabbling as they spoke of their families, living down by the water, lost sisters, lost parents – tears streaming down Deepak's fat face as the whole horror of the previous tsunami relived itself in his mind . . . and suddenly it was mayhem – a stampede through the house, up and down the stairs, grabbing precious things together . . . photographs, food, passports . . . and out into the driveway, squashing into the cars, any which way . . . Deepak's great body bulging over the sides of Jay's jeep, and Marianne squashed randomly beside him, clinging to the bars for balance as she turned to reassure the two bleary-eyed older children now huddled in the back.

Lola had refused to join them. Refused to let go of

her warm, solid father. She clung with monkey determination as George – concerned, now, as the general fear gathered momentum – approached his stepmother at the far end of the driveway. Anusha was sitting at the wheel of her car, checking the petrol level with an irritated expression.

'You really think this is necessary?' he said, in a low voice.

Anusha looked round, shading her eyes from the evening sun.

'You survived the last tsunami,' he pressed. 'You were here then. I know you were, Anusha. You were high enough.'

Silence.

'Don't get me wrong. I can see it's understandable. Of course it's understandable. After the last one, no one wants to take a risk. But if the ground up here was good enough before, I don't see what point there is –'

'Yes, I know, George. I agree.'

'So . . .?'

Anusha sighed. She looked further round, to where Jay was frantically stuffing bedding and food into the back of his jeep. George followed the direction of her gaze.

'He needs to act,' she said, reaching round into the rear footwell for her can of emergency petrol. 'He needs to do something. This ground . . . it's high, but it could be higher. Lady Hill is higher.'

'Not much.'

Anusha shrugged.

George shifted Lola round a little. He squatted to Anusha's level. 'So you're telling me you prefer to go Jay's way – mislead your household, give in to this madness – just to keep your little boy happy?'

'It isn't that simple.' Anusha shook the emergency can. It sounded pretty full. She wasn't looking at George any more. 'And who's to say he isn't right? He could be right.'

George was silent.

'Better safe than sorry.'

'And you think you're safer, dashing off to Lady Hill?'

'It's higher, George. It's further from the coast.'

'Sure. Fine. If you can get past the crowds on the road.'

George returned to the steps of the *walawe*. He sat down. And, with Lola still silently clinging to his collar, he took out his BlackBerry mobile. This was all too much for Helen, who ran over, screaming at him to get into Anusha's car, pulling the tenacious baby-fingers from his shirt. Hearing the commotion, Jay stopped what he was doing and turned. He spotted the BlackBerry.

'Jesus,' he muttered, slamming shut the boot of the jeep. 'Can he do nothing without consulting that thing?' And then – getting in behind the steering wheel, starting the engine – Jay leant through the open window, shouting, 'Think of your wife – your *children*, George! You *want* them to die?'

Pale with anger, George got to his feet. Shaking Helen to one side, he strode towards the jeep – with Lola's arms still tightly wound round his neck. For a mad, wild moment, Marianne thought he was going to take a swipe at his brother . . . but then Lola wriggled, her hands lost their grip, and the moment passed. George stopped in the driveway. Adjusting his hold on the little body, he relinquished Lola to Helen – who took the scarlet screaming child to the safety of

Anusha's car. Then, returning to his BlackBerry, George dialled in a number and held it to his ear – glancing at his brother as he waited for the connection.

'I'm not trying to be difficult, Jay. Really, I'm not. I see why you're scared. I'm just—'

'*Scared?*'

George closed his eyes. 'I didn't mean—'

'Then what, exactly, did you mean?'

'Just – just that . . . don't you think, as earthquakes happen all the time out here, and as it would be a complete freak of nature if we had two tsunamis in the same decade, don't you think we should at least check? It's—'

'No! No, I don't! And nor to do I want to hang around while you risk our lives –'

'Except it's not a risk,' George replied. 'Not when we must be at least five hundred feet above sea level here, and—'

And then he stopped mid-sentence as, attention all on the BlackBerry once more, he explained his enquiry to the voice at the other end and listened to the reply.

'I'm sorry, would you say that again?' he was asking, his voice barely audible over Jay's invective and Lola's fury. Marianne watched as he turned his back and listened again to the voice at the end of the line. 'Right. So it's an *alert* and not a *warning*, and I'm presuming a warning is more serious? Of course. And what about the NDMC? Have they altered their position too?' Long silence. 'So that's . . . sure. I understand . . .'

Anusha's car was full now, ready to go, waiting only for Minnendra to finish filling it with petrol from the emergency cans. His hands shook. Petrol was leaking and spilling, splashing over the bone-dry ground. Anusha tried the engine. She tried again. It worked the third time. Minnendra jumped into the back. And with car doors opening and closing on either side, with the engine up and running and the general mayhem, Anusha realised – too late – that Sunitha was no longer in the passenger seat beside her. Looking round, she saw the elderly figure making for the house – something precious, something forgotten –

'Sunitha!'

'Leave her, mother.' Jay was close to tears. 'Please. There's no time. We can't—'

But Anusha was out now, followed by Helen – hurriedly thrusting the kicking, scratching Lola into Minnendra's slippery petrol-hands as she went back for George . . . who, finishing his call, calmly put aside his BlackBerry and walked round to the front of the cars.

'Could you listen for a moment?'

His tone was low – so quiet, it seemed impossible that anyone would hear him at all. And yet, to Marianne's astonishment, it worked. Everybody listened. Lola stopped screeching, and Deepak stopped weeping, Helen stopped jabbering and Anusha stopped shouting after Sunitha – for Sunitha, too, had stopped and turned to hear what George had to say.

'There's no tsunami.'

Jay snorted. 'And that's according to – ?'

'The Met Department. They're saying it's a false alarm. It – yes, Jay, there was an earthquake in the Indian Ocean. And they did put out an official alert – you're absolutely right. But they're now saying they overreacted.'

Nobody said a word. Nobody moved. Not even George, who stood for a moment in the driveway, observing the same maddening group-paralysis that

Jay had experienced in the dining room . . . and then, with a brief shrug, he turned and made his way back, past Sunitha, into the empty house.

Marianne couldn't bear it. She looked at Deepak, sitting beside her in frozen indecision. She looked round at the children in the back of the jeep, and then across the driveway, at the others round Anusha's car – all of them waiting, waiting for a sign. Then she opened the door at her side of the jeep, and jumped down – out of the rickety vehicle, on to good, firm ground. Safe, certain, secure. Opening the boot on her way past, releasing the children, she followed George inside. And, one by one, they joined her until it was just Jay left sitting at the wheel of his abandoned jeep, with the deserted driveway before him, and only the splashes of petrol to show what had just taken place.

George was right, of course. Right about the high ground. Right that there was no tsunami. And Marianne, packing her bags that night in preparation for tomorrow's journey back to London – couldn't stop thinking about it, about the way George had handled the matter in contrast to his brother.

Later still, with the lights turned off and Jay sleeping beside her – Jay, who'd eventually come back inside and spent the rest of the evening in front of the television, watching the local news reports as map after map showed the limits of the Sumatra earthquake while reporters praised the Sri Lankan emergency reactions, as if the whole exercise had been some sort of deliberate test . . . with George eventually joining him, both brothers drinking beer together and getting increasingly outraged at the Met Department's incompetence, until it seemed that they'd been in agreement all along . . . Marianne was relieved. Relieved, and – again – impressed that, instead of crowing, George had been big enough to find a way of helping his brother save face.

Jay slept on. And as he slept, she found herself wondering what George and Helen were doing in their room down the passage. Were they sleeping too? Were they talking? Were they making love? She thought of George's elated expression as he'd greeted Helen last weekend. She thought of the unguarded things that Helen had said on the verandah that afternoon, with the bottle of rosé between them and Lola asleep upstairs.

Odd thoughts, odder scenarios, kept floating into her mind.

No doubt it was the holiday setting, the unfamiliar scenery, the exotic sets of fears and challenges that would never present themselves in London . . . all these things must have touched her, altered her. With the very real disintegration of her bond with Jay, with her eyes fully open and the sense of herself as single again – for Marianne, knowing now that there was nothing left to save, had already resolved to end it with Jay tomorrow at the departures gate . . . perhaps it was only natural that she should be susceptible to this sort of thing. It was a temporary state of affairs. The fantasies of a restless mind.

She forced her thoughts to the work that would be waiting back home. She thought of the mess that Gabby would have made in her absence. She thought of Lee and his team in Hatton Garden. She even thought of Paul – hopeless, insubstantial Paul, whose desire to be all things to all people had forced whatever real personality he might have had into mere service of

340

a series of false identities. She thought of the showroom exhibition – now set for July – and the final pieces she needed to get on with designing just as soon as her holiday clothes were put away . . .

Only her mind kept flitting back to George: George as he'd been that evening, standing on the driveway in the evening light. She'd never really noticed how tall George was. She'd never really noticed how authoritative he could be . . . never even thought that an air of authority might be something to value, that she might find it attractive instead of kicking against it all the time. And this particular authority of George's – authority dressed down, with a complete absence of ego . . . Marianne knew suddenly that she'd never admired anyone so much in her life. George Franklin was better and wiser and smarter and kinder than anyone she'd ever met. He was – to Marianne, lying there that night – a revelation. Not so much because he had qualities she hadn't noticed before (although that was certainly part of it) but because – simply through his example – he'd caused something fundamental to change within Marianne herself. She'd never been so interested in, and driven by, the approval of another. And, acknowledging this, she knew now that nobody and nothing mattered more to her than George – who, with a wife and children he adored, could never be more than a friend.

Marianne longed to be able to erase the memory of George's face the night he arrived at the *walawe*, the moment he laid eyes on Helen: obviously mad about her, obviously in love. Helen might be having second thoughts about their marriage, but there was no doubt in Marianne's mind that George was completely committed.

And yet . . . was that enough?

Marianne thought once more of that sultry afternoon on the verandah. She remembered every detail: the glug of rosé into the glass, the rustling of a humming-bird in the bushes beyond the wall, the bitter timbre of Helen's voice. *I'm just not cut out for the kind of life George thinks we can live . . .*

And then Jay muttered something in his sleep, and the bubble burst. Marianne felt a fool. It wasn't just the depth of George's love for Helen that made these thoughts of hers so totally absurd, it was the sudden cringe-making recollection that it was George – *George* – who'd caught Paul kissing her on the steps of the showroom back in November. How would a man like that, so upright and so straight, ever be interested in someone so blatantly irresponsible, so evidently unfit as a mother? Even if he were single, it was an absolute non-starter.

Telling herself that it would all get back to normal when she returned to London, Marianne found a more comfortable position, concentrated on her breathing, and finally – at four in the morning – achieved an hour or two of hot, unsatisfactory sleep.

PART V – LONDON

Chapter Twenty-Two

Helen didn't mess about. Within a week of getting home, she was back with Messrs Gibson & Dent at 12 Lincoln Lane for further legal advice. She hadn't met Rory Dent before. He was surprisingly well dressed for a solicitor, with a bespoke suit and a substantial watch, the kind that suggested regular scuba diving, and a need to know – at a glance – what time it was in New York and Tokyo while simultaneously checking his navigational co-ordinates. There was nothing sombre about the way he looked, nothing dull, nothing that she'd come to expect from men of his profession. Dent wasn't interested in looking like an undertaker – didn't see divorce as a death, with himself as some sort of dreary officiator. On the contrary, he saw it as a game to be fought and won and celebrated. And there was something very pleasing, almost chivalric, about such a man acting as her champion – jousting for her, winning for her . . . all with a merry swagger. Helen loved it. He took away the guilt.

Within another week she'd assembled the recommended evidence. She'd prepped the nanny and the schools. She'd set up her own separate bank account – and had even managed to fix an appointment with her hairdresser before the next campaign meeting in Lincoln Lane. By Friday evening, everything was in place. Pouring herself a large glass of wine, Helen went upstairs to deal with the final item on her list.

George was in the bath. After a gruelling week in London, he was just beginning to feel normal again when Helen poked her head around the door.

'Mind if I come in?'

'Of course not. Here –'

His wet hand trailing bubbles, George reached out to where a book lay open on the white wicker chair by the bath, and knocked it to the floor. He indicated the empty space. But Helen – standing, now, with her back to him so that their eyes only met through the mirror above the basin – showed no interest in coming any closer.

George lay amongst the bubbles, playing with his sponge as he listened.

And an hour later he was driving back to London. He couldn't stay in Hampshire – Helen had been adamant about that. She'd pulled together a few things she thought he might need. She'd even made sure there was enough petrol in the car. He was going back to London, and he was going tonight.

George had sat half-dressed on the edge of the bed, feeling numb. Too stunned to think about finding fresh clothes, he'd simply got back into the crumpled day-worn shirt and pants that he'd left on the bed before his bath. In Helen's eyes, such blatant lack of care in himself was pathetic – repellent, even. She turned quickly to the neat little suitcase she'd been packing. It was part of a set they'd been given as a wedding present. Too small to take on holiday, too big for a weekend. It was the only one they'd never used. Briskly, she lifted the lid.

'Now I've put in your pyjamas and your slippers, and some spare clothes – see? There's room for your washbag here, and your book . . . we'll get the rest sent up next week.' She looked up, briefly. 'I'll tell the children you're working.'

Their eyes met. His very lack of expression expressed his disgust.

'For now, at least,' she added. And then, getting crosser, 'What? You'd prefer to wake them now and drag them downstairs in their pyjamas and break the news to them right this minute?'

'No,' said George. His chest hurt. It was as if he was in a lift that was plummeting, floor after floor – whip-fast down the narrow shaft, cables snapping and flying . . . but at the same time oddly still inside the chamber. 'But I don't think it's a good idea to keep it from them. If you really want a "quickie", as you put it . . .'

Silence.

'. . . if you truly believe it's over –'

More silence.

'. . . and you really can't be bothered to try a little harder?'

She couldn't.

'Not even counselling?'

George looked at his wife for a moment – a final, fading moment, made up of total stillness on his part and narrow bustling, rustling on hers. She was removing the cardboard care labels from the suitcase. Untying the strings, throwing them away. She wasn't going to reply.

'All right,' he said, quietly. 'Then we should speak to them soon – certainly Claudie and Fred – and speak to them together. It's not fair to leave them in the dark. They'll only—'

'Fine.'

'It's—'

'I said fine, George.' Yank-yank went Helen's hand on a final plastic tag. 'We'll do it tomorrow, if you like. You let me know what time you think you'll be here, and I'll try to make sure we're in. They've got Pony Club in the morning, so it would need to be after lunch. But that won't be a problem, will it?'

George closed his eyes.

'You're not staying here.'

He couldn't believe what she was saying – the air of injured righteousness she'd acquired, the total absence of apology . . . almost as if he were the one at fault.

'I'm serious,' she went on. 'And if you try to insist, then I'm afraid I'll have no choice but to—'

'Of course I'm not going to insist,' he said, bending forward to tie the laces on his shoes.

Helen finished her battle with the suitcase. She pushed it to one side and waited for him to say something else, but he didn't. He merely pulled on his suit trousers and went into the bathroom for his washbag and his book. And ten minutes later he was gone – red tail-lights disappearing into the night.

But it was still only nine o'clock when his car pulled into Fitzroy Place, and George – looking up at the large dark windows of his grand London house, at the lifeless Regency shell that was now his full-time home – felt suddenly desperate for company. Gab's company. Mad, unstable Gab, who'd always needed

348

him and depended upon him – and yet whose very need, for the first time in his life, George realised he needed in return. He sat in the car outside, and dialled his sister's mobile.

'George!'

He reeled at the pleasure in her voice. Helen never said his name like that. Not for years, at any rate. And – recognising this – George saw in a flash that his wife's love for him, if love it was, had vanished long ago. He saw, too, that the ensuing desert of indifference (nothing as vigorous or flattering as hatred . . . God, no) had shrivelled his sense of self-worth. It made love from another source – even simple, sisterly love – overwhelming. He felt a piercing gratitude.

'Where are you?'

'I'm at work!' Gab said, laughing. 'Can you believe it? You've actually caught me working on a Friday night!'

George swallowed to speak, but the lump in his throat wouldn't go away . . . and he was suddenly aware of a tightening in his lungs. There was cloudiness at his ears, straining round his heart, pressure in his head . . . a real physical sensation of being deep down, under an immensity of water. His whole being welled with emotion. He could barely inhale, far less reply.

'. . . it's true,' Gab insisted, a tone of indignation creeping in. 'I promise you. I'm at the showroom and we're just on the last page of the exhibition catalogue, which has to be back at the printers by Monday. So Marianne, slave-driver that she is, is forcing me to stay late so that we can get the thing nailed—' And then, with uncharacteristic intuition, Gab sensed something amiss at the other end of the line. George should have spoken back by now. Something disparaging, no doubt, but –

'Are you all right?'

More silence.

'What's wrong?'

Marianne didn't mind stopping early. Their work was as good as done. George's marriage crisis was clearly more pressing than a catalogue and, in any case, she could finish the thing by herself tomorrow – or on Sunday, it didn't matter. Her main aim for the evening had been to reignite Gabby's involvement in the business – and to that extent it had been a success.

For Gabby's business focus – which was, at best, erratic – had suffered in recent months and it was all too easy to see why. For Dexter had moved to London semi-permanently. And for all his claims to be a director of this company and that company (directorships that seemed oddly pointless, certainly undemanding – more a way of feeding Dexter's ego, as if an effortless inheritance entitled him to an air of real importance and success, as if he'd earned that fortune himself), it was obvious to Marianne that the man's main occupation was Gabby. On the rare occasions when Gab was working, Dexter was simply round the corner in a café – reading *GQ* magazine behind the *Herald Tribune* – waiting for his girlfriend to knock off so that he could take her out to lunch. And Gab – far from finding this behaviour tiresome, bordering on stalking – was revelling in a sense of herself as the object of someone else's obsession. It was a real concern for Marianne that her business partner would one day drift away with Dexter, off to the land of the lotus eaters, and never return.

True, no particular disaster had occurred while Marianne had been in Sri Lanka: the showroom premises were still standing on her return, the business was still functioning – no suppliers had been alienated, no clients lost; and yes, Gabriella had proved herself a perfectly reliable custodian. But it was also abundantly clear that her heart wasn't in it any more. Gab no longer seemed desperate to prove herself, no longer craved approval and recognition – not in a business context, at any rate. There was no urgency, no passion, no air of industry. Marianne had come back from Sri Lanka full of plans and ideas – newly inspired, her fingers itching with new designs – and it had come as something of a shock to her to feel no corresponding push from Gabriella's corner. And while there were times when this new dynamic suited Marianne – Gab never questioned her judgement, never blocked a new idea . . . in all but name, Marianne was very much the boss – there were also moments when it drove her mad: this habit of dependence, this passenger-quality, this absence of initiative and creative energy. Yes, Gab was still her friend – would always, to a greater or lesser extent, be her friend. But the partnership, the sense of themselves as professional equals in this enterprise, seemed barely tenable these days.

And so, sensing that a rupture might happen before their all-important exhibition took place – sensing a shift in her friend's priorities – Marianne knew that the only way to ensure Gab's continued interest was to leave her in charge of the glossy presentation elements of the enterprise: the catalogue, in other words; and the invitations to the private view. Tonight had been critical. The exhibition might not be until July, but the ground still needed to be prepared – especially when it

351

came to generating advance publicity – and the catalogue was vital to that process. So if that meant Gab needed a bit of extra nudging – and, on this occasion, supervising – then Marianne decided it was time well spent. It wasn't as if she had anything better to do that evening. Quite apart from anything else, she, too, had an interest in the superficial side of the business. She cared that the catalogue looked right. She wanted it ready in good time . . .

Not that any of those concerns remained long at the forefront of her mind once Marianne heard that George was on his way to the showroom – and, more significantly, why.

The news threw her into turmoil. Her hands shook as she packed away the catalogue proofs. For while there was a part of Marianne that revelled in the collapse of George's marriage, there was another part that couldn't bear the thought of him suffering. She was excited beyond measure that he might now be free, yet couldn't help thinking that George would never get over this rejection – that he would never be anything more than technically single, and that any subsequent woman in his life would only ever rank second to his Helen. She longed to see him, yet feared it too – not least because of the things that Helen had said to her on Anusha's verandah that hot afternoon and the sense that she was wrong to have listened to Jay, wrong to have remained silent instead of warning George.

She fretted, too, about the way she was looking – and fretted that it was shallow to have such thoughts when George's world was falling apart. But after five hours of uninterrupted work, with no trace of make-up on her face, and the man she admired above all others about to walk into the showroom, *free, single* . . .

Marianne hurried into the bathroom with her bag.

Her skin was dull. Her lips were dry. Her eyes were small and tired. She took the stick of mascara, untwisted it, and put it to her lashes – wanting to bring back the glow and give herself the outward look of the inner person, but not so that it was slick or obvious. She didn't want Gab to see her trying. It wasn't easy – especially when her hands were shaking and – damn it, he was early. She could hear the car on the cobbles.

'Marianne?' Gab was calling her.

'Just coming.'

Grabbing the kohl pencil, Marianne suddenly stopped caring about what Gabby thought. Boldly, freely, she darkened the edges of her eyes so that they were vigorous, defined. Make-up wasn't about hiding things – not to Marianne. She didn't have much in the way of foundation and concealer in her armoury. She had colours and highlighters and strong black edgings. It was about bringing something out. It was self-expression.

Gab rapped at the bathroom door. 'Marianne, he's here.'

George was standing alone by the desk when Marianne reappeared. Gabby was in the kitchen, opening a bottle of champagne – it was the only alcohol they had.

George kissed the newly blushered cheek. 'I'm sorry,' he said.

'Don't be silly. We were finishing. And anyway, it's hardly *your* fault –'

The bottle popped in the kitchen.

George smiled a bitter smile. 'That's true enough,' he said. 'Yes, you blame my wife – ex wife, I should say – if that catalogue of yours falls short. Although I'm sure it won't,' he added, accepting a fluted glass from his sister. Raising it in an ironic salute, he took a good slug of the contents.

Gab returned the salute. 'Well, I never liked her,' she declared showing loyalty theory why she knew how.

George finished his glass. 'More credit to you,' he replied. He sounded tired. 'Clearly your judgement is better than mine when it comes to spotting cunts.' He reached for the bottle. 'You don't mind, do you?'

'No, no. Go ahead. It's—'

'Thanks.' George refilled the glass. His ugly word hung in the air. They all felt it.

'I'm not apologising,' he muttered. But the glance he shot at Marianne – a glance that betrayed more regret than he was prepared to admit – said otherwise. She smiled.

'No need.'

Gab nodded, vigorously. 'You say what you like. You go for it, George. Get it off your chest.'

'Oh, I will.' George took a fresh gulp, closed his eyes, and followed it up with another. 'I will,' he repeated, with new determination in his voice. 'With a bit of help from this—' he drained that glass as well. 'And this . . .' He couldn't refill the next glass quickly enough – froth and bubbles were getting in the way. But his purpose could could not have been more obvious.

Gabriella watched him – fascinated. She'd never seen her brother reckless . . . and while she knew she should be feeling sympathetic, there was another part of her that was oddly excited by the transformation.

'I wish I didn't have to go,' she said, with feeling, as she checked the time. Dexter would be waiting. He'd already rescheduled their table that night, so that she and Marianne could finish the catalogue. She couldn't let him down.

'Gab –'

'What?' Gab muttered, sensing criticism – sensing, uncomfortably, that it was perhaps deserved. Only . . . George would be all right, wouldn't he? Marianne was here. Marianne would take care of him – much better care than Gab could ever offer. Gab was no good at this sort of thing. Probably better that she *wasn't* here, in fact. Leave Marianne to it. 'I'm sorry,' she sighed. 'It's not ideal. I see that. But Dexter's expecting me now. I can't just . . .' – eyes pleading now – 'I can't . . . you know how much he hates it when –'

'Yes, yes, okay.' George sank into one of the sofas. He glanced at Marianne. 'We'll manage, won't we?'

Will we? thought Marianne – increasingly desperate, both for herself and for George. It was typical. Typical of Gabby to absent herself in this way. Marianne was reminded of Maya's funeral – of the message Gab had left for her that day. It made her sick to the core.

'You'll look after him for me, won't you?' Gab whispered as she left.

'You should be here, Gabriella.'

'I know, darling. Of course I should.' She opened the door. 'I owe you one.'

'Except it's not *me* you owe,' Marianne hissed back, unable to contain her disapproval.

Gab could smell the cool night air. Over the far wall, an underground train was gathering momentum – screeching and sliding along the tracks. Another moment, and they wouldn't be able to hear one another at all. 'I – I've gotta run, Mazza. I'm sorry. I'll call you tomorrow . . .'

*

355

. . . Which was how Marianne came to be alone with George – drunk, bitter, disconcertingly undone – at ten o'clock that Friday evening, with nothing but a fridgeful of champagne to help them see out the night.

Fantasy or nightmare? She honestly couldn't say.

Joining him in the kitchen as he tore off the foil on the second bottle, Marianne listened to his chatter: his affectionate mutterings about his sister's flakiness, her time-keeping, her terrible taste in men . . . moving into progressively indiscreet opinions about Dexter Rawlinson as a potential brother-in-law. Slowly, she smiled. George might be drunk and bitter, but he was also increasingly entertaining. She began to relax. Still smiling, still listening to him, Marianne watched George's hands round the neck of the bottle. She watched him ease the cork free. She held forward her glass – and then he said something funny; something that made her laugh out loud. And catching his eye in that bright brief moment – a moment of unguarded warmth that generated a surge of unexpected heat between them – Marianne probably knew right then how the evening would develop . . . certainly, she knew it an hour or so later, after the second bottle of champagne had disappeared, along with the pizzas they'd ordered in, and half a bottle of whisky they'd found at the back of a cupboard.

Of course it was a bad idea. It was much too soon. He was much too drunk. There was never any future for the Rebound Girl. Marianne knew all that – and, in her defence, she did try to put on the brakes. She didn't sit next to him on the sofa. She sat opposite. But how was Marianne to know just how sexy it could be to sit face to face, with a table in the way, instead of side by side? With Jay, it had all been about touch. With George – drunk and funny and taking full advantage of their relative positions to hold and play with her gaze – it was all about eye contact. She'd have been safer sitting on his lap.

So she tried a different tack: confessing all about the things that Helen had said to her in Sri Lanka, about how she'd known that Helen was considering divorce, about how Jay had convinced her to say nothing . . . how bad she felt, how guilty . . . letting him down, not a good friend . . .

'Rubbish.' George wiped a smudge of tomato from his shirt.

'But—'

'What possible good would it have done for you to tell me?'

Marianne wasn't sure. 'You – you'd have been prepared,' she said. 'Wouldn't you? Or . . . I don't know, George. You might have been able to stop her somehow . . .'

'Unlikely.'

Their eyes met.

George sighed. 'Helen is leaving me because I'm not rich,' he said. 'Period. She's leaving me because I can't keep her properly any more. The business isn't going quite the way we expected it to go . . . we – we won't have the lifestyle she was banking on. I've let her down. And now she—'

'*You?*' spluttered Marianne. 'You let *her* down?'

George finished a mouthful of pizza. He reached for his champagne glass. 'She does have a point, Marianne. There's no getting away from the fact that I'm not the – er . . . the asset I once was. And Helen needs money. Really. Needs it. There are things in her past, things that . . . well, anyway, there's nothing that you or I or anyone could have done to change the way

357

she's wired now. She was always going to bail out. You were right not to tell me. It would only have complicated things.'

He fell silent. For a moment, neither of them spoke. Marianne bit her lip. She couldn't look at him – couldn't bear to think of what it must be like for him to understand that he was merely a source of cash for the woman he loved, to be valued in that way. She swilled her glass – looking at the whirlpool of bubbles – and racked her brain for another subject. Something to distract him . . .

'So what went wrong?' she said at last. 'You've got a good business, George – a great business. You're Mr Successful, aren't you? We all assumed you were raking it in. You worked hard enough –'

George looked at his feet. 'Not enough to keep my marriage,' he replied. 'Not enough to stop those assholes at Kau Lung choosing Nick Malloy over me, and trashing the business in the process. I should have been smarter – less gullible, less trusting.' Sitting back against the cushions, he lit a cigarette. 'When your business goes sky-high,' he said, 'which it will Marianne, I can tell it will – you've got the wind in your sails, you have some great ideas and, vitally, the right business attitude . . . it's rare, you know, for someone creative – and when some massive luxury conglomerate gives you an offer you can't refuse –'

Marianne rolled her eyes.

'– just make sure you learn from my mistakes and add a few conditions to the handcuffs clause. Don't end up like me. It's not like I don't know how to make money, or do my job. But when I'm shackled to a business that's no longer my own – when they bring someone in, over my head, with no sense of what

Franklin's is actually about and no real feel for the clients or the—'

'Sod the contract.'

George smiled at this, at the innate insubordinate thinking.

'I'm serious,' she went on. 'You'd have handled the fallout – I'm sure you would. You could have bought your freedom – walked away. It's not as if you—'

'Possibly,' he agreed. 'Except it wasn't just me. I had the children and Helen to consider as well. We'd have had to sell the house, let go of the nanny, cut back on the holidays – that sort of thing. Straight away. And, believe me, Helen couldn't have dealt with that. And while, of course, there's no future for me at Franklin's now – we can all see that . . . but with everything already going pear-shaped, you can see why Helen insisted I stay on to the end of the contract. Keep the income for a year or two. Avoid a whopping penalty. It was the least I could do – from her point of view – and I—'

'Fuck Helen.'

Marianne reached for the champagne bottle. 'Fuck her,' she repeated, amused by George's reaction – by the brightening face, by the way he was suddenly sitting up and forward. He was listening, really listening. 'Correct me if I'm wrong, George, but – as I see it – the woman's irrelevant. She's just taken herself out of the equation and, like it or not, you're free of her now. You can do what you damn well like!'

And George, smiling, did exactly that. He put aside his cigarette, got up from his sofa, and came round to Marianne's. It was supposed to be a grateful kiss – a spontaneous, happy, grateful, straightforward kiss on the cheek – firm and heartfelt, with a hug maybe: an uncomplicated display of affection towards Marianne for pointing out the silver lining, for lifting his spirits, for staying on here with him tonight. But something swerved in the process, something to do with Marianne – the unexpected effect of her closeness – a gravitational pull . . . and by the time he reached her, it was clear to them both that this would be no kiss of friendship.

Marianne did nothing to resist. She kissed him back. *Sod the contract.*

Sod the rules. Sod anything and everything and . . . kiss me now, George! Kiss me here! Get rid of that jacket, that tie, that shirt . . . so much material in the way. So many obstacles . . . so many fastenings – buttons and zips and catches and . . . here, let me . . .

A table shifted, a lampshade rocked, both pizza boxes slid messily forwards. A glass flute toppled. The empty champagne bottle rolled to the edge and fell soundlessly to the carpet – not that either of them noticed. Only George's half-smoked cigarette – smouldering in its ashtray, its wispy line of grey drifting upwards – seemed detached from what was happening, observing from the sidelines like a jaded critic.

And if it hadn't been for the state-of-the-art smoke alarms that Marianne and Gabby had conscientiously installed on their arrival – smoke alarms attached to those low mews-house ceilings; smoke alarms that, only last week, had finally been fitted with batteries – who knows what would have happened. As it was, a sudden whooping siren cut through the moment. George pulled back.

'What the—'

'I'm on it,' said Marianne. She found the cigarette, stubbed it out, and pulled on her shirt. Then, climbing up on to the sofa, she reached for the offending circle of plastic and found the switch. The siren bells subsided. Still standing barefoot on the sofa, she looked down at George: wonderfully dishevelled, wonderfully kind – picking up the champagne bottle, removing the pizza boxes, putting the cushions back on the sofa – making it comfortable for her, making a nest.

He looked back up at her, smiling. 'Come on, then!'

But the moment had vanished – as quickly as it had materialised. Freed from his distorting proximity, Marianne's good sense returned. She looked down sadly at the tousled head, the crumpled clothes, the cushiony nest he'd made . . . and suddenly it was all too clear to her that this was a mistake. He might not look it, but George was miserable – devastated – and he was dealing with the trauma in a good old-fashioned manly way . . . alcohol, sex, whatever it took to reach oblivion. It wasn't as if he was pretending anything different. Indeed, he'd said as much about his needs and intentions when he'd first walked in that night. She'd been warned. And while there was a part of Marianne that longed to give him what he wanted, there was another part – the part that was falling in love with him – that knew something vital was missing. George wasn't himself. And while Marianne was desperate for him to kiss her, it had to be when he was in full possession of his right judgement. It had to be the real George choosing her. Otherwise, it was meaningless. Worse than meaningless.

'Marianne?'

'I'm sorry.'

Clambering down, Marianne put on the rest of her clothes. In sinking silence, George set about doing the same.

*

He went home shortly afterwards – apologising to Marianne for getting drunk, for misreading the moment, for allowing himself to think that she –

'It's okay,' she insisted, accompanying him to the door. A taxi was waiting in the mews outside. 'Really, it is.' She smiled at him – one of those bright, flat smiles that, more than any other expression, put the other person at a distance. 'With any luck, neither of us will remember a thing about it tomorrow morning!'

George didn't smile. 'I'll remember,' he said.

'No you won't.' She was laughing now. 'Not with the amount you've drunk! And nor will I, I promise. We'll just carry on as before – we'll still be friends – and it will be as if tonight never happened. Okay?'

George looked at Marianne – so sure of herself, so certain – and wished his head was clear. Why had he drunk that whisky? Blurred and befuddled, he was finding it just too hard to stand up to her, too hard to argue against what she was saying or to read beneath the smiling surface. He sensed that something wasn't right about this sudden dismissal – something contradictory about the way Marianne was standing, the colour in her cheeks, a certain gaucheness in her body-language, in the way she was avoiding eye-contact – something that belied the certainty of her words. Or was that merely wishful thinking on his part? And, even if it wasn't, what could George do about it? Right now, he simply didn't trust himself.

Marianne stood watching as he got into the taxi – her body aching with frustration, her head perfectly satisfied.

Chapter Twenty-Three

She told herself that the ache would subside and, in a way, it did – but only because they saw each other so rarely. In the months that followed, George was clearly too immersed in the whole nasty business of instructing divorce lawyers – lawyers that were a match for the impertinent Mr Dent – to think of Marianne. She heard via Gabby that he was resigning from his job, severing all ties with his old business and paying the substantial penalty that breach of 'golden handcuffs' incurred (a move that sent Mr Dent and his underlings into overdrive). She also gathered that he'd accepted a position in the investment management department of a well-known international bank which, no doubt, would be delighted to have the benefit of his experience, not to mention his list of loyal clients. Gab couldn't recall the name of the bank but it was a good one, she knew that much. George would be substantially poorer than before (especially with the levels of alimony that the charming Mr Dent was bent on securing for his client), but at least he was free, properly free. He was doing well.

And Marianne was pleased for him. She deduced that although George probably hadn't forgotten about the evening they'd shared, he'd clearly decided to behave that way. So while he'd called from the car the following afternoon to thank her for the previous evening, for putting up with him in such a state, for making sure he got home all right, there was no mention of that other matter. He explained that he was on his way back down to Hampshire to break the news to the children –

'Oh God.'

'I know.'

It was all too awful. Neither of them could think of anything to add that wasn't trite or inappropriate.

'I'd better ring off,' he said, eventually. 'I'm sorry. I just—'

'Sure. You go. Good luck, George.'

'Yeah.'

And that, pretty much, was that. Switching jobs meant a forced leave of absence – George was obliged to take a specified period of 'gardening leave', with immediate effect, from the moment he left Franklin's – but Marianne could see that there were infinitely more important claims on his time than herself. His children, for a start. And that elusive divorce settlement.

George still dropped by the showroom from time to time. He would come to see Gabby, or he'd leave something for her, or meet her there on a Friday night so that they could drive down to Hampshire together for a weekend with their mother. On one occasion, he came specifically to look through the company accounts. But at no time did he linger. He was friendly to Marianne while he was there, and she was friendly back, greeting him cheerfully on arrival, waving when he left. Neither of them looked at the empty sofas in the corner, or the cushions neatly arranged along their lengths, or the discreet smoke-alarm disc attached to the ceiling above.

And Marianne, seemingly indifferent, would bend over the latest design and look unseeingly at the page . . . her grey pencil merely following the pre-existing lines she'd made, incapable of adding anything coherent while he was in the room. And an interior voice would howl with silent frustration at the absurdity, at the madness of behaving in a way that was so directly contrary from what she was feeling. The divergent pulling – internal from external; heart from head; emotional turbulence from physical stillness – it gave rise to a certain silent pressure that was sometimes more than she could bear.

She realised with a jolt that however intrigued she'd been by Jay's elusiveness, however flattered she'd been by Paul's attentions, none of it touched what she was feeling now. It wasn't about solving riddles or wanting some sort of security. It was about a simple and certain longing to be on the inside of George's life, and to have him on the inside of hers . . . to be the person he confided in, the person who could take care of him, ease his problems, fight his battles, share his victories. Hell, wash his underpants, cook his suppers, undergo any kind of intimate drudgery . . . the whole sexist framework of what it was to be a wife . . . of what her mother had done, and her mother's mother, and so on, all the way back to the caves . . . it all made madly perfect sense when love was involved. You actually wanted to do those things. You wanted the right to do them. You wanted the job.

But the offer never came. Instead, George would go

home, or off out to dinner, or wherever it was he went these days, and Marianne would feel a stab of pain. Muted by circumstance, like the mermaid in the story, she could only watch in silent anguish as the door closed behind him.

And as time passed, she understood that she would have to let it go. It wasn't just the infrequency of his visits, his obvious lack of interest, it was his continued love for Helen that really broke her hope. For Gabriella – oblivious to Marianne's feelings – never tired of worrying about her brother's love for his ex-wife, and what the split was doing to him. She was desperate for him, and would speak to Marianne at length about the way poor George was struggling.

'Worst of all is the way he pretends he's over her. He makes out it's all water under the bridge and perhaps it's even a *blessing in disguise* and all that crap – acting happy and jolly when we can all see that he's breaking up inside.' She sighed. 'It's awful, Marianne.'

'Of course. It must be.'

'If only he'd just stop being proud and *admit it*!' Gab cried, working herself into quite a passion. 'We – all of us – we can see it on his face that he's barely sleeping these days. He hasn't taken a single photograph down – even the wedding ones. He says he wants to keep it just the same *for the children* – it's always *for the children* – but it can't be healthy, can it?'

Marianne shrugged.

'I reckon he thinks he can win her back. I reckon he's still—'

'Sorry, Gab. I must call Lee before he leaves the workshop . . .'

It didn't help that Gabby was so damn happy these days. For Dexter – provoked into action by the

366

increasing demands of this jewellery exhibition on his girlfriend's time – had decided that a wedding was the answer. After one particularly tedious spring morning and his third lunch alone in as many days (the waiters at La Grenouille were starting to look at him with pity, not respect, no matter what fancy wine he ordered), Dexter could bear it no longer. He rang the future Mrs Rawlinson from his mobile.

'Have lunch with me.'

Gab glanced across the room at Marianne, with her lists. 'I can't, Dex. You know I can't.'

'Yes you can. They've got lobster on the specials, today. And I've got a beautiful bottle of Meursault in the ice bucket – and something rather particular to ask you . . .'

'What?'

'Meet me for lunch, and you'll discover.'

'What? Discover *what*?'

'I'll order the lobster then, shall I?'

'*Dexter!*'

Gab was overjoyed. Now that he'd asked her, now that she had a socking great sparkler on her finger – a sparkler oddly similar to the one Paul had given Marianne all those years ago (not that Marianne would ever be so tactless as to mention it now, not when even she had to admit that it actually looked very *right*, and very Gab, glittering there beside the manicured nails and the TAG Heuer watch) – now that it was all settled, Gab had no need to hide her love for Dexter any more. And even if there was a slightly unsettling degree of gratitude about it, an element of need, and a physical interaction that seemed more fond than sexual, Marianne didn't think that such things necessarily made it wrong. Not in this case. Gabriella had found the right person. She was, perhaps for the first time in her life, genuinely and completely happy – and who was Marianne to begrudge her that?

But while Gabby was ecstatic in her love, she was also – more than ever – filled with pity for her poor brother, for being at the opposite end of the happiness scale, for losing his soul-mate just as she'd found hers, for being cast off and discarded just as she was being loved and wanted, for having his whole world fall apart just as hers was pulling together. She felt his pain. Now that she had Dexter, now that she knew what it felt like to be wanted *for ever*, Gabby could hardly bear to imagine how she'd feel if Dexter were to turn around at some point in the future – as Helen had done to George – and brutally tell her to get lost.

Marianne listened to Gab's anxieties on the subject, and drew the inevitable conclusion. A picture would come into her mind: George standing in the doorway of Anusha's dining room after his long-haul journey – searching for his Helen, searching, searching down that long length of table, and then his face lighting up when, at last, he saw her . . . it haunted Marianne. Recalling his expression – such open devotion, such vulnerability – how could she fail to agree with Gabriella?

So she began the slow process of forcing George from her thoughts. No point wasting time on a man who didn't return her feelings. She needed to get a grip and move on. Yes, it would be difficult. It was always difficult. And some losses were certainly harder to process than others. Some losses, indeed, she had no wish to forget . . . that of Maya, for instance; there would always be a hole, and it was only right. But a situation such as this – misplaced passion – had no need of a shrine. It hadn't been this hard with Paul, or even Jay. So what the hell was the problem? How could she have allowed what was – face it – one drunken fumble and a bunch of daft fantasies about a man to whom she was entirely unsuited get so completely under her skin? She didn't understand how it was she'd grown so weak, so incapable of exerting her will over her heart . . . and thanked God for the exhibition, for the distraction it afforded her, and the way its anticipated success would bolster her self-esteem.

All the early responses – generated from Marianne's decision to circulate that limited preview edition of their catalogue – were excellent. From magazines willing to promote her pieces in editorials to a number of major retailers showing real interest in commissioning a limited line from Cooper Franklin . . . all of it was positive.

And it helped that matters were improving with her mother. Something had changed between them since Marianne's return from Sri Lanka – something had softened. Perhaps it was the split with Jay. Certainly, Patricia had been worried enough to come up to London when she'd heard the news . . . was Marianne all right? Was she really okay, living all alone in that flat of hers? Didn't she want to come back down to Kent for a while? Let herself be pampered for a month or two? Or – no. Of course. That wouldn't work. Patricia understood. But might she come to London for a bit? Stay on the sofa? She didn't like the idea of Marianne all by herself . . . not after everything that had happened. She – yes – she knew that Jay had hardly been a constant presence, even at the best of times, but Marianne had been through a lot recently.

Was there nothing Patricia could do? What about money?

In the end, they'd agreed that she would come to London for a long weekend. And while, afterwards, Patricia had laughingly admitted to her friends in the parish that it had actually been quite a strain – having to sit there, even for that short stretch of time, in the haphazard space that Marianne called home, resisting the urge to get out the duster, find cupboard space for all the rubbishy bottles and vases on Marianne's kitchen worktops – worktops that looked more like an artist's studio than a place for preparing food . . . while Patricia was guiltily grateful that her daughter had not needed her to stay the full week, Marianne was genuinely sorry to see her mother go. She'd loved being able to enjoy Patricia's company without feeling oppressed by her household habits. She'd loved having her mother on her own territory, loved being able to give – instead of always having to be grateful. It had been a revelation. And Patricia's interest in the upcoming exhibition, the way she seemed, finally, to understand how much it mattered to Marianne, how serious she was . . . it was all very healing – and helpful, when it came to convincing herself that there was life beyond George.

A date for the private view had been set for the second Thursday in July and, by June, the invitations were ready to send out. They sat on Marianne's desk ready for dispatch, along with the remaining catalogues. There was still quite a bit of work to do – for Gabby was far more interested in wedding invitations these days – but Marianne wasn't overly bothered. She had all the relevant names and addresses for her guest list on the computer. She knew how to print labels. A couple of late nights, and the job would be done.

Looking again at the long list of names, which included those of their all-important professional contacts, both from the press and those in the trade, as well as those of their clients, past and present, and, finally, their families and friends, Marianne worried that there were still far too many for the showroom space. She and Gab had done their best to keep it down, culling family and friends to an absolute minimum.

But the other names – the contacts and the clients – were impossible to cut back. And tempting as it was to strike off the names of certain awkward clients – Paul's and Sophie's, amongst them – Marianne wasn't prepared to take on the ill-will that such a gesture would provoke. Better to invite the lot and hope that most refused. The party could always spill out into the mews if it really got too cramped – so long as the weather stayed fine.

Chapter Twenty-Four

Paul and Sophie accepted their invitation. Sophie, in particular, was keen to support Marianne – encourage that undeniable talent, as well as the rather more fragile soul that hid beneath the confident personality. Sophie remembered visiting Marianne in hospital. She remembered the service held for Marianne's stillborn child. She remembered noticing Marianne's absence at their wedding and – far from feeling snubbed – was simply ashamed for being so insensitive as to have invited her at all. Poor Marianne. The last thing she'd have wanted, then, was an afternoon of forced smiles at the wedding of some ex-boyfriend. No wonder she'd decided to give it a miss. And when Sophie heard that Marianne was no longer with Jay – that she didn't even have a boyfriend to help her through the darkness – Sophie was filled with frustrated compassion. She knew it wasn't her place to comfort Marianne (who clearly had closer friends than Sophie and no need for extra sympathy), but nor did she feel comfortable merely letting it go, as Paul seemed happy to do. It seemed cold, somehow – and Sophie racked her brains, without success, for a way of renewing the connection that didn't come across as patronising, or openly smug . . . especially when she discovered she was pregnant. The contrast of her own fulfilment beside Marianne's emptiness was only too apparent.

So naturally Sophie was delighted to open the Cooper Franklin invitation, not just because it showed that Marianne still had something positive in her life – that she hadn't given up, hadn't allowed troubles in other parts of her life to affect her career – but also because it provided Sophie with an opportunity to show a bit of warmth. Perhaps even rekindle the friendship. She was determined to accept.

And, for a while, Paul was happy to oblige. Even as close as the week before the exhibition, he had no objection to the plan. He still experienced the odd twinge when he thought of how things had been left with Marianne: occasional flashes would appear uninvited in the forefront of his mind, but they were flashes that – like a dream half recalled – he found easy to dismiss as unimportant. Senseless. Blips on the screen. Paul simply wasn't capable of the kind of personal honesty that – in another man – would have involved admitting to himself that he loved Marianne. Far less, that he loved her more than the woman who was now his wife, and – thwarted in his primary love, doubly thwarted, in fact – had grabbed at the alternative without giving any thought as to whether it was fair to Sophie to treat her in this way. Paul needed to like himself. He needed to see himself in a better light. And, to do that, he needed to muddy the past. Or – even better – not think of it at all.

And so, with a reaction so ingrained it was more like instinct, Paul turned his thoughts to something nicer:

the baby due in September, the sensible family car he'd bought in its honour, the idea of himself as a wonderful father. And if that didn't work, then it wasn't hard for him to find some other distraction – something mildly troubling but inherently solvable, like fixing the aerial or clearing the drains . . . and ultimately effective, in terms of tricking himself into a more comfortable frame of mind. Paul 'solved' a lot of household things that month. Even Sophie noticed the improvement. Assuming the renewed focus was down to impending fatherhood, she freely praised his efforts.

Which meant it was really quite a shock for Paul when – the very evening before Marianne and Gabby's party – he suddenly realised that there was a problem, a real problem, and that he had less than a day to make it right.

He was sitting up in bed, playing with the new digital camera he'd bought last week – a camera they'd be needing for the baby . . . really, an essential. Nothing to feel guilty about. They had enough money. Indeed, Sophie was pleased he'd got it in good time to master any technical complications before the baby arrived. Well done, Paul. Good husband. Tick.

Sophie was standing at the wardrobe, looking at her clothes with a despondent expression. Then she sighed.

Paul looked up. 'What is it?'

'Oh, nothing,' she replied. 'It's nothing . . .'

But Paul knew her too well. He put the camera aside. 'Come on.'

Sophie hesitated.

'Tell me . . .'

Sophie sat on the bed. 'It's stupid,' she said, snuggling close to him and toying unthinkingly with her ring. 'And it's not as if anyone else at Marianne's party will care – or even look at me, for heaven's sake. I'm pregnant! I can't expect to look slim or pretty or—'

'You're beautiful, Sophie.'

'You're kind.'

'Not kind,' he insisted.

And Sophie – now wishing fervently that she'd never raised the whole painful subject of her looks – fell silent. Nothing was going to stop her from looking like a carthorse next to all those svelte women tomorrow night. But boring Paul about her expanding shape – drawing his attention to it, forcing him to deny the obvious – was hardly a constructive way to deal with what should, in any case, be a source of celebration. Embarrassed, she looked away – down to the ring she was twiddling.

Her beautiful ring.

'Still,' she said, turning it slowly. 'It's nice to know that I can go on wearing *this*, at least, no matter how big I get. And I'll be able hold my head high tomorrow night – in front of all those trendy people – all those bohemian designers and international gem experts, and dealers like Jay, and fashion reporters, and so on – and not feel a total misfit!'

Oddly, Paul did not respond.

'I really do love it, darling . . .'

Silence.

'Darling?'

Paul looked at her. 'Are you sure it's going to be that sort of party?' he said.

Sophie smiled. 'Marianne's hardly dowdy! You remember what she looked like when *she* was pregnant!'

'Yes . . .'

'– and Gabriella Franklin's so thin and glam, it's terrifying. Truly. And no doubt their friends will be every bit as scary.'

'But the trade people,' said Paul, no longer really listening to her. 'The experts and dealers and so on. You don't think they'll be there as well, do you?'

Except he already knew the answer to his question. Even if Sophie told him what he wanted to hear – that it was a private social party, nothing more – Paul would not have believed it for a second. He lay awake all night, working through his options. There was always the chance that those gem experts would never notice the problem with Sophie's ring. And if Paul hadn't felt so guilty, he probably would have taken the risk. The chances of anyone spotting the discrepancy were tiny. Even if Marianne picked up on it – and she was really the only person at all likely to do so – she was hardly going to blow the whistle. Not when she herself was so deeply involved. Yes, she'd changed her mind. Yes, she'd eventually sent him the true padparascha in an identical setting, but the fact she'd complied at all with Paul's original plan was hardly to her credit. So if he'd then decided, on balance, that it was better to leave Sophie with the inferior version and raise money from the other – and what in God's name was so very wrong with investing family funds in a sensible car instead of fancy jewellery? – who was Marianne to criticise? It wasn't as if he intended actually to sell the padparascha. The pawnbroker was simply helping him through the immediate demands of married life – and then, in time, when cashflow was a little better, he'd redeem Sophie's real ring and nobody would be any the wiser.

That, at least, had been the original plan. The fact that his six-month contract with the pawnbroker had recently expired, leaving Paul with the option of either redeeming the ring (which, clearly, he couldn't afford to do – not now, not with a baby on the way), renewing the arrangement and continuing to pay the interest on his loan (which was getting increasingly hefty and awkward to handle with each passing month), or else abandoning the ring altogether, leaving the pawn-broker to sell it at a fair market price – and perhaps even win for Paul the cash benefit of the balance between the broker's original valuation and the true proceeds of sale . . . in the end, it had been all too easy for him to deviate from his original plan. Nobody would ever know. And there were just so many expenses these days.

So Paul, simply by letting the matter drift, by failing to respond to the notice he'd been served, effectively gave the pawnbroker permission to sell his wife's ring. Somewhere in the back of his mind, he allowed himself the idea that it wasn't really his decision. And some day, he told himself, some day soon, he'd win it back. Those brokers wouldn't be able to sell a ring like that instantly. There were repeat valuations and whatnot to be made. And anyway, who else had heard of a padparascha stone? How easy were such things to trade? He imagined it languishing – forgotten – in the pawnbroker's vault, and went on telling himself that all would be resolved. They'd get the ring back. It was just a matter of time . . .

Except, of course, it wasn't. Not any more. Not with Marianne's exhibition party tomorrow evening. And Paul, fired up by guilt, fear, pride . . . Paul couldn't merely accept his fate. He couldn't just do *nothing*. He had to try. And so, in spite of his current position with the pawnbroker, and in spite of knowing that the risk of being caught – on the night, by one of Marianne's gem experts – was tiny . . . Paul resolved any do his best to get the damn thing back. Apart from anything else, it was the only way he was able to get any sleep that night.

He waited until Sophie left for work the following morning; waited for the ticking of her bicycle wheels to fade, before opening the door to the drawing room, treading silently over to the desk in the corner, and lifting from the wall above it a small watercolour that had hung there ever since he'd first known Sophie and her parents. He replaced it with a landscape from the spare room and told himself that, if Sophie asked, he could say he was getting the frame on the watercolour repaired. Something like that. Then, wrapping it in an old overcoat, Paul took the painting down to the Earl's Court pawn shop just as quickly and discreetly as he could.

It wasn't an attractive painting. Nobody liked it. Sophie's great-grandmother – a portly woman, sitting in an armchair – was hardly the most desirable of subjects. In no way could it be described as one of the artist's most desirable works. But the signature of John Singer Sargent, he knew, was worth enough. There was an auctioneer's certificate stuck to the back – verifying the authenticity, and giving an estimated value. It might have been dated a decade ago, but that was surely to Paul's advantage. In any case, it would only be for a day *at most*. He'd return first thing tomorrow to swap them back again. It would all be fine. Better than fine. In Paul's opinion, it was his only chance of reclaiming the padparascha – albeit temporarily . . .

. . . except there was no padparascha to redeem. Paul stood in the pawnshop, clutching the Sargent while the news sank in. It was gone. Sold last week, in strict accordance with the National Pawnbrokers Association procedures, all of which . . . a perky assistant with very short red hair and a shiny suit rustled back a few pages in Paul's file . . . yes, that's right, all of which had been outlined on the original notice documents which had been duly served on Mr Farage, in person, at his offices, on the twenty-third day of June. Paul glanced down – his eye resting on the smart vintage Rolex on the man's wrist, a trophy that sat at odds with the cheap shiny suit and struck Paul as most distasteful in the circumstances. Observing the watch, he listened as its owner explained how – it now being the eleventh of July – those fourteen days had elapsed. The brokers were entitled to sell the item at fair market price, and Paul was entitled to whatever balance might arise from that sale, which – rustling forward in the file again, the assistant lifted a relieved face to his customer – '. . . which took place last Thursday and which, Mr Farage, I'm sure you'll be delighted to hear, after the usual deductions, has produced a balance in your favour! See here?'

Paul looked at the original valuation figure on the invoice, the subsequent sale price and the balance owed: £215.38. He had to concede it was fair. They hadn't undervalued the ring. It was just . . . when he thought of how quickly the original loan had vanished, of how the interest payments had escalated, of all the future demands on his purse . . . was this really all that was left?

'Well, that's a turn-up, isn't it? We can give it to you now, if you like – in cash . . .'

'Is Michelle here?'

Michelle, the friendly woman that Paul had dealt with in the past, was summoned from the vaults below the shop. After a minute or two, she appeared – looking rather less approachable than before, if not entirely unsympathetic.

'. . . come on, love. You really want me to go through it again?' She looked at the sickened face. 'If,' – sighing – 'if, after fourteen days you fail to renew your contract or respond to the notice served . . . which I'm sorry to say is exactly what has happened – then we do have the right to sell.' The contract was produced for Paul. The relevant clause identified. 'We're not running a charity, here.'

'Who bought it?'

Michelle shook her head. 'Even if we had that information,' she said, sifting through the remaining paperwork to check, 'and we don't, it's not customer policy to give out private details. I'm sure you understand . . .'

'So – so that's it?' Paul spluttered.

'I'm afraid so. You want me to take a look at that painting, then? We won't be able to deal with it directly, I'm afraid – not until we can get our fine art expert over from the Bond Street branch, which may take a few hours. And we'll want all the usual documents, of course: proof of ownership, recent valuations . . . that sort of—'

Paul shrank away. 'No – no . . . no, thank you. It's all right . . .'

He hurried home with his £215.38, and hung the painting back in its place above the desk. Great-Grandmother Mostyn looked down at him from the comfort of her armchair. She wasn't a pretty subject, but something of the woman's spirit had undoubtedly been caught in the flick of Sargent's brush. It was a look of utter disdain.

Paul toyed with the idea of letting Sophie go to the party alone. He could easily leave a message saying he was detained – the car breaking down, a meeting running on, a sudden blinding headache . . . his options were plentiful. But the expression on Great-Grandmother Mostyn's face was having a strangely compelling effect on him. Paul felt observed. Reminding himself that the chances of exposure were – in any case – extremely slim, he checked the urge to run. He wasn't going to let his wife turn up, alone, at a party she was clearly going to find intimidating. He wasn't going to let her down. He wasn't that sort of man.

Chapter Twenty-Five

Marianne arrived early at the showroom on the morning of her exhibition, partly because there was much to do, but mainly because she'd woken light-headed in a fluttery state of hypercreativity – as if she'd already had three cups of coffee. Lee had completed all his polishing over the weekend and the pieces had arrived yesterday in a security van – gleaming, finished, ready to exhibit. Marianne had glanced at one or two before packing them back in their silken boxes and locking them away in the showroom safe: row after row, box after box, of elegant catmint-green . . . sitting there now, in the dark.

There was really only the party left to pull together now. That morning, Marianne would be taking delivery of a series of hired cabinets that would display their work to maximum advantage. A storage company would be taking away the sofas and the coffee table to create more space for their guests. She and Gabby would then make sure that the place was spotless before the florists and caterers arrived.

Marianne was outside – standing on the cobbles of

the mews, with her sleeves rolled up, smiling and laughing and waving her hands as she helped the storage company driver back his van up as close as possible to the showroom steps – when the telephone rang.

'You okay now?' she shouted to the driver. 'You mind if I get that?'

The driver waved agreement – he was close enough. Marianne went back inside.

'Hello?'

'Marianne . . .'

Marianne frowned in semi-recognition.

'It's Helen Franklin!'

'Hello, Helen.'

Helen registered the neutral tone. It wasn't unfriendly, exactly. But nor was it overjoyed. 'Is this a bad time?' she said, giving Marianne the benefit of the doubt. 'I did hear on the grapevine that you have an exhibition coming up, so if you're busy at the moment—'

'I am a bit. What's this about?'

Helen smiled. She couldn't help it. Her recent news – sharing it, going public – was just too thrilling to be negated by whatever it was that was eating Marianne that morning. 'It's still early days, of course,' she said airily, 'and there's certainly no hurry, but I was hoping I might be able to speak to you about a commission . . .'

Commission. The word was impossible to ignore. And for all her misgivings about the idea of taking work from such a source, Marianne couldn't quite bring herself to the point of voicing them. She had no problem being cold and short to Helen, but found it strangely difficult to reject – actively – an approach for work. Especially when Helen was being so warm.

Because, for all the woman's disgraceful behaviour towards George in recent months, for all her selfishness when it came to the big picture, it still went against the grain to meet friendliness with hostility.

So Marianne, disarmed by Helen's sudden charm – and blinded by the moment, by professional nicety, by the micro-demands of the present – Marianne sat at her desk with the telephone to her ear and a pencil in her hand, taking notes, while Helen explained what was wanted, and the storage men began heaving the first sofa towards the door. There was a fair bit of crashing and banging. At first, she thought she might have misheard. What was it? A necklace? A bracelet? Some earrings? With the way Helen was already talking about rococo styles and the specific gemstones she'd be considering, it was as if she'd missed a vital section of the brief.

'. . . needless to say, he's wanting diamonds – preferably two or three – but I thought maybe you'd be able to suggest something more unusual, something like that stone Jay found for those friends of yours in Sri Lanka last year, maybe? I don't think Rory's averse to the idea. He'd just need a bit of convincing, which I'm sure you'd be able to help me with, if—'

'Rory?'

'Rory Dent. My fiancé.'

Marianne paled.

'I know it's a bit quick.' Helen was giggling. 'But what are we supposed to do? Creep about like teenagers? George and I will be divorced by the end of the year – sooner, with any luck. So I'm good as free to marry again, I'm not getting any younger—'

'I can't do it,' said Marianne, as the shock subsided and her faculties returned. 'I'm sorry, Helen. It – it's just . . . just not . . .'

384

'Yes?'

Silence.

'You disapprove?'

Marianne squirmed. 'I'm sorry, Helen. Really I am. But – but after everything you've done, and what with Gabby being George's sister . . . I mean – what did you expect me to say? You can hardly have thought that I—'

'I'm not asking Gabriella to do it, Marianne. I'm asking you. And – and not just because I think you're good – although of course that's a factor! No – it's also because you understand . . .'

'*Understand?*'

Helen coughed. 'At least, you seemed to understand . . . back in January? In Galle, remember?'

How could Marianne forget?

'I told you I was going to leave him, Marianne. And' – she was laughing again – 'I can't say I recall you having any sort of problem with it back then . . .'

'That's only because—'

'And looking at the way you were happy to dump poor Jay less than a week later, you're hardly a model of constancy. You – come on, Marianne! Who are you trying to fool? Being a good girl and living by other people's rules . . . it's hardly your style, and it certainly isn't mine. Neither of us is going to waste time on someone we don't love any more. We've got lives to lead. We're the *same*, you and me, it's why I confided in you back then and – frankly – it's one of the reasons I'd like you to make this ring for us now.'

More silence.

A tone of petulance crept into Helen's voice. 'You might at least sound pleased for me.'

'Pleased?' Marianne laughed in disbelief.

'It's not as if Rory doesn't have the means for something pretty glitzy, something that'd make you a fair bit of cash. It's supposed to be a compliment!'

Marianne looked down. Her hand was tight around the pencil. Her knuckles were white. 'I'm not doing it,' she said grimly. 'Nothing would induce me. And for the record, you and I are absolutely *not* the same. I didn't abandon a kind, dear husband and three innocent children simply because he lost a bit of money. I didn't break his spirit – insisting he go on working with the new management at that place when it was clear that they were humiliating him. I didn't live like a parasite while he worked like a dog. I didn't destroy every ounce of confidence that a good, decent, intelligent man like George should have in spades.' And then, sensing she might have said too much, sensing stunned astonishment at the other end of the line, Marianne reined back. 'I'm sorry. I shouldn't be talking like this, I know – not when you've only ever been nice to me – but, honestly, Helen, I just can't think why you're leaving him! Any woman would be thrilled to find herself married to someone as talented and funny and kind and – and family-minded—'

'Good God,' spluttered Helen. 'What is this? The George Franklin Fan Club?'

Marianne stopped.

'Since when did you switch sides?'

'I never switched sides.'

Silence.

Marianne sighed. 'If I was silent back in January,' she said, picking her words with care, 'if I didn't object to the things you were saying about him back then, I'm afraid it was only because I was hoping and praying that you weren't serious. I hoped you were simply letting off steam.'

'Hmm,' said Helen. And then, suddenly aware of an unpleasant combination of stupidity on her own part and some yet-to-be-defined betrayal on Marianne's – and needing, for the sake of her own self-esteem, to believe in giving weight to the latter – she went into full defensive mode. 'Either that, or you wanted him for yourself, right? Which, of course, would explain why you—'

'*What?*'

Helen laughed. 'Well I never . . . to think you've got the hots for *George*!'

'You really think that?'

'Don't hear you denying it. Although I can't – for the moment – think quite *why* you'd want that loser after all things I told you about him. But, as they say, there's no accounting for—'

'Stop it, Helen. Don't be absurd.'

'Absurd.' Helen's laughter disintegrated into silence. 'I called you, Marianne, in friendship, to ask about a ring . . . and now you're saying I'm absurd?'

'I think what you just said was absurd, Helen. And insulting, and typical of someone who's prepared to behave as you've behaved in the past few months.' Marianne took a deep breath, before explaining that George was merely her friend. 'Like Gabby is my friend. Nothing more. I care about him.'

'You certainly do,' came the whipping reply. 'And you're welcome to him. Goodbye.'

Chapter Twenty-Six

In other circumstances, Marianne would have carried Helen's call about with her for days – relived it, pondered it, imagined all the things she wished she might have said differently . . . it was too unpleasant, too accusatory, and – in parts – too close to the truth for her merely to scrumple up and toss into the waste basket of encounters best forgotten. This time, however, she couldn't linger. There was no time for private ponderings. With the exhibition upon her and the party preparations building towards an inevitable climax, Marianne had no choice but to turn to matters more pressing, more immediately to hand – and save the memory of Helen's call for a time when she'd be able to process its effect on her more thoroughly. For now, tonight – and only tonight – occupied her mind.

Everybody came. If it had been raining – if there had been no natural extra space afforded by the enclosed mews, which was now almost as full of guests as the showroom was itself – Marianne dreaded to think what a disaster the evening might have been. As it was, the spontaneous overflow had charm. Guests were clustered around the old car bonnets and propped-up bicycles that made up the mundane scenery of Marianne and Gabriella's everyday life – yet now looked more like intentional, even groovy, party props. Marianne thanked God that Mr Chevening in No. 5 had such a very beautiful Bentley in sleek racing green; thanked God that he liked to clean his car obsessively, and happened to be away in Spain that week. And while the wheelie bins at the far end weren't exactly fragrant and the potted plants outside No. 7 were yellowing and dry, it somehow didn't matter. Nobody else seemed to notice or mind. With the sun disappearing and the mews in purple shadow, the air was getting cooler – people were reaching for their coats and shawls – but nobody looked like leaving. When another train crashed by on the other side of the wall, the guests simply raised their voices, or bent a little closer, or stopped to enjoy the champagne. Watching them from her vantage point on the showroom steps, Marianne munched another canapé, grinned at the security guard, and felt her misgivings disappear. Some might think it unprofessional for a promotional party to have turned out this way – it wasn't tidy, it wasn't comfortable – but there was still something special about the way everybody wanted to stay in spite of the jumbled result.

Turning the other way – looking inside the showroom, to where the displays were rendered almost invisible by the wall of guests crushed around them, heads bent to examine the contents, faces caught in the bluish cabinet lighting – Marianne's sense of pride intensified. She couldn't see the jewellery – but then, she didn't need to see it. Not tonight. What mattered now were the various reactions of her guests – in particular, those of the journalists and the important buyers from places like Fenwicks, Selfridges and Harrods. And from brief conversations she'd had with those individuals, together with the way they were staying on – talking to one another, making notes on the catalogue, speaking into dictaphones – Marianne could tell it was good. Better than good. On the back of the things they'd said to her, the contracts they were offering, the exposure, the international possibilities, it was suddenly clear to Marianne that her career – her life – was going to change for ever. After tonight, she wouldn't have to rely on Gabriella's financial backing. It wouldn't matter if Gab and Dexter ran off into the sunset. Marianne was strong enough now to make it on her own.

'I'm impressed,' her mother had said, earlier.

'Really?' Marianne glowed. 'You like it?'

Patricia nodded. 'Yes,' she said, looking out across the party. 'I do, as it happens – although that's neither here nor there. It doesn't matter what *I* think of your designs. What matters is—'

'Of course it matters.'

'All right.' Softening. 'If you like. But the thing I'm trying to say to you, Marianne – and saying it very badly, as usual – is that I was wrong . . .'

Marianne looked away. She felt an urge to cry.

'I thought your father would be disappointed. I thought it would all come to nothing.' Patricia gave a rueful smile. 'How wrong I was! Coming here now and seeing you, and looking at all of this – all of *them* . . .' She gestured towards the magazine photographer, and a couple of men just beyond him – one of them on his mobile, reading out the blurb from the catalogue and translating it into Italian, while the other, who had all but signed Marianne to create a line for their next season, pushed three Cooper Franklin catalogues into a briefcase.

'Dad would have been proud, darling.' Patricia bit her lip. She couldn't quite look at Marianne. 'All right? That's what I wanted to say. And I'm sorry for not believing in you.'

Patricia left shortly afterwards – needing to get back home to Kent before dark, needing to feel safe on the road, safe in the comfort of her own space and her own routines. And Marianne understood. It was great that her mother had come at all. And after the things she'd said – the things about her father – how could Marianne complain? On the contrary, she was floating. In an otherwise-perfect evening, only George – poor ignorant George, who was looking happier and more relaxed than she'd seen him in months, and who still, presumably, given his cheerful mood, knew nothing about Helen's recent engagement – only George remained a source of concern.

Looking over to where he was standing at the far end of the mews – he was talking to some people she didn't know, some friends of Gabby's – Marianne was struck by the fact that George wasn't in a suit. And while the jeans he was wearing were still dark and new, the rest of his attire was decidedly informal – and, in Marianne's opinion, all the better for it. The linen shirt was attractively crumpled, the Pumas nicely trodden in, and there was no doubt in Marianne's mind that 'gardening leave' – or perhaps it was the absence of Helen's rigid domestic order in his life? – whatever it was ... it suited him. The genetic link to Jay – which had always been obscured by the half-brothers' divergent tastes in clothes – was now overwhelmingly present. And Marianne, noticing this, realised to her shame that much of Jay's physical appeal – for her – had come from the superficial way he presented himself: scruffy, low-key, off-beat.

She glanced for a moment in Jay's direction. He was standing with Lee and Lee's wife, lighting a cigarette as Lee opened the catalogue to show him something. He looked exactly as he'd looked the day they'd met – same clothes, same hairstyle, same air of restlessness. No older. No wiser. With that old nomadic quality she'd once found so mesmerising . . . only now it just seemed fidgety. Unrelaxing. Until he'd strolled into the party half an hour ago, they hadn't known for sure if Jay was even in the country. And while Marianne was relieved that there was clearly no resentment over her decision to split up, no bad feelings, not even any wistfulness – he'd kissed her warmly on arrival, praised her designs, passed on good wishes from his mother – she was starting to understand that, in all the time they'd spent together, Jay had never completely engaged. Good to be with her. But really just as good to be apart – free again, free to pursue his great true love . . . his adored precious stones that, where Jay was concerned, were special enough in themselves and needed no elegant neck, no kissable earlobe, no significant fourth finger, to show them at their best.

Not that any of this mattered to Marianne. Not any more. For with George now equally dressed-down – George looking, at last, like a match for the kind of woman Marianne felt herself to be – she knew at once that there was no comparison between the two men in terms of sexual attraction. George won. Every time. His decision not to wear a suit that night – a suit, for so long, that had kept him safely off her radar . . . it now placed him completely, dramatically, at the centre.

And then, sensing the scrutiny, George looked round and – seeing it was Marianne – he smiled . . . a smile that sent her hurtling so far round the emotional spectrum it felt as much like fear as love. Perhaps it was fear. Certainly, there was a quickening of adrenalin, a sense of something critical thundering towards her in time – some moment of immense personal challenge – giving rise to feelings that, in spite of the intense privacy of the exchange, were oddly like stage-fright . . . as if the cosmic spotlight had finally swung its beam on her, as if the whole universe was watching, and this was the moment – the moment above all others – when she absolutely could not afford to forget her lines.

George left the people he was talking to – left them almost instantly – and made his way across the mews, weaving in and out of the various chattering groups, directly towards Marianne. They'd spoken earlier. There was no need for him to be coming back towards her. And Marianne, knowing instinctively that he was feeling what she felt – that he was picking up all the little messages and nuances, the imperceptible body signals and semi-telepathic connections that drive two people towards one another with confidence – Marianne knew suddenly, and with a great lift in her heart, that there was still hope. Any residual feelings of concern she felt for him evaporated in that moment. Gabby was wrong. George didn't need pity. He wasn't a man in mourning for his ex-wife. On the contrary, he was a man who'd seen the light . . . and was travelling towards it as fast as he possibly could.

But before George could reach her, Marianne felt a tap on her arm and turned to see the catering manager

393

– holding an empty champagne bottle. They were running out.

'I would offer to send one of my lot to buy more,' the manager explained, 'but we're stretched to breaking point – what with all your extra guests – so it might make sense for you to go yourself, or ask a friend. Or—'

'Sure.' Marianne scanned the party for Gabriella's newly streaked hair. It was Gab's damn fault they'd run out. She could jolly well go for more. Or get that good-for-nothing Dexter to go. Or—

'Everything all right?' said George, finally reaching them.

'We're out of booze.'

'Can I go?'

He made it sound so simple. She looked at him warmly. 'Would you?'

'Of course.' He was smiling again, and Marianne was off into orbit once more – *Oh God. Please . . .* 'No problem. So long as you promise to have dinner with me afterwards.'

Marianne couldn't speak.

'Or—'

'No – no! Of course I will!' she said, recovering. 'I'd love to.'

And so, with an expressive press at her elbow – a gesture that told her he wasn't finished, not even remotely – George went off for more champagne, and Marianne, watching him, was filled with a wonderful and unfamiliar sense of being supported. After years of Jay leaving her to deal with things alone, the sensation – far from making her feel suffocated – actually made her feel able to breathe more deeply. It was liberating. For George's gesture wasn't patronising, or swamping, or muddied by some hidden agenda. He wasn't like

Paul. He simply wanted to make things easier for her. And Marianne – observing the innate generosity – realised that there had always been something inherently stingy and small about the way Jay had loved . . . that there was all the difference in the world between standing back and giving space, and abandoning the person altogether.

She was filled with amazement at the way it made her feel. I love him, she thought – as George passed under the archway, out of the mews. I really, truly love him. She was as much struck by a new understanding of what it meant to love and be loved – a love which, after Marianne's previous loves, had an almost dazzling authenticity – as she was by the fact that this transforming miracle related to George.

And so it was that – lost, for a moment, in her thoughts – it took a while for Marianne to register the commotion that was taking place back inside the showroom.

'It's a pretty ring,' someone was saying, most politely. Marianne recognised the South African accent of Charles le Floch – one of the most important buyers there that night. 'Of course it is,' he went on, 'as are all her pieces. The setting is beautiful, and typical, and genuine enough. But you must know that this stone, lovely as it is, isn't actually a real padparascha.'

'But we—'

'You'd need to conduct a few tests, of course . . . to be a hundred per cent certain. Check it out in a proper laboratory setting. But I'm willing to bet that stone's a pink sapphire. I'd swear to it in fact,' le Floch's voice went on – with all the authority of decades in the trade. 'It's a nice enough pink sapphire which has been specially treated, at a very high temperature, to give it a superficial covering that makes it look exactly like a padparascha. So there's no shame in you thinking that it is. These stones are still very striking – and easily mistaken. Only an expert would smell a rat. It's probably much better value to go for something like this instead of wasting money on something that looks almost exactly the same . . .'

Marianne turned to see Sophie Farage deep in conversation with the man who was on the verge of making her career. Sophie's left hand was spread out flat – her head bending forward to examine the ring while she listened to le Floch's analysis. The unmistakeable bump of a honeymoon baby was visible through her dress.

'Except we were there when they found it in the ground!' Sophie protested, removing the ring now and offering it over, as if to prove her point. 'Or practically there. Certainly Jay was in no doubt that it—'

'Jay?' said le Floch, taking the ring. 'Jay Franklin?'

Sophie nodded.

Le Floch was now the one to look puzzled. He'd known Franklin for well over a decade. The man's reputation as a stone dealer was solid. Taking out his own little loupe, he stared at the stone for a second or two – squinting into the glass. 'Jay Franklin sold you *this* stone as a padparascha?'

'Well, he sold it to my husband, who gave it to me –'

Le Floch put his loupe away. He handed back the ring. 'And your husband is here tonight?'

'Of course!' said Sophie, relieved. Paul would deal with it. Paul would know. 'Let me find him for you . . .'

It didn't take her long. And Paul – listening with a sinking heart, as she introduced le Floch and explained the nature of their conversation – knew now that he had only one option left, and that was to brazen it out.

Le Floch smiled. 'And do you mind me asking how much you paid for it?' he said.

Paul coughed, discreetly. 'I'd rather not,' he replied, 'if that's all the same to you. It's not really—'

'All right, all right. But if you paid a padparascha price for this, my friend, then – I hate to be the one to tell you this – but you've been well and truly shafted.'

'I doubt it,' said Paul, perfectly calm. 'And, in any case, we're still very happy with it – aren't we, darling? So—'

'No!' cried le Floch, incredulous. 'Please! You *can't* tell me you're not bothered!'

'I'm telling you we're happy,' said Paul.

But Charles le Floch couldn't let it go. Brain buzzing with unanswered questions, he looked around for Marianne and saw her at the door. 'You know about this?' he mouthed, jabbing his finger at the ring on Sophie's hand.

Marianne came over. She kissed Paul and Sophie 'hello' – congratulated them on their bump – and turned to look at the ring. 'What's the problem?'

'Well, I can see it's one of yours, of course,' said le Floch. 'No problem there. But these nice friends of yours seem to be under the impression the stone's a pad—' He glanced swiftly at Marianne's face. She was looking at Paul. 'They said Jay Franklin found it for them –'

'That's right.'

'And that Jay told them it was a pad.'

'That's right. It was.'

'So what in God's name happened, darling? I mean, unless my instincts are completely up the spout . . . why are we now all looking at a pink sapphire?'

Marianne bit her lip. 'I think Paul is probably in a

397

better position than me to answer that particular question,' she said. 'Although—'

'Am I?'

Marianne stared at him.

Paul felt queasy.

'You – you're saying you didn't get it?' she said, horrified – not ready to believe what was happening, what Paul was willing to do to her.

'Of course we got it, Marianne. And we thanked you at the time, didn't we? I'm sure Sophie wrote . . .'

Marianne was very pale. 'I'm talking about the other one,' she said, her gaze still fixed on Paul.

'Other one?'

'Other one! Jesus, Paul – the one that you wanted to . . . the one we discussed! The one that I then couriered to your office? In January?'

'We married in December, Marianne.' Paul's voice was suddenly very distant to his own ear, as if someone else were speaking. 'We had our ring by then . . .'

Marianne was speechless – speechless at his audacity. Yes, Paul was dodgy. Ever since that decision to go ahead and marry Sophie at the end of last year while simultaneously declaring love for Marianne . . . ever since that moment she'd known what Paul was really like. She had the measure of him. But still. Jaw open. This was another league.

'You did have a lot going on at the end of last year. You're probably confusing us with someone else.'

Still Marianne said nothing – and then, somewhere on her outer register, she realised that le Floch, too, was silent. Turning, she noticed a shadow of regret passing over the man's face and – understanding what this signified – felt sickened to the core. Reputation was everything when it came to selling jewellery. Reputation and trust. If Charles le Floch doubted she was telling the truth about these stones – if he believed that she'd somehow defrauded Paul and Sophie – it wouldn't just be the end of any future dealings with him. It would be the end of Marianne's career. Realising that Paul wouldn't help her – realising he must have sold the good ring, or kept it hidden, or given it to someone else? Who knew . . . the point was: he'd lied to Sophie about the ring she was wearing tonight. And nothing – *nothing* – would induce him to come clean. Looking at Sophie's altered physique, Marianne understood that now. Too much was at stake.

And in the end it was this – more than the paralysis induced by initial shock at the lengths Paul was prepared to go to; more than the party-hostess role she was obliged to play, the reluctance to make a scene, the instinct to tone it down, at least until the party was over . . . more than either of those things, it was this sense of Sophie's innocence, and the innocence of the child she was carrying, that made Marianne so ultimately impotent, so incapable of fairly and freely fighting back. For she could see that every attempt she made at self-defence – every attempt to reveal the falsity of Paul's story – would be a blow to the heart of that marriage. It wasn't that Marianne intended to sacrifice her career for Sophie's dream – she wasn't that selfless – she just couldn't believe it wasn't possible, with a bit of tact, to save both.

'What's going on?' said Gabby, joining them.

For a moment, Marianne brightened. But all Gabriella could say, with any certainty, was that the stone she verified back in Galle – the stone that Paul and Sophie had brought back with them to London –

was, absolutely, the genuine article. So if this stone here was some sort of fake—

'Not fake, exactly. It's a perfectly decent pink sapphire. It's just—'

'So where's the pad?' said Gabby, looking at Marianne as if she didn't quite know her any more. 'Where is it, Marianne?'

Marianne put a hand on her friend's arm. She'd no desire to expose Gab's ignorance, not in front of all these people. No need to humiliate her. 'The stone you saw in Galle, Gab – the stone you *thought* was a padparascha . . .'

Gab shook her off. It was clear she'd been drinking. 'You're saying I don't know my stones?'

'Please, Gab. Not now . . .'

'Not now?' Gab raged. 'Don't you *not now* me! You—'

'It's not something you need to be ashamed of. You're a designer – not a gemmologist. Jay should never have asked you to verify something as difficult as a padparascha. He—'

'I'm telling you: it was a pad.'

'And I'm telling you, it wasn't . . . not that it matters, to be honest.' Marianne turned to le Floch. 'Paul and Sophie brought the treated sapphire back to London with them, and came to see me about a ring. I spotted the discrepancy. I spoke to Jay – who, needless to say, was appalled . . .'

It didn't take long for the party to disperse, for the majority of guests to sense trouble and drift awkwardly away.

Poor Marianne . . . poor Gab . . .

How embarrassing.

Marianne was barely conscious of the exodus. With

400

a few remaining stalwarts from the trade gathered close – a group that now included the Harrods buyer and the magazine reporter – she stumbled to the end of a story that, with every complicated twist and turn, became increasingly difficult to believe. With Paul mechanical, Sophie bewildered, le Floch suspicious, and Gabby downright furious (how dare Marianne question her judgement? How dare she suggest to all and sundry that Gab was somehow incompetent?) Marianne's confidence faltered. Even Lee, dear Lee, was unable to do anything more than confirm that he had made two identical rings. He did his best, reminding anyone who'd listen of Marianne's unblemished reputation and saying that, in all the years he'd worked with her, there had never been any question of foul play . . . but it wasn't enough. Lee could barely say the word, 'padparascha'. Far less, identify one. He had no hard evidence.

And while Jay was rather more credible when it came to providing Marianne with a good defence – he certainly had no problem exposing his sister's shortcomings when it came to gemmology, and was more than willing to side with Marianne on the whole issue of her good reputation. He'd happily call Tariq Ibrahim, even bring him to London and make the man explain his 'joke'. When it came to the whole strange story of the good rough stone being cut to match the 'fake' – and establishing that there had always been two stones in the balance – Jay was convincing. But none of this was going to help Marianne fight Paul's implication that, at some later point, she must have kept the genuine stone for herself, and merely delivered the inferior. It was Paul's word against hers.

*

George returned from his errand. Heaving three half-cases of champagne from the boot of his car, he piled them one on top of the other and carried them back into the mews . . . only to find the place eerily silent. Almost all the guests had left and, looking at those who were still there, it was clear to him, standing in the archway, that something was badly wrong. Further down the street, he saw one of the reps unlocking his car. Gabby was with him. And Dexter. George couldn't hear what his sister was saying, but she seemed to be pleading with the man – who merely shrugged and got into his car.

Noticing the jewellery magazine reporter he'd met earlier in the evening – who was now standing on the kerb, texting busily as she waited for a taxi – George approached the girl, who looked up from her mobile and smiled. George smiled back. He rested his three half-cases of champagne on a nearby bollard, and asked what had happened to the party. The girl was more than happy to enlighten him. Unaware of George's family connection to Gabriella, far less his closeness to Marianne, and failing to make the rudimentary conclusion that a more experienced reporter would have reached from observing those cases of champagne, she explained with some glee that there had been accusations of fraud. She'd be writing a fuller piece on it in due course but – in the meantime – the story was too good not to pass on the basic facts to her cousin, who was trying to make a name for himself in a broadsheet gossip column. She owed him a favour – and, as everybody knew, there always was a market for a good old-fashioned scam . . .

Grimly, George suggested that the girl check her facts before exposing herself and her cousin to accusations of defamation – which, in his book, was every bit as despicable as fraud, not to mention ruinously expensive. And leaving her there with her mouth wide open, he picked up his champagne cases and carried them back, under the archway, into the mews, and up towards the showroom. He climbed the steps, went through the open door, past the security guard, to see only the caterers silently clearing the mess. There was no sign of Marianne. Leaving the champagne in the kitchen, George returned to the deserted mews. Only Gabby and Dexter remained – returning, arm-in-arm, from their failed attempt to salvage something from the arrangement with le Floch. Someone had to oversee the final clearing away, discharge the security guard, and lock the whole place up. They explained to George what had happened – adding that Marianne had grown increasingly distraught, and that Jay had taken her home.

Sophie sat quietly as Paul drove back to Ifield Road. It was almost dark outside. Paul had switched on the headlights of their new car, and the dials along the dashboard – the speedometer, the petrol level, the rev counter, the clock, all now had a sleek bluish backlight. And even though the car was strictly second-hand, it was still in very good condition, retaining something of that special smell – no doubt a toxic chemical in the carpets – that carried oddly soothing associations of newness and comfort. Slowly, deeply, Sophie inhaled.

'. . . so strange,' Paul was saying. 'I just don't understand how she – I mean, what did she mean? *Other* stone . . .?'

In the darkness, Sophie's hands pressed into the cushiony sides of her passenger seat. It was made from some sort of leather, or faux leather, perhaps. It was nice.

'You think she mixed us up with someone else?'

There were packages in the back of the car, boxes of baby stuff – a plastic tub, a nappy bin, two changing mats, multi-packs of newborn baby-grows, muslins, towels, bedding – all bought from John Lewis that afternoon, all ready to unload and take up to the newly painted baby room. Sophie and her mother had had a happy day together, choosing it all.

'I can't get my head around it,' Paul went on. 'I mean, was that le Floch guy really accusing Marianne of something dodgy? It doesn't seem credible somehow . . .'

Sophie looked at her ring. She looked at the setting and the stone. Still beautiful, still special. Still hers. In the semi-darkness, between the brief rhythmic bursts of orange from the streetlights they passed, at that precise moment, the colour of the stone was almost grey. It changed, constantly. In different lights, at different times of the day – sometimes lovely, sometimes quite plain . . . but wasn't that part of the charm? How often, if ever, did it – did anyone – need to stand in the unforgiving brightness of a gem-lab microscope? And if she, Sophie, was no expert, no judge, if she was happy with what he'd given her – and, ultimately, the person he was . . .

'Darling?'

'Mm?'

Pulling up at a set of traffic lights, Paul turned to his wife. 'You're quiet,' he said.

Sophie smiled. 'I'm fine.'

'Not worried about your ring?'

Her smile grew – not so much broadening as

showing sudden, startling depth, shot through with a quality of understanding, of protective love, that Paul – his soul so tiny, so frail, so damaged – could only vaguely fathom.

'Not in the slightest,' she replied, ruffling his hair.

Paul smiled back, relieved. And then the lights changed to green again, and the family car moved forward.

Chapter Twenty-Seven

It wasn't until she woke the following morning that Marianne – recalling the horrors of the night before – realised that, on top of everything else, she'd forgotten about dinner with George. She pictured him coming back to the showroom with all those extra bottles of champagne only to find the party over, in every sense of the phrase. Guests gone, sun down, reputation shattered, career destroyed, partnership with Gabby good as finished . . . all in ruins in under an hour. Pulling the duvet over her head, Marianne curled into a downy ball and willed the world away.

But the world would not retreat. And there was nothing that her cocoon of bedding, with all its fine white cotton and feathery padding, could do to block out the sunlight, or the sound of the doorbell of the neighbouring house, or the incipient fear that – as a result of last night – everything that mattered would be forever beyond her reach.

Pushing aside the duvet, Marianne left her bed and stumbled towards the shower. Blankly, she stood in the hard stone cubicle with water crashing over her.

*

Two hours later – dull, pale, emotionally absent – she was back at the showroom, mechanically and silently going through the various tasks she had to do that day. In truth, there wasn't much. The only essential thing was her physical presence at the showroom – to oversee the departure of the display cabinets and the return of the sofas.

Gabriella had called a little earlier while Marianne was drying her hair. And, for a moment, Marianne had softened at this gesture of solidarity. Gab might not have been the most reliable of partners over the years. She didn't have talent, or judgement, or even much of a brain. She'd got it wrong last night. She'd let Marianne down. But she was still, when it mattered, a friend. She'd bothered to pick up the telephone. She wanted to know how Marianne was. She cared.

'You okay?'

Marianne took the telephone over to the bed. 'It's fine, Gab,' she said, sitting up against the pillows and cushions. 'I'll be fine.'

'You sure?'

'Absolutely. I mean, it isn't ideal, of course. And there's—'

'Strong enough to go in this morning?'

Marianne shut her eyes.

'I did close up last night,' Gab reasoned, 'after Jay took you home. And Dexter was kind enough to pay off the security guard and those caterers. We owe him one thousand, five hundred pounds – something like that – the receipts are on the windowsill. I wasted half an hour looking for the company chequebook—'

'It's in the drawer with the petty cash, Gab. Where it always is.'

'Well, anyway – we paid them off and locked the place up. It took for ever. We were there until ten, which meant we lost our table . . . and I just think it would be kind to Dexter, if nothing else, if you could do the decent thing and offer to—'

'All right. All right.'

'Great. Thanks. And – I'm sorry, Marianne – but Dex is pressing for us to fix up a meeting. He thinks we need to look at where the business is going, that sort of thing . . . sooner, rather than later, if it's all the same to you. He thinks – and I agree with him – that there isn't much point in dragging things out if—'

'Just tell me when you want it, Gab, and I'll be there. Any time next week is good for me.'

'Monday, then? Ten o'clock?'

Marianne now sat at her father's desk, smoking a cigarette – the first she'd had since losing Maya – waiting for the removal men to show up. There were various bland administrative tasks she might have tackled, but the energy just wasn't there. In any case, what was the point in cleaning a showroom that, very likely, would never see another client? What was the point updating a filing system that would never be needed again?

The first time the telephone went, she decided to ignore it. Whoever it was could leave a message. A minute or so later, her mobile buzzed in her bag – and she ignored that too. It was only when the office line rang for a fourth time that Marianne picked up.

'At last,' said a familiar voice, not bothering to announce himself. 'Now listen, love. It's important. I've been speaking to Mike and we both think that you're—'

'Not today, Lee. Please.'

'Sorry, angel. But if you don't get on with this thing *now*, then you'll lose that contract with Selfridges, or Fenwicks, or whoever it is you've got lined up, and word will get out, and before we know it you'll be out of work and I'll have lost one of my best customers and – and while you might be okay with your business going belly-up without a fight, I most definitely am not. All right?'

Marianne was silent.

'Now. Can you remember which couriers you used for those rings? Because they'll have records of the deliveries – you see what I'm saying? And then all you have to do is show the slips to le Floch . . .'

'And what?' said Marianne, dully. 'Apart from the fact that I hand-delivered the first ring – so there's only one recorded delivery – they still won't be able to say *what* it was they carried that day. It's only my contents-description on the delivery slip – that's all they need for the insurer. No one verifies it, Lee. Least of all some delivery guy. It won't prove anything.'

'It'll prove the date of the delivery, won't it? And if they already had that first ring, the one you hand-delivered, in time for the wedding – which was December, right? – what else could the courier have been delivering in January?'

Marianne sighed. She wasn't convinced. There was still nothing to prove what the courier's package contained the second ring.

'It's a start, love. It'll show the man signed for *something*. And I can't help thinking – your reputation being what it is, and the rest of us happy to back you up . . . it's got to be worth a try.'

Marianne sat on in silence, smoking and thinking.

She could see Charles le Foch flapping the courier's delivery schedule in her face, saying 'And? And?' Was it really worth the effort?

Lee coughed. 'Never took you for a quitter, Marianne.'

'*Quitter?*'

'It's all right, love. I just thought for a moment you were different, that's all. Most women coming into this business – the design end, that is; birds like your Gabriella, and Flora de whatsit and that Amanda Kerr down in Battersea – they're all right in their way. They're friendly. They pay up – on the whole. Never any trouble . . . but not what I'd call serious – you get me? And the second it gets tough, or someone wants to marry them, or kids come along, they're out. I've seen it time and again. You, on the other hand, in spite of that other stuff, and the way you speak, and your rich friends . . . but I guess we were wrong. You're no different, are you? Better at hiding it, maybe, but – fundamentally . . .'

Marianne made the call. It wouldn't help, she knew that. Not where Charles le Floch was concerned. The man had made up his mind and nothing short of a signed retraction from Paul would make things better, and how likely was that? Still – dialling in the courier's number now – Marianne reminded herself she had nothing to lose from looking into the matter. For a quiet life, and to get Lee off her back, it was simpler to do as he asked. And better, surely, than staring into space while she waited for those lorries to arrive.

Half an hour later, however – and in a state of growing irritation – Marianne began to wonder if she wouldn't have preferred staring into space. As her enquiry related to a past delivery, she was told to ring a call centre in Leeds, and then asked to hold for twenty minutes only to find herself re-explaining the entire story – for a third time – to yet another operator . . . who then explained that she needed the Cardiff records department if she wanted a copy of the relevant slip. She was speaking to Angela from Customer Services when the doorbell went. Still listening to Angela – droning on about complaints procedures – Marianne got up from the desk to let in the removals men.

'. . . except I'm not making a fucking *complaint*,' she snapped, opening the door.

George stood, smiling, on the step.

Marianne swallowed.

'Hello?' said Angela's voice in her ear. 'Hello? Ms Cooper?'

'I – I'm not suggesting the delivery wasn't made,' Marianne stumbled on, embarrassed, beckoning George in. 'I'm just asking for evidence that it happened so that I can prove to a third party that it . . . yes! That's right! To the address on the file if that's . . . Great. Thank you. No, no – nothing more . . .'

'Everything all right?' said George, as she replaced the receiver.

'What do you think?' she retorted.

George's smile vanished. 'I'm sorry.' He came a little closer to the desk. 'Jay told me what happened,' he said, pulling up a chair and sitting opposite – almost a prospective client, as if he and Marianne were doing business. 'It sounded appalling –'

'It was.'

'I'm sorry,' he said again. 'I'm sorry I wasn't with you.'

411

Sorry? Disarmed by the apology, by the gentle tone of voice, by the fact that he was there at all . . . very slowly, Marianne – who was still recovering from the shock of discovering that it was George, and not a random deliveryman – began to understand. She still couldn't quite believe it. After everything that had happened, and everything that had been said, and the terrible thing that she was supposed to have done – even Gabby thought she was guilty . . . this morning, standing in the shower, it had seemed to Marianne that her entire world had caved in, that everything she'd worked for was lost, that everyone she cared about – including George, especially George, so upright, and so decent – would want nothing more to do with her.

And yet, for all that, here he was. And – thinking more clearly now . . . and Lee, bless him, Lee wasn't letting her sink without a fight. And Jay had stood with her. And – and she could hardly blame her mother for failing to show support when the poor woman had left the party before the problems began. The important people – the ones she really minded about – they hadn't deserted her.

'You couldn't have helped,' she said, softening. 'Nobody could. Not even Jay. And,' – indicating the telephone – 'yes, I'm following up a couple of ideas, but nothing decent. Nothing that's going to turn it into anything more than Paul's word against mine. Somehow, that bastard has managed to trash my life overnight and I – I suppose I'm—'

To her horror, Marianne realised she was close to tears. She couldn't speak.

'I'm sorry.' She reached for her bag. 'I'm not myself. It's been a difficult morning – not that that's an excuse or anything. I'm just—'

And suddenly George was coming round to her side of the desk. He was picking her up from the chair and pulling her close and holding her there – safe and calm.

'You're shattered,' he said, stroking her hair. 'But it's going to be all right. Really. I promise you. It's all going to be fine . . .'

'No it's not.'

'It is,' he insisted.

'It's not! It's not!'

'Just *listen*,' said George, frustration breaking through the calm. 'Listen to me, will you? Let me tell you why.'

Marianne fell silent. She listened as George explained that he'd been doing a little research on her behalf. He told her how he'd noticed Paul and Sophie arriving last night – not on their bikes but in a smart new-model BMW. And to George, who had an eye for these things, and who was only too aware of how Paul had spurned the filthy lucre of the City for a softer occupation, living off his wife, and giving part-time financial advice to the kind of organisation that couldn't afford the real deal, and with all the added expense of a baby on the way . . . to George, it all seemed a little odd.

Marianne pulled back to see his face – her eyes were sparkling from a combination of tears and fascination.

'Go on.'

'Odd,' George went on, 'but ultimately forgettable, except for what we all now know about the – er . . . the true value of poor Sophie's ring.'

'You think he *sold* the padparascha?'

'Pawned it. Jay and I did some digging about this morning, and we've managed to find the broker he used – a shop just round the corner from his place in

Earls' Court, which only goes to show exactly how lazy, and frankly *stupid*, the man is . . . trying to shift something like that on his own doorstep. And while the owner says she sold the ring on recently, and can't help us trace it, she does have the paperwork from January and, bless her, she keeps CCTV tapes . . .' George passed Marianne a brown package. 'It's all in there.'

She took it with shaking hands.

'. . . and I've spoken to that reporter, and that friend of hers at the *Telegraph* – so there's no problem there. And Jay tells me you'll have no trouble with le Floch. It's sorted.'

Marianne nodded, taking it all in, trying not to cry again.

'She took a bit of persuading,' George added. 'That pawnbroker. Refused to say anything, at first – all very high and mighty about customer confidentiality. But Jay clearly knows how to handle such situations . . .'

Marianne rolled her eyes. 'How much do I owe him?'

'Dinner, apparently,' George replied. 'Although I have to say I wasn't so taken with the idea . . .'

Marianne suddenly found her attention fixed fast to the brown edge of the pawnbroker's package, to a bit of sellotape that was coming off. She couldn't look at him.

'. . . so we compromised on lunch,' George went on. 'Somewhere expensive, we both agreed. But no atmosphere. I thought maybe a sushi restaurant. Only, no cosy banquettes. Preferably, no alcohol –'

'You can talk.'

George laughed.

Then, leaning over the desk, he gently took the package from her grasp and placed it to one side. He held her hands in his. And in a voice that was suddenly serious, said what he'd come to say ... all the things he'd been planning to tell her over dinner last night; all the things that – in the stony misery of her shower cubicle that morning – Marianne thought she'd never hear.

He explained how it was really only when Helen had left him that he realised what was going on: that his interest in Marianne – the pleasure he had just from being in her company, the excuses he kept finding for seeing her again – it wasn't mere fondness, or friendship, or brotherly concern; it wasn't simply the burgeoning professional respect he now held for her, or neutral admiration for the way she dealt with the respective challenges posed by his unreliable siblings. It was something far greater. Something actively disturbing. Something that, if acknowledged at the time, would have blown his world apart – his family, his principles, the stability of his children ... something he absolutely couldn't afford to admit. And it was only Helen's sudden departure, and the bizarre way it made him feel – not miserable and downtrodden, not shattered and pained, rejected, abandoned, insulted, degraded, not dragging himself through a fog of misery ... but strangely relieved in the clean light air, like someone waking up from a nightmare – only then did he understand the degree to which that one desire – for a principled life – had all but prohibited the rest. Only then did he feel able to understand what Marianne meant to him: how absolutely precious she was. And suddenly the idea of her being pregnant by another man, or in hospital, or attending a service for her stillborn child without him at her side ... suddenly, those things had become completely intolerable to him.

Not that he could do much about it, of course. For

George, convinced that a vibrant girl like Marianne wouldn't consider – not for one moment – a washed-up has-been like him . . . it was only too easy for him to see why she should have decided to take advantage of the smoke alarm that intoxicating night, see sense, and send him on his way – insisting that it had all been a monstrous mistake.

'Yes, but only because you were drunk, George. Drunk, and—'

'It's all right.' Smiling, he kissed her hands. 'I know now. I understand. When Helen told me how you felt, when she collected the children yesterday morning – *livid* because you'd refused to make that ring for her, and—'

'Helen?'

George stopped, suddenly. An unpleasant thought ran through his mind. He and Marianne looked at each other over the desk. Then George closed his eyes.

'George –'

'She was lying, wasn't she? When she said she was certain that you wanted me for yourself, that you were *desperately, pathetically in love* . . .' George slumped forward, mortified, over their entwined hands. 'Oh God.'

Marianne was laughing now. 'You really think I'd have trusted Helen with something that private?'

George groaned.

And Marianne – her smile softening – looked down at the ruffled head. His cheek was warm against her hand. His clasp was tight. She leant closer in – close enough to kiss him – and, doing so, said, 'You don't think I might have wanted to tell you about it myself?'

Gabby brought Dexter with her to Monday's meeting

416

at the showroom. Neither of them was convinced that she'd be able to stand up to Marianne on her own. She needed Dexter's confidence, his clarity, his certainty that winding up the business was now the only way to go. They parked in a slot outside the mews and, walking in under the archway, passed George, whistling, on his way out. He waved and smiled at their astonished faces. For there was something about the glow in his eyes, the tousled drying hair, the way he was moving, the jangling of his car keys . . . some transformation in the man that, for all its implausibility, could only suggest one thing.

'George?'

'Gotta run, Gabs. I'm late as it is . . .'

'But—'

'She's there. She's waiting for you. And I suggest you guys don't hang about. There's some appointment at Selfridges, I think she said, for midday . . . from what I can gather, she's not going to want to be late for that!'

'But—'

George opened the door of his car. 'Good to see you, Dexter,' he said and, grinning, slid inside.

EPILOGUE

'. . . Nearly there,' said the agent as Jay followed him across a third baking quadrangle – past a group of uniformed gardeners at work on a faulty irrigation system – and on, through another set of double-doors, back into the relief of the palace air conditioning. He then led Jay down a long marble corridor and into an office, where a security guard was waiting for them.

The room might have been an office, but there was no sign that it belonged to any one individual. There were no loose papers, no photographs, no random items of stationery . . . just a large map of Dubai on the wall above the desk, a set of beige filing cabinets below the window, and a tray of iced water on a table by the door. It was all spotlessly clean.

'Go on, then,' said the agent to the guard, closing the door and leaning against it in a way that was somehow disrespectful. He flapped a hand. 'Go on.'

The guard turned and bent to the skirting. Pressing down on a concealed stone panel, he caused the map of Dubai to roll back and reveal a state-of-the-art safe, which he then proceeded to open. And while Jay watched the security wizardry with intent fascination – he'd always have a soft spot for 007 paraphernalia – he was rather less struck by the thousands of pounds' worth of jewellery that lay within the system. It was, after all, Dubai. Nor was he surprised to note that all of it was dated, in terms of design. Not vintage. Not antique. Just dated. In twenty or thirty years, this collection would start to regain and then exceed its original value – the pieces were all perfect specimens of their time – but that wasn't enough for this particular client. For now, he simply wanted to get rid of the old stuff – and Jay, by all accounts, was the man to do it for him.

Jay took out his notebook, loupe and torch. He pulled the nearest case a little closer, and – lifting a necklace from its cushion – began compiling his inventory. It was going to take at least an hour to work through all the items. Maybe two. The agent decided he had better things to do. Making his excuses, he left Jay there with only the guard for company, and promised to return again at four.

So Jay worked in silence, with only the rustling of the guard's newspaper to disturb him – and the occasional hack-hacking of some desert bird, outside in the courtyard garden. He worked his way through a blaze of gold, through priceless gemstones with extraordinarily vivid colours that – after the subtle neutrals in the sands of the Arab landscape he'd driven through that day – had an almost psychedelic quality.

And then he saw it – not even with its own special case, but sitting quietly in the corner of a velvet tray along with a mass of gaudier pieces. And while it was Marianne's design that he recognised first, it was the stone that caught his breath and held his eye. There it was – unwanted, unloved – on a tray of discarded trashy clutter in the heart of Dubai . . . but still with the same mesmerising gleam, the same dawn light, the same unique beauty he'd always known would be there – even when the thing was nothing more than a dull, rough lump that day in Ratnapura.

Hack-hack-hack went the noisy desert bird.

Jay picked up the padparascha. He didn't need to shine his torch. He simply held the stone forward so that it was caught in a natural line of afternoon sunlight – sunlight that was now low enough to have found an angle across the palace courtyard and in, through the window above the filing cabinets – and observed the mysterious warmth in its depths, while the security guard turned a page of his newspaper and took another sip of water.

Honor & Evie

Susannah Bates

Does growing up have to mean growing apart?

Privileged and beautiful, intelligent and popular, life's gifts come effortlessly to Honor Montfort. If only things were that simple for her prickly cousin, Evie.

Yet in spite of their differences – or perhaps because of them – the bond between Honor and Evie is strong. They are the very best of friends.

But which of them is really best-equipped for the challenges ahead – the one who appears to have everything, or the one who's had to learn to fight? And how will their unusual friendship survive when Honor's charms start working against her will . . . upon the only man that Evie has ever loved?

'Charming and beguiling' Penny Vincenzi

arrow books

ALSO AVAILABLE IN ARROW

All About Laura

Susannah Bates

Mel Ashton – hardworking and reliable – is tired of her image. Bored with her flat and exasperated by her job, the only thing she's not planning to quit is her relationship with David.

David, a talented artist, likes Mel the way she is. With Mel, he is finally growing up. He's even growing out of his passion for women called Laura – a secret fixation inspired by one particular life model he could never quite forget.

But Mel is changing. And when wealthy Joss Savil commissions a portrait of his new wife, David's relationship with Mel is thrown into crisis. For Joss's wife is the original Laura . . .

arrow books

ALSO AVAILABLE IN ARROW

Charmed Lives

Susannah Bates

Kate Leonard is a high-flying young lawyer. Smart, sexy and successful, she seems to have it all, except a life outside the office . . . until she meets Tom Faulkener.

Tom comes from a different world: the privileged, idle world of private incomes, breathtaking bills and the pursuit of pleasure. The last thing he wants is a relationship . . . until he meets Kate.

But as Kate tries to juggle her hectic existence with the temptations of Tom's exclusive circle – irresponsible society photographer Charlie, shy but kind-hearted Douglas, and Tom's lovely but neurotic ex-wife Arabella – she begins to see through the careless glamour of their charmed lives . . .

'Penny Vincenzi fans will devour this – unputdownable'
Louise Bagshawe

arrow books